SHE WAS AT THE MERCY OF THE MAN THEY CALLED THE LEOPARD. SHE COULD ONLY HOPE HER FATE WAS KINDER THAN THAT OF HIS NAMESAKE. . . .

A large spotted cat lunged forward, snarling at them through the bars of the cage. Astra stepped back quickly, and even Richard flinched.

"Is he not magnificent?" Richard asked.

"Aye," Astra whispered. She had never seen such beauty and power melded into one form. The cat's eyes were like brilliant jewels, his fur as rich and finely-ornamented as the most expensive cloth. Yet he was not just a lovely object or an elegant plaything. His sleek flanks quivered with strength; his huge, hungry-looking mouth opened to reveal gleaming ivory teeth that looked as though they could easily bite off Astra's arm. He was danger and death personified. Astra found pity arising in her. "All his beauty and grace is wasted. Such a creature is meant to be free, not caged up in London's gloomy Tower." She turned to Richard. "Can you not feel it? They call you The Leopard—how would you like to be imprisoned in a place like this? Would it not make your soul grieve, your heart ache with discontent?"

"I am a man, Astra. This animal does not have a soul nor a heart as you speak of it. He is a cold-blooded killer, an instrument of death."

"Are you so different from him?" Astra demanded.

HE WAS LARGER THAN LIFE, AND HE HELD HER LIFE IN HIS HANDS. . . .

* * *

Praise for Mary Gillgannon's *Dragon of the Island:*
"A lusty tale of love and betrayal!"
—*Romantic Times*

If you liked this book, be sure to look for others in the *Denise Little Presents* line:

MOONSHINE AND GLORY by Jacqueline Marten	(0079-1, $4.99)
COMING HOME by Ginna Gray	(0058-9, $4.99)
THE SILENT ROSE by Kasey Mars	(0081-3, $4.99)
DRAGON OF THE ISLAND by Mary Gillgannon	(0067-8, $4.99)
BOUNDLESS by Alexandra Thorne	(0059-7, $4.99)
MASQUERADE by Alexa Smart	(0080-5, $4.99)
THE PROMISE by Mandalyn Kaye	(0087-2, $4.99)
FIELDS OF FIRE by Carol Caldwell	(0088-0, $4.99)
HIGHLAND FLING by Amanda Scott	(0098-8, $4.99)
TRADEWINDS by Annee Cartier	(0099-6, $4.99)
A MARGIN IN TIME by Laura Hayden	(0109-7, $4.99)
REBEL WIND by Stobie Piel	(0110-0, $4.99)
SOMEDAY by Anna Hudson	(0119-4, $4.99)
THE IRISHMAN by Wynema McGowan	(0120-8, $4.99)
DREAM OF ME by Jan Hudson	(0130-5, $4.99)
ROAD TO THE ISLE by Megan Davidson	(0131-3, $4.99)

Available wherever paperbacks are sold, or order direct from the Publisher. Send cover price plus 50¢ per copy for mailing and handling to Penguin USA, P.O. Box 999, c/o Dept. 17109, Bergenfield, NJ 07621. Residents of New York and Tennessee must include sales tax. DO NOT SEND CASH.

MARY GILLGANNON

LEOPARD'S LADY

PINNACLE BOOKS
KENSINGTON PUBLISHING CORP.

PINNACLE BOOKS are published by

Kensington Publishing Corp.
850 Third Avenue
New York, NY 10022

First Printing: July, 1995

Printed in the United States of America

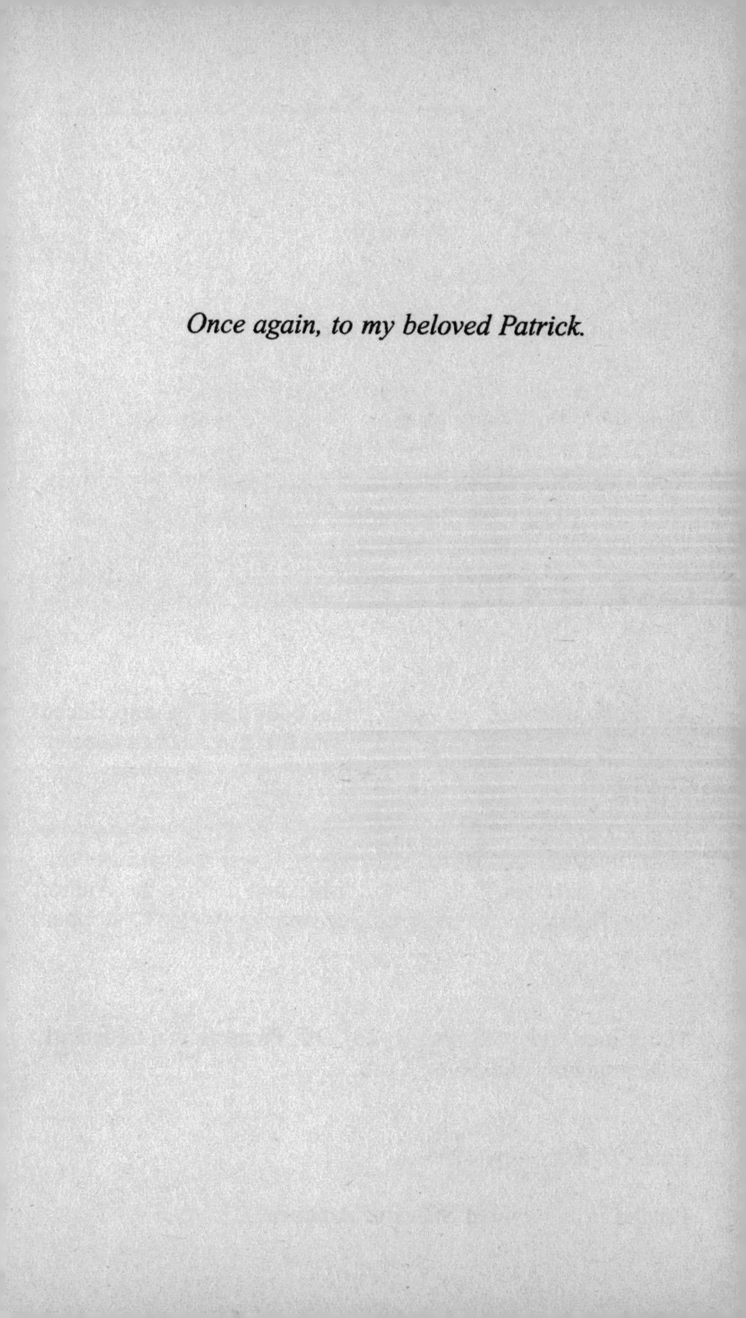

Once again, to my beloved Patrick.

Acknowledgments

I am indebted to the many friends and fellow writers who encouraged me and supported me during the beginning of my writing career. (And still continue to do so). I would especially like to thank:

Ed and Ann of the Laramie County Writers Group—for your ruthless criticism, unflagging encouragement, wit and humor, and computer advice and assistance.

My critique group—Deneé, Jessica, Margaret and Barbara. Your love and wisdom continues to enrich my life as well as my writing. The power of sisterhood is amazing.

My friends and coworkers at the Laramie County Library—for believing in me when it was all just a dream.

And finally, my wonderful editor, Denise Little, for making my dream come true.

Prologue

The sound of feminine laughter came to his ears, peals of girlish delight. He pushed through the lush green growth cautiously, trying not to scratch his hands on the brambles. His breath caught as he spied the two maidens bathing not twenty paces away. They were cavorting and frolicking in a small pool, and the shimmering water was not deep enough to hide their nakedness. His eyes took in dripping hair, smooth, young skin and two pairs of buoyant breasts floating on the water's surface. They laughed and shrieked like children, splashing each other playfully.

The nunnery of Stafford was nearby. These lovelies were likely young noblewomen who had been sent to the convent for schooling and protection. The tingling desire in his groin deepened almost unbearably. Unlike the whores and serving wenches who usually serviced him, these *demoiselles* were fresh and innocent, their skin clean and fragrant, their breasts firm, their faces guileless.

With near desperate impatience, his hand gripped the small tree hiding him. If only they would get out so he could really see them. Will would likely be along any minute. Unless his friend approached quietly, the girls would realize they were being watched and make a dash for their clothes. The thought of it made his breath catch again.

"God's blood," he whispered. "Hurry up! Get out so I can see you!"

As if she heard him, one of the girls made her way to the edge of the pool and stepped out gracefully, the water dripping from her small upturned breasts and trailing down her long slender legs. She is as dark as a Saracen, he thought with a greedy smile. Her hair was glistening black with wetness, her skin dusky even in places the sun seldom saw. She walked to her clothes with languorous ease, and he memorized the shape of her pert, muscular bottom, the enticing black triangle of hair between her legs, the berry color of her nipples.

He turned his eyes expectantly back to the water and was not disappointed.

A Venus—he thought as the second young woman rose slowly out of the water. His eyes widened as each stunning inch was revealed. Strands of rosy blond hair slid away to bare skin the shade of buttermilk and ripe, pink-tipped breasts shaped to fill a man's hand. He held his breath as her tiny waist was exposed, then the rounded curve of her hips. His gaze fastened on the tops of her thighs, where the soft shadow of hair the color of strawberries made his mouth water for a taste.

She stepped clear of the water and shook herself, her body undulating provocatively. His mouth went completely dry. She was made to look at—her small form opulent with the promise of pleasure. The pliant delectable flesh, the flawless blooming skin, the swirl of bright hair—if he had designed the perfect woman himself he could have done no better than this. He was tantalized beyond endurance by the very sight of her.

The other girl had dried herself and begun to dress, but the Venus remained naked, as if enjoying the feel of the sun upon her skin. She fluffed her hair, twirling her fingers through the cascade of dazzling rose-gold tresses. The other girl called teasingly to her, and she turned to respond, affording him a glorious view of her backside. Twin dimples winked at him just below where her hair met her hips, accenting the most splendidly rounded little bottom he'd ever seen. The cheeks of it were firm and smooth, but so temptingly full they made his fingers ache to cup them.

He was rock hard, and when she sat down at the edge of the pool and stretched out her exquisitely formed legs, he nearly came in his chausses. The only thing that saved him was Will's harsh whisper in his ear:

"King's knight or not, you could be strung up for spying like this."

"It would be worth it," he answered with a low moan. "Sweet Jesu, did you ever see anything like that one. She looks so deliciously pure."

"She is pure, you fool, she's probably a nun."

"God would not be so unjust. A woman like that is meant to be enjoyed."

Will put a restraining hand on his shoulder. "Not by you. You'd best get away while you can. Our excuse that we were pursuing a hind and got lost would sound pretty lame right now."

"In a minute," he whispered. "I only want to look at her a while longer. She's bound to get dressed soon anyway."

Except she didn't. She continued to sit on the rock, sunning herself as unconsciously as a child. Every little while she would shake out her hair or turn to speak to the other girl. The slight movements made her breasts jiggle enticingly. The sweat trickled down his chest.

Will sighed. "Stay then. When they hang you, I won't even remember your name."

Time seemed to stand still. He was not ten paces away from where she sat, and his eyes drank in every inch of her. He could almost see the pulse beating in her creamy neck, the last few drops of water drying on her sun-warmed skin. Her eyes were blue, clear and pure as the summer sky. Her features were soft and delicate, their childish sweetness contrasting with the lushness of her body.

For a moment he closed his eyes, imagining her ripe, beautiful body opening up to him—her pink lips moist and parted, her soft breasts crushed against his chest, her slender legs spread wide for his shaft.

Something made him open his eyes. She was standing up, staring directly at him, as if she could see him through the hawthorn bush. He froze as she advanced toward him. What should he do? Run? Greet her and tell her how beautiful she was, how much he had enjoyed watching her? He did nothing—just let her walk up to him. When she reached his hiding place, he stepped aside so she could see him.

A scream started in her eyes but never made it to her lips. He smiled at her. She stared back at him. Then she realized that she was completely naked and gave a little squeal of terror. He was surprised how fast she ran away. Who would have thought those slender legs could move so quickly? He treasured one last glimpse of her beautiful little bottom bobbing up and down as she ran. Then he turned and walked off into the forest.

One

England, a.d. 1248

She would never see Stafford again, Astra de Mortain thought ruefully as she turned back for one last look. In the distance, the priory seemed like a holy vision, floating ethereally above the veil of mist shimmering over the green valley. The soft morning light made the stonework gleam golden, and the transept vaults of the small chapel reached toward the sky like the very archways of heaven.

She straightened her spine and turned away. She had made her decision; there was no point indulging in regrets. Despite her resolve, the tears began to flow, leaking from her soft blue eyes and trickling down her cheeks. She wiped them away with impatient fingers.

"Sweet Jesu, you promised you wouldn't cry!" Marguerite Fitz Hugh exclaimed, guiding her fine white palfrey next to Astra's mule.

Astra gave her friend an exasperated look. "I've spent my whole life at Stafford," she reminded Marguerite. "It's only natural that I experience some sorrow at leaving."

Marguerite made a face. "I can't imagine why. Do you want to end up a sour-faced, dried-up old biddy like them?"

Astra smiled faintly. It was obvious Marguerite considered taking holy vows a fate worse than death. She could never understand how hard a choice it had been for Astra. Stafford represented security, peace . . . and love. The sisters had been the only family she'd ever known. If she had not discovered how ill-suited she was to the holy life, she would never have decided to leave.

How much Marguerite was to blame for that discovery, Astra thought wryly. If Marguerite had not come to Stafford and shown her a glimpse of the world outside the priory—and a frightening insight into her own sinful nature as well—she would never have had the courage to forsake the cloistered life. The truth was that she was unfit to be a bride of Christ, and she would not be a hypocrite. If she could not keep to her vows, she would not take them.

The mule she was riding stumbled slightly, and Astra struggled frantically to right herself. The animal quickly resumed its plodding pace, but Astra's stomach did not recover so easily. She had only to think about what was ahead of her, and her insides twisted in forboding. She had no preparation for the secular life, and the nuns had filled her mind with stories about the violence and evil that awaited her outside the priory. If it had not been for Marguerite's assurances that she would take care of Astra and help her realize her dream of a husband and a family of her own, Astra would never have dared to leave.

She glanced fondly at her friend, who had urged her horse ahead and was conversing with one of the knights escorting them. A charming smile graced Marguerite's lips, and her manner suggested blatant flirtatiousness. Astra shook her head. Marguerite was everything she was not—tall, elegant, assured. She sat a horse as if she had been born to it, and her gestures were as dramatic and graceful as Astra imagined a queen's would be. Next to her, Astra felt hopelessly awkward and gauche.

Perhaps Marguerite also had that effect upon the knight she was now flirting with, for as Astra watched, the man leaned away from Marguerite and spurred his destrier forward. Marguerite laughed teasingly after him, then let her mount slow until she was beside Astra.

"What wooden-headed dolts my father has for knights," she complained. Then she glanced at Astra, and her amused look turned to concern. "Still brooding, sweeting? Please don't fret anymore. You'll soon see that things have turned out for the best. We'll go home to my father's castle, Ravensmore, behave ourselves for a few months, and then, when Papa has grown tired of having us underfoot, we'll convince him to send us to King Henry's court."

A twinge of excitement stirred beneath Astra's gloom. Marguerite had been to the courts of both the French and English kings. Astra, on the other hand, had never been further afield than the market at Lichfield—and that in the company of a group of elderly nuns who hovered around her like hens guarding an orphaned chick.

"I'm afraid I would make a fool of myself at court," she told Marguerite. "I have no idea how to talk to ladies and noblemen."

"Never fear," Marguerite announced grandly. *"I* shall teach you everything you need to know. While we're at Ravensmore, I shall impart to you all the subtleties of dealing with kings and queens, barons and knights. I'll also have my mother instruct you in the arts of running a noble household. After you charm some wealthy and gallant knight into making you his wife, you'll need to know how to manage his *demesne."*

Astra shook her head at Marguerite's ridiculous plans. Most marriages were contracted for money or land, and she had neither. She was hardly a likely choice for a nobleman's wife, and even in her dreams, she had not dared to aim so high. When she imagined herself married, it was to a modestly successful clerk or an older merchant. With the skills in writing and sums she had learned at Stafford, she knew she could be an asset to such a man. Her ability to help her husband with his accounts might be enough to overcome her lack of a proper dowry.

"We'll begin your education this very day," Marguerite enthused. "It's Saturday, and there will undoubtedly be a fair at Tudbury. When we pass by this afternoon, I'll insist to our escort that we stop and take refreshment. With a tournament scheduled there in a fortnight, there's certain to be some knights in the area. We'll make their acquaintance, and you will have your first lesson in conversing with the opposite sex."

Astra turned and cast one last regretful glance toward the distant priory. It was too late to turn back now. Her new life was about to begin.

"Mother of God, what a smell!" Astra exclaimed as they rode into Tudbury. The combined odors of offal, cooking food, sweat and perfume which exuded from the town fair were already ripening in the summer heat.

Marguerite gave a peal of laughter before responding in her husky, heavily accented voice: "That, *ma petite,* is the smell of adventure!"

Astra nodded, a shiver coursing down her body in response to her friend's tantalizing words. This was why she had left the priory. She wanted to see a fair, to buy something useless and extravagant, to rub shoulders with the nobility and the peasants—in truth, an adventure was exactly what she yearned for.

They reached the crossroads outside the town, and the leader of their escort tried to turn them east on the road toward Repton Abbey. The old knight, Sir Thomas de Chilham, was reluctant to see his young charges exposed to the base merrymaking of a town festival. Only by arguing strenuously did Marguerite manage to convince him that she was near faint with hunger and could not endure waiting a moment longer to eat.

The booths and pavilions of the fair were spread out on a green meadow dotted with poppies and cornflowers. The flowers were now mostly trampled; the field strewn with refuse. As they approached, the odor of cooking food intensified, almost but not quite overpowering other less enticing scents. Astra's stomach growled noisily, and as soon as one of the men helped her dismount, she hurried with Marguerite to the food booths. The stalls seemed to overflow with food—succulent meat pies, roast fowl, spicy sausages, nuts and sweetmeats, even oranges from Morocco. Marguerite was lavish with her pennies, and Astra's foremost problem was deciding what to eat next.

"Don't stuff yourself," Marguerite warned. "If you aren't used to rich fare, it's easy to make yourself wretchedly ill."

Astra nodded as she took another bite of divinely flavored sausage. The food at Stafford was nothing like this—fish in plain sauces much of the year, salted pork the rest, with a tough stringy chicken or fresh cheese from the nearby monastery as an occasional treat. She rolled her tongue in her mouth and savored the foreign flavors she'd just experienced.

Their hunger satisfied, the two young women set out to explore the merchant booths. Astra's senses were areel. She'd never seen such beautiful things—bolts of exquisite cloth: cottons from France and Flanders, silks from the East, bright wools from native looms; buttersoft leather boots and shoes from Spain; finely wrought jewelry of silver and gold set with pearls, jet, rubies and lapis lazuli. There were also booths and tents offering more practical things: weapons and armor, farm tools, and ropes.

The people attending the fair were as interesting to Astra as the merchandise. She saw ruddy-faced peasants in wooden clogs and plain brown tunics which hung to their bare, dirty knees; prosperous townfolk in bright wools of saffron, green and scarlet; monks with their tonsures and coarse robes; clerics resplendent in samite, velvet and silk; even a nobleman with a fine embroidered surcote over his armor and an elegant, gold-coifed lady at his side. Astra took in everything, trying not to stare.

"Now to find some knights," Marguerite announced when they had made a quick tour of the merchant area.

"I really don't think . . ."

"Nonsense. It's exactly the same as anything else at a market, Astra. You must look over the merchandise before you decide what you want. Myself, I fancy a big, lusty specimen. I'm tired of being reminded that I'm too tall for fashion; I want a man I can look up to instead of hunching over and trying to pretend I am some dainty feminine thing." She grimaced.

"I also have a special fondness for blond men," she continued. "Maybe even one with Saxon blood. I've heard that they make good lovers, that they are willing to woo a girl with a fine piece of talk. Not like the Normans." Marguerite made an even more disgusted face. "They are too grim and dreary, always obsessed with war, and next to that, land. What of you, Astra? What sort of husband do you fancy?"

Astra thought a moment. "Someone loyal and kind, and pious of course."

"Bah! You are not picking out a confessor, Astra, but a husband. Surely you can think of qualities you desire more than those. What of his features? His form?"

"I don't know, Marguerite," Astra answered uncomfortably. "I've had so little experience with men."

"Indeed," her friend whispered teasingly. "What about the day we spied upon the monks? Did you learn nothing then?"

Astra's face flushed. She had tried to force the memory from her mind, but she could not forget the sight of a dozen naked men bathing in the river. Their bodies were pale and hairy, their private parts odd, dangling things that revolted Astra as much as fascinated her.

"In truth, the monks were not such fine-looking creatures, were they?" Marguerite admitted. "What we seek are handsome, virile young knights. Perhaps over there."

Marguerite set off briskly for the part of the fair reserved for entertainments—jugglers and minstrels, cockfighting and dicing. Astra's heart sank as they neared the crowded scene. If any young knights were to be found at the fair, it would likely be there. She hesitated, suddenly realizing she was not ready to learn about men quite yet. "Marguerite!" she called after her friend. "Can we not look for the spice booth now?"

Marguerite turned, frowning. "Since it is your first fair,

Astra, I will humor you. But as soon as we are done there, I mean to discover some gentlemen."

They followed their noses to the source of the alluring scents that wafted above the crude odors of people and food. Drawing near to a booth which offered rare condiments such as cinnamon and ginger, Astra closed her eyes and breathed deeply, enthralled by the sweet odors which brought to mind foreign, exotic places. Her reverie was broken when Marguerite whispered teasingly in her ear:

"Astra, time for your first lesson."

Astra opened her eyes to see three knights approaching. They did not have on full armor, but they wore hauberks and carried swords at their sides, swaggering with the bravado of fighting men. To Astra they appeared threatening and evil. She reminded herself that no harm could come to her and Marguerite. The Fitz Hugh knights would protect them, wouldn't they? Astra looked around and uneasily realized that their escort was nowhere in sight.

"Marguerite," Astra whispered. "Where are they? Where are your father's men?"

"Those tiresome fools," Marguerite scoffed. "They're all as old as my father—and nearly as easy to deceive. We gave them the slip back by the cloth merchants."

"We're alone and unprotected!"

"Exactly," Marguerite answered.

The knights continued to approach. Astra ducked into the spice booth and pretended to examine a packet of peppercorns, praying frantically that the knights would pass them by. Her hopes were in vain, for as the three soldiers tread toward them, Marguerite deliberately dropped one of the velvet slippers she had just purchased. "Oh, how clumsy of me!" she exclaimed.

The three knights halted, and the largest one reached down and retrieved the dainty object.

"My lady," he said. He handed it to Marguerite with a flourish.

"You are most kind, sir." Marguerite smiled. She turned to Astra. "Oh, cousin, if only we had not lost track of Sir de Chilham and the rest of our escort. I have no one to carry my purchases, and I am so affeared I shall lose something."

Astra gaped at her friend. It was bad enough they were unprotected, but to draw attention to their vulnerability before these dangerous-looking men—was Marguerite mad?

"My lady, we would be honored to serve you," the nearest knight asserted. "Pray, spend your money freely, we will be happy to carry all that you buy."

Astra looked the man over critically. He was not unpleasant to look at, with tousled fair hair and pale gray eyes. But there was something malevolent about him, an insincerity to his smile. The warmth of it did not reach his shrewd, unsettling eyes.

Astra put a hand on Marguerite's arm, begging her silently to refuse. Of course, it was not to be. Marguerite was determined that Astra should spend some time in the company of men.

The three soldiers trailed along as they walked again among the merchant booths. Marguerite chattered merrily. Occasionally she stopped to purchase ribbons and combs and thread, inconsequential things that she and Astra could have easily carried themselves. Once, they almost ran into one of the Fitz Hugh knights, but Marguerite deftly steered Astra into a leather shop before she could get the man's attention.

Astra endured their masculine companions glumly. She'd had a chance to observe the three knights more closely and proximity hadn't enhanced her opinion. They seemed like coarse, ill-mannered louts, and their leader's inept conversational skills made it clear that he was not accustomed to escorting ladies. Marguerite carried the conversation, nay, dragged it along.

Astra's alarm intensified when the tall, fair-haired knight suggested they take a respite in the shade of the nearby forest. Astra looked at Marguerite, sure she would refuse the offer. To Astra's horror, her friend fluttered her long dark lashes. "What a lovely idea," she cooed at the man. "I'm sure the woods would be much cooler and more comfortable than the open meadow."

Astra reluctantly followed Marguerite and the three men into the shadowy, sunlight-speckled woods. She tried to reassure herself that they were really only a short distance from the outer edge of the fair. If, God forbid, something unpleasant happened, they could call out and someone would come to their rescue.

They were barely a few paces into the humid, green foliage when Marguerite allowed the golden-haired knight to take her arm. After they had gone a short ways further, she leaned into him, pulling him into an awkward embrace. The man looked startled, then recovered. He bent over and kissed Marguerite enthusiastically. Astra could only stare. She'd worried that the knight might make improper advances toward Marguerite, not the other way around! What was she to do now?

She glanced at the other two men, noting their hungry, speculative looks. Something in their faces made a scream form in her throat. Before she could actually find her voice, one of the men grabbed her and clamped a heavy hand over her mouth. Astra began to struggle, certain she was on the verge of being ravished. She caught a wedge of flesh in her teeth and bit down. At the same time, she clawed the man's face with her nails. The man cried out and landed a blow on the side of her head. The impact made her dizzy, and for a time she could not think clearly. When she came to herself, the fair-haired knight was chastising the man who held her.

"Damn you, Tom, don't hurt her! How will we collect the ransom if she dies!"

"Ransom! You mean to ransom us?" Marguerite's voice rose, furious, utterly outraged.

"Aye, my lusty little vixen," the blond knight answered. He directed his attention back to her. "You have just told me how dear your father holds you and how rich he is. I'd be a fool not to test Lord Fitz Hugh's devotion."

"Why . . . you . . . bastard!" Marguerite flung herself violently at the knight she had embraced only seconds before. The man did not endure her pummeling long. He pulled a wicked-looking knife from his belt and pointed it directly at Marguerite's heaving bosom.

Two

"I tell you, Richard, you're ready. If you train much more you'll only lose your edge."

Richard Reivers shook his head. "You don't understand. I mean to be perfect, absolutely magnificent for this tournament. They say Lord Darley is offering a manor to the victor."

"Winning land—is that all you think of?"

"What else is there?" Richard asked. His dark eyes glowed.

"I know it sounds lame, coming from me, but wealth and power aren't everything. You cannot buy happiness."

Richard laughed uproariously and slapped his friend soundly on the back. The blow was hardly felt, for both men wore full armor, except for their conical helmets—which they carried.

"You're right, Will, it does sound lame. You're so filthy rich you can't even imagine what it is like to be a poor, landless knight."

"I've told you before, Richard, I'd be pleased to speak to the King about awarding you a manor . . ."

"The King!" Richard's dark eyes flashed with contempt. "Since I'm not from Provence, Henry isn't likely to give me anything. He's so busy handing out castles, manors and bishoprics to his wife's relatives he can't be bothered with his loyal knights."

Will sighed. Richard wasn't exaggerating. King Henry's shameless promotion of his Provencal relatives was the talk of England.

"When I think of all the battles I've won for him . . ." Richard grumbled.

"Look sharp, Richard—what's that ahead of us?"

The two men froze, then strained to see through the budding green foliage. A short distance away, a group of rough men appeared to be guarding two plainly dressed women. The women's faces were pale and strained; the men watchful and furtive.

"God's blood, Will, they're prisoners!"

"It does indeed look that way. Worse yet, the women are dressed like novices. What kind of men would harass holy sisters?"

"They're obviously sacrilegious as well as unchivalrous," Richard growled. "It'll make killing them even better sport."

"What say you then—the count of three?"

Richard nodded, then silently pulled on his helmet and drew his heavy sword.

Astra didn't even see their rescuers arrive. As she prayed silently, the man guarding her abruptly fell over backwards. She turned and gaped at the man's pale, slack face. A stream of crimson darkened the leaves around his scalp, and Astra realized he'd been hit over the head.

The rest of it happened almost as quickly. The big, fair-haired knight grabbed Marguerite again and held his knife to her throat. While Astra's horrified eyes were fixed on the glittering blade, the knife abruptly dropped and Marguerite's attacker also slumped to the ground, his head nearly cleaved in two by a massive sword blow. Later, Astra would learn that the third man hadn't lingered, but immediately bolted into the forest. At the time she was too overcome to care. The sight of so much blood undid her. She bent over and began to retch, heaving up the rich, spicy food she'd recently eaten.

As she spat out the last sour dregs, Astra felt a steadying arm at her elbow. Assuming that it was Marguerite, she nearly gagged again when she looked up and saw a helmeted knight regarding her. With a shiver of dread, she shook off the mailed arm that supported her and stared in dismay at the hideous visage of the tall knight. With his conical helmet and nose guard he looked like a terrifying, evil being—a devil.

The knight stared back at her. She could see his eyes at least. They were dark, almost black, and they watched her with an intensity that was utterly unnerving.

"Is she all right?"

They both turned to see another knight approach. He gently braced Marguerite against his armored chest. Even though he wore the same ferocious-looking armor as the dark-eyed knight, this man didn't seem nearly as intimidating. He was smaller than Astra's rescuer, and his movements were refined and graceful. When his companion didn't answer, he released Marguerite and pulled off his helmet, revealing long, straight brown hair, blue eyes and fine, almost delicate features.

"God's toes, Richard, take off your helmet. You're scaring her."

The dark-eyed knight made no move to comply. The

other man frowned, then approached Astra and bowed politely.

"My lady, are you well?"

Astra managed to nod. She was still trembling and dazed. She'd never been exposed to violent death before, and the ugliness of it appalled her.

Marguerite clutched at the smaller knight's arm. "How can we ever repay you? If you hadn't come along just then . . ." Marguerite gave a dramatic shiver. "They said their intentions were to ransom us, but I was afraid . . ." She fluttered her long, dark lashes demurely. "I feared their intentions were much worse."

"They meant to ransom you?" the dark-eyed knight named Richard spoke up abruptly. "How can that be? How could they hope to ransom a nun?"

Marguerite gave a soft, seductive laugh. "You thought we were nuns? Oh, no, my lord. While we travel from Stafford Priory, we aren't bound by holy orders. I am Lady Marguerite Fitz Hugh, and this is my cousin, Astra de Mortain."

Astra felt the man holding her stiffen at the mention of Stafford, but she was too surprised by Marguerite's words to ponder why. Marguerite had again introduced Astra as her cousin. It was a blatant lie, and it made Astra exceedingly uncomfortable. It was one thing to tell a falsehood to the group of disreputable louts, another to deceive well-born knights—especially after they had rescued you. Astra opened her mouth to protest; Marguerite silenced her with bright, pleading eyes.

The smaller knight bowed again, this time with a regal flourish.

"We are honored to be at your service, *demoiselles*. I am William de Lacy, Baron of Thornbury. And my companion . . ." he gestured to the dark-eyed knight, ". . . is Richard Reivers, also known as the Black Leopard—one of the bravest and fiercest knights in Christendom."

Astra could only stare. Sweet Jesu! They had been rescued by a baron! A baron and a devil! She glanced again at Sir Reivers. He still had not removed his helmet, and he appeared as deadly and dangerous as ever. The Black Leopard—how many men had he killed to win that horrifying appellation?

Marguerite seemed slightly taken aback by the prominence of their rescuers, but she recovered quickly. "You must be here for the tournament," she suggested. "I told my cousin that there would be knights in the area, that someone would come to our rescue."

"But where are your men?" Sir Reivers asked. "Surely you don't travel without an escort."

"In the confusion of the fair, we became separated from my father's knights. Then those awful men . . ." Marguerite glanced with a shudder at the slaughtered pair laying gruesomely nearby, ". . . they offered to help us." Her lower lip trembled. "I feel like such a fool. We should have known better than to trust such ill-mannered knaves."

"Aye, you should have known better," Lord de Lacy agreed dryly. "You were very lucky we came along when we did." He gave Astra a concerned look. "Can you walk, my lady?"

Astra nodded.

"Very well then, I think we'd best be finding your men."

Sir de Chilham spotted them as soon as they left the woods and neared the fair. He rushed up, his face flushed, his thinning hair sweaty and disheveled. "Lady Marguerite, where have you been? Who are these men?"

De Lacy stepped forward, bowing gracefully to the older knight.

"Your mistress came very near to being kidnapped by a group of ruffians. My companion, Sir Reivers, and I arrived just in time to prevent the abduction."

The blood drained from de Chilham's face. "Lady Marguerite, is this true?"

With a chagrined look, Marguerite nodded.

For a moment de Chilham stared at her, then he exploded: "This time, *demoiselle,* you have gone too far. Your father will hear of your adventures as soon as I deliver you to Ravensmore, and I promise you, he will not be pleased. Get yourself to your horse this minute—and see you do not get into any more trouble on the way!"

Marguerite managed another dramatic shift. She suddenly appeared as meek and contrite as a chastised child. She bowed politely to de Lacy and Reivers, then walked off with dainty, mincing steps. She lifted her skirts fastidiously to avoid the muck of the fairgrounds.

Astra would have followed her friend, but Sir Reivers continued to hold her arm. She turned and stared at him in puzzlement, wondering if he thought she would be ill again. His helmet did not entirely hide his face, and she could see his mouth below the nose piece. His surprisingly full, sensual lips were formed into a smile.

She frowned back, disturbed by his expression. Was he mocking her? Astra abruptly pulled her arm away, then offered a shaky curtsy to Lord de Lacy. She was halfway across the maze of booths and tents before she realized that neither she nor Marguerite had thanked their rescuers.

* * *

"Will, about those young women . . ." Richard began as the two men walked toward the ale tent.

"Odd, wasn't it. . . ." Will mused. "The way de Chilham lost control. They did behave stupidly, but still . . . to shout at a lady like that, the daughter of your liege lord . . . I can only think de Chilham was so overcome with worry that he forgot himself."

"William, I'm trying to tell you—I know those women."

"Know them?" Will turned in surprise.

"You remember the luscious young ladies we saw swimming near Stafford last summer?"

"No! It couldn't be!"

"I was skeptical too. But when they mentioned they were traveling from Stafford, I looked them over thoroughly. I'm sure Lady Marguerite was the tall, dark-haired girl who got out of the water first, and Lady Astra—she is . . ."

"Your Venus," Will finished.

Richard nodded. "It strains the imagination, but it's true. I've found her. I know her name. And the best part is . . ."

"She's not a nun!" Will finished brightly.

Richard shook his head. "No. The best part is that she's undoubtedly rich. Lord Fitz Hugh has land in Kent, Brittany and Wales as well as Westford. I can't imagine that his niece would not be well-dowered."

"Rich, innocent and beautiful beyond compare—it seems you have found the woman of your dreams."

"And she's on her way north this very minute, damn the luck," Richard grumbled. "Besides, she's probably betrothed—that's likely why they're leaving the nunnery."

"For shame, Richard, it's not like you to give up so easily."

"You're right, Will," Richard agreed with a mischievous smile. "Although I may never lay claim to Lady Astra's dower lands, I might yet claim her body. After all, 'tis mine by rights. I'll wager I was the first man to look upon her glorious nakedness."

"I had almost forgotten the incident. As I recall, the young woman caught you watching her. Is that why you refused to remove your helmet?"

Richard nodded. "I thought Lady Astra had had enough shocks today without recognizing me. Watching a man killed caused her to lose her meal. She'd have likely fainted dead away at the sight of me."

"What an odd day it's been. We rescue two nuns from brigands, only to find that they're not nuns at all, but beautiful young heiresses. It almost makes you wonder if there isn't something to the saying that 'virtue is its own reward.' "

"Don't be a dolt, Will. It was blind chance that we came upon those women when we did. Besides, we haven't received any reward. Sir de Chilham hardly even appeared grateful that we returned his delectable young charges safely."

"If you ask me, de Chilham has his hands full, at least with Lady Marguerite. I wouldn't be surprised if she wandered off on purpose. She risked her own life and Lady Astra's for the sake of a lark. Anyway, while de Chilham may not have had the decency to thank us, Lord Fitz Hugh is another matter. I'd wager he will offer us some boon for rescuing his daughter and niece from the clutches of those animals."

"By God, you're right!" Richard responded enthusiastically. "Perhaps it was divine will that they appeared in our pathway. Perhaps Fitz Hugh will reward my bravery with a small manor, or at least another suit of armor or a warhorse."

"God's toes, Richard. Do you think of nothing else? Your greed wearies me."

"Weary are you? I know just the thing." Richard gave his friend a merry smile and gestured toward the refreshment booths. "I fancy a drink myself. Saving damsels in distress is damn tiring business."

Three

"I've done it again, haven't I?" Marguerite sighed as they rode toward Repton Abbey. "Papa will be truly wroth with me this time. I don't know how I'll ever explain."

Astra nodded, unsure whether to comfort her friend or scold her. Marguerite had accomplished one of her astounding changes of mood. At this moment at least she appeared contrite.

"I truly didn't mean to get us into such a plight. How was I to know those men were little more than criminals?"

"Really, Marguerite," Astra admonished. "I grew up in a convent, and even *I* knew they were untrustworthy. Why ever did you allow them to lead us into the woods, away from everyone?"

"You could have said something, Astra. If you were worried, why didn't you insist we return to our escort?"

Astra pressed her lips together and didn't answer. Why indeed?—she wondered. Was she so eager for an adventure she was willing to risk being kidnapped and ravished? Mother of God! She should never have left the convent if she was going to act like such a fool.

"I'm sorry Astra," Marguerite said after a moment. "You are right. You trusted me to take care of you, and I failed you."

"That's not true," Astra protested. "You did not mean

to lead me into danger. The rest of the day was wonderful . . . the fair, the food, all the pretty things. . . ." She could not resist smiling at the memory of the delights she had experienced.

Marguerite smiled back. "Speaking of pretty sights," she teased. "Were those young knights not thrilling? I've never seen such shoulders as the one called Richard had. No wonder they call him the Black Leopard!"

Astra's smile faded. "I thought he behaved very oddly. He kept staring at me. I can almost feel his eyes upon me even now." She gave an involuntary shudder.

"Perhaps he was so bedazzled by your beauty, he could not look away."

Astra gave her friend a disbelieving look. Their plain gray bliauts and white wimples were spattered with mud and blood, and Astra's face felt so sweaty and filthy she could hardly bear it. Compared to the stunningly attired women she had seen at the fair, it was inconceivable that any man would look twice at her. Still, Sir Reivers's interest in her had been unmistakable. He had watched her so intensely, his eyes had seemed to burn through the slits of his helmet. And the way he held onto her arm—Jesu, she had been afraid he would never release her!

"I didn't see the other man's face, but Lord de Lacy is certainly handsome," she told Marguerite.

Marguerite nodded. "Handsome, aye, but too pretty for my taste. I would have liked to have seen the other one, Richard, without his helmet. Odd that he didn't take it off, even when his companion asked him to. You might think he was hiding something."

Astra shivered again. What *did* Sir Reivers's face look like? Was it as fierce and deadly as his battle epithet—the Black Leopard?

* * *

The rest of their journey was uneventful, and they arrived at Repton soon after sunset. The tranquil, quiet atmosphere of the priory filled Astra with relief. The bells announcing vespers, the quiet chant of prayers, the sense of order and peace—Astra felt as if she were coming home. They ate a plain, sparse meal, then an elderly monk led them to the guest quarters.

"Mon Dieu, you would think we were back at Stafford." Marguerite wrinkled her nose at the tiny austere cell they were offered. She poked one of the pallets on the floor with her foot and swore in disgust at its obvious hardness. "We are noble guests, not penitents, surely they could have offered us more comfortable accommodations."

"Prior Grosbert believes that comfort is an enemy of the pure in spirit," the old monk replied gravely. "He offers his guests a quiet refuge to examine their sinful lives and pray for forgiveness."

Marguerite rolled her eyes and quickly dismissed the man, then flopped down on one of the pallets with a sigh. "I am so tired, I think I could sleep anywhere, even on this wretched rock of a bed."

Astra sighed. She was exhausted as well. The day had begun very early and been filled with more excitement than she had experienced in months. She removed her wimple and bliaut and stretched out on one of the lumpy pallets, then pulled up the thin, rough blanket.

Long minutes passed. Next to her, Marguerite's breathing slowed and deepened. Astra twisted restlessly and tried to find a comfortable position. A sense of anxiety crept over her as she recalled the danger she and Marguerite had faced in the forest. They could have been raped, even murdered! Astra's heart pounded and her tense muscles tightened even further as she contemplated what might have happened. Perhaps she should never have left the priory. She was obviously too naive and foolish to avoid the evils of a country fair. What would happen to her when she faced the dangers and depravities of a king's court? It might be best if she returned to Stafford before something truly awful occurred.

Astra clutched her chest and felt her heart thundering beneath her fingertips. Jesu, what a coward she was! One little scare and she was ready to go fleeing back to Stafford. If she did, it would be the end of her dreams of a husband and family. The rest of her life would be spent in the narrow, numbing world of the cloisters. No, she thought resolutely, she would not be so spineless.

As she had many times before, Astra thought of her father. She could not remember him, but she knew he had been a brave man, not only a courageous soldier, but also a man of strong convictions. Many years ago, Brian de Mortain had defied evil King John and refused his request to murder a man who had offended the king. His defiance had eventually ruined him, but de Mortain had never expressed regret over his choice. Recalling her father's life—he had drowned crossing the channel in 1233, only months after Astra's mother had perished of childbed fever—Astra could not help but be inspired. Her father had stood up for what he believed, despite the cost. She, too, must follow her convictions.

A sense of determination began to replace her panic. To return to Stafford would be to choose the easy path, the safe one. For the sake of her father's memory she could not do that. She must continue to search for the destiny she was meant to pursue.

She sighed and willed herself to relax. As the tension left her body, she thought again of the knight in the forest. She recalled his hand upon her arm, his dangerous dark eyes staring at her. The memory made a warm tingle rush down her body. The sensation surprised her. What did it mean? Was she afraid of the evil-looking knight, or was it something else? She considered asking Marguerite about it in the morning, then decided she would not. Her friend would only tease her mercilessly.

Will de Lacy felt a vague apprehension as he gazed around the dingy, sweltering alehouse. The tournament had attracted knights from the nearby shires, along with a less savory element of ruffians, gamblers and petty criminals. The very air of the Boarshead Tavern seethed with menace. Will could not help feeling for the dagger at his belt; he wondered if he would have need of it.

Across the greasy plank that served as a table, Richard conversed animatedly with another knight, arguing various fighting techniques and their relative merits on the tournament field. Will scarcely listened. To his mind tournaments were dangerous and foolish, and he had tried without success to dissuade Richard from entering this one.

He took another swig of bitter ale and surveyed the room gloomily. His eyes met those of Guy Faucomberg, a hard-eyed young man who was said to be one of the richest men in England. For a moment their gazes locked, and Will's uneasiness increased. His body tensed, and a wave of grim weariness washed over him. It was always this same battle.

Four feet away Richard gave a delighted laugh. The conversation had turned from weapons to women, and on that subject the Black Leopard was truly an expert.

Will glanced toward the door, planning his escape. From the look in Faucomberg's eyes, there was going to be trouble, and Will didn't want Richard drawn into the unpleasant business. He stood. Richard looked up, regarding him with curiosity.

Will schooled his face to a calm, unconcerned expression and tried to slow his racing pulse. Then he began to walk toward the door, pushing his way through the mass of sweaty, drunken soldiers who blocked his way.

"Fleeing again, de Lacy? Too much of a coward to face me?"

Will paused and turned stiffly toward his challenger. Faucomberg stood about ten paces away, his orange-colored hair bristling above his high forehead, his sneering mouth a red slash in his pale face.

"If you have something to say to me, Faucomberg, I suggest you join me outside." Will turned back toward the door and edged carefully past the men in his way. They took note of his rich velvet tunic and the heavy gold chain at his neck and moved aside.

"Oh, aye, you queer bastard. Go outside where your men can defend you."

The harsh loathing in Faucomberg's voice carried remarkably well in the suddenly quiet tavern. Will could hear the indrawn breaths and excited whispers behind him. The confrontation was becoming a public event. Two barons facing off in a grubby Tudbury alehouse—it was a thing not to be missed.

A third voice rose above the hush: "What's that, Faucomberg? Did you say something to Baron de Lacy? I thought you called my friend a coward, but I must have misunderstood."

Will turned in dismay. Of course Richard would come to his defense, damn him. It was just like him to risk his neck in a hopeless cause. Didn't he realize that there was no fighting Faucomberg? The gist of his words was true, and getting into a brawl over them would only fan the flames of the man's hatred all the higher.

"No misunderstanding, Reivers. I did call de Lacy a coward. I hadn't realized you would be fool enough to defend him. Can it be that you have forsaken your whoring ways and become a lily lover like him?"

There was a collective gasp from the bystanders. Faucomberg enjoyed some protection because of his wealth and title, but everyone knew that the Black Leopard was a vengeful man and one who feared nothing. All eyes turned to Reivers. He looked exactly like his animal namesake—tense and deadly, ready to spring upon his opponent with unbridled savagery.

Will thought he saw a flicker of fear in Faucomberg's eyes, but it was nothing compared to what he felt. He couldn't stand by and watch Richard throw away his career and perhaps his life.

"Stop them!" he called out. "If they fight and someone is killed, Lord Darley will cancel the tournament."

The hard-eyed, half-drunk men around him muttered knowingly. Tournaments were already denounced by the Church. If blood was shed here, there would be even more reason to outlaw their favorite entertainment. The crowd watched the two combatants uneasily. Richard had drawn his knife, and no one appeared brave enough to take it away from him.

The knife flashed, shimmering like a silver fish in the

dim tavern light. Faucomberg jumped back, fear making his white skin grow whiter still. He gave a slight, imperceptible nod, and the group of men behind him surged forward like a menacing tide. Richard was surrounded.

The Black Leopard eyed his assailants disdainfully, then fixed his cold, pitiless glance on Faucomberg.

"Cowardice? I give you cowardice—ten men against one."

A murmur passed among the spectators, unfriendly, mocking. Faucomberg gained color rapidly, his face flushing almost as red as his hair. "Seize him!" he hissed.

Will pushed forward, only to see Richard disappear in the midst of a flurry of flailing arms and grim faces. When he could finally see him again, Richard's knife was gone, and three men had his arms pinned behind him. His eyes were black whirlpools of hate.

"Face me on the tournament field, you bastard. I dare you!" Richard taunted.

Faucomberg's mouth twitched, but he didn't respond. He jerked his head toward the door. His men abruptly released Richard and followed after him.

Will was finally able to reach Richard. His friend was glaring toward the door and cradling his right hand against his chest. Blood trickled down his fingers in a dark stream.

"Jesu, it's only a scratch, Will. I won't even notice it by tomorrow." Richard lay on a pallet before the fire while one of the de Lacy squires rubbed goose grease into his thick muscles. Will glanced at his friend's bandaged hand morosely. The wound wasn't deep, but it was in the worst possible place—cutting across the palm of

Richard's sword hand. It was sure to weaken his grip on the heavy lance he must wield in the tournament.

"You shouldn't have gotten involved, Richard. All you did was make a dangerous enemy and get yourself hurt."

"I wasn't going to stand there and let that arrogant sack of shit call you names!"

Will shook his head. "You must learn to ignore it. I can't change what I am, and there will always be men like Faucomberg who can't resist taunting me."

"But he called you a coward!"

Will shrugged. "In his mind those who share my aberration are something less than men. I've grown used to it."

"Miserable wretch—if only he would meet me on the tournament field. We'd see who was the coward then!"

"It will never happen, Richard, and it's just as well. You have your own reputation to consider. If you appear as my champion . . ." Will hesitated. "People might say that you and I . . ."

Richard's eyes hardened. "Pathetic, gossiping fools."

The slap of the squire's palms on Richard's sleek, oiled skin was suddenly the only sound in the room. Will's taste in lovers was a subject that neither man wanted to discuss.

"Let me get someone to look at that hand, Richard. I want to make sure you don't need it stitched."

"Stitched!" Richard sat up abruptly. "God's blood, Will. I told you, it's only a little scratch."

"Still . . . I'd feel better if you had it looked at. I could ask the serving wench if she knows of a physician . . ."

"A physician! You must be mad! I wouldn't let one of those murdering bastards near me if I was on my deathbed!" A slight smile quirked his lips. "But perhaps you should get the serving wench up here anyway. I have this ache in my groin that needs attending."

Will groaned. "You're hopeless, Reivers. The next thing I know you'll be asking for a skin of wine to kill the pain. Get some rest. You have a tournament tomorrow."

Richard frowned as he rolled out of the sagging bed. His hand was sore and throbbing. He pulled off the ragged bandage and stared at the wound. It was clean, no festering. Still, it hurt. The thought of clutching a heavy lance made him wince.

He shrugged his shoulders to ease the morning stiffness from them and tried to banish his doubts as well. He needed to win this tournament, and he had no intention of letting a sore hand interfere with his plan. He'd fought with much worse injuries before, and this time he was competing for something he'd dreamed of all his life. Land—his own land.

A thrill went through him as he considered the rich hill country around Tudbury. Already he could envision it: his own small but formidable fortress and surrounding it, rich, ripe fields gleaming golden in the sun, sheep grazing peacefully in the meadows, with cattle down by the river. In the fall, the produce of his prosperous lands would fill up a dozen sturdy carts and be taken to market. There it would be changed into gold, and the gold used to buy exquisite things to fill his hall.

Richard sighed. He had dreamed of possessing his own *demesne* for so long. It would make up for everything: the danger and wretchedness of soldiering, the galling years of deferring to vain, stupid noblemen who considered themselves superior to him, even his lonely, fatherless youth.

He clenched his hand tightly and ignored the burning pain of the knife wound. He would not fail now—not when he was so very close.

The tournament ground was already busy when Richard arrived. Carts and booths were being set up by peddlers and farmers. In a few hours they would be offering joints of beef, meat pasties, sausages, and pails of ale, milk and water to the hordes of spectators. At one end of the long oval field, knights, squires and horses gathered near the brightly-colored pavilions, while along one side, workers put the final touches on the canopied enclosure where the nobility would sit. Richard glanced scornfully at the rows of wooden seats covered in gold and purple cloth. Faucomberg would likely watch the tournament from there, a velvet cushion under his bony, worthless arse. And he had the nerve to call Will a coward!

Richard made his way to a pavilion marked by a banner of deep crimson embroidered with a gold dragon. He would fight under the banner of Deaumont as he always had. It seemed the least he could do for the family who had given him a chance at knighthood.

Inside the pavilion, his squire was rubbing down his huge warhorse, Sultan. The youth smiled at him, showing the slight gap between his front teeth.

"Splendid day for a tournament, sire."

Richard nodded. Absurd as it seemed, he was nervous. He was never nervous in battle, and he could not fathom why he felt so skittish now. Perhaps it was because this tournament meant so much to him.

He approached a pile of armor and weaponry near the tent entrance. He poked at it with his foot, then reached down to pull out the huge lance he would begin the joust with. It was much longer than he was tall and formidably heavy. He hefted it in his right hand, ignoring the pain the motion caused. It would be better with gloves. Besides, it didn't matter; pain or no pain, he would win.

Four

Will stood by the edge of the field, a few paces from the covered seating area. He wanted to be close to the combatants—to feel the dust, to smell the sweat, the blood. He wanted to be right there when Richard won. He used the sleeve of his tunic to wipe a trickle of sweat from his brow. It was hot out under the merciless sun. For now, it was peaceful too. He could hear plovers and blackbirds calling from the edge of the fields; flies buzzed around the piles of horse dung near the pavilions.

The harsh blast of trumpets sounded, and Will's tranquil mood evaporated. As the nobility took their seats in the stands, gaily-decked pages marched onto the field carrying huge canvases depicting biblical scenes: Samson bringing down the temple, Daniel in the lions' den, the serpent entering the Garden of Eden. The knights followed, resplendent on their massive warhorses. Beside them, squires carried the banners of the royal houses: lions, dragons, serpents and stags cavorting on streaming pennants of green, gold and scarlet silk.

The procession circled the field and slowed as they reached the royal seats. Will caught a glimpse of Richard. His face wore a calm, almost languorous expression, and he looked as if he were going for a ride in the woods instead of preparing for deadly combat. Will could not help marveling how Richard always managed that carefree, nonchalant look—no matter what horrors lay ahead of him. Richard's hair shimmered blue black, and his armor winked and glimmered in the sunlight. On the brilliantly caparisoned black charger, he looked like an anointed prince. He easily outshone all the wealthy nobles who were gathered to watch him.

As Richard passed the stands, a young woman in a brilliant gown of gold cloth called out to him. Smiling, he guided his horse close to the wooden rail and reached out for the glittering veil she offered. He tied the piece of gold cloth around his upper arm, and a titter went through the crowd. Richard's armor was already adorned with the favors of half a dozen other ladies who had made him their champion. The thought of Richard seeking kisses and other boons from all those women brought a grin to Will's face. It would be just like his friend to survive the tournament and get himself murdered by a jealous husband afterwards!

The knights circled around to the end of the field, and another bray of the trumpets announced the first match.

Hours later, Will shifted his weight from one leg to the other, rubbing his bleary, dust-sore eyes. The tournament field was now rough and offal strewn, and in places the ground was stained black with blood. The earlier matches had been brief, lackluster affairs. The crowd had been roused to excitement only when blood was spilled or an injured combatant was carried from the field. Now they were impatiently waiting for the final contest: the Black Leopard facing William Fitz Geoffrey, whose symbol was a silver griffin.

Will stiffened as the two men entered the field. Fitz Geoffrey rode an enormous bay stallion bedecked in blue satin trimmed with silver. Even from a distance, it was obvious that he was larger than Richard, his reach much greater. Will felt a cramp of fear deep in his belly. Richard was a formidable warrior, a superb fighter, but against this giant of a man, what chance would he have?

The two men met solemnly in the center of the field, then moved to the ends. The tension of the crowd mounted. Will glanced to the stands and saw that many of the ladies were on their feet, calling out encouragement to their favorite. The crowd was all for Richard, shouting "the Leopard, the Leopard" and waving blood-colored cloths.

Will shook his head. Leave it to Richard to capture the people's hearts. For all that he was a penniless, untitled knight, he charmed them all, noble and commoner alike.

Darley, Earl of Wickingham, leaned out of the stands and dropped a purple cloth. The two knights spurred their warhorses and the immense creatures took off, gaining terrifying speed as they neared the center of the field. Will felt his body go rigid as he waited for the impact. At the last moment, both knights shifted their weight, and their horses passed within inches of each other. Again the knights retreated to the ends of the field. Again they charged. This time, Richard struck a glancing blow at Fitz Geoffrey as they passed. The huge knight faltered but managed to keep his seat.

The two warriors retreated and caught their breaths, then charged a third time. The tournament field grew eerily silent as the knights approached each other; the only sound was the pounding of the horses' hooves. Their lances struck with a thunderous clash that tore both men from their horses. They landed cleanly, free of their horses and the flying lances.

Encased in their heavy armor, neither of the men was able to rise very quickly. They appeared stunned, and both swayed slightly as they found their legs. It looked to Will as if Fitz Geoffrey was limping. He prayed it was true.

The two men took their swords and shields from their squires, then moved slowly toward each other. Their movements were sluggish, ungraceful. They circled each other with a cumbersome, awkward rhythm, while Will clenched his fists in anxiety. On foot, the towering Fitz Geoffrey had the advantage. His reach was longer, and he was likely stronger as well. Richard's success on the battlefield and tournament field had always depended upon his blazing quickness and unerring instinct for guessing his opponent's next move. If he was as winded and befuddled as he looked, he would be easy prey for the bigger man.

The crowd grew restless as the two men circled and slashed. They managed to do little more than dent each other's mail. The mob wanted blood and battle fury, and they began to shout insults at the two beleaguered champions. Richard responded first. He shook off his muddle-headedness and went after Fitz Geoffrey with the ferocity that had earned him his battle epithet. Fitz Geoffrey parried Richard's sword thrust with his shield. The crowd erupted with catcalls and hisses.

Richard lunged, and again Fitz Geoffrey met his blow, this time with his sword. The impact seemed to jar Richard, and his sword wobbled in his hand. His opponent reacted quickly, bringing his weapon down on Richard's shoulder while he was off balance. He staggered and slipped to his knees; his sword crashed to the ground. Fitz Geoffrey dropped his own sword and pulled his misericord from his belt. He moved warily toward Richard.

Richard was not ready to concede defeat. He struggled to rise, his hand on his own dagger. The crowd held its breath. Richard made it to his feet and drove forward. His dagger aimed for the lower part of Fitz Geoffrey's face, the few inches that his helmet didn't cover. The blow fell short, deflected by the heavy mail protecting his neck. Richard faltered backwards, and only then did the crowd see that Fitz Geoffrey's dagger had caught him in the leg. Bright blood spurted from the wound.

Fitz Geoffrey turned to the stands where the nobility sat and raised his dagger triumphantly. Silence reigned over the tourney field for a moment, then cheers of "Fitz Geoffrey, Fitz Geoffrey, the Griffin, the Griffin" rang out.

Richard had fallen backwards on the grass. He lay there, apparently unconscious, while Fitz Geoffrey mounted his warhorse and rode toward the stands. Will hesitated a moment, then rushed onto the tourney field, hurrying toward the prone body of his friend.

Richard's squire reached his master first, and by the time Will arrived, Richard had wrenched himself to a sitting position and pulled off his helmet. He was cursing and threatening the boy with his dagger.

"Get away from me, Nicholas. I'm not hurt so bad I cannot run you through!"

"Sir Reivers, please! If only you will let me help you to the tent."

"Have I not made myself clear!" Richard snarled. "Get away!"

Reluctantly, his shoulders slumping and his eyes morose, the squire left. Will took a step forward.

"Richard . . . I . . ."

For a second the two men's eyes met, then Will turned away as the squire had done. There was such bitterness in his friend's eyes—it made his blood run chill to see it. He feared Richard blamed him for the loss of the tournament. Indeed, he blamed himself. If Richard's hand had not been wounded, he might have fared better. As it was, it had been very close. Richard had fought the more valiant fight, although Fitz Geoffrey had been declared the winner.

Will walked from the field, feeling leaden, miserable. He would give Richard time to let his temper cool, then he would make sure his wounds were properly treated.

On the way out of the tournament grounds, he chanced to see Guy Faucomberg. Will gave the man such a menacing, murderous look, Faucomberg stepped backwards, and, for once, said nothing.

Will searched first one tavern and then another, his eyes rapidly scanning the crowded, filthy tables. Sodden men with dull, bloodshot eyes looked up at him and regarded him with curiosity. He paid them no heed, intent on finding Richard. The Leopard had left the tournament field bleeding and furious, and Will guessed he now drowned his sorrows in some sordid aleshop. Recalling the blood he had seen seeping through Richard's mail, he shuddered. His friend might be bleeding to death and not get help before it was too late.

Almost empty of hope, he returned to the inn where they had their lodging. Relief flooded him when he saw the familiar dark head and massive shoulders slumped over a table in the corner. He rushed to his friend and shook him. Richard's head hung forward limply. His face was startlingly pale in the dim rushlight. Will gasped as he saw a puddle of congealed blood on the table. A few inches away, Richard's purse lay open and half-empty.

The serving wench approached. Will grabbed her and shook her until her teeth rattled.

"What the hell did you do to him?" he snarled. "Rob him and then leave him to bleed to death?"

"Oh, no, my lord," the girl whimpered, her brown eyes huge in her pale face. "I tried to help him, truly I did, but he was having none of it." She swallowed hard, her slender white throat quivering. "After I brought him the wine, he threw the money on the table and began to rage like a madman. He called me vile names—'whore' and 'witch' were the least of them. After that I left him alone. I was just now going to see if he be all right."

"What about the money? Where's the rest of it?"

Trembling, the woman pointed toward the floor where Will could see silver pennies glittering in the filthy sawdust.

"I'm sorry. I didn't mean to frighten you." He lifted her small, pointed chin with his fingers. "Will you help me?" he asked softly. "He needs a bath and some stitching up."

The girl looked up at Will's fine, aristocratic features and smiled nervously. "Of course, my lord," she whispered. "Anything you ask, my lord."

Will and two other men dragged Richard up the stairs, leaving a sickening trail of blood behind them. As they heaved Richard onto the bed, Will got a good glimpse of his friend's gray and drawn-looking face. His heart went cold with dread. Richard couldn't die now—not after all they had been through. He couldn't be killed in some damn tournament!

The serving wench ordered an old battered wooden tub brought up and placed before the fire, then filled with heated water. Then two of them wrestled Richard's clothes and armor off—the heavy boots and greaves, the massive hauberk, then his hose and the padded gambeson. They dragged him over to the tub and heaved him in. Richard stirred and mumbled but didn't rouse.

"Wash him," Will said harshly. The girl began to bathe Richard hesitantly. Will heard her intake of breath as she reached the ragged wound on his upper arm.

"It's deep," she gasped. "And it still bleeds."

"Can you wield a needle?"

The wench's eyes widened. "You mean *me* to sew him up?"

"If you can. I know no surgeons in these parts, and I've heard a good seamstress does almost as well."

The girl bit her lip. "It may scar."

"I don't give a damn if it scars, as long as his arm works when you're done."

The girl sighed. "He is so handsome, his skin so smooth."

Will glared at her. It might be a good thing if she was besotted with Richard's looks and had a care in mending him. Still, right now it irritated him.

"There's another wound on his thigh."

Will nodded. "That one too. Can you do it?"

"Aye," she whispered. "Let me finish washing him, and I'll get my needle."

She seemed to take a long time bathing him. Will turned away, gritting his teeth in aggravation. It would be a fine thing if Richard bled to death because the wench enjoyed stroking his smooth skin!

Finally she was done. They managed to drag him out of the tub—spilling at least half the water on the floor—then get him on the bed. While the girl went for her needle and some silk, Will covered Richard with blankets and sat down, staring at his friend's still, ashen face. He couldn't help wondering again if the wound on his hand had been a factor in Richard losing the tournament. The thought filled him with anguish.

The girl was back. As soon as she approached Richard, Will got up and took the needle from her. While she watched him with surprise, he took one of the rushes from the floor, lit it and waved the needle through the flame.

"Why did you do that?"

Will shrugged. "I've heard it helps keep the wound from festering."

The girl nodded, then pulled the covers back. Blood still seeped from the two wounds, and Richard's normally tan skin was bleached and grayish. The girl took a seat on the bed and began to sew. Her pink tongue peeked out of her mouth as she concentrated. Will went to the table and took a gulp of wine from the wineskin Richard had purchased before he collapsed. It was thin, sour stuff; he poured the rest of it into the fire and went back to the girl.

She seemed to be doing a good job. The stitches were straight and neat. He thought again that it might be well that she admired Richard's body. She would not mar him if she could help it.

When she was done, Will stood up. "I have to see to some business for my friend, or all this will be even more of a waste. Will you stay with him?"

The girl hesitated. He tossed her the rest of the coins. "Watch him. If he wakes, get him more wine—some decent stuff this time."

She nodded, and Will slipped out the door.

* * *

The serving girl slipped the covers back, taking another peep. The knight's shoulders were impossibly broad, his chest massively muscled. Despite his pallor, his skin gleamed bronze in the rushlight. Glancing quickly at the door, the girl pulled the blanket down further, feasting her eyes on the wounded knight's private parts.

His face drew her eyes again. She admired his fine features, the hard look to his jaw that kept him from being too handsome. Then she noticed the scar and reached out and traced the pale, pinkish line that curved down his cheek. Something stirred within her, a longing, a tender instinct. Without thinking, she began to hum. The knight moaned softly. To soothe him, she began to stroke his hair. It was soft and thick and black as soot.

She paused in her crooning as she remembered the words to the song. It was a lullaby, she could recall her mother singing it at night to quiet her younger sisters. She smiled slightly and began to hum again.

The girl was asleep on a stool by the bed when Will returned. Richard looked as if he hadn't moved the whole time, but the dead, muddy color had left his skin. Will leaned over him and listened for his breathing. It was even and deep. Will sighed in relief and went to wake the girl.

She jerked in surprise when he shook her, then gazed at him sleepy-eyed and scared until she remembered who he was.

"How is he?"

She gave him a wary look, then shrugged. "He seems well enough now, considering all he's been through."

Will let out a sigh, relieved.

"Was he wounded in the tournament?" the girl asked.

Will nodded. "Richard's won quite a name for himself over the years as a fighting man. They call him the 'Black Leopard.' "

The wench gasped. "He . . . he's the Black Leopard?"

"Not so fierce now, is he?"

"He was one of the champions, wasn't he?"

Will grimaced. "He lost narrowly, winning a fine horse for his trouble. That's where I went, to see to his new mare. A beautiful creature she is—delicate, spirited and reputed to be as fast as the wind. Lord Darley brought her back from the Holy Land."

He glanced again at the bed. "I hope Richard finds her some consolation for losing the tournament. He can be so bullheaded sometimes. Only a fool would leave the tournament field without having his wounds tended. He's lucky he didn't bleed to death before I found him."

The girl looked at the unconscious knight speculatively. "He seems peaceful enough now, for all that he acted like a madman earlier."

"You mean downstairs?" Will asked, suddenly worried again.

The girl shook her head. "A while ago, before you came back."

"God's wounds! Why didn't you tell me he had roused? What did he say?"

The girl shrugged and looked as if she wished she hadn't mentioned it. "Out of his head he was, talking nonsense, calling me by some other woman's name."

"What name?"

"Maude, he called me Maude."

Will tensed. "What else did he say?"

"He was out of his head, I told ye. Swearing at me,

calling me filthy names like he did afore." The girl seemed to shiver at the memory. "It took me awhile to quiet him."

"What made him wake? Did you speak to him?"

The girl shook her head. "It was naught. I was only . . . I was singing to him."

"What?"

She shrugged. " 'Twere a lullaby. I thought it would soothe him. 'Stead it made him go all wild-eyed and raving."

The wench fixed Will with a sharp, accusing look. " 'Tweren't just the fever or the wine working on his mind that beset him, 'twas something else, wasn't it?"

Will said nothing.

"I've a right to know," the girl said stiffly. "I saved his life for you, after all."

Will looked at the girl's face, her intense brown eyes making him uncomfortable. She was likely pretty if you cared for the sort. At any rate, she had done right by Richard—sewing him up, singing to him. She was probably halfway in love with him already. Even unconscious and raving, Richard managed to charm the ladies.

"Maude was his mother's name," he told her. "You probably reminded him of her when you sang to him."

The wench looked more puzzled than ever. "But why did he scream and yell at me if he thought I was his mum?"

Will grimaced. "His 'mum' was a whore. Richard's never forgiven her."

Five

"Marguerite, you did not tell me it was a fortress!" Astra gasped as they approached the towering walls of Ravensmore.

"Fortress, nay. It is no more than a small country holding. My father's castles in Chirk and Kent are much grander."

Astra merely stared in awe at the wide moat, the formidable gray curtain walls, the imposing towers. She had never seen a castle before, and it impressed her as much as the cathedral at Lichfield.

The drawbridge was lowered and they transversed the moat. Astra was disappointed to see the water surrounding the castle was cloudy and stagnant. A faint stench rose from the greenish depths.

The inside of the fortress was crowded and chaotic. Servants ran to and fro, fetching animals and baggage. A squire helped Astra from her horse, and she joined Marguerite, who was flirting with the man assigned to her palfrey. They both jumped as a booming voice echoed across the courtyard.

"Lady Marguerite!"

A squat, powerful man strode toward them. Marguerite dipped into a graceful curtsy, and Astra did likewise. She regarded the man through lowered lashes. He was nearly as wide as he was tall, with massive shoulders and arms and a huge head crowned with wavy black hair streaked liberally with white. He reminded her of an enraged bull—right down to his dark, bulging eyes and the curl of hair that fell over his broad forehead like the forelock of a shaggy steer. Her body stiffened in apprehension as she anticipated the bull's charge.

"Marguerite!" the man bellowed again. "The whole shire is abuzz with rumors of your disgrace, whispering that you were all but banished from Stafford. What explanation do you give for your appalling behavior?"

Astra cringed. She could sympathize with her friend's shame as she confronted her father's wrath in the crowded courtyard. For once Marguerite looked well and truly cowed. She was biting her lips nervously, and her stricken eyes were as large as pullet eggs.

"Father . . . I . . ."

"Silence! We'll speak of this later." Lord Fitz Hugh gestured curtly toward the towering keep. "Wait for me in the solar."

Lord Fitz Hugh dismissed them and went on to berate some young squire who had the misfortune to dawdle in unloading one of the packhorses. Astra slunk across the courtyard after Marguerite, feeling like a whipped hound. As soon as they entered the Great Hall, Marguerite turned and faced Astra.

"You'll come with me, won't you?"

Astra licked her dry lips; her voice seemed to fade in her throat.

"Marguerite . . . I . . ."

Marguerite grasped Astra's bliaut beseechingly. "Please, Astra. He won't dare let loose with his full fury if you are there."

"I really don't see how . . ." Astra's voice trailed off uncertainly. As much as she feared Lord Fitz Hugh, it did not seem right to desert her friend. "Of course, Marguerite. I will come."

They followed the narrow staircase to the solar on the third floor of the keep. Astra could not help gaping in admiration at the splendid decor of the Fitz Hughs' private quarters. The walls were hung with elaborately worked hangings of velvet and gold, embroidered with the Fitz Hugh emblem of a magnificent ram. Plushly-upholstered furniture of blue velvet was arranged around a massive hearth. Astra followed Marguerite's lead and sank down on a bench of cloudlike softness.

The two women stared at each other. Marguerite twisted her long fingers restlessly, while Astra sat very still and tried to calm herself with long, deep breaths. She looked down at her own hands, noticing with dismay that they were streaked with dust.

They did not have a long wait. There was a rumbling sound in the stairwell, and Lord Fitz Hugh thrust himself into the room, his bulky body seeming to vibrate with anger. Astra clutched at the soft fabric of the cushion and steeled herself for the coming confrontation.

As if his size and demeanor weren't intimidating enough, Lord Fitz Hugh fixed himself directly in front of Marguerite and tapped one of his big feet impatiently.

"I am waiting."

Valiantly Marguerite opened her mouth. Her father cut her off before she could get a word out.

"The stories I have heard, child! I could have sworn the nuns were speaking of a changeling. Surely *my* daughter would never replace the communion wine with vinegar nor steal a poor sister's underdrawers from the clothesline."

"They were just pranks, Papa. No one was hurt . . . and Sister Blanche . . . she deserved it. She was cruel to me, Papa, truly she was."

"Pranks, were they?" Fitz Hugh muttered, finally lowering his voice below a shout. "What of the other stories? Do you call spying on a group of monks as they bathe and then hiding their clothes a prank?"

Fitz Hugh's voice had risen in a terrifying crescendo. Astra repressed the urge to dart for cover beneath one of the huge pieces of furniture, but Marguerite faced her father resolutely. Her normally pouting mouth was drawn into a tight line.

"But there is more, daughter. Explain this to me—how could a young lady who has been raised at the courts of kings, whose education and wardrobe and jewels would have beggared a poorer man—explain to me how she could plan a rendezvous in the forest with a common servant boy?"

"It was not like that, Papa! Nothing happened. No more than a few innocent kisses. Ask Astra—she was there."

Lord Fitz Hugh wheeled to face Astra. She gripped the bench fiercely and wished she could vanish into the floor.

"Lady Astra." Unbelievably, Lord Fitz Hugh bowed. "I am afraid I have not properly made your acquaintance."

Astra merely stared at him, too stunned to remember to rise and curtsy.

"I knew your father, you know," Lord Fitz Hugh continued conversationally. "An exceedingly brave man. Exceedingly. I fought beside him in Wales. There was one time the Welsh bastards had us backed up against an old stone wall. Thought we were bound for our last reward then, truly I did. But old de Mortain—Little Cockerel—we called him. Never gave up. They kept coming, and he kept fighting. When our relief came, all that was left was myself and de Mortain and a handful of men." A broad smile split Fitz Hugh's craggy face at the memory.

"You see, Papa," Marguerite broke in. "Astra is like her father—stalwart and virtuous—the perfect escort. I would rather die than embarrass her. I would never dream of doing anything unseemly in her presence . . ."

"That is the other matter," Marguerite's father interrupted, pointing a meaty finger at Astra. "I was told you corrupted Lady Astra. Because of you, this innocent and pious young woman was led astray, tricked into the devil's own wickedness."

Marguerite paled, her sense of guilt finally overcoming her endless supply of excuses and explanations.

"That is not true!" Astra protested.

Both Marguerite and Lord Fitzhugh looked at Astra in amazement, as if surprised that she actually had the power of speech. In truth, Astra had startled herself with her outburst. She *was* afraid of Marguerite's father, terrified right down to the roots of her hair. Even so, she could not let her friend take all the blame. She would not be a coward.

"Marguerite did not force me to do those things. I . . . I joined her willingly." Astra hung her head, her voice but a whisper in the large room. "I am just as guilty as she is."

There was a long silence. When Astra looked up, Lord Fitz Hugh was regarding her with perplexity, his heavy dark brows drawn into a puzzled *"v."*

"Loyal," he pronounced. "Exactly like her father. In that, Marguerite, you have done well. A loyal friend is worth a thousand marks."

Marguerite ventured a smile. "You see, Papa, that is why I wanted Astra to come home with me. I cannot bear to be parted from her."

"For shame, child, you are being selfish. This young woman has paid a high price for her association with you. Because of your so-called 'pranks' she has lost her home and what humble station her poor father—God rest his soul—could afford to buy for her. Now, you seek to bind her to you as a handmaiden, with no future of a husband and family of her own."

"No, of course I do not intend that. I plan to take Astra to court with me and find her a husband."

Lord Fitz Hugh frowned. "Certainly Lady Astra is comely and well-born enough to interest many men. But few knights are willing to set aside their ambitions to wed a pretty and virtuous woman who cannot hope to advance their fortunes."

He hesitated, as if embarrassed to confront Astra's poverty so bluntly. "I cannot say that I would approve of the sort of man Lady Astra is likely to attract. Better that she should toil in a noble household than wed a man who is beneath her."

Marguerite shook her head emphatically. "Of course we will not allow Astra to wed beneath her. All she needs is a modest dowry. With that and her beauty, she will wed well—perhaps better than me. She is a sweet-tempered thing," Marguerite smiled warmly at Astra. "You have always told me that men prefer sweet-tempered women."

"The Prioress at Stafford told me that Lady Astra has no relatives, no source of income. How do you propose she come by a dowry, daughter?"

Marguerite's smile grew radiant. "Surely you can spare

a manor as a wedding gift for your daughter's dearest friend, can you not, Papa?"

Lord Fitz Hugh frowned again, as if unsettled by having his daughter manipulate him into honoring his earlier rash words. Astra opened her mouth to protest, horrified that Marguerite would drag her into this humiliating situation. It was too late. Lord Fitz Hugh nodded his head decisively.

"By the heavens, you are right. Such a move would likely gain me a strong young knight I could count on to stand at my side. Besides . . ." He startled Astra by turning to her with a benevolent smile. "It is clear that you have been a good influence on my daughter. Without you as a friend, Marguerite would likely have involved herself in even worse scrapes. A wedding gift it is then. No land too dear—that would arouse King Henry's ire, and in the end he must approve of this. Perhaps a manor in the south, along the Thames where I need a man to protect the waterway."

"But Lord Fitz Hugh, I could not possibly . . ."

"Nonsense," Fitz Hugh barked, silencing Astra instantly. "You can and will accept my offer. As Marguerite says, we owe you this. I'll have the papers drawn up anon."

Astra stared after Lord Fitz Hugh as he departed the solar as abruptly as he had come. She felt dizzy, her head awhirl with half-finished thoughts.

"You see?" Marguerite pronounced gleefully. "I told you that it would all work out."

"Marguerite, you know I cannot possibly accept your father's incredible generosity."

Her friend laughed. "Don't be a dullard, Astra. You cannot refuse my father any more than I can. He is like a force of nature. People don't refuse him *anything*."

"But it isn't right! You all but tricked him into making me an offer of land."

"Don't try and tell him that. By now, my father thinks it was all his idea, and he'll never hear of you gainsaying him."

"But Marguerite, your father misunderstands the situation completely. He thinks I am some poor innocent that you led into sinfulness. That's simply not true. You know I left the priory willingly. I have had doubts for some time, and after the . . . the incident with the boy in the forest . . . after that I could no longer ignore the fact that I am unworthy to serve Our Lord."

Astra bowed her head, confronting the shameful memory. For all her guilt and remorse afterwards, she couldn't deny the thrilling warmth that had enveloped her as she watched the servant boy's soft pink lips press down on Marguerite's deeper rose ones. After that she had known that she was too weak, too in thrall to the base urges of her body to ever become a nun.

"Pooh!" Marguerite scoffed. "You are no more unworthy than any of those fat, old hens who run Stafford. Lust is no worse a sin than avarice or gluttony or vanity, and the priory is overrun with proud, vain and greedy women. As for cruelty and lack of Christian charity—I have known hardened soldiers who looked like saints next to that bitch Sister Blanche."

Astra fidgeted uncomfortably. There was truth in what Marguerite said. Some of the nuns did not seem to truly follow the Christian precepts of meekness and self-denial.

"At any rate, it is a silly thing to argue about," Marguerite continued as she rose from her seat. "Whatever reason you decided to leave the priory, I am very glad you did.

We will have great fun here at Ravensmore . . . and even greater fun when we go to court."

She grabbed Astra's hand, pulling her up from the plush cushion. "But the first order of the day is a bath. My mother would slay me alive if I went down to dinner like this, and your face is so filthy you look like a Saracen!"

Astra reached for her dusty face in mortification even as Marguerite half-dragged her from the solar. Marguerite led Astra to another large, well-appointed room, this one with a huge raised bed surrounded by curtains. A big wooden tub filled with steaming water stood in one corner.

"Your bath, my lady," Marguerite announced, gesturing elegantly.

"This . . . this is how you bathe?" Astra asked in wonderment.

"Aye, did you think that a dip in a scummy pond or a miserable scrubbing in a tub of cold water was the only way it was done? Ah, Astra, you have much to learn. Baths can be more than a way to get clean, they can be pleasurable as well. Take off your clothes. I'll have the maid fetch one of my old gowns for you while I attend you myself."

Hesitantly, Astra removed her clothes, feeling vaguely uncomfortable.

"Don't be such a silly goose," Marguerite said, noticing Astra's unease. "I've seen you naked plenty of times."

Astra nodded. It had never bothered her to have another woman see her unclothed before. Perhaps her embarrassment had something to do with all the strange tingling sensations she felt at night in bed.

Astra stepped into the tub and sank down into the heavenly warm water. She adjusted herself on the stool carved into the tub and leaned against the back of it, feeling the soothing heat ease her sore legs. She was unused to riding, and two days on the road had left her thigh muscles and buttocks a quivering bundle of knots.

"Now for the soap." Marguerite held out a carved ivory bowl. Astra took a handful of the slippery paste.

"Oh! How lovely it smells!" Astra exclaimed as a sweet, spicy fragrance wafted to her nose.

"My mother makes it with sandalwood and lavender. It is nothing like that rank, greasy mess they gave us at Stafford. Use as much as you like, Astra; there is plenty more."

Gingerly, Astra began to smooth the soap over her skin. As she soaped her breasts, she was horrified to see her nipples harden and thrust out. She glanced at Marguerite and was relieved to see that her friend was turned away.

"Your hair needs washing too," Marguerite noted. "Get it wet and then hang it over the back of the tub so I can soap it."

Astra obliged, ducking her head under the water. She shivered slightly as the cooler air struck her skin.

Marguerite squeezed the excess moisture from Astra's hair and rubbed soap through it. Marguerite's touch was gentle, soothing. Astra felt herself slipping into a peaceful state of relaxation.

"It is a good thing we have all summer to get you ready for court," Marguerite announced briskly. "Not only must we look to your manners and household skills, but your wardrobe from Stafford is fit for naught but burning. We'll have to have everything made new—right down to your shifts. It's a pity that full surcotes are all the fashion at court now. The style is flattering to tall women like myself and the Queen, but a little thing like you is likely to be lost in a heavy, ample gown. You would do better in a fitted bliaut that gives some hint of your figure."

"I assure you I have no intention of dressing so that

men can imagine my form beneath my clothes," Astra answered stiffly.

"You have left the nunnery behind, Astra," Marguerite reproved. "Modesty won't help you catch a husband. My father is right when he says that most noblemen seek a wealthy wife. The estate Papa means to gift you with will be respectable, but not extravagant. To attract an appropriate suitor, we must make use of your beauty."

"Surely a Christian man should be more interested in his wife's virtue and character than her appearance."

"Aye, they *should.* But the truth is that women have been snaring men with their beauty since Eve. How do you suppose the Queen came to be queen? Do you truly think Henry married Eleanor solely for her bloodline and character?"

Astra nodded grimly. Marguerite was right. She had left the nunnery behind, and she must learn to face the unpleasantness of a world ruled by the crude values of men.

"You may be poor in land," Marguerite continued, "but your wealth in beauty is as great as any woman at court. The knights will be drawn like bees to honey by your angelic features and exquisite coloring. If they were to catch a glimpse of your lovely breasts as well, I imagine some of them would be on their knees proposing in a trice!"

"Marguerite—you're jesting!" Astra gasped.

"Aye, I am," Marguerite chuckled. "Still, there is some truth to it. I recall a certain Lady Veronique at Louis's court who said she had only to undo her gown and let her husband press his face into her generous bosom, and he was soon willing to gift her with whatever jewels or new gowns she desired."

Shocked beyond words, Astra slid down in her bath water, trying to hide the objects of their discussion. It did no good. The water wasn't deep enough, and her breasts seemed to float to the surface, the deep cleft between them plainly visible above the soapy water. For a moment Astra imagined a man's dark head resting there. The image unleashed a painful ache deep within her.

"Perhaps I should not go to court at all," Astra murmured. "If men of character tolerate their wives manipulating them in such a disgusting manner, it is clear I am not fit to be a nobleman's wife. A wife has a duty to endure her husband's attentions for the sake of producing heirs, but she certainly should not encourage repulsive carnal acts."

Marguerite's hands paused for a moment in soaping Astra's hair. Then they began to tremble as Marguerite indulged herself in a fit of exuberant laughter. When she finally calmed, her voice still bubbled with amusement.

"How true my father spoke, Astra. You are an innocent. It's going to be great fun watching you lose that damnable purity you carry around like a shield. And you will lose it, mark my words. The court is full of men, *ma belle,* and you're bound to find at least one of them irresistible."

Astra slid down in the water even further. Marguerite's warning words echoed in her head, vibrating down into some deep secret place inside her. She shivered, though the bath water was still warm. Here was a new danger, a new temptation she must guard against. The nuns had been right. The world outside the priory was a virtual quagmire of hazards to her soul.

Six

"Still sleeping? Why, you lazy slug-a-bed!" Astra strode purposefully into Marguerite's sleeping chamber and pulled the curtains back from the bed so that the daylight streamed in on her friend.

"I'll get up now, I promise," Marguerite answered sleepily as she untangled herself from the covers and stretched. "It is not so late, is it?"

"Late! The rest of the castle has been up for hours. Lady Fitz Hugh and I have already seen to the evening meal, started the buttermaking and supervised cleaning out the rushes in the Great Hall. This afternoon we will review the supply lists and then she's to teach me how to make her special soap."

"Soap!" Marguerite made a horrible face. "Astra, you have no idea how awful soap-making smells. You have to boil the wretched grease for hours, and it stinks up the whole courtyard. You'll get the smell on your hair, your skin . . ."

"Then I'll wash," Astra answered briskly. "Surely any decent wife must know how to make her own soap. Your mother promised me she would share her special recipe of herbs with me so I will know how to make the wonderful-smelling concoction you use here at Ravensmore."

"You are taking this housewife business utterly too seriously." Marguerite pouted. "A chatelaine does not have to learn to do everything herself. She has plenty of servants to do her bidding."

"You forget, Marguerite, that I am not destined to be mistress of a great castle as you are. If I, indeed, find a man at court willing to marry me, we will likely live in a small house and have few servants. I need to know how to do these things myself."

"Oh, bother! I had planned on us going riding this afternoon. It has been days since you've had time to spend with me, Astra. You must admit you've neglected me shamefully."

Astra fixed her friend with a look of exasperation. There was so much to learn if she were to ever know how to manage even a small household, and Marguerite kept dragging her off to go riding or swimming or other idle pursuits. She was torn between spending time with Lady Fitz Hugh—or Lady Bea, as the castlefolk referred to her—and trying to keep Marguerite entertained.

"Perhaps we can compromise," she suggested. "Lady Bea can show me the basics of soapmaking, and then I will go riding with you."

Marguerite nodded. "That will have to do, I suppose. Then you could take a bath as you suggested, and afterwards we could practice your dancing and fixing your hair for court events. I wish your new clothes were finished. We cannot try out wimples and headdresses without knowing how they go with your new gowns."

"The seamstress has finished them. I had her put them in the big chest."

"Your court clothes are ready? Why didn't you tell me?"

Astra shrugged. "I didn't know it mattered. Certainly I

couldn't wear them for riding, or cleaning and soapmaking for that matter."

"But don't you want to see how they fit?" Marguerite asked as she went over to the chest and impatiently dug inside, throwing bliauts and undertunics everywhere. "Don't you want to know how exquisite you will look in them?"

"I'm sure there will be time enough for that. We have the whole summer after all."

"The whole summer? Why should we wait until fall to go to court? Why not go now?"

"Now?" Astra was aghast. "I have only begun to learn how to manage a household. It will take me the rest of the summer at least to feel confident that I can do things half as well as Lady Bea."

"There you go again, Astra, harping on that boring 'mistress of the keep' nonsense. You don't even have a husband yet. Why are you worried about managing his household?"

"It does not hurt to plan ahead. If—God willing—a man does ask for my hand, I want to do right by him as a wife."

"If you worry about nothing except cleaning, cooking and keeping accounts, there's no point taking you to court at all. Most men marry for land and money, but those that don't are more interested in a comely face than soap recipes!"

"You make it sound so . . . so base, as if I were a prize cow being taken to market!"

"You can see it that way if you wish. Consider me the farmer who has taken on the responsibility of 'taking you to market.' I assure you I intend to see you are the comeliest little heifer there."

Despite herself, Astra couldn't help smiling at Marguerite's absurd comparison. The idea of fastidious Marguerite as a farmer gave her the giggles.

"Please," Marguerite coaxed. "I can't wait to see you in your new finery. If we can't make you the most dazzling creature to grace King Henry's court, why, I . . . I'll stir up a batch of soap myself!"

London—the great city loomed ahead of them. Astra could see the massive battlements of the old Roman walls as well as the stately spires of churches rising above the sprawl of shops and houses. The sight took her breath away. She longed to stop and savor the moment, but it was impossible. The roadway was crowded with knights, pilgrims and farmers, and she dare not rein in the fine-boned gray palfrey she rode for fear she would impede traffic.

Her first sight of London was the culmination of their long journey from Ravensmore. They had been on the road for nearly a week, riding through the brilliant green of the summer countryside. Astra had almost grown accustomed to life on horseback, but she had not resigned herself to the other chief discomfort of traveling—the dirt. She decided that the first thing she would do when they arrived at the palace was take a bath.

They entered the city through an arched gateway and exited onto a broad avenue. The mounted traveling party—headed by Lord Fitz Hugh himself—progressed quickly south. Astra had little time to observe the sights, for she was occupied with guiding her horse through the thronging streets. Around her people shouted and cursed with vigor, rudely jostling each other in their hurry to pass.

"What think you, Astra?" Marguerite called. Her voice

barely rose over the thud of the horses' hooves and the din of the crowd. "Is it not exciting?"

Astra smiled back but made no attempt to answer. She was not sure what she thought of London. It was much noisier and dirtier than she had imagined, smellier too. She had never seen so many buildings, nor so many people. The crude, aggressive crowd made her want to find someplace quiet and catch her breath. And yet she was fascinated too. She had never felt so alive, her senses overwhelmed by the new sights and sounds all around her. The crowd increased, and down the street to her left, Astra caught a glimpse of the shops and food stands which drew them.

"That's the Cheapside market," Marguerite shouted helpfully. "We'll visit it sometime. It's great fun."

The Fitz Hugh party passed by the great cathedral of St. Paul's and turned west. As they journeyed away from the marketplace, the houses grew richer, more elegant, and Astra could smell the river—the vague odor of water, mud and salt rising above the stench of offal and garbage. They followed the river's course. Ahead of them the towers and spires of Westminster gleamed golden in the sun.

They reached the royal complex and passed through the gate into a large courtyard abustle with activity. It appeared that the King was preparing to depart on a hunt. There were valets busily polishing hunting spears, horns and other implements of the chase; grooms leading magnificently caparisoned chargers and palfreys; falconers seated on the stone benches allowing their hooded falcons to bask in the sun's rays; huntsmen leashing in shaggy wolfhounds, slender coursing dogs and wiry vulperets.

Astra gaped at the splendid confusion, feeling like more of a backwards country girl than ever. Despite the fine horse she rode, she was sweaty and disheveled, her plain bliaut coated with a layer of dust.

They left their horses at the palace stables and set off on foot toward the part of the palace that housed the Queen's chambers. Foot-sore and weary, Astra lagged behind. By the time she caught up with Marguerite and Lord Fitz Hugh, she could hear shouting.

"What do you mean there is no room?" Marguerite's father bellowed at a put-upon looking royal official. "I have brought my daughter to wait upon the Queen. She must stay at the palace!"

"I'm sorry," the small man said. His fingers plucked nervously at his soiled crimson tunic. "Many of the Queen's relatives are visiting London, and she insists they be housed at Westminster. There is very little space left."

"This is outrageous! I sent word of my arrival weeks ago. I have a good mind to take this to the King himself." Lord Fitz Hugh started to brush by the man.

"Wait!" the clerk begged. "There must be something left, perhaps a small chamber. Please stay here while I inquire."

As soon as the man left, Marguerite leaned close to her father and grumbled: "The Queen's relatives—they are not even English—how dare Henry allow them to take precedence over his own nobles?" Lord Fitz Hugh nodded, while Astra stared, amazed that anyone would dare to criticize the King of England.

In time, the man returned and informed Lord Fitz Hugh that sleeping chambers had been found. Fitz Hugh thanked him heartily, and a servant came to lead them into the palace. They were escorted down a narrow, moldy hall to a small corner room. It contained little more than an unlit brazier, some cupboards, a curtained bed and a smaller pallet on the floor. The servant departed to fetch them water. Astra sank down gratefully on the bed and began to remove her soiled linen headdress.

"I suppose it will do," Marguerite groused. She glanced around the tiny room critically. "Last time we were in London, we had much finer accommodations." She made a sour face. "It seems the steward spoke the truth—the better rooms are all taken up by the Queen's relatives. They have descended upon London like a plague of locusts, and neither of the royal couple will turn even one away."

"Surely it is normal for the King and Queen to want their family around them," Astra ventured.

Marguerite raised her eyebrows. "There are many who feel that positions of power and influence should go to Englishmen instead of greedy foreigners. It is one of the reasons King Henry is in trouble with his barons."

"In trouble?" Astra asked in surprise.

Even though they were alone, Marguerite lowered her voice as she answered. "There are those who talk of dealing with Henry as they did King John at Runnymede. They say Henry should be forced to abide by the Magna Charta as his father was compelled to promise."

Astra felt a tightness in her chest. "Forced? Do you mean there will be war?"

Marguerite shrugged. "If it happens, it will be a long time coming. The barons are too busy squabbling among themselves to unite for a common cause. Still, it is true that Henry is not a popular king, and Queen Eleanor is liked even less."

Astra felt her stomach grow tight with dread. Her father had lost nearly everything during the intrigue of King John's reign, and she had determined some time ago that she would have nothing to do with politics. Now she wondered if that were possible.

A servant arrived with a large bucket of water and a basin, and Astra hurried to wash away the grime that covered her face and hands. The day was hot, and she was sweaty as well as dusty. She decided to freshen up before she changed clothes and stripped to her chemise. To keep from getting it wet, she pulled the thin linen undergarment down to bare her breasts. She was nearly finished washing when she heard the door open again. She turned, expecting to see the chambermaid arriving with fresh water, and stared in astonishment at the sharp-featured young woman in the doorway. She was elegantly attired in a pale pink gown of patterned silk, with a gold and rose headdress to match.

The woman gaped openly at Astra's breasts. Her eyes fixed there with such shock and amazement Astra wondered if she'd ever seen another naked woman before.

"Holy Mother of God!" the woman gasped, still staring at Astra. "What are you doing in my room?"

"Your room?" Marguerite stepped forward and glared haughtily at the intruder. "We were shown here and told we were welcome to use the chamber during our stay."

"Who are you?" the woman demanded rudely.

"I am Lady Marguerite Fitz Hugh, come to court for a visit with the Queen. My father is Reginald Fitz Hugh, Baron of Westford."

The woman met Marguerite's icy look with her pallid gray eyes. "I am Isabel Vipoint, third cousin to the Queen. She herself assured me that this room would be available to me as long as I wished."

The two women stared at each other a moment, each

taking the other's measure—like a pair of dogs preparing for a fight. Nervously, Astra stepped between them.

"It seems there has been a mistake, Marguerite. The chambermaid obviously did not realize this room was being used by Mademoiselle Vipoint."

Isabel's glance flicked to Astra, regarding her as one would a noxious, repulsive insect. "And who might this sluttish-looking creature be? Your serving girl?"

Astra sucked in her breath, completely stunned. She had done nothing to this woman; why should she speak so cruelly?

"This *lady* is Astra de Mortain," Marguerite answered. Her dark eyes glittered dangerously. "She is a dear *friend* of mine, and she will be sharing this room with *me.*"

Astra glanced from one angry woman to the other. They looked as if they might come to blows at any minute, and the thought horrified Astra. They had only arrived at court. It would hardly do for Marguerite to provoke a fight with one of the Queen's relatives. She had to intervene.

"Ladies, please!" she remonstrated. "There is no reason to quarrel. I'm sure something can be agreed upon." She looked anxiously around the tiny chamber. "There is plenty of room. I could sleep upon the pallet, and the two of you could share the larger bed."

Marguerite looked at Isabel as if she would rather sleep with a snake. Isabel was not much more enthusiastic. Astra continued to reason with them: "It appears that there is a shortage of bedchambers in the palace. If we make a fuss, it will likely distress the Queen. I'm sure neither of you would wish that."

Marguerite's eyebrows rose, and she assessed Isabel disdainfully. Then, abruptly her full mouth curled into a smile.

"Astra is right, of course. We would never dream of distressing the Queen, would we, Lady Isabel?"

The other woman's angular features twitched, as if she could not decide if Marguerite were mocking or sincere. Finally, she returned Marguerite's smile with a taut one of her own. "No, of course not. We would not dream of it." With those words, Lady Isabel cast a last hostile glance at Astra, then quit the room.

"What a snake!" Marguerite exclaimed. "You are right that we must not inconvenience the Queen, but still . . . I hate to think of sharing a chamber with such a nasty little tart. She's bound to make trouble. Did you not see that look she gave you when she first entered into the room? Already she despises you."

"But I've done nothing . . ."

"Nothing except be beautiful, and she'll never forgive you for that. If you hadn't noticed, Lady Isabel is extremely plain—pointed nose, horrible, pale, freckled skin, colorless eyelashes. She'll never turn a man's head with her looks, so naturally she resents a woman like you who doesn't have to do anything to be beautiful."

For a moment, Astra was speechless. It was ridiculous to think that someone might dislike her because of how she looked. And yet, Lady Isabel had appeared decidedly hostile, actually referring to Astra as a "sluttish creature." Recalling the demeaning phrase, she flushed with embarrassment and anger.

"How unfair of Isabel to hold my appearance against me. It is not as if I can help how I look. She is naught but an ill-tempered shrew!"

"It is good to know that you can get angry occasionally," Marguerite chuckled. "I was afraid you were going to make up some excuse for Isabel's appalling rudeness. Of course, one has to pity her a little for her obvious plainness. No amount of jewels or finery can dress up such a drab, little rabbit face and bony body."

Astra felt a sudden prick of conscience. Perhaps it was unfair to criticize someone so ill-favored. Still, Isabel had begun things, and Astra knew her own dislike went beyond mere appearances. There was something mean-spirited about Isabel. For a moment, she regretted that she had played the part of peacemaker. It was going to be hard enough to make her way at court without having the Queen's cousin against her.

"The royal party is back from hunting," Marguerite announced as she looked out the one tiny window. "In a few hours, Astra, you will be meeting the King and Queen of England."

Astra's stomach fluttered with a nervous thrill as she went to the window and stared down at the swarming courtyard. Now, for good or bad, her new life was truly beginning.

"A grand hunt, wasn't it?" Will put in as he and Richard dismounted and turned their horses over to their squires.

"Oh, aye," his friend answered coldly. "I so enjoy riding in the forest with the King and an intimate group of fifty or so, chasing after a small, terrified animal."

"You're in a foul mood today, Richard. What's happened to turn you into a snarling beast? Do your old wounds pain you?"

"I told you, I'm completely healed. No, it's this stupidity which irritates me." He gestured toward the mass of nobles crowding the courtyard. "All these people pandering to Henry, slavering over any little nod or smile he deigns to throw their way. I'm a soldier, Will. I'm not cut out to be a simpering, groveling courtier."

"God's wounds, Richard. Lower your voice. You want a manor, don't you? I tell you, this is the way to earn Henry's trust—hunt with him, break bread with him, pray with him . . ."

"And piss with him too, no doubt," Richard snarled. "Damnation, Will, I have more pride than these fools. I've won wars for Henry—that ought to count for something. I shouldn't have to kiss the royal arse as well."

"I'm afraid that Henry is one of those men who can't be reassured enough. He scents treason everywhere, and his memory is as short as a two-year-old's. He forgets who did him a favor last year, last month, probably even last week."

"I don't care what Henry's problems are. I've had a gutful of scraping and bowing. There has to be another way for me to win land. I have half a mind to pay a visit to the French king . . ."

"Oh, certainly, Richard, go to Louis," Will answered caustically. "He'll know you come to him as a faithless traitor, but he'll trust you anyway. Use your head, man. It's pure foolishness to throw away everything you've fought for because the rewards are a little long in coming. If you can't abide court, offer to go off to Wales to guard the Marches. Henry certainly needs help on that battlefront. If you keep him from losing more ground there, he might finally recognize your value to him."

"Perhaps there's another way to win what I want," Richard said thoughtfully. "If I could find an heiress willing to marry me, I might be able to make my fortune that way."

"Where are you going to find a rich woman willing to wed a landless knight? I grant that you're a superb fighter, and you certainly know how to charm women, but marriage is another matter."

"I could be useful to a wealthy widow," Richard said defensively. "I could protect her property, warm her bed."

"Would you really be happy living like that? Does being rich mean so much to you?"

"It's done all the time. Besides, it's really not about wealth, but power. If you'd been cursed and spit upon as much as I have, you'd understand."

"That was years ago. Now, men respect you—for your battle skills if nothing else."

"It's not the same," Richard answered, his face suddenly hard and dangerous-looking. "They may fear my skill with a sword, but they know I'm really only a poor, untitled fighting man. I want to have real power someday, to be a force men must reckon with. Someday I want even old Henry to court my favor."

"You don't ask for much, do you, Richard?" Will shook his head as the two of them walked to the knights' quarters.

Seven

"You look perfect!"

"You really think so?" Astra squinted into the polished silver mirror Marguerite held up for her. "You don't think the gown is too elaborate?"

"You are meeting the King and Queen of England for the first time—I hardly think you could dress too elaborately."

"But I feel so strange," Astra pulled at the bodice of her bliaut. "I've never worn anything so snug."

"Stop tugging at it! Your chemise fills in the neckline quite modestly. You needn't fear that you will fall out of it."

That was exactly what she did fear, Astra thought nervously. The gown was laced up the front so tightly it made her breasts spill out over the top; even though the linen of her undertunic hid them from view, she felt only half-dressed. She looked down and wished for a larger mirror so she might better admire the effect of her long, bell-like sleeves and full, trailing skirt. She smoothed her hand over the lustrous rose velvet; it was as soft as the petals of a flower.

She turned to the mirror and scrutinized her face beneath the white wimple and delicate gold circlet. Her eyes sparkled deep blue next to the white, and her cheeks were flushed pink with excitement. Even to herself she looked pretty.

"If you are done admiring yourself, we'd better go. My father is waiting for us."

"Don't you want a turn at the mirror?"

"There isn't time. Anyway, I'm quite satisfied with my own attire. This gown was made for my aunt, who resides at Louis's court. Even the Queen will have nothing so fine."

Astra smiled as she admired the diapered gold and black pattern of Marguerite's voluminous surcote. With her pearl-encrusted gold headdress, Marguerite looked like elegance personified.

"I wish Papa hadn't insisted on making the trip," Marguerite grumbled as they left their bedchamber. "He's bound to embarrass me. The way he carries on about his battle escapades!" Marguerite rolled her eyes.

"I suspect he doesn't trust us to travel by ourselves after Tudbury."

Marguerite nodded. "What a disaster. It would have been better if I had told Papa about it as soon as we arrived at Ravensmore. The way it came out, with Sir de Chilham insisting that we lured those men into the forest on purpose . . . I could almost believe that man was deliberately trying to rile Papa."

The two women went out into the hallway and waited to join the other courtiers in the Painted Chamber, where the King and Queen were greeting their guests before the meal. Lord Fitz Hugh appeared, and his blustery bulk reassured Astra. But when it was finally her turn to curtsy before the royal pair, she was too overwhelmed to do more than nod at King Henry and Queen Eleanor.

The Queen was quite lovely—with beautiful dark eyes and exceptionally clear, creamy skin—but there was a hard set to her jaw that suggested she possessed a force of will quite in contrast to her delicate features. The King was moderately tall and rather stoutly built, with reddish brown hair and a long face and regular features. His most distinguishing characteristic was a drooping right eyelid that made him look sleepy.

"What a charming, sweet, young woman," Queen Eleanor pronounced as Astra stood before them.

"She is that indeed," Lord Fitz Hugh agreed. "Lady Astra was raised in a convent, and at one time intended to take vows."

"Is that true, child?" the King asked. "Did you seriously consider becoming a nun?"

Astra nodded.

"What caused you to give up such an admirable ambition?"

Astra did not know what to say. She had heard that King Henry was extremely devout. Would he be displeased that she had been unable to commit herself to a life of devotion and self-sacrifice?

"I think that a young woman of Lady Astra's beauty and charm might better serve her God and king by marrying and raising a family," Lord Fitz Hugh answered when Astra didn't respond. "Don't you think so, Your Grace?"

The King smiled. "Certainly being a wife and mother is a worthy ambition for any young woman. And now that Lady Astra has come to court, we will make it our business to see that she marries well. Won't we, dear?" The King squeezed the Queen's arm affectionately.

The Queen nodded and returned his smile. Astra received the impression that the King and Queen were genuinely devoted to each other.

Thankfully, Astra's time before the royal couple was over quickly. She and Marguerite moved out of the hall and joined the procession to the Great Hall where they would dine.

"The King seemed quite interested in you," Marguerite whispered as they broke away from the crowd. "That won't hurt your prospects. Most knights are anxious to please Henry in hopes he might gift them with a manor or other property. That you stand in the King's favor makes you even more desirable as a wife."

"But I did nothing to impress the King," Astra protested. "That I was raised in a convent is due more to my family's poverty than my own piety. I truly don't understand why the King would single me out for his special attention."

"The King is easily impressed by expressions of devotion. Then too, he is a man. . . ." Marguerite winked broadly. "I'm sure he was also taken with your feminine charms."

"That is pure silliness, Marguerite. I've heard you babble on for weeks now about how I will steal the heart of every man at court. Looking around, I see many refined, beautiful women. I can't imagine anyone taking notice of me."

Marguerite again winked and then laughed.

They seated themselves at the long trestle tables, and servants immediately began to bring them food. The exotic dishes compared favorably to the delicious fare Astra had enjoyed at Ravensmore. Astra queried Marguerite constantly on the dishes she was sampling. Was this heavily spiced meat venison or beef? And this delicate fowl—was it chicken or goose? Heron, peacock, wild boar—there were so many flavors she had never tasted before. Then came the custard and sweetmeats; it did not take Astra long to realize she must stop eating or she would make herself ill. She put aside her eating knife and twisted slightly in her seat, the better to watch the spectacle of the King's banquet hall.

Her eyes took in the rich gowns of the women—flowing ripples of rose and blue, burgundy, violet, shimmering gold and deep green—a hundred different styles and colors adorning the room like wildflowers in a field. The men were decked in hues almost as dramatic. The few that favored simple blacks and grays often set them off with jewels and dazzling trims of silver and gold.

Not everyone seemed comfortable in their splendid attire. No one was allowed to carry weapons in the King's Hall, but Astra reasoned that she could easily pick out the fighting men. The younger knights in particular shifted restlessly in their seats, reminding Astra of village children—cleaned and dressed up for church, pulling at their stiff tunics and squirming in their confining shoes as if they longed to be dirty and barefoot once again. Her eyes lingered on the knights as she recalled the two men who had rescued them at Tudbury. A familiar face caught her attention and sent a ripple of excitement coursing down her spine.

"Marguerite, there's Lord de Lacy! He's sitting at the table next to us."

"Where? Oh, I see him. I wonder if that big, dark-haired man next to him is Sir Reivers."

Astra watched the man who sat beside de Lacy. He was conversing with the man on his left, and Astra could make out only the knight's extremely broad shoulders and the back of his head. She waited expectantly and wondered if she would see the face of the Black Leopard at last.

De Lacy caught them watching him and smiled their

way. He turned and said something to his companion. The dark-haired knight's head jerked around. Astra stared at him a moment, eye-to-eye, not ten paces between them.

"Do you think it's him? Sir Reivers, I mean," Marguerite whispered.

"Mother of God," Astra answered in a strangled voice. "It's him. The man in the forest!"

"It is Sir Reivers, then. How wonderful! I have always regretted that we did not have a chance to thank them for their bravery before we were dragged off by de Chilham. Now we will be able to converse with them at length."

"No!" Astra cried. She grabbed Marguerite's arm in a panic. "You don't understand. It's not Sir Reivers, or perhaps it is. Either way, I have no intention of going near that man. Ever!"

"What? What's wrong with you, Astra? Your face is flushed. Are you ill?"

"I said he was the man in the forest. I meant the summer before this . . . that day when we were swimming at the pond. Remember? I felt someone watching us, and I went into the woods . . . and *he* was there."

Marguerite lost two shades of color. *"Mon Dieu!* Are you sure? Could it not be a man of similar size and coloring?"

"He had a scar on his cheek," Astra muttered through clenched teeth. "Exactly as that man does—Sir Reivers or whoever he is. I would know that scar and those mocking eyes *anywhere."*

Marguerite sagged back against her seat. "I cannot imagine that a well-born knight would do such a thing. Spying on women in a convent—why, we might have been nuns. And we were completely naked. He must have seen *everything!"*

Astra nodded, feeling sick to her stomach. The man had seen everything. She had been too stupid to dress before she confronted the spy. She had thought it was an animal or, at worst, one of the nuns come to reprimand them. She had never dreamed it was a man—a huge young knight with hot, dark eyes and a twitching, hungry smile. She had stared at him long enough to memorize the evil slash that marred his smooth cheek. Then she had run away like a simpering coward. The thought of what her naked backside must have looked like made her sick all over again.

"We must leave," Astra whispered to her companion. "They might come and speak to us, and I could not bear . . ."

"Don't be silly! It would be very bad manners to leave the hall. You have nothing to be ashamed of; you did not spy upon him. It is Sir Reivers's duty to beg your pardon."

"No!" Astra cried again, utterly aghast. "I could not possibly face him . . ."

"Ladies, it is unseemly to keep whispering so," Lord Fitz Hugh admonished. He leaned toward them. "If something is wrong, tell me now, and I will deal with it."

"Nothing is wrong. Astra was merely noting that our rescuers from Tudbury are here. Sir de Lacy and Sir Reivers are seated at the table next to us." She motioned discreetly to the two men.

"What a stroke of good fortune! I will go and speak to them immediately. I have not yet had a chance to express my gratitude to the gentlemen personally."

Astra watched in horror as Lord Fitz Hugh rose and strode purposefully to where de Lacy and Reivers sat. The two knights stood and greeted the baron politely. Astra was too far away to hear Lord Fitz Hugh's words, but she could guess what he was saying. She sighed miserably, wishing she could disappear into the floor.

"Don't be upset, *ma petite,*" Marguerite murmured. "If you want, I will tell my father the whole story. He will know then that Sir Reivers isn't quite as gallant as he appears."

"You wouldn't! You promised me you wouldn't tell anyone!"

Marguerite shrugged. "As you wish, sweeting. It's your choice. If you keep silent, Sir Reivers will be treated as a hero by my father and the rest of the court."

It was true, Astra thought glumly. If she kept silent, the man would never be punished for spying. On the other hand, she could not bear the thought of anyone else knowing what he had done to her. It seemed better to say nothing, to pretend that the incident in the forest had never occurred.

"I have no choice! I cannot disparage Sir Reivers's reputation without damaging my own. I can only hope that his guilty conscience punishes him as fiercely as he deserves."

"I suspect your hopes are in vain," Marguerite said with a slight smile. "Sir Reivers is headed this way, and it does not look like his conscience troubles him in the least. Why, the bastard looks absolutely smug!"

Astra's whole body stiffened with tension, and she stared fixedly at her hands and prayed for strength. Amid the low murmur of conversation around her, she heard the tread of boots approaching and strong masculine voices near. She did not look up until she heard Lord Fitz Hugh clear his throat and the rustle of Marguerite's skirts as she stood to greet her father's companions.

Astra forced herself to rise slowly. Even more slowly,

she raised her eyes and steeled herself to face the dark mysterious gaze she remembered so well.

Sir Reivers stood directly in front of her. As Marguerite had said, he was smiling. Astra avoided the smile and the dangerous, mocking eyes. Instead, she focused her gaze on the crooked scar on Reivers's cheek.

"Lady Marguerite, Lady Astra—what a pleasure it is to see you again." De Lacy gave a small bow. Astra was aware of a slight movement in front of her as Reivers mimicked the gracious gesture.

"Of course we are delighted to see you as well," Marguerite answered. "And under much more pleasant circumstances. We must apologize for taking leave of your company so abruptly in Tudbury. You risked your lives for our safety, and we never had a chance to thank you properly." She dipped into a graceful curtsy.

"No thanks are necessary." De Lacy turned to his companion. "We believe that the chance to do a good deed is reward enough in itself, don't we, Richard?"

"Of course. Not to mention the opportunity to be in your presence, to enjoy your beauty once again. That is a reward beyond measure," de Lacy's companion added silkily.

The irony in Reivers's deep voice was so pronounced, Astra looked up at him sharply. His eyes gleamed with laughter, while his mouth curled into a smooth smile. She gritted her teeth, amazed at his audacity. Could no one else see that he was mocking them? She glanced at Lord Fitz Hugh. He was nodding and smiling benevolently. Astra suppressed a groan and wondered how long she would be forced to endure this humiliating charade.

"Gentlemen, as I told you, I cannot stay long in London," Lord Fitz Hugh said. "It would ease my mind greatly if you would consent to look after my daughter and Lady Astra during their stay at court. Lady Marguerite does not always have the best judgment. It would be a relief to know that someone was looking out for her."

"Oh, Papa, I m sure these men have better things to do with their time," Marguerite protested with a seductive smile. "We will be quite safe. The Queen will see to it that we are properly chaperoned at all times."

"Nonsense. There must be a dozen women attending the Queen, and she cannot possibly keep track of all of them. These men have proven their chivalry and honor beyond doubt. It would be a great burden off my shoulders to know that they were personally looking to your safety and well-being. Sir de Lacy, Reivers—would you be willing to grant me this additional kindness?"

De Lacy appeared surprised. He did not answer immediately but looked to his friend, as if waiting for his response. Sir Reivers smiled broadly. "Of course, Lord Fitz Hugh," he answered with a low bow. "We are honored by your trust, and we will do our best to merit your faith in us."

"Marvelous!" Fitz Hugh boomed. He gave Sir Reivers a mighty thump on the back. The brutal blow did not appear to faze the man called the Black Leopard in the least. If anything, his gloating grin widened.

"Well, then, there is much I must do in the little time I have remaining here. I'm off to see the King. I'll leave you young people to your own devices."

Lord Fitz Hugh strode off rapidly, leaving the two knights and two ladies standing silent, each taking the measure of the other. De Lacy spread his hands in a gesture of mock regret. "Alas, *demoiselles,* it appears you are stuck with us."

"As you are with us," Marguerite answered coyly.

Astra said nothing; in fact, she doubted she would ever speak again. Her stomach was a coil of knots, her knees on the verge of collapsing beneath her. She looked steadily at the floor. Perhaps if she prayed hard enough and long enough, God would take pity on her and make Sir Reivers disappear.

"Lady Astra seems distressed, does she not?" Reivers said softly. "Perhaps I should see her to her sleeping chamber so she can lie down and rest."

Astra jerked her head up, ready to protest. She met Reivers's dark eyes and felt the words die in her throat. This man had some terrible effect on her—his very existence seemed to render her mute.

"Richard, I think it is your presence which distresses Lady Astra. Perhaps we should take leave of these ladies for now," de Lacy suggested.

"Perhaps that would be best." Marguerite placed a soothing hand upon Astra's arm. "Lady Astra was raised in a convent, and she has just begun to explore the delights of the outside world. We must give her time to grow used to the freedom and opportunities of the King's court."

"Of course," Reivers said softly. "I would not wish to overwhelm Lady Astra."

He took Astra's hand and lifted it up so he might kiss it. Seeing that Astra's fingers were clenched with tension, he gently unbent each finger and pulled it back like the petal of a flower. Then he leaned down and tenderly pressed a kiss into her exposed palm.

The touch of Sir Reivers's lips sent a tingling warmth coursing down Astra's arm. She snatched her hand away, but it was too late—the warmth spread. A hot flush swept over her cheeks and her insides filled with an aching heat.

She felt almost faint, and she stepped away from Reivers unsteadily.

"Astra, are you well?" Marguerite frowned; her dark eyes filled with concern.

"I'm well, but I would like to rest. It has been a long, tiring day."

"Of course, *ma petite,"* Marguerite consoled. "We'll go to our bedchamber now."

De Lacy and Sir Reivers bowed, and Astra followed Marguerite from the hall. Her heart seemed to thud with every step.

Eight

"Sir Reivers and Lord de Lacy can wait in the hallway for the rest of their lives for all I care. I'm not leaving this room." Astra plopped stubbornly onto one of the Queen's plush settees and crossed her arms over the rich green velvet of her riding habit.

Marguerite rolled her eyes upward, as if beseeching the heavens for strength. "Don't be obstinate, Astra. The Queen can be quite patient and sympathetic, but she won't tolerate your hiding away in the ladies' chamber . . . unless you tell her the real reason you don't want to come out."

"Sir Reivers would well deserve it if I did tell the Queen. He's insufferable! I think he actually enjoyed seeing me blush and stammer in his presence last night!"

"He is a bit smug, isn't he? It might do him good to be brought down a notch or two. All that is required, Astra, is for you to spread the word that Sir Reivers is a worthless rogue who spies on ladies as they bathe. The Queen—despite her extravagance—is really quite prudish; she'll likely have him banished from court."

Astra uncrossed her arms and sighed. "I don't want to see him suffer complete disgrace, only make him squirm a little. Why, to think that that man stood there, so polite and kissing my hand, and all the while he knew exactly what I looked like naked—every blessed inch of me!" She gave a little shiver.

"If you were ill-formed or displeasing to look it, Astra, you might have cause for embarrassment, but the truth is, your body is so well nigh perfect, I've always thought it was a shame to cover it up. It is not such ill chance that Sir Reivers saw you naked. Having seen you thus, he may be willing to overlook your modest dowry and ask for your hand anyway."

"Are you suggesting I consider Sir Reivers as a husband?" Astra came to her feet, her blue eyes wide in horror.

Marguerite shrugged. "Why not? He's not rich yet, but his prospects are good. He appears to be a formidable warrior, and he stands high in the King's favor. In time he could win much land, and he certainly is handsome. With those big shoulders and dark eyes, I think he is utterly irresistible."

"Then you marry him! I want nothing to do with the devious, ill-mannered lout!"

"I don't think he wants *me,*" Marguerite pointed out. "Besides, my father would never permit it. He has his heart set on my wedding at least an earl."

"Oh bother." Astra sank down on the settee again. "Can you not see that I despise Sir Reivers, that I hope never to lay eyes upon him again?"

"You hardly know the man. He may have many good qualities that you have not yet discovered."

Astra's mind leapt to the thought of Sir Reivers kissing her hand, the feel of his silky mouth on her palm. Was it a good quality for the mere sight or touch of a man to make her swoon? God help her, she was right to try and stay as far away from him as possible.

"Marguerite, you must help me out of this coil. I know

that your father expects Reivers and de Lacy to keep company with us, but I simply cannot do it. The mere thought of being near that man makes me ill."

"As you wish," Marguerite agreed, heading toward the door. "I will tell Sir Reivers that you will not be attending the hunt because the very sight of him sickens you."

"Nay, do not tell him that! I do not want to be cruel. Can you not make up some other excuse?"

"But that would be lying. Surely you do not want me to lie for you?"

"Of course not." Astra twisted her hands together uneasily. "But perhaps you could soften the truth a little. Explain how upset I am over the . . . the incident in the forest. Surely he will understand my ill-ease."

"I will try, but I know Sir Reivers will be disappointed. In truth, I think his interest in you is sincere."

Marguerite left the room. Astra got up and began to pace. Now that the thing was done, her conscience bothered her. She did not want to hurt Sir Reivers. For all that he had rudely spied on her, he had also rescued her from those dreadful men. Perhaps she owed him something; perhaps she was being unfair not to offer him a chance to redeem himself.

She went to the oriel window and sat down heavily on the cushioned seat. She could see out into the palace gardens, and the sight of the lush foliage reminded her that she was missing the excitement and pageantry of a royal hunt. Her lovely new clothes and all the weeks of riding lessons were going to waste, and it was only the first of many sacrifices she would have to make if she continued to shun Sir Reivers's company. She was being a coward, avoiding things because she did not have the courage to face them. Perhaps it would be better if she confronted Sir Reivers and insisted that he apologize to her.

The sound of the door opening behind her made Astra turn in surprise. She came quickly to her feet when she saw Sir Reivers in the doorway. He looked even more formidable than she remembered. For a moment Astra just stared at him, too shocked to speak. Then she cleared her throat and spoke as calmly as she could. "What are you doing here?"

"I've come to ask your pardon."

Astra tried to think of what to say next. The realization that she was alone with this huge, threatening man seemed to blot out all her other thoughts.

"You shouldn't be here," she finally managed.

"Why not?"

"Because . . . because we should not be alone together."

"I had no choice. You would not see me otherwise, and I must talk to you."

Astra noticed that his wicked smile appeared to be missing. Somehow, without it, he seemed even more frightening. She stepped back toward the window seat. She felt trapped.

"Please, my lord, say what you have come to say."

Sir Reivers quickly closed the space between them; he did not stop until he was only a hand's breadth away. Then he sank to his knees at her feet.

"What are you doing?" Astra gasped.

"I am begging your pardon." He reached for her hand.

"Don't!"

"Alas, you hate me."

"Nay, I do not!"

"You will not speak to me. You will not let me touch your hand. You must hate me." He bowed his head.

"It is not that. It is . . . I am afraid of you!"

Sir Reivers looked up, his beautiful dark eyes wide with surprise. "Afraid? What do you think I would do to you?"

Astra stared at him. What, indeed? This man had saved her life. Why should she think he would hurt her? "I don't know," she answered.

Once again, he gave her that look: bewildered, perhaps even a little hurt. It pierced Astra's heart. She suddenly felt she had wronged him.

"I wanted to explain . . ." Sir Reivers began, ". . . about that day you were swimming and I watched you."

Astra felt herself blush to the roots of her hair, and she turned away. She did not want him to remind her of her folly, to make her relive the horror of finding him in the bushes.

"I know it was a disgraceful, abominable thing to do." He sighed. "I would not blame you if you never forgave me."

"Why did you do it?" Astra's voice caught. "Why did you stay there, watching us?"

"Why? Can you not guess? I wanted to leave, but I could not tear myself away. You were so beautiful, so exquisitely pleasing to look at. You reminded me of an angel."

"An angel?" Astra gaped at him, too surprised to remember her anger.

He nodded. "You were all pink and white and glimmering gold. I can still recall how your hair shone flaxen in the sun. Your skin glowed as white and smooth as a marble statue; your eyes were as sweetly blue as the clearest summer sky." Sir Reivers's voice grew husky, ragged with emotion. "Is that not how angels are described—so dazzlingly fair they near hurt your eyes?"

"I cannot imagine that you could have mistaken me for an angel," Astra said in a disbelieving voice.

Sir Reivers sighed, his face suddenly sad and weary. "Perhaps I mistake beauty for goodness. I have seen so much ugliness in life, the blood and pain of the battlefield, the horror of torture." He paused, and Astra had a vision of the wound on his face before it healed—a raw and bleeding slash. How much it must have hurt!

"You cannot blame a man for being inspired by a vision of purity and innocence. When I saw you . . . laughing with your friend, so happy and carefree . . . it reminded me that there are other things in life besides death and destruction."

Astra felt her heart softening. A soldier's life often was harsh and brutal. It was certainly possible that such a man might be drawn to things that allowed him to forget the grimness of his profession.

"I realize now how much I frightened you. I am sorry for that. The truth is that I am a weak, selfish man. Sometimes I do loathsome things."

Astra nodded. She knew what it was like to do things she was ashamed of. "We all do things we regret. The important thing is to ask God for forgiveness and to try and do better in the future."

"I have asked God for forgiveness. But I must know—will you forgive me?"

Astra stared at Reivers, torn by her conflicting emotions. The man seemed genuinely contrite. He was kneeling at her feet, begging for her forgiveness; she even thought she caught the glitter of tears in his dark eyes. Having the means to soothe his pain and knowing it was blessed to forgive, how could she deny him the soothing balm of absolution?

"I . . . I will try."

Sir Reivers got to his feet rapidly, his dusky countenance lit with a bright smile. "I knew you would not withhold your pardon. I knew that you would be generous." He grabbed her hand and pressed it fiercely to his lips. Astra tried to pull away, but he was too quick for her. He leaned over and kissed her on the mouth. She jerked back, staring at him.

"Sir Reivers. Please!"

"Call me Richard," he said, still holding her hand.

He was so big, so dark, so handsome. His glowing eyes, as deep and lustrous as ebony, mesmerized her.

"Say that you will go on the next hunt with me. Say that you will let me show you London."

She nodded slowly. She felt as if she were in a dream. Her will seemed to leave her as she gazed into his rapt, strangely sensual face. He leaned toward her and his lips came down upon hers again. She could feel the heat of his breath, the fiery hunger of his mouth. His hands gripped her shoulders fiercely.

A sob escaped her lips. "No, don't! Please—you mustn't!"

He pulled away, his chest heaving. His mouth was wet. When his eyes swept her body, she knew he was remembering what she looked like without her clothes. The thought made her ache all over.

"You are so good, so sweet," he whispered. "I want to devour you."

She could feel his need. It terrified her. What had happened to the contrite penitent who begged for her forgiveness? Had it all been an act, an elaborate lie to weaken her defenses? If only he would go away. She needed time to think, to decide what kind of man he really was.

"Sir Reivers . . . you must leave."

He nodded, then reached out and touched her cheek. She flinched. He smiled sadly and walked toward the door. She watched him, admiring his gleaming dark hair, his broad shoulders, his long, well-muscled form. He reminded her of an animal, lithe, graceful . . . dangerous. When the door closed behind him, she realized she was not relieved to have him gone. Instead, she felt a sense of loss. She wondered immediately when she would see him again.

When Marguerite returned, she found Astra sitting on the window seat, staring pensively out at the gardens.

"Ma belle, I wish you would have come. The hunt was great fun."

Astra turned huge, troubled eyes toward her friend. "He came to see me."

"Who came to see you?"

"Sir Reivers. He begged me to forgive him."

"Holy Mother! What did you do?"

"I . . . I said I would try."

A sly smile crept over Marguerite's face. "So you do fancy him, don't you? You admit he is handsome and charming."

"God help me, Marguerite, I don't know what I think. He seemed so sincere, so genuinely aggrieved that he had offended me. He even got down on his knees." Astra turned away, her lower lip trembling. "But when I said I would try to forgive him, he . . . he pounced on me . . . like an animal. He even kissed me on the lips. I do not think it was a kiss of friendship."

Marguerite's brown eyes danced. "Did you like it? How did it make you feel?"

"I . . . I am ashamed to say."

Marguerite laughed loudly. "This is wonderful! We've only been at the court a day, and a fine, young knight is pursuing you. And you, Astra, I believe you are falling in love."

"Love! I hardly know the man. I am appalled to admit it, but . . ." Astra turned away again; her long auburn eyelashes swept down to hide her eyes. ". . . what Sir Reivers makes me feel can only be lust. I dare not be alone with him again."

"But there is no reason you cannot spend time in his company if you are properly escorted," Marguerite reasoned. "Will has offered to show me the sights of London tomorrow. You and Sir Reivers could serve as our escort, and we could serve as yours."

Astra looked doubtful. She had told Sir Reivers that she would see him again, but she was not sure it was wise. Still, why had she come to London, if not to experience the sights of the city? She would be more careful this time. De Lacy and Reivers had vowed to protect her and Marguerite, and she believed Lord de Lacy at least was a man of his word. A sudden thought came to Astra, and she turned to regard her friend intently.

"You seem quite interested in the Baron of Thornbury, and he is certainly wealthy enough to please your father. Could it be that you consider de Lacy a prospect as a husband?"

Marguerite frowned. A slight crease marred her smooth, tan forehead. "I do like Will, but I'm not sure he returns my interest. In all the time we spent together today, he never attempted to kiss me, or to even touch me except in a brotherly way." She shrugged. "Perhaps he does not find me pleasing."

"Perhaps he has too much respect for you to paw you as Sir Reivers did me." Astra shivered. "That man reminds me of an animal, a beast. No wonder they call him the Black Leopard. There is something absolutely ferocious about him."

Marguerite smiled, thinking how lucky Astra was. Ferocious—it seemed a likely word to describe a man who would be a marvelous lover.

The moon was a bright crescent in the sky, the air balmy and soft. Still, the loveliness of the evening was not enough to banish the squalor of the row of rough taverns that hulked on the edge of the river. Richard grimaced as he walked beside them. Usually the ugliness and danger of Southwark excited him. Tonight was different. His mind was filled with the image of a pale, glimmering creature whose mouth was as fresh as springtime. By comparison, the rough side of London seemed repellingly sordid and crude. He could not block out the stench of piss and rotting garbage that rose from the gutters, or ignore the harsh voices and cackling laughter that emanated from the darkened alleys.

His mouth twisted hungrily as he thought of the woman he had just left. Lady Astra had turned out to be everything he had dreamed of. She was incomparably sweet and tender-hearted, but he also suspected a core of molten passion burned beneath her demure exterior. One kiss and she had been deeply aroused, near beside herself with desire. If a kiss could do that, what would she be like when he had a chance to properly seduce her? The image of her ripe, full breasts resting in his hands, her slender thighs spread to receive him, made him ache. For a moment, the ugliness of his surroundings fell away. It was almost as if she had enchanted him and redeemed his jaded soul. Perhaps she truly was an angel.

Richard ignored the beggars and half-naked whores who called out to him and turned into the Black Swan Tavern. He pushed by the drunken, raucous sailors filling the main room and made his way to a back table where his companion sat.

"Been waiting long, Will?"

"Not nearly so long as Ruby. She's been back here a dozen times, looking for you. I think she's in love."

Richard laughed. "Are you suggesting that she prefers me to this group of depraved misfits? I'm not even sure that's a compliment."

"At least you don't smell as bad as the rest of this lot." Will wrinkled his nose in distaste.

"Always the fastidious one, aren't you? I must say that tonight I share your disgust for this crowd. After having sipped ambrosia from Lady Astra's luscious lips, I may never be satisfied with a crude whore again."

Will's eyes widened. "It went as well as that? Lady Astra let you kiss her?"

"Aye, she let me—after a fashion. I suspect she was simply too startled to repulse my attentions effectively."

"You're a miracle worker, Richard. From what Lady Marguerite said, Astra intended to hide away in the Queen's chamber for the rest of her life rather than face you. Whatever did you do to change her mind?"

"I spent a few minutes on my knees begging her pardon, and the lady melted like butter in the sun. She's a genuine innocent, Will, as sweet and guileless as a lamb. I mumbled some nonsense about her reminding me of an angel, that her beauty and goodness was pure balm to my soul after my gruesome life as a soldier. She went all pale and starry-eyed; I honestly think she believed it was her duty to forgive me."

"Jesu, Richard, what a wicked devil you are. Don't you feel a little guilty about deceiving her so ruthlessly?"

"I wasn't really deceiving her," Richard protested. "I meant at least half of what I said. Besides, if she's anywhere as rich as Lady Marguerite, I intend to make Lady Astra my wife."

"Your wife!" Will put down his ale cup with a thud. "You're serious about this, aren't you?"

"Why not? I'm not likely to ever meet a woman as beautiful and desirable as Lady Astra, and she's rich in the bargain. I can scarce believe it, Will. It's like a miracle, as if the answer to my prayers had suddenly dropped into my lap."

"I didn't know you believed in miracles," Will answered with narrowed eyes. "How do you know Lady Astra will accept your offer? More to the point, what will Lord Fitz Hugh think about someone like you wedding his niece? He likely has other marriage plans in mind."

"He may be reluctant at first, but I feel sure I can convince him. I intend to take Lady Astra to bed, then see to it that old Fitz Hugh learns of it. He'll not refuse my offer of marriage then."

"You're going to seduce her? Good God, Richard, Fitz Hugh will kill you!"

"I think not," Richard answered smugly. "I made a few inquiries, and it seems the old man's naught but bluster and bluff. He caters shamelessly to his daughter's whims, allows her to run all but wild. He has no more backbone than Henry does. If I compromise Lady Astra and she admits to it, I believe Fitz Hugh will make his mark on a marriage contract."

"What about Lady Astra, has she no say in this?"

"I'm not going to ravish her, if that's what you mean. She's going to enjoy every minute of the seduction, I assure you."

Richard leaned forward, intending to share the specifics of his plan. He started when he felt a caressing hand upon his cheek.

"Jesu—Ruby?"

"Oh, so the bastard admits he knows me," a comely, hazel-eyed woman smirked as she tossed her copper-colored curls and then leaned over to brush one of her big breasts against Richard's arm. "I thought perhaps you had decided you were too good for me and were seeking your pleasure in the arms of one of the haughty bitches of the King's court. Don't even think of it, darling. You know they'll never please you like I do."

"Damn it, Ruby! You ought not sneak up on me like that! I swear you took a year off my life."

"Better than an inch off your cock," she purred. "And how is my sweet pet this evening?" She dropped a hand to Richard's crotch.

"Get your hands off me," Richard growled as he grabbed her wrist and pushed her away. "I don't belong to you or any other woman, Ruby, and don't you forget it."

The woman put her hands on her hips and pursed her full lips into a pout. They were heavily painted with the particularly vivid shade of lip rouge that had earned Ruby her nickname.

"Touchy tonight, aren't we? What's wrong with your

friend?" she asked Will in a sharp voice. "Has he spent so much time with you that he's taken up your filthy habits?" She eyed Will malevolently. "If I find you a couple of boys, will you leave Richard alone?"

Quick as a flash, Richard's hand snaked out and grabbed a handful of Ruby's hair.

"Apologize," he snarled. "Now!"

Ruby's hazel eyes glinted with defiance, then she shrugged her shoulders. "All right. I apologize, Lord de Lacy," she said insincerely. She cast Will another scornful look, then, as Richard released her, turned and sashayed off.

"That wasn't necessary, Richard. I don't really mind anymore."

"Well, I mind, by God!"

"But you hurt her!"

Richard gave Will an incredulous look. "She asked for it. Besides, I'm a regular saint compared to most of her customers."

Will leaned back and took another sip of his ale, regarding his friend intently. Even after all these years he'd known him, Richard was an enigma. He could be sweet and charming one minute, devious or even violent the next. Will had personally never known Richard's wrath, nor did he want to. Considering Richard's plan to seduce Lady Astra, he decided he didn't relish what it would be like to experience Richard's compelling charm either.

He had only recently met Lady Astra, but already he felt sorry for her. The sweet-faced, innocent young woman was no match for the Leopard's stealth and cunning.

Nine

"I'm not sure it is a good idea to let Sir Reivers and Lord de Lacy show us London," Astra said as the two women dressed the next morning. "Remember what happened to us at Tudbury?"

"Don't be silly," Marguerite scoffed. "Those men were low-born knaves. Will and Richard are gentlemen. They would never let harm come to us."

"We should at least take some of your father's knights for protection."

"I can hardly think of a greater deterrent to romance than having a group of armed knights breathing down my neck."

Astra paused in pulling on a fresh chemise and regarded Marguerite in surprise. "Romance? I didn't realize you saw the Baron of Thornbury as anything other than a friend."

"You mistake my words. I said Will treated me like a sister. I did not say I was not interested in *him.*"

Astra nodded. "He is handsome, well-mannered and rich. Even your father approves of him."

"He is also something I like better—a challenge."

"What do you mean?"

Marguerite gave Astra a sly smile. "So far, Will has been rather cool to me, but I intend to change that. I'll wager you that by the end of the day, I will have Sir William de Lacy fawning over me the way Richard does you. Tell me—what odds will you give me?"

"Gambling is a wasteful vice," Astra answered severely. "And furthermore, I don't think much of your plan to entice poor Lord de Lacy. If he acts like a friend, perhaps that is all he wishes to be. Must you see every man as a conquest?"

"Tush, tush. You're always so serious. Some day I will be a wedded woman—sober, proper and dull. In the meantime I intend to enjoy myself."

"I can hardly imagine you ever being proper and dull." Astra shook her head, then her eyes widened as she saw the gown Marguerite had pulled from the heavy oak wardrobe.

"The saints preserve us—surely you're not going to wear that!"

"Why not?" Marguerite smoothed the wrinkles from the exquisite surcote of deep blue samite threaded with gold. "Don't you think it is becoming?"

"Becoming? It rivals the Queen's own ceremonial robes. But you saw the streets when we arrived, Marguerite. How can you think of dragging that beautiful thing through the muck of London. It will be utterly ruined before the day is over!"

"Then I'll have it sent to the fullers or trimmed off to make a shorter overtunic. I intend to look my very best today, Astra, and I don't have the advantage of your stunning figure."

"Wear what you wish then, but don't expect me to spoil my new clothes. I'm wearing my plain gray bliaut."

"Oh, no you aren't." Marguerite again dug in the chest. "I'll not go out looking like the peacock and you the little wren. You'll wear something elegant as well. This . . ." She fluffed out a gown of saffron-colored sarcenet, the bodice delicately studded with pearls. "This will be perfect."

Astra stared in dismay at the vivid garment. Not only was it garishly bright, she also considered it much too tight and revealing to wear in the daytime.

"I couldn't possibly go out in that."

"Oh, but you will," Marguerite insisted. "You'll wear it to please me, won't you, *ma petite?"*

Astra sighed. It was because of Marguerite's generosity she had all these beautiful clothes. It seemed ungrateful to refuse to wear them. With resignation, she reached for the yellow garment.

The two women finished dressing and were fixing their hair when one of the Queen's man-at-arms announced that their escort had arrived. Astra gave one last careless pat to her hair—Marguerite had insisted that she wear it covered with only a thin veil and circlet—then followed her friend to the door to greet Sir Reivers and the Baron.

As soon as she saw him looming in the doorway, Astra's heartbeat quickened and her knees began to wobble. For all that Sir Reivers was attired like a gentleman—his dark clothes clean and brushed and only a short sword in his belt—there seemed to be an aura of menace and danger surrounding him. She stepped forward hesitantly and acknowledged his low bow with a quick nod of her head.

"Demoiselles, you look exquisite today."

"Indeed." Beside Reivers, de Lacy smiled warmly. "We will be the envy of all of London when we are seen in the company of these beauties."

Astra flushed, acutely aware of her inappropriate attire. Marguerite had no such qualms—she gave de Lacy a seductive look and reached out to pat his elegant crimson tunic. "You two gentlemen look equally dashing. Of all the gallant knights that serve the King, I can think of no others I would rather spend the day with."

Sir Reivers seemed pleased by Marguerite's words, but Lord de Lacy looked embarrassed. Astra felt a stirring of sympathy for the young nobleman. She was intimately acquainted with Marguerite's forceful nature, and she did not envy de Lacy if his plans for the day ran counter to Marguerite's intentions.

They set out to see the sights of London, first taking a wherry to Queenhithe. As they disembarked the small boat, their noses were assaulted by odors from the fish-market of Billingsgate. It was a hot, muggy day, and the odor of decaying fish was almost unbearable. The ladies held scented pomanders to their noses, but Astra was still greatly relieved when they turned north and the air grew fresher.

Marguerite and Will chatted companionably, but Astra and her escort remained silent. Astra had no gift for small talk, and she was too busy watching her step to make conversation. In places the gutters had overflowed, sending wash water, kitchen refuse and god-knew-what-else into the street. As she grew more adept at keeping her gown safely out of the mire, she began to admire the sights they passed: massive, tiered houses that crowded over the street, churches, convents and schools, as well as guildhalls and shops of workers in metals, leather, cloth and fur.

The streets were filled and everyone seemed to be in a hurry. The variety of people bustling by reminded Astra of the fair at Tudbury. In addition to the familiar nobles, clerics, farmers and merchants, Astra saw cripples and beggars in rags, bands of filthy children who roamed the streets in packs, as well as armed sergeants and beadles in striped robes who were charged with keeping order in the city. At one street they met a group of sheriff's men leading a prisoner. His hands were bound and the ends of the rope that tied him were attached to the wrists of his captors.

"What has he done? Where are they taking him?" Astra asked her escort.

"Hard to tell. Whatever he's been convicted of, he's likely headed for Newgate. You have to pity the poor bastard. I'd rather be hung right off than spend a night in that hellhole."

Astra shuddered. She was curious about the horrors of Newgate, but she also realized she really did not want to know of them. They reached the market of Cheapside, and she had another shock. Two men and a woman were bound in stocks outside the marketplace. They looked utterly wretched, their tongues hanging out in thirst, their faces bespattered by the garbage and dung which the crowd had hurled at them.

"And these poor unfortunates . . ." Astra asked, stopping to stare in pity. ". . . what have they done to deserve such torture?"

"The one man's likely a fishmonger who sold bad fish," Richard answered, gesturing at the rotting sturgeon that hung from the older man's neck. "As for the others," he shrugged dismissingly. "They probably cheated someone as well. You must not feel too sorry for their kind, Astra. If the authorities did not punish people this way, the greedy merchants of this town would poison the lot of us."

Astra turned, unconvinced, and looked uneasily for Marguerite and Will, who seemed to be lagging behind.

"Should we not wait for them?" she asked as Richard guided her into the noisy crowd.

"Perhaps they want to be alone. Have you not heard the saying, 'two's company, four's a crowd'?"

"That's 'three's a crowd,' " Astra answered stiffly. "I think we should all stay together. We would be safer that way." Astra slowed to let Marguerite and Will catch up. Her apprehension was genuine. With their shifty eyes and hardened faces, Astra guessed that some of the ragged men and women in the crowd around them were pickpockets, thieves and other unsavory characters. She wondered if she was truly safe even with Richard at her side.

Will and Marguerite continued to lag behind as Marguerite stopped to examine the merchandise at nearly every booth they passed. Astra's attempts to keep them in sight fell by the wayside when she was distracted by the sight of a large crowd gathered around a huge wagonlike structure. It was the stage of a miracle play, the back of it grotesquely painted to resemble the flames of hell. Before the backdrop, a man in a flowing white robe and unnatural golden locks appeared to represent Christ, while another man with a purple cloak and flaming red hair portrayed Pontius Pilate.

Astra stared in amazement as the two actors worked the crowd—the shabby Christ inspiring praise and sympathy, while Pilate was greeted with jeers and catcalls. She could not decide if what they represented was blasphemy or merely a gaudy form of worship. By the time she thought to look for Marguerite, she realized her friend had well and truly disappeared. Richard had stayed watchfully by her side the whole time. Now he drew even nearer, taking her hand in his.

"Are you frightened, Astra, now that you are alone with me?"

Astra pulled away slightly, regarding him with a disapproving frown. "You promised to protect me. If you are a man of honor you will guard me from evil influences, including those you harbor in your own heart." Despite her cool words, Astra felt her heart pounding. She had dreaded being alone with Richard. She was afraid he would try to kiss her again.

He laughed delightedly. "What a spirited little thing you are! I find your primness refreshing after the honeyed seductresses of court. I was not wrong about you, Astra—you are as delightfully pure and untouched as I had imagined."

Astra watched him warily, unsure whether he was flattering or poking fun at her.

"Alas, the sun has gone behind the clouds. Tell me, Astra, what makes you frown? Don't you like what you have seen of London?"

Astra shook her head, her forehead puckered slightly in thought. "In truth, I cannot tell. I see many beautiful things, but I see much ugliness too. There are so many poor people. The peasants around Stafford have little, but they do not seem so hungry, so desperate."

"The city brings out both the good and bad in people. It can be a desperate place if you are one of the unfortunate ones."

Astra nodded, feeling a cold shiver down her spine. What must it be like to slip into the hellish netherworld she had just glimpsed?—the emaciated beggars with twisted limbs and open sores, the raggedy, sharp-eyed children who lurked at the edge of the crowd, waiting for a cart to topple or a distraction to lure a shopkeeper away from his wares, the skulking, grim-faced men who were surely criminals, capable of any cruelty or depravity.

Astra allowed Richard to take her arm and guide her through the jostling crowd. She could only gape as he led her swiftly past more delights and corruptions: reeking meat and poultry shops surrounded by pools of blood and piles of rotting entrails; goldsmith shops, the counters bright with the gleam of gold and jewels; clothiers displaying bolts of damasks, sarcenets and velvets; rude cookshops that stank of stale ale and rancid grease.

They stopped at St. Paul's Cathedral. The courtyard was crowded with ragged, hollow-eyed people, and as they walked toward the entrance, a group of scrawny children surrounded them. When her escort moved to push them aside, Astra stopped him.

"No, please—I want to give them something." Astra reached to her girdle for the small leather purse Marguerite had pressed upon her earlier. She pulled out a handful of coins. As she attempted to pass them out to the children, a black-haired, bony child who was bigger than the rest grabbed the coins from her hand and ran off.

Richard laughed. Astra turned indignantly to see him regard her with a sardonic, self-satisfied smile. "Now you see the futility of doing good works, Astra. You can't help the genuinely needy ones, because they'll only be robbed. London is a cruel world, and only the strong survive here."

"At least I tried," Astra said coldly. "At least I can go into the church in good conscience, knowing that I did not turn away completely, that I tried to help my fellow man."

"Perhaps they'll have you give a sermon while we're here," Richard suggested. "Lady Astra de Mortain speaks upon the subject of loving thy neighbor—I'm sure the people of London would fill the cathedral to bursting to hear you expound on that theme."

Astra pushed ahead of him, trying to quell the anger

that Richard's sarcastic words roused in her. How could he be so cold-hearted and cynical? Was that what living in London did to you?

She walked slowly through the crowded cathedral. The nave was filled with clerks and solicitors doing business. Astra moved past them, seeking the peace and sanctity of the altar. She knelt at the rail and prayed, asking God for the strength to avoid temptation, for the patience and tolerance to turn her anger to compassion. In a few minutes she was finished. She rejoined Richard, feeling much calmer and almost at peace with herself.

"You seem to take your devotions quite seriously," Richard gibed. "I'm surprised you saw fit to leave the nunnery."

"I found I was not suited to be a nun."

"Why not?"

Astra glanced at Richard, her tranquil mood deserting her. She was once more ensnared by his burning, midnight eyes. "Because I am weak," she answered as calmly as she could. "I could not forsake the base desires of the flesh."

He grinned at her. "I believe you, Astra," he said softly. "For all your piety and urge to do good works, I can't imagine you as a nun."

He took her arm and led her swiftly from the cathedral. Out in the streets again, the odors and noise of the city assaulted her. A part of her longed to return to the cathedral, to the contentment and security she found there. Another part was enthralled with the bustle of London, the raw vitality that seethed all around her. This was life—the enticing energy that made her body tingle all over, that filled her veins with bubbling warmth. She could not deny that it fascinated her, that she had waited years to feel this way.

They headed back toward the marketplace, passing food vendors offering hot bread, warm meat pies, fresh milk and buckets of ale. Astra's stomach growled. When she looked especially longingly at an open air shop selling pastries, Richard leaned close. "Hungry?"

She nodded.

"I'd rather not eat standing out in the street. Let's go inside."

He guided her to a dingy-looking building with a gaudy sign announcing it as The Red Lion. The cookshop was crowded and looked none too clean. Astra paused in the doorway, noting with distaste a group of rough-looking men dicing in the corner. As Richard led her past them, they stopped their game to stare at her with bold, assessing eyes. Astra pressed closer to her escort, wishing she were not so brightly dressed.

"Must they stare so?" she whispered.

"They're admiring you," Richard whispered back. "They're probably trying to decide how much you're worth."

"Worth? What do you mean?"

"For a tumble in bed."

Astra felt her face flame. It was repulsive—all these men having carnal thoughts about her! She wanted to leave. Then she realized that if she did, she would have to walk past them again. As Richard led her to a table in the back, Astra kept her face down, struggling to control her mortification.

"What's wrong, Astra? Your face is as red as a poppy."

Astra glanced at Richard, infuriated by his obvious amusement. She wanted to slap him. Instead, she fixed him with a look as cold and disapproving as any Mother Marie had ever given an errant novice.

"It was very unchivalrous of you to bring me here, Sir Reivers. I want you to escort me out of this place—by the back entrance if possible!"

Richard sat down and continued to smile at her benevolently. "Never fear, Astra, I will guard your beauty with my life." He reached out his hand to help her down to the bench. Without thinking, Astra slapped it away.

Richard laughed delightedly. "Why, the kitten does have claws!"

Astra brought her fingers to her lips, appalled by what she had done. What was wrong with her?—she was behaving like a spoiled child! Shaken, she slid into the seat by Richard.

"Are you all right, my lady?"

Astra nodded. "Please, Sir Reivers, will you make it quite clear to these men that I am not for sale?"

"Richard . . . call me Richard." He shrugged. "They already know that. They can tell from your manner and bearing that you are a lady . . . and since you're with me, you're completely safe."

Richard's voice was calm, matter-of-fact. Astra felt even more foolish. Was she being too sensitive? Marguerite had told her more than once that it was natural for men to stare at an attractive woman. It was rather a compliment of sorts. She sighed. "It does not seem right that men should look at every women as if she . . . as if she set a price on her virtue."

Richard's eyes narrowed. "But they do—all of them. I know no woman—from the highest-born princess to the poorest peasant—who does not have her price."

"I certainly do not!"

"Oh, no? Would you marry a beggar, Astra? Can you tell me that a man's wealth or lack of it does not influence whether you will consider him as a husband?"

"But you're speaking of marriage—not men's filthy thoughts!"

"Marriage is an exchange of property, and use of the woman's body is part of the man's share. When a man takes a wife, he buys her favors in bed. How is that different than what a whore does?"

Richard's harsh words shocked Astra, but she could not deny there was some truth to them. Many marriages were little more than business transactions.

Richard's mouth twisted scornfully as he continued. "To me, an heiress who barters her body like a rich prize is no better than the whore who sells herself on the street. Nay, she is worse, for at least the whore honestly admits what she is doing."

"How cynical you are! Marriage does not have to be like that. It can be a sacred bond between two people who truly care for each other."

"Are you speaking of love, my lady?"

Astra looked away, unable to meet Richard's laughing dark eyes. She knew he thought her a foolish, silly romantic.

"Please don't mock me, sire."

"For shame that I should ever mock someone so sweet and good." As he spoke, Richard reached out and took her hand. Astra glanced down shyly, watching his gloveless fingers cover her own. There was something startling in the contrast between his calloused brown skin and her own pale delicacy, and the sight of her small fingers enveloped in his big hand made her feel weak.

She shook off the strange, giddy mood just as their food

arrived, served by a bulky woman with a bored, plain face. Richard had ordered them each a meat pie and a glass of ale. Astra looked at the pastie suspiciously, worrying about the cleanliness of the inn's kitchen. Richard had no such reservations; he bit into his pie greedily, a trickle of juice dribbling down his chin.

"It's good, Astra. Think you that I would take you somewhere that served bad food?"

Spurned by his chastening words, Astra took a dainty bite and found that the pastie was indeed delicious. The crust was tender, the filling piping hot and succulent, full of exotic flavors and spices.

They did not talk at all for the next few minutes. Astra watched Richard between bites, noting that he ate with the swift, serious concentration of a boy. With a trickle of meat broth still embellishing his chin, he seemed touchingly young, not dangerous or threatening at all.

The salty food made Astra thirsty, and afterwards she downed her glass of ale quickly. Too quickly—the bitter liquid was more potent than she was accustomed to. She felt the blood rush to her head; her body relaxed so completely she felt as if she might slide off the bench.

"Astra, what's wrong?"

She shook her head, trying to banish the languorous, dreamy feeling that had overtaken her.

"Perhaps you need some fresh air."

Astra nodded and let Richard escort her from the crowded tavern. When they reached the street, Astra leaned against him and took a deep breath, her head spinning slightly.

"You *are* ill," he murmured, sounding alarmed.

"Nay, I am fine. It is only . . . the ale." Astra felt another wave of weakness overtaking her. She clutched at Richard's tunic, leaning her face against his chest. "Oh, I am sorry. You must think me a terrible nuisance."

"Nuisance! You must be jesting! I am enjoying this enormously."

Astra straightened and jerked away from Richard's warm, reassuring body. One glance at his smug, sensual smile told her that he had indeed been taking pleasure in touching her.

"How crude of you! To pretend that you are helping me, when all you have on your mind is . . ." She stopped, unable to finish. She dare not even think about what Richard likely wanted of her. Unbidden, the image sprang to her mind of him lying on top of her, her skirts asprawl around her bare legs.

She swallowed hard and looked down at the street, watching the flies buzz around the garbage in the gutter. It had been a mistake. She should never have agreed to be alone with this man. He was simply not to be trusted.

"Take me home," she said coldly. "Take me back to Westminster."

Ten

Damn his wicked tongue! Richard cursed silently as he and Astra walked toward the quays. What was it about this woman that brought out the worst in him? He couldn't seem to help mocking Lady Astra's sweetness, her innocence. It was hardly the way to win her favor, to entice her into allowing him to bed her.

He cast a look side-ways at her, wondering again at Astra's beauty, at the sheer perfection of her delicate form. He wanted her—in the worst way he wanted her—but so far he had succeeded in angering rather than charming her. He'd never had so much trouble seducing a woman before. His tongue kept betraying him, letting slip cynical, hard-bitten words that revealed the ruthless side of his nature. It was as if a part of him were trying to warn Lady Astra away, to keep her from falling in love with him.

Could it be true? he wondered. Did he really want to protect Astra from himself? Why should that concern him? She was a woman, and likely as deceitful and manipulative as the rest of her sex. Besides, his intentions were not really dishonorable. He wanted her wealth, but he would not ill-use her to get it. She could do worse than him for a husband. He would appreciate her beauty and give her a great deal of pleasure.

The thought made him smile, and when he looked over,

he found Astra watching him, a puzzled look on her lovely face.

"I was thinking," he said softly. "There is much of London you have not seen yet. Perhaps you would allow me to escort you again sometime?"

Astra's eyes widened. She opened her mouth, as if to protest. For some reason, though, she said nothing.

"Visit London with them again tomorrow? Surely you jest! Sir Reivers is one of the most ill-mannered men I have ever met! I have absolutely no desire to endure another day in his company."

"Please, Astra," Marguerite cajoled. "I need more time alone with Will. I'm convinced it is only a matter of time before he falls under my spell."

"Mayhaps he doesn't want to kiss you. As a gentleman he may consider it improper to seek favors of a young woman he has only recently met."

"My point exactly—Will is likely afraid I will be offended. Once he grows used to my company, he will relax and grow bolder."

"If you were a man, Marguerite, you would be a despicable rogue. You view every knight you meet as a conquest."

Marguerite shrugged. "What if I do? It does no harm and keeps me entertained. So, will you?" she asked again. "Will you agree to having Reivers and de Lacy escort us around the city tomorrow?"

Astra sighed, already suspecting Marguerite's pleading would win out. "Why must I go?" she protested weakly. "Why can't you and Will see the sights by yourselves?"

"It would not be fitting for us to be seen leaving the

palace alone together. Besides, Will won't go without Richard. They seem to be fast friends—almost as close as we are."

"Mother of God, help me," Astra murmured. "I must be mad to agree to this."

Marguerite smiled in delight.

Their journey began much as it had the day before. Reivers and de Lacy joined them in the Queen's chambers and escorted them to Kingsbridge Quay to hire a wherry. They traveled by boat to a dock near the main part of London and disembarked to walk to Cheapside. When they reached the market, Marguerite did not bother to hide her intentions. She grabbed Will's hand and pulled him off into the swarming crowd. Astra stared after her friend, shaking her head in amazement.

"Lady Marguerite seems quite determined," Richard observed in an amused voice. "But I rather think she has met her match this time."

"What?" Astra turned to him with a perplexed expression.

"Nothing. I don't wish to worry about Will and Marguerite. I'm very pleased that you have agreed to give me another chance."

"Another chance?"

Richard turned toward her. His eyes caressed her with languid warmth. His mouth curved up in a tender smile. "I am afraid I offended you yesterday. I'm sorry. I didn't mean to be rude. I hope you will give me an opportunity to make it up to you."

Astra stared at him. All her resolve melted away as she gazed into the depths of his black-brown eyes. Despite her haughty words to Marguerite, the truth was that she wanted to see Richard again. There was something about him that made her heart rise in her chest like a soaring bird, her legs turn to quivering aspic. She could look at him for days, admiring the clean lines of his features, the burnished glow of his skin and hair, the formidable grace of his powerful body. He was so shockingly, alluringly male—he seemed to affect her like too much of a heady vintage of wine.

When she didn't answer, Richard took her hand. "Come, I want to show you something."

He led her through the jostling marketplace, hurrying her past the busy stalls and heaping carts so rapidly Astra had no time to observe the merchandise. They left the crowds behind them and progressed down a dim, narrow street. Astra clutched Richard's hand tightly. She was far from comfortable in this dirty, teeming world of the city. The sheer impact of it made her want to go somewhere quiet and catch her breath.

Richard paused before a tiny shop that was almost hidden at the end of the street. He guided her ahead of him through the dark doorway and whispered in her ear: "Welcome to fairyland, Astra."

She blinked, then drew in her breath. The small shop seemed to glow with light. The shelves and counters were covered everywhere with bowls, cups and fanciful objects made out of clear and colored glass. They caught the faint light from the street and the cresset torches on the walls and turned the room into a glittering spectacle.

"I . . . I've never seen anything like it," she gasped.

"It's from a place called Venice. The shopowner told me how they make it. They heat a special kind of sand, then blow into it to create these beautiful shapes. See, it comes in different colors: blue, red, green, a kind of violet." He picked up a small cup. "Touch it. It feels cold, but it glows like the hottest fire."

Gingerly, Astra reached out and felt the delicate object. It was smooth, and as Richard said, cold.

"Sir. Madame."

Astra started as a small, balding man appeared from the back of the shop. His bland, doughy-looking face contrasted sharply with the brilliance of the merchandise; with his tiny blue eyes he reminded Astra of a near-sighted mole.

"I was just showing the lady your wares," Richard answered pleasantly.

Astra shook her head in amazement as she slowly walked around the shop. She had never seen such beauty. One shelf held small glass pieces shaped like jewels. Some were round, others oval or teardrop-shaped. She picked one up, admiring how it caught the light. It was exquisite, not much bigger than her thumbnail. She wondered how much it cost.

"Let me purchase it for you," Richard murmured in her ear.

"Nay, I could not," she whispered back, disturbed to think what the shopkeeper thought of them. He probably imagined them to be lovers.

"It is perfect for you," Richard urged. "See how there is a tiny star floating in the center of it? That is you, Astra—an exquisite star." When she gave him a surprised look, he added: "Astra means star in Greek—did you not know that?"

She shook her head. "I learned to read and write Latin at Stafford, but not Greek. The nuns told me that my father chose my name, but I never sought to find out what it meant."

"Your father chose well. Like a star you are—pure and gleaming, inspiring men to wistful longing and dreams of mystery and enchantment."

Astra blushed. She knew she should not let herself be affected by Richard's intemperate flattery. In fact, it was not his words which stirred her, but the sound of his voice—husky and velvety. A shiver chased down her spine at the sound of it.

"Please, Astra, I feel I owe you for the unfortunate circumstance of our first meeting. Let me make it up to you. Let this be my peace offering."

Astra's resolve wavered as she held the glass jewel in her fingers, feeling it warm to her touch. How beautiful it was—so hard and perfect. "Perhaps," she whispered. "If you are sure . . ." She looked at Richard doubtfully. His eyes glowed deep and dark as jet; his full mouth was pulled into a warm smile.

"Done." Richard produced a small sack from beneath his tunic and removed silver pennies from it one by one until the shopkeeper nodded, then thrust the bag back.

"Thank you, Sir Reivers," Astra murmured.

"Call me Richard," he answered, still smiling.

Astra clutched the precious glass teardrop tightly. "How will I keep it safe? What if I lose it?"

"It is meant to be worn on a necklace," the shopkeeper pointed out.

"I have just the thing." Richard reached beneath his tunic again, this time drawing out a long gold chain. He lifted it over his head, then took the glass jewel from Astra and deftly threaded it onto the chain. He held the necklace out to her.

"I couldn't . . ."

"Why not? It has no great value to me. I found it on a battlefield and began wearing it on a whim. The other knights jest that the chain gives me luck, but I don't believe in that sort of nonsense."

Richard held out the necklace, waiting. When Astra reached for it, he shook his head. "I'll put it on you."

Stiffly, Astra turned and gathered her veil out of the way. She felt Richard's calloused fingers on her neck, and the chain slid down her chest. The gold was still warm from Richard's body. The thought made Astra flush. There was something strangely intimate about donning something that had just rested against a man's skin. She knew Richard felt it, too. He grinned and his eyes glowed with delight. She looked down and felt her flush spread. The necklace was really too long, and the glass jewel had settled deep between the cleft of her breasts. Richard's eyes focused there with a fascination that unnerved her. She could feel the pendant—hot, burning, an emissary for Richard's own erotic imaginings.

Irritated with herself and him, Astra reached into her bodice and yanked out the necklace. It dangled wildly, swinging back and forth across her bodice, then came to rest at a point below the swell of her bosom.

"It suits you well, madame," the shopkeeper offered. "It is the perfect complement to your own beguiling beauty."

Astra gave the little man a distracted smile. She had almost forgotten he was there.

"Will there be anything else?" he added in a timid voice.

"Not today. Perhaps another time we will return and the lady will choose something else."

The shopkeeper bowed as they departed, his small furrowed face lit by a vague smile. Astra felt relieved to be back on the streets, as squalid and filthy as they were. The small shop had begun to seem too small, almost oppressive, and Richard's presence so close filled her senses to bursting. She could not seem to escape the breathless ache his nearness aroused.

They wandered back to the market, but saw nothing that matched the splendors of the tiny glass shop. Richard paused by a cart of ripe apricots, and Astra leaned against it with a sigh.

"Are you weary, Astra?"

"I am not used to . . ." she gestured, ". . . all of this."

"My poor little butterfly. I forget you are not yet accustomed to the bustle and stink of the city." Richard brought his hand up to touch her shoulder, then slid his fingers beneath her veil to rest on her nape. He began to stroke her neck, his strong, probing fingers skillfully easing the tension away. Astra closed her eyes and sighed again, oblivious for a time to the noise and confusion that swirled around them.

"I know a place we can go," Richard murmured. "Would you like to see the Tower of London, Astra?"

Astra opened her eyes, considering. The Tower was one of the oldest buildings in London, dating back to the days of William the Conqueror. It had served as the King's palace until only recently, when Henry had moved most of his household to the new palace at Westminster a short time before he wed Eleanor.

"It is not too far," Richard coaxed. "We can take a wherry back to Westminster from there."

Astra nodded, her curiosity making her forget how hot and sweaty she was and how much her feet hurt. She allowed Richard to take her arm and guide her through the maze of the marketplace. They turned southeast toward the river. In the distance they could see the Tower, the royal standard waving from the highest turret. When they reached the quays, they walked along them for a while, watching the ships: wine ships from Gascony, scuts from Flander, Essex and Kent, the great vessels of Almain and Norway. Finally, they entered the royal complex and beheld the Tower rising above them, majestic and gleaming white.

"The King spends most of his time at Westminster, but he's renovating the Tower and building up the defenses around it," Richard explained, gesturing toward the busy courtyard where workers were unloading stone and gravel from wagons. "Once it is finished, the Tower will be a well-defended palace. A moat and stone wall will surround the north and west, and the river will guard it on the south."

When Astra coughed at the dust and held her veil to her face, Richard added: "Queen Eleanor stays away because the dirt and noise of construction bother her, but Henry visits the site fairly often. Sometimes he brings Prince Edward to see the animals in the royal menagerie."

"The menagerie?"

"The Emperor of Germany sent Henry three leopards in honor of the three beasts emblazoned on the English flag. Since then the King has added a tiger, some water buffalo and several bears. There was an elephant, but he died. The King insisted he be buried at Westminster as if he were royalty."

Astra could only nod in amazement. She had never heard of such animals existing outside of books.

"Would you like to see them, Astra?"

"Could I?"

Richard shrugged. "Why not? Hardly anyone goes

there. Most of the nobles think the menagerie is only another of the King's foolish extravagances."

The menagerie was housed in a separate building, called the Lion Tower. Richard was right, Astra noted, for as busy as the rest of the complex was, the dreary stone building where the animals were kept was deserted. They had gone a few paces inside when a deafening roar emitted from the darkness ahead of them. Astra froze, her limbs rigid, the hair on her neck prickling with fear.

Richard laughed. "They're in cages, Astra. There's no way they can eat us."

Astra nodded, but gratefully clung to Richard's hand as he led her forward. The first cage housed the bears. They looked much like the bears Astra had seen at bear baitings, except they appeared to be better fed and more docile. Indeed, there was an air of lethargy, almost melancholy about them.

She scrutinized the small space the animals were crowded into, a dank dark room with only one small window. "Are they happy here?" she asked. "For all that they are well-cared for, they must miss the forest, the fresh air and freedom they once knew."

Richard laughed. "My sweet, tender-hearted Astra, they are only animals. It not as if they can reason about their lot in life."

"But they can feel," Astra protested. "Look at their eyes—do you not see the hopelessness there?"

Richard laughed again, but this time he sounded less confident. He led her on to the next room. The cage there held only one bear, a gigantic creature with fur of pure white. "This is 'Bruin,' the King's favorite. Is he not a handsome specimen?"

Astra nodded, still troubled by the regal-looking creature's gloomy surroundings. Another rumbling roar came to their ears—even nearer this time. Astra shivered.

"The big cats are next." Richard pulled at her hand. They moved on to another chamber. As they entered, the torches on the wall flickered, casting eerie shadows into what appeared to be an empty cage. There was a low growl and a large spotted cat lunged forward, snarling at them through the bars of the cage. Astra stepped back quickly and even Richard flinched.

"This is the male; the two female leopards are smaller. Is he not magnificent?" Richard asked.

"Aye," Astra whispered. She had never seen such beauty and power melded into one form. The cat's eyes were like brilliant jewels, his fur as rich and finely-ornamented as the most expensive cloth. Yet he was not just a lovely object or an elegant plaything. His sleek flanks quivered with strength; his huge, hungry-looking mouth opened to reveal gleaming ivory teeth that looked as though they could easily bite off Astra's arm. He was danger and death personified.

"Do you feel sorry for him, Astra? Do you worry that he is unhappy in his bare, boring cage?"

Astra didn't answer. The leopard growled again, then began to pace, padding delicately from one end of the cage to the other. There was a restless frustration in the cat's movements, and Astra again found pity arising in her.

"I do feel sorry for him. All his beauty and grace is wasted. Such a creature is meant to be free, not caged up in some gloomy tower." She turned to Richard. "Can you not feel it? They call *you* The Leopard—how would you like to be imprisoned in a place like this? Would it not make your soul grieve, your heart ache with discontent?"

"I am a man, Astra. This animal does not have a soul,

nor a heart as you speak of it. He has no conscience, no morality. He is a cold-blooded killer, an instrument of death."

"Are you so different from him?" Astra demanded. "I saw you kill those men in the forest—without a care, without even a twinge of regret. You are a killer too!"

Richard stared at her, startled by her vehement response. "I am a knight. It is my duty, my *Christian* duty, to protect defenseless women, to smite down evil with my sword."

Astra sighed, knowing suddenly that she had started an argument she could not win. Richard had been trained from boyhood to believe in the rightness of violence and war, while she had been taught the opposite.

There was silence between them for a moment, then Richard put his hand on her arm. "Do you want to see the rest of the animals?"

Astra shook her head. She could not really explain why it distressed her to see beasts in cages, but somehow it did.

"There is another place you must visit while we are near the Tower, Astra," Richard said, his voice again soft and mesmerizing. "And I promise that this place will not grieve you, but gladden your heart."

Eleven

They traversed the busy courtyard and followed a pathway behind the Tower. It led to the neglected ruins of what once must have been a splendid garden. Formerly elegant hedges had returned to their wild, sprawling state, and masses of knee-high vegetation encroached upon the pathway. Most of the flowers and herbs had been choked by the rampant weeds, but there were still roses, gillieflowers and daisies sparkling among the disordered green. Their perfume mingled with the soft scent of earth and sunshine.

"In the days of John and Isabella, this was the Queen's privy garden," said Richard. "It has been abandoned since then, but it is still a pleasant refuge from the city."

"It is wonderful! You would never even know we are in London. It reminds me of the woods near Stafford. It even smells like it—the scent of flowers and water, not dung and garbage." Astra wrinkled her nose in disgust at the remembrance of the stench of the markets.

Richard laughed. "I suspect you will never be a city girl, Astra de Mortain. You belong here, a bright butterfly among the flowers." He idly picked one of the daisies that grew in profusion and used it to tickle her under the chin.

She giggled, then paused, uneasy. A disturbing tension moved in the air between them, and her heart had started to race again. Richard was only inches away. She could almost smell the salty, sweaty maleness of him. Up close, he was even more astonishingly handsome; soft black hair curling around a sculptured, arrogant face, dazzling dark eyes, a sensuous, expressive mouth. His tanned velvet skin was marred only by the pale scar on his cheek. Without thinking she reached up and traced the faint line it made, slanting sharply across his cheekbone.

"How did it happen?"

"An unlucky sword thrust. Or perhaps it was lucky after all." He grimaced. "Usually when a man gets his weapon under your helmet, he drives it straight through your skull."

Astra could not repress a shudder of horror. "I hate war. I don't understand why men insist on fighting stupid battles over land and kingdoms."

"If there were enough land and wealth for everyone, there probably wouldn't be any wars, but there isn't. A man has to fight to protect the things he cares about."

Richard's fierce words surprised Astra. "What do you care about, Sir Reivers?"

"Wealth and power, of course. What else is there?"

"Much more! There is love and children . . . peace . . . happiness . . . security . . . living a Godly life . . . caring for the less fortunate . . ."

"Spoken like a true little novice," Richard interrupted, his voice suddenly sharp. "You live in a dream world, Astra. Outside of Stafford, many of those things don't exist. The real world is made up of greedy, selfish men who don't give a fig for your pretty ideals. They take what they want, and if you aren't strong enough to fight them, you're left with nothing."

Astra stared at Richard for a moment, startled by the bitterness in his voice. She could hardly reconcile this harsh philosophy with the playful, easy-going man who teased and flattered her.

Richard caught her watching him and smiled, the charming mask slipping back into place. "Here we are quarreling again. Surely this is too pleasant a place for an argument. Why don't we find some place to sit and rest?"

Astra nodded. For all that her slippers were made of soft leather, they were still new and stiff enough to rub her feet raw in a day of walking. As they reached the trees that grew between the overgrown garden and the river, she looked longingly at the soft grass beneath a sprawling chestnut. "I'd delight in sitting, but I'm not sure I dare. I'm certain to get grass stains on my gown."

Richard glanced at the elegant rose velvet bliaut she wore, then jerked his tunic over his head. He shook it out and arranged it carefully beneath the tree. "Your couch, my lady," he announced with a grand gesture.

Astra gaped at him. Richard's torso was completely bare, the smooth brown skin glazed with a faint sheen of sweat. She could see the sleek muscles rippling across his chest. The sight made her feel strange.

"Please, Richard, it's not decent!"

"Why not? I'm sure you've seen peasants laboring in the field without their tunics. Why is this different?"

Astra shook her head. She didn't know why it was different. Perhaps it was because she found Richard so irresistibly attractive. Surely it was sinful to be alone with a man who made you feel so exhilarated and alive.

"Come. Sit down," Richard coaxed as he settled himself beside the tunic. "Don't look at me if it bothers you."

Astra sat down cautiously, then gradually leaned back against the tree. She sighed. It felt wonderful to rest, and it was such a tranquil, lovely place. She closed her eyes and listened to the soft sounds of the river and the faint breeze whispering through the boughs overhead.

"Don't fall asleep."

Astra opened her eyes. Richard was leaning over her, his face inches from her own. His teeth were very white against his dusky skin, his lips rose-brown and moist.

She closed her eyes when he kissed her. She felt so dreamy, so relaxed. Her body floated away. All she could feel was the warm, gentle pressure of his lips on hers.

She shivered when she felt his tongue on her lips. His arms came around her—hard, imprisoning. She could not move when he put his tongue deep within her mouth. The sensation startled her. In some forgotten part of herself she knew what this bold, probing kiss meant. Her body responded with a restless fire as she fought the doubts that worried at the edges of her mind. It was just a kiss. Wasn't it?

She was gasping for breath when he released her. She stared deep into Richard's eyes. They were darker than ever, almost black. The wry, amused softness was gone from his face. He looked intense and serious.

She blinked and tried to catch her breath.

"Did you like it?" His voice coaxed with silky smoothness. It sent another shiver down her spine.

She nodded, and her face flushed. He did not wait for more, but abruptly kissed her again. His tongue flicked and glided over her mouth and between her lips. He found the tip of her tongue and played with it. It seemed to take all her concentration to think about what he was doing to her mouth. Her body turned to liquid. She hardly noticed that she was no longer sitting, but lying on Richard's tunic beneath the tree. He leaned over her, and her fingers rested against the smooth, damp skin of his chest. Without thinking, she slid her hands around to stroke his back. It was firm but silky; the thick muscles flexed slightly beneath her fingertips.

His mouth left hers and trailed down over her neck, nuzzling softly just below her collarbone. Astra let her fingers wander to his neck, then stroked his thick, soft hair. His mouth found the hollow between her breasts. Astra squirmed. Her breasts seemed to throb. A tingling ache radiated from each nipple and rippled down her body like a fierce, greedy flame.

Her eyes were closed, but suddenly she could feel Richard's hands on her breasts. He touched them with a rough possessiveness that she could feel even through the fabric of her gown. The throbbing pleasure she felt unsettled her. She had to stop this. It had gone too far. Soon he would have her gown undone and his fingers would touch naked skin! The thought brought her to her senses. She pulled Richard's hands from her breasts and struggled to sit up.

"Richard!" she cried and tried to push him away. He released her slowly, looking surprised and rather puzzled. She wanted to chastise him for making improper advances, but somehow it did not seem quite fair. She had not protested when he kissed her. Nay, she had encouraged him. Astra pressed her hands to her flushed cheeks, horrified by what she had just allowed to happen. She had behaved like a wanton. After her priggish words the day before, Richard must think her a terrible hypocrite. Tears gathered in her eyes, eloquently proclaiming her distress.

"Shhhh, lovey," Richard soothed. " 'Tis nothing to cry over."

"I am a dreadful, sinful creature."

"Nay, you are beautiful and sweet."

"I . . . I don't know what came over me. I have never been like this before. In truth, I have never even kissed a man until you."

"And was it so awful that you must cry?"

Astra shook her head. He did not understand. She had liked his kisses—far too much she had liked them.

"Then what distresses you, Astra? Why do you cry?"

"I . . ." she started again. She couldn't tell him. It was simply too shameful. Even with Marguerite she had not shared the extent of her impure thoughts. And this man—she scrutinized Richard through the blur of her tears—she was afraid he was not above taking advantage of her fleshly weakness. Hadn't he already admitted his weakness to her?

"I think perhaps, Sir Reivers, we should not see each other again," she forced out in a quavering voice.

For a moment he just looked at her, as if he were stunned. Then she saw the hurt fill his eyes.

" 'Tis not your fault, truly," she added, hoping to soften the blow. " 'Tis mine own weakness that I guard against by shunning your company."

"But Astra, I thought we shared something special. Already I feel a rare bond between us, and you admitted to me that you believe in love. How will we ever know what might have been if you thrust aside our budding friendship before it has a chance to blossom?"

He made it seem that she was cruelly rejecting his offer of friendship. Was there not something to what he said? Perhaps it was not lust she felt, but strong affection, the first stirrings of what could grow into love.

"I don't know," she answered, more confused than ever. "I will have to think upon it."

"Of course, my dear." Richard helped her to her feet.

"We must get back to Westminster. You likely should rest before it is time to dine."

"It's time we returned to the palace," Will suggested as he led Marguerite toward the river.

She nodded, too distracted by her thoughts to argue. The day had certainly not gone as she had planned. William de Lacy had turned out to be more than a challenge—he was a baffling puzzle. She had flirted and teased all day, and he had not responded with anything more than pleasant smiles and polite rejoinders. Time and time again she had tried to entice him into out-of-the-way corners, hoping he would finally try to kiss her, but to no avail.

When they passed a small alcove between buildings outside the market, she had pulled him into the vacant space and brushed his arm deliberately with her breast. When he turned to look at her in surprise, she gave him a bold, inviting look and pursed her lips provocatively. Will had hesitated, then leaned over and gave her a light, passionless kiss. After he released her, she had been more confused than ever.

The rest of the day had been pleasant, if slightly strained. They had talked and eaten and continued to be unfailingly polite to each other. It was as if the kiss had never been. But Marguerite could not get the memory of it out of her mind. She had never had a man behave this way with her before. They might act shy or uneasy at first, but once she offered them her lips, they always warmed to her. This man was obviously not interested; he kissed her as if it were a duty!

Could it be that Will did not find her attractive? She dismissed the thought from her mind. She knew most men found her comely, if not beautiful, and she was confident that any man would at least want to kiss her. Unless he was in love with someone else, and too loyal to betray them? Marguerite frowned. If that was the case, why didn't Will just tell her?

She glanced sideways at her escort. Will was not as tall or muscular as Richard, but he was well-built and apparently a good soldier. He seemed in every way a virile, masculine man. She again considered the possibilities—that Will did not like her, that he had sworn himself to celibacy—then discarded them. No, there had to be something else, some other reason. The truth dawned suddenly.

"Sweet Jesu," she gasped, stopping in the middle of the crowded street. "You don't like women!"

Will looked around uneasily, then took her arm and pulled her forward. "It is not a thing I wish the whole city to know," he muttered.

"It's true!"

Will glanced her way, then nodded. "I wish it weren't, Marguerite, but it is. If I could have spared you this knowledge, I would have."

"You're a. . . . Oh!" Marguerite gasped. "I've never known anyone like that before."

Will grimaced. The day was ruined, and likely also the sense of companionship and acceptance he'd begun to feel with this woman. He turned wearily as Marguerite spoke again: "Tell me—do you find the same things pleasing in a man that a woman does?"

He gaped at her in astonishment. "I don't think that is something I should be discussing with you."

"Of course you should. We obviously have something in common—we both like men. Why shouldn't we compare our tastes?"

"Marguerite, I don't think. . . ."

"At least tell me what you do when you find someone you like."

Will searched her face. Finding no scorn in her expression, just frank interest, he answered in a low voice. "I must make sure that the man feels the same toward me. It can be dangerous to approach a man if you're not sure he shares your desires."

"And then what?"

"What are you getting at, Lady Marguerite?"

She gave him her sweetest smile. "I want to know what you do in bed with a man."

Will burst out laughing, the tension between them abruptly dispelled. "I'm surprised your father ever let you out of the convent. I suspect he made a grave mistake in doing so."

"You're making fun of me," Marguerite pouted. "You're not going to tell me, are you?"

"No, I'm not. You'll just have to use your wicked imagination."

Marguerite frowned. "I've tried, but I don't really understand. A man and a woman fit together nicely, but a man and a man . . ." She shook her head.

"Perhaps some day, when you're older, I'll give you a hint," Will teased. "For now . . ." his face grew sober again. "I would appreciate your discretion about this. Richard knows, obviously, but he is a much more open-minded man than most."

Marguerite gasped. "Richard and you . . . are you . . ."

"Lovers?" Will finished for her. "No, Richard does not share my aberration. If anything, he goes the other direction. He likes women as much as any man I've ever known."

"But you appear to be so . . . so close."

"Aye, Richard and I *are* close." Will's handsome face twitched with a wry smile. "We have both saved each other's lives so many times we can't count them all. Women aren't always aware of this, but there are bonds formed in battle that are stronger than even passions of the flesh."

Marguerite nodded thoughtfully. "How do you hope to hide your . . . your difference as time goes on? Your family is one of the richest and most powerful in England. There is bound to be pressure on you to marry, to father heirs for your line."

"Perhaps some day I will marry. In the meantime . . ." he gave Marguerite a warning look. "I must ask you to keep this knowledge to yourself. You could cause me a great deal of trouble if you were to spread this information at court. I'm not sure King Henry would understand."

"Of course. I am good at keeping secrets, Will, truly I am."

He nodded doubtfully, wondering if this impulsive, flighty woman would be his ruin. His unease increased when Marguerite gave a whoop of laughter.

"What? What is it?"

"I was just thinking, Will, how funny this is. For once my father was right. He gave me into your care, thinking that you would be the perfect escort, and by God, you are!"

Will smiled back, his spirits lifted by Marguerite's infectious laugh. "I am pleased that you are so understanding. I wonder if you would allow me the honor of continuing to serve as your escort?"

Marguerite shrugged. "You're good company, and now that I know that it's not my fault you don't want to kiss me, I feel much better. Besides, I had another reason for dragging you off alone. I think Astra is falling in love with Richard, and I wanted them to have some time together."

Will shook his head. "I may be harmless, but Richard more than makes up for me. I wonder if it is wise to leave him alone with Lady Astra."

"Why? Don't you trust Richard?"

"For myself, I trust him with my very life. But with Lady Astra's virtue . . ." He rolled his eyes.

"Astra will manage, I'm sure. For all her ethereal beauty, she's no fool. At Stafford, I depended on *her* to keep me out of trouble."

Will's smiled faded. "While we are sharing confidences, Marguerite, I must warn you—Richard intends to seduce your cousin. He thinks by compromising Lady Astra, he can force your father to allow them to wed."

"If Richard wants to marry Astra, why doesn't he just ask her?"

"Richard did not think Lord Fitz Hugh would look favorably on the match. Despite his success on the battlefield, Richard has been unable to convince the King to grant him any land. Except for his horse, his armor and a chest of war booty, Richard owns almost nothing."

"That is something of a problem, but it's not insurmountable. My father has agreed to give Astra a small manor near Wallingford as a dowry. It's not much, but it would be a place for them to live until Richard can increase their fortunes."

"A small manor—that is all Lord Fitz Hugh offers for his niece? What of her own family? Surely Astra has dower lands of her own?"

"You misunderstand my relationship to Astra. She's not my cousin, but rather, a dear friend. Her father and mother are dead, and there is no family fortune. She is as poor as

Richard. My father offered her the manor because I asked him to."

"What? Astra is not related to the Fitz Hughs? She is not an heiress?"

Marguerite shook her head. "I love Astra like a sister, and I intend to see that she weds a man who loves her and cherishes her as I do. But he need not be rich. If he truly cares for her, Richard would make a perfectly acceptable husband."

"I don't think you understand. Richard has his heart set on marrying for wealth. If Astra is poor . . ." Will's voice trailed off, and his fine features tensed with worry. "You must not continue to encourage Lady Astra's feelings for Richard. He may be bewitched with her beauty, but I doubt any woman can make Richard forget his ambitions. Astra will likely be hurt, her reputation ruined before she has an opportunity to attract a more suitable husband."

"Oh, bother, Will. I think you worry for nothing. I would not be surprised if Astra is able to entice Richard into marrying her despite her lack of dowry. If there is true love between them, they will find a way to be together."

Will shook his head but did not speak. Beneath her bluff practicality, Marguerite was obviously as naive about life as most women. He didn't have the heart to shatter any more of her illusions today.

Twelve

"It was astonishing. One kiss and Astra gave herself to me like a flower opening its petals to the sun," Richard exulted as soon as he was alone with Will in the knights' quarters.

Will groaned. "What did you do?—try to debauch her in some filthy alley?"

"Of course not." Richard sat down on a bench and yanked off his rumpled tunic. "A jewel like Astra deserves the proper setting for romance. We were down by the river, near the Tower. Her lessons in love are only beginning. All I did today was teach her how to kiss properly."

Will fidgeted with the cross-garters on his braies, trying to decide what to do. Richard had to know Lady Astra's situation, and the sooner the better. Still, he dreaded telling him the truth. Richard was bound to regard Astra's poverty as another galling set-back in his plan to amass a fortune.

"Richard, I'm afraid there is something you should know. I learned today that Astra isn't related to the Fitz Hughs at all. She's just a comely young woman Marguerite befriended at Stafford and decided to take under her wing."

The smug, self-satisfied look on Richard's face faded. "What do you mean?" he asked in a puzzled voice. "If Astra's not kin of the Fitz Hughs, who is she?"

"No one, apparently. Certainly not an heiress. As I understand it, your new ladylove is penniless."

"Penniless? The girl has nothing?"

"I believe Fitz Hugh has promised to grant her a small manor when she weds."

"A small manor. God's blood, Will, that's not nearly enough!"

"Actually, Fitz Hugh is being quite generous. He offered the manor to Astra as a favor to his daughter. It is rare such a gift is made to someone outside a family."

Richard appeared too stunned to respond. He stood abruptly, his hand rubbing the short sword at his side with a thoughtful, almost sinister motion. Will watched his friend uneasily, wondering if he had been unwise to blurt out the truth. He did not like the cold, bitter look on Richard's face. The scar on his cheek twitched—a sure sign he was wroth.

"Of all the damnable, wretched . . ."

"Calm down, Richard. This isn't that grievous a setback. Your visit to London might still yield benefits."

"I should have known she was too good to be true," Richard fumed, ignoring Will's attempt to soothe him. "Most heiresses are ugly as sin or betrothed nearly at birth. The really comely women are always poor."

Will nodded sympathetically. "I'm sorry, Richard. Perhaps you'll have to endeavor to win your fortune by other means."

"I hate this hellish, miserable city!" Richard cursed. "I wish there was a good war I could go fight in. Perhaps I could finally win some land that way—or get my guts cut out trying!"

"God's teeth, don't take on so! Surely things will work

out eventually. If nothing else, I will see to it that you are made castellan of one of my family's castles."

"Oh, that would be grand, wouldn't it? Then I'd never live down the whispers that I'm a nellie like you."

Will blanched. Richard cursed again, then began to pace. "I'm sorry, Will. I shouldn't have said that. I don't care what they say—I know you're as good a man as any that's walked the face of the earth."

He paced a few moments more, then continued. "I appreciate your generosity, but it wouldn't work. It wouldn't be *my* land or *my* castle. Lady Astra may be willing to accept a friend's charity, but I am not."

Will wanted to argue that a grant of land from him was no different than one from the King, but decided against it. Richard was very stubborn, and for all his cynical words about wealth and power being everything, Will suspected that deep down Richard sought something more in his life.

"What will you do now?"

"What can I do?" Richard snapped. "I'm right back where I was a month ago when I first came to London. Again I'm reduced to begging for favors from my liege lord." His eyes narrowed suddenly, and a dark look passed over his face. "I have half a mind to go to Henry and ask straight out for a reward for my years of loyal service."

"I wouldn't advise it. The King doesn't like to be forced into decisions. That's the reason he gets on so poorly with his brother by marriage, Simon de Monfort of Leicester. De Monfort insists on backing Henry into a corner and rubbing his face in his shortcomings. They say that's why King Henry sent de Monfort to Gascony to quell the troubles there. They say he wanted Leicester out of his sight."

"Still, the King owes me, and I doubt that he'll have the guts to refuse me before a roomful of knights. It would make him look too much the greedy, conniving bastard he is."

"Richard, I think . . ." Will began, then paused as he saw the look on his friend's face. When Richard was in this mood, it was better to distract him than argue. "What about Lady Astra?"

Richard's mouth quirked bitterly. "You were right. She was too good to be true."

"Will you drop your pursuit?"

Richard shrugged. "I must. There's no way I can wed Astra if she's poor."

"It seems a shame. I thought perhaps you were beginning to care for her."

Richard shook his head. "The part of me that could care for a woman was destroyed long ago. What I feel for Astra is naught but lust, and I am far too old and cynical to let my cock get the better of my wits."

"Are you sure? The way you talk about Astra is different than the way you usually speak of women. You seem to genuinely like her, even admire her. You once likened her to an angel."

"She is an innocent, but after all, she only arrived in London a few days ago." Richard's face hardened. "I don't doubt that her innocence will tarnish over time. She'll end up whoring around like the rest of the women at court."

Will shook his head, depressed by Richard's bitter words. Marguerite had been wrong. There was no such thing as true love. Marriage was a grim, practical business. Those who denied it was so were fools.

"Well, you certainly took your time," Marguerite teased as Astra entered the small sleeping chamber to dress before the banquet. "This morning you were afraid to be alone with Sir Reivers. After spending nearly the whole day in his company, do you still think he is ferocious?"

Astra blushed and glanced uneasily at Isabel. Astra was embarrassed enough to tell Marguerite what had happened—she was certainly not going to share her transgressions with Isabel, who already disapproved of her.

"Actually, he was most polite," she answered softly. "He took me all over the market, then down to the quay."

"You were alone with Sir Reivers?" Isabel asked in a shocked voice. "How could you do such a foolish thing? The Queen is a pious and virtuous woman. She won't tolerate her ladies being involved in scandalous dalliances."

Marguerite rolled her eyes and turned away, but Astra met Isabel's accusation with calm politeness. "Sir Reivers and Lord de Lacy were asked to act as our escort by Marguerite's father. As for being alone with Sir Reivers, that happened by mistake. We simply became separated from Marguerite and Will at the market."

"A mistake!" Isabel snorted. "I'll wager it wasn't a mistake at all. Sir Reivers has a notorious reputation with women. He probably took you off alone so he could make improper advances."

"As I said, Sir Reivers was extremely polite and well-mannered. Anyway, you shouldn't listen to gossip, Isabel. Most of it is untrue, and you only shame yourself by repeating it."

Isabel looked startled, then made a sour face. "You must be more of a simpleton than I thought. Ask anyone at court. Sir Reivers is an outrageous womanizer, not to mention an unscrupulous fortune hunter." She stalked abruptly out of the room, leaving Astra to glare after her.

"Oh, Astra," Marguerite giggled. "That was marvelous. Isabel is a terrible gossip. I loved the look on her face when you told her she shamed herself by repeating it."

Astra shook her head. "I couldn't allow that whey-faced shrew to imply that Richard . . . that he . . ." Astra broke off, her delicate features abruptly draining of color. "Oh, Marguerite, do you think it's true? Do you really think Richard might have intended to seduce me?"

"Well . . . I . . ." Marguerite chewed her lips thoughtfully. "Given the opportunity, most men will attempt to entice a woman into loveplay. My father assures me that it is simply part of men's nature. He believes they have much less control over their physical urges than women."

"God help me, I truly am a hypocrite."

"Ma belle, what's wrong?"

"Oh, Marguerite! After calling Isabel a liar, I realize her words are likely true. Richard did make improper advances toward me. And I . . . I let him. I let Richard compromise me."

Marguerite's eyes widened with horror and fascination. "You didn't! Surely you didn't. What did he do—take you to some dirty inn?"

"No," Astra moaned. "We were under some trees in a garden by the Tower."

"You let him futter you right there on the grass?"

"Of course not!" Astra gasped. "That much of my virtue I still retain. But I did let him . . . touch my breasts." She flushed scarlet.

"Oh! Well, that is only natural," Marguerite responded, sounding relieved. "It seems to be the next step beyond kissing. Unfortunately, I am so skimpily endowed, I cannot usually distract a man that way." She glanced ruefully at her own less-than-ample bosom.

"I have done such sinful things, Marguerite. First, I let him kiss me, then I touched the bare skin of his back and chest. Then he put his hands upon me."

"Were you naked?"

Astra shook her head vehemently.

"Then it hardly counts. Don't look so glum, sweeting. Letting a man feel up your titties hardly means you have lost your virtue."

Astra groaned. "Isabel's right. I am a simpleton. I let Richard do those things, then convinced myself that he hadn't planned it, that it was my own sinful nature that led me into temptation. Isabel insists that Richard has a terrible reputation with women, and I have seen the proof of it. How could I be so dense not to know what he was up to?"

"Perhaps you didn't see the truth because you didn't want to. I suspect you are falling in love with Richard, and it goes against your nature to think badly of those you love."

"Falling in love!—what a horrible thought! I don't want to fall in love with a man like Sir Reivers. He is very much lacking in virtue and honesty. Isabel called him 'an unscrupulous fortune hunter!' "

"You can't control your feelings, Astra, only your actions. If you have fallen in love with Sir Reivers, there is naught you can do about it. Still . . ." Marguerite put a consoling arm around her friend. "I don't want to see you hurt. It might be best if you were not alone with him too soon."

Astra nodded, then reached to touch the small glass pendant that hung from her neck. "I suppose I should give this back to him."

"What is it?" Marguerite asked, leaning down so she could see better.

"A glass jewel that Richard purchased for me at a little shop in Cheapside. He gave me the chain so I wouldn't lose it."

"It doesn't look valuable. Although it is exceedingly pretty, and somehow suits you."

"But I must give it back, mustn't I?"

"Why? It was a gift. Besides . . ." Marguerite smiled slyly. "It appears that Richard obtained what he wanted as well. I imagine he considers the sweet kisses and caresses you granted him more than fair payment for the few pennies he spent on the necklace."

"Don't say that!" Astra cried. "Richard said that every woman had her price—that you could buy any woman's virtue if you had enough gold." She snatched off the gold chain, crushing it in her trembling fingers. "I almost sold mine for this cheap trinket!"

Astra stared at the necklace for a moment, then flung it down on the bed, trembling. How close she'd come to disaster. A few moments more of kissing, and she might well have given in to Richard and let him take her maidenhead. Despair washed over her as she wondered again if she had made the right decision in leaving Stafford and coming to London. Did she risk her immortal soul by remaining in this dangerous world of flatterers and connivers?

Sighing, Astra turned from the bed and began to dress. She must not give up now. Tonight was another banquet, another chance to meet a decent, worthy man. She would not forsake her goal simply because the way was difficult and treacherous. She had more pride and courage than that.

Thirteen

The Painted Chamber was crowded with courtiers and noblemen. Will looked around nervously and tried to suppress his rising anxiety. He had to find Richard and warn him that Guy Faucomberg was at court. There was no telling what trouble the villain might try to stir up. It would be best if he and Richard avoided Rathstowe altogether.

Will hurried forward, making his way through the press of bodies. He reached the far end of the room in time to see King Henry rise from his ornately-carved chair. The crowd parted as the King made his way among them, his long, green brocade robe edged in sable swirling as he walked. For a moment Will's view was blocked. When he could see again, he almost gasped aloud. Richard was down on one knee, directly in the King's pathway.

My God, he's really going to do it! A sickening wave of premonition washed through Will. This was not a good time. He had failed to warn Richard that the King had been very irritable and short-tempered lately. Rumor was that the Queen was in the early, unpleasant stage of pregnancy and taking out her discomfort on her husband.

Will could not hear Richard's words, but he could easily guess what his friend was asking. He watched the King's face. Henry looked intent, but not hostile. A surge of hope lifted Will's heart. Then he saw Guy Faucomberg move beside the King, and his hope shattered.

Faucomberg's voice echoed loudly through the now-quiet room: "Begging your pardon, Your Grace, but I think it unwise to set the precedent of allowing baseborn knights to take charge of your castles. What's next—appointing peasants to your Chancery?"

Furtive snickers rippled through the room. Will closed his eyes and cursed God for allowing men like Faucomberg to rise to positions of power. When he opened them again, King Henry was glowering like an angry bear.

"You're wrong, Rathstowe," the King said shortly. "I will award guardianship of my property to anyone I see fit." His hooded eyes flicked from Faucomberg to Richard. "But I demand more than a few years' battle service for such an honor."

The King gave Richard a meaningful look, then brushed by the kneeling knight and swept from the room. Will licked his lips, relieved and despairing at the same time. It could have been much worse, but it was bad enough. Richard had not sprung up and throttled Faucomberg, though Will knew he must have wanted to. Somehow Richard had controlled himself, but at what cost? Will shuddered, thinking of Richard's fury. Rage like that could destroy a man, and it had already burned inside Richard for years.

Will walked cautiously toward his friend. Richard had risen and was staring after the King. He was utterly still, his face expressionless. Only the twitch of the scar on his cheek betrayed his inner turmoil.

"Richard, I . . ."

"Don't," Richard warned. His dark eyes flashed like live coals. "Don't say anything."

* * *

"Bless the heavens the King has finally arrived," Marguerite murmured as Henry strode into the banquet hall, trailed by a crowd of nobles. "Now we can finally be seated. I'm utterly starved."

Astra didn't answer. Food was the farthest thing from her mind. Since her arrival in the hall, she had been scanning the crowd, searching for a certain dark-haired knight. She intended to speak to Richard at the first opportunity. She would tell him that she was aware of his wicked plan and no longer willing to endure his attempts to entice her.

Astra perused the gathering around the King. The men all wore lavish robes that reached below their knees. Despite the warmth of the crowded hall, the elegant garments were trimmed with coney, fox and sable fur. King Henry favored the formal style, but Astra suspected that a serious fighting man like Richard would never attire himself in such a cumbersome robe. The men around the King must be rich noblemen, she decided. Her thoughts were immediately confirmed by Marguerite.

"My word," her friend whispered. "Half the barons in England must be here tonight." She pointed discreetly. "Those are the men you should attempt to beguile, Astra. They're all so rich they needn't worry about marrying for wealth. A beauty like you might well catch their eye." She tugged on Astra's blue velvet sleeve. "The King seems to be dawdling again; this would be a good time to introduce you to some titled noblemen."

Before Astra had a chance to protest, Marguerite grabbed her hand and led her across the hall, weaving in and out among the clusters of elegant ladies and gentlemen waiting for the King to take his place at the high table. Marguerite did not slow until they reached a straight-backed older man with short, iron-gray hair.

"Lord Darley," Marguerite enthused. She bobbed a curtsy, then extended her hand. "My father will be sorry to have missed seeing you."

The man stared at Marguerite a moment, then smiled warmly. "Little Marguerite Fitz Hugh—how you've grown. Last time I saw you, you were small enough to bounce on my knee."

"You could still try," Marguerite answered with a boldly flirtatious look. "Although I daresay I am slightly heavier these days." She touched Lord Darley's robe with an intimate gesture and purred: "It's a pity my father has left London already. I know he counts you among his dearest friends."

"Still the little flatterer, aren't you?" Darley said wryly. "It's sweet of you to favor an old man like me with your charming company. Your time might be better spent in cultivating the young gallants." He turned to the two men beside him. "Faucomberg, Ferreres—have you had the pleasure of making Lady Marguerite Fitz Hugh's acquaintance?"

"I think not," the stocky, red-haired man immediately to Lord Darley's left replied. He reached for Marguerite's hand and lifted it to his lips. "I am Guy Faucomberg of Rathstowe. Charmed, of course," he murmured. Astra watched him, thinking that he had the reddest hair she'd ever seen. In contrast, his eyes were a flat, pale green.

The other man, who was very small, wiry and dark, leaned forward. "Adam Ferreres of Montgomery. It's my pleasure to make your acquaintance." He took Marguerite's hand and kissed it. All three men looked at Astra expectantly.

"Where are my manners!" Marguerite exclaimed. "You must meet Lady Astra de Mortain, my dearest friend. Astra, this is Lord Darley, and his companions, Lords Rathstowe and Montgomery."

Astra curtsied briefly, then awkwardly held out her hand. Lord Darley brushed it with a light kiss, then gave her a warm, fatherly smile. Ferreres's kiss was polite; his eyes disinterested. In contrast, Faucomberg grasped Astra's hand very tightly in his thick, sweaty fingers, then lingered his wet lips far too long against the back of her hand.

"A great pleasure, *demoiselle,*" he said, smirking. "I cannot recall seeing you at court before. Where has a beauty like you been hiding away?"

"Astra grew up at the Stafford Priory," Marguerite volunteered. "This is her first visit to court."

"You've never been to London before?" Lord Darley asked.

Astra shook her head. "I have been fortunate to see quite a few of the sights in the several days I've been here. It is an amazing place."

"Lord Fitz Hugh took you around?"

"Not my father," Marguerite interjected. "William de Lacy and Richard Reivers were kind enough to show us the city."

"De Lacy!" Lord Rathstowe's face wore an aghast expression. "Does Fitz Hugh know you are spending time in de Lacy's company?"

"Of course," Astra answered, anxious that their unchaperoned adventures in London not be misconstrued. "Lord Fitz Hugh expressly asked de Lacy and Sir Reivers to look after us."

"That is a little like asking a wolf to guard your flock,"

Rathstowe murmured, his green eyes narrowed. "Among his other faults, Reivers is an appalling lecher, and de Lacy, he is . . ."

"It looks as if the King finally intends that we should eat," Marguerite broke in abruptly. "Shall we be seated, Astra?"

They returned to their usual table, and Astra slid down on the bench beside Marguerite, puzzled by her friend's rudeness but also relieved that she hadn't asked the three noblemen to join them. Astra suspected having such important men nearby would make her too nervous to eat.

"Why did you leave so abruptly?" she asked Marguerite as a servant poured their wine. "I know you are hungry, but we could have taken leave of Lord Darley and his friends a little more politely."

"I suspect that Guy Faucomberg mislikes Will for some silly reason," Marguerite said lightly. "I didn't want to stay and hear him ridicule a man I call a friend." She shot Astra a piercing look. "Court politics can be unpleasant business. I avoid involving myself in men's stupid quarrels. Really, they can be even more petty than women!"

Astra looked down at her trencher, dismay replacing her appetite. Court life was overwhelmingly complicated. How would she ever figure out how to act?

"Where's Sir Reivers?" A coy, feminine voice disrupted Astra's gloomy thoughts. She glanced across the table to see Lady Isabel regarding her with a smug smile. "He's been your constant companion these last few days, but I don't see him tonight." Isabel laughed snidely.

Astra gritted her teeth and tried to recall what the Scriptures said about turning the other cheek. In truth, there was nothing she could say. As much as she hated to admit it, Lady Isabel was likely right. Sir Reivers was distinctly absent from the banquet hall, and she suspected he was seeking companionship elsewhere.

Astra repressed a sigh and choked down a bite of spiced venison.

The Black Swan was crowded as usual, except for the area around the dark-haired man with his back turned to the door. Looking at the conspicuously empty tables, Will guessed that the tavern's inhabitants had already had a taste of Richard's violent temper and were staying out of his way. He wished he could do the same, but his conscience dictated otherwise. Richard was his friend, and he was honor-bound to do what he could to help him.

He approached Richard cautiously, wondering if his mood had mellowed since the encounter with Faucomberg two days ago. Richard scarcely moved as Will edged onto the bench across from him. Then he looked up and regarded him with flat, expressionless eyes.

"What do you want?"

"I've come to talk some sense into you," Will replied. He had decided a firm, brusque approach would be the best way to scald his friend out of his self-pitying anger. "How long do you intend to hide away here?"

"Hide?" Richard snarled, his eyes suddenly flashing. "Would you have me go back to the palace and kill Faucomberg with my bare hands? I assure you, that is the only outcome that will result if I am forced to be in the same room with that devil's spawn again!"

"You'll let him win then?" Will goaded. He held his breath. Richard's eyes grew even blacker and more deadly, until Will thought he must be looking into the very pits of hell.

Richard's body tensed, then slowly relaxed. He turned away. "How can I hope to defeat a baron?" he asked bitterly. "All my life men like Faucomberg have ground me beneath their boots, and there has been naught I can do about it but grit my teeth and endure. I am sick unto death of holding back, of choking on my fury. The anger burns so deep inside me—sometimes I think it will consume the flesh off my bones."

He looked back at Will; his dark eyes no longer gleamed with hate, but raw pain. "I cannot win this battle. Henry's court is Faucomberg's territory, not mine. He has all the advantages."

"Not so," Will argued. "Henry hates to be mocked and challenged, and Faucomberg has done just that. If you continue to be patient and dutiful, the King may finally decide to award you some property, with the goal of putting Faucomberg in his place. But you must remain in Henry's presence, subtly reminding him that you are a dutiful subject, a man he can count on."

"God's teeth, it sickens me to think of groveling before the King again!"

"You have no choice, Richard. If you don't return to court, Faucomberg will claim you have run off like a whipped hound with its tail between its legs."

"That puling whoreson! I have more courage in my smallest toe than he does in his whole flabby, worthless body!"

"Then show it, Richard. Walk into Westminster with your head held high and proud. Let them know the Leopard is not yet beaten."

Richard nodded, his eyes agleam with the brilliant glow of vengeance. Despite himself, Will shivered. Sometimes the white-hot fury that burned inside his friend frightened even him.

The Queen's ladies were sewing quietly in her outer chambers. Queen Eleanor arose and left to see her children in the nursery, and pert, green-eyed Lady Nell turned to Lady Isabel and whispered something in her ear. The two laughed delightedly. Lady Isabel smoothed the embroidery in her lap and announced: "I haven't seen Sir Reivers around the palace lately. Have you heard nothing from him, Astra?"

Astra stiffened, sensing the malice underlying Isabel's seemingly innocent remark. Before she could reply, Isabel continued: "Perhaps he has grown tired of you and moved on to more interesting conquests." Her eyes widened as she feigned shock. "Oh, Astra, surely you did not already give him what he wanted!"

Astra's tongue failed her. It was Marguerite who answered, her voice light and deadly sweet. "Don't be silly, Isabel. Richard isn't ignoring Astra. He's away on the King's business."

"The King's business?" Plump, dowdy Lady Sybil frowned. "That seems rather unlikely. Sir Reivers is a soldier, not a diplomat!"

"Nevertheless, it is true; he told me so himself," Marguerite said haughtily.

Isabel gave Astra a sharp, condescending look. Astra ignored her, blessing Marguerite for her convenient lie. She would die if Isabel found out that Richard had taken advantage of her and then abandoned her. Even thinking about his manipulations made her feel sick. Richard was a liar, a conniver, a silver-tongued snake. She was fortunate he had dropped his pursuit before he could shame her further.

"Sir Richard must stand high in the King's favor if he entrusts him on such an errand," Nell purred. "Perhaps Henry means to gift him with some property. Would that not make him absolutely irresistible?—handsome, charming and possessing land and a title as well. Reivers would truly have to fight off the ladies then."

"Aye, if he had some property, Sir Richard would no longer have to amuse himself with cheap little country wenches." Isabel looked down her long nose at Astra, then both she and Nell began to twitter.

Astra felt her face flame, and she fought to come up with a dignified response to defend herself. She had no chance, for Marguerite rose and said pointedly: "Perhaps Sir Reivers finds such women refreshing after the conniving opportunists he has met at court." She gave Lady Isabel a sweetly innocent smile, then gestured to Astra. "Come, *ma belle.* It appears the Queen no longer requires our company, and besides, it has grown unpleasantly close in here."

"Oh, Marguerite, thank you," Astra whispered when the two of them had escaped to the hall. "I never know what to say when Isabel attacks me. It is so unfair. I've never done anything to her!"

"The ill-tempered little wasp is so jealous of you, she near sickens with it."

"Jealous!" Astra looked astounded. "Is that why she is so cruel to me?"

"Of course. I think she is half in love with Richard herself, and she knows he'll never spare her a second glance as long as you're around."

"Then her fears are groundless. Richard has obviously tired of me."

"Perhaps not." Marguerite shrugged. "From what Will told me, Richard has been too ill-disposed to think of pursuing women."

"Richard's ill!" Astra's eyes widened with alarm.

"Not seriously," Marguerite reassured her. "A stomach ailment, Will said. He's much better now. Will thought they would both dine in the banquet hall tonight."

Astra stiffened. The thought of seeing Richard again panicked her.

Marguerite discerned her discomfort and laughed. "What is it, Astra?" she asked teasingly. "Has something distressed you?"

"I . . . I'm not distressed. Indeed, I am relieved to know Richard is not seriously ill."

Marguerite raised her dark brows. "Why should you care? I thought you were finished with Richard, that you intended to snub him coldly the next time you saw him."

"I could not do that, not if he's been ill!"

"How clever it was of Richard to guess that there is no surer way to Lady's Astra's heart than to arouse her pity."

Astra glared at her friend. Marguerite laughed again. "I wonder what Richard will do when he discovers he has a rival. From what I've heard, Richard and Guy Faucomberg despise each other. It should be interesting to see what happens when they find themselves in the same room—with you."

"I'm sure Guy was merely being polite when he offered to sit by me the last two evenings."

"Polite!" Marguerite gave an unladylike snort of amusement. "He was all but drooling over you. I'd watch out for that one. Rathstowe's even slyer than Richard."

Astra sighed. She'd been startled and a little flattered when the Earl of Rathstowe had sought her out and asked to join her in the dining hall. It had seemed innocent enough at the time, but now she wondered. Guy had been persistently flattering and charming, but she found she trusted him even less than she had Richard. There was something calculated in the way the earl attempted to turn her head with pretty words. Faucomberg wanted something from her, and her instincts told her that his goal was something more sinister than mere seduction.

"Sweet Mary," Astra muttered as they entered the tiny bedchamber. She sank down wearily on a stool. "If I had my way, I'd skip the banquet tonight altogether. I'm not sure I'm up to handling Faucomberg or Richard—either one of them."

Fourteen

It was worse than going into battle, Richard thought grimly as he walked toward the banquet hall. He hadn't even seen his enemy, and already his body throbbed with tension. It took more courage to face that gloating bastard Faucomberg across a trestle table than it did to fight a dozen murderous soldiers. His hand went instinctively to his side, feeling for the sword that wasn't there. It was probably well and good that no man was allowed to enter the King's Hall carrying anything more dangerous than an eating knife. It would help him resist temptation—although he suspected he was strong enough and ruthless enough to tear Rathstowe's throat out with his bare hands if he had the chance.

No, he thought resolutely, his fingers twitching with strain. Will was right. To let Faucomberg goad him into losing control was to fall prey to his enemy's devious strategies. He must rein in his temper at all costs.

He paused in the anteroom outside the hall and braced himself for the stares and whispers. He should have arrived earlier; then there would have been fewer people to gawk at him. As it was, it appeared most of the courtiers were already seated. All eyes would be upon him as he entered.

"Sir Reivers."

He turned and felt his grim mood softening as Lady

Astra rushed up. It was obvious she had been running. Her face was flushed, and she still held her skirts clutched in her fingers.

"You're late."

"I know." She blushed an even deeper shade of rose. "And you? Are you well?"

Richard cocked a brow. "Well? What do you mean?"

"I'd heard you were ill. Will told Marguerite you were suffering from a stomach ailment."

He smiled and silently blessed Will for his tact. "I am completely recovered. Thank you for your concern."

He watched her blush again, and a wave of longing swept through him. She was so sweet, so beautiful. It did not seem fair he could not have her. But then life was not fair, not fair at all.

He extended his arm. "We should go in. We can sit in the back if you wish."

She hesitated and stared uneasily at him. "I do not think . . ." She swallowed. "I am supposed to sit with Marguerite and . . . and . . . some gentlemen."

So, she had found another paramour. The thought infuriated him, but he refused to let his anger show. He had no claim upon her, no right to be jealous. He shrugged. "As you wish, *demoiselle.*"

She gave him a stricken look, then turned and entered the hall with a flurry of her saffron satin skirts.

He followed after her, struggling to appear nonchalant and composed. He entered the hall and forced himself to meet every eye. He was a warrior going into battle, proud, dangerous. There was not a man in the place who could defeat him.

The strategy worked. People glanced his way warily, then went back to their food and conversation. He walked over to a table of knights near the rear. They nodded and made a place for him in their midst.

"Reivers—good to have you back."

"Aye, we've missed you."

"Rumor was that you'd given up on Henry and turned mercenary—went and hired yourself out," one man said mischievously.

Richard grinned and shook his head. "Not yet. Henry has my loyalty for a while longer."

He took a gulp of wine and felt himself relax. It had not been unendurable. He would ignore them, the arrogant nobles who had made his life miserable for so many years. This was where he belonged, surrounded by the companionship of honest, stout-hearted fighting men. To hell with barons and kings.

A broad, freckled-faced knight leaned across the table toward him. "You shouldn't have stayed away so long, Reivers. I don't think you'll be pleased to see who's taken your place at Lady Astra's side."

Richard felt the sudden tensing of the men around him, and a chilling dread clutched at his heart. Unable to stop himself, he jerked around and faced the direction the knights stared.

Astra was near the front, surrounded by ladies and noblemen. Directly beside her sat a man with vivid red hair. Richard swallowed. He could feel it collapse, his facade of cool confidence shattering like Venetian glassware. It could not be a coincidence. Faucomberg had found out about his interest in Astra and deliberately singled her out for seduction.

"If it's any consolation, Reivers," a man beside him murmured, "I don't think any woman who'd let that whoreson cozen her has much value. Faucomberg's a rich bastard, but he's a coward. A good knight like you is worth a dozen of him."

Richard's mood slumped further. The little fool would let Faucomberg charm her and flatter her. Innocent Astra would fall right into his trap. For a moment Richard couldn't decide who he was more furious with—Faucomberg for cruelly using Astra to get at him, or Astra for being so gullible she would let him.

"Damn," he cursed. "Damn them both."

"Is something wrong, Sir Reivers?" a lilting female voice cooed beside him. Richard looked up to see a plain-faced young woman dressed in an extraordinary costume of alternating bands of crimson and gold. Even her headdress was fashioned of the gaudy fabric. She fluttered her sparse eyelashes at him and said demurely, "We've missed you at court, my lord. It's delightful to have you back."

For a moment, Richard was too startled to speak. Then a brittle smile curved his lips. "Lady Isabel. How kind of you to remember me." He moved aside on the bench. "Pray sit beside me and tell me everything I've missed."

Astra kept her head lowered, pretending to concentrate on her food. She dare not look up and meet Lord Faucomberg's gaze. He had given her such a strange look a few moments ago. It was almost as if he guessed she'd met Richard in the antechamber and spoken to him. Was he jealous? Did that account for the dangerous glance he'd given her? Jesu, if he only knew!

She took another bite and forced herself to calmly chew the cod in sauce. She was still shaking from her encounter with Richard. It had only taken a few moments alone with him, and it had all come back to her—the vivid recollection of his warm, wet tongue teasing her lips, his possessive hands stroking her breasts. The mere memory of that afternoon made her body ache. It was shameful, obscene, and yet she could not forget it. She could not help hoping that it would someday happen again.

But not with Guy. Her lips pursed in involuntary distaste. As much as Richard drew her, Guy repelled her. There was something unappealing about his eerie green eyes and stubby, white fingers. It was difficult not to flinch when he kissed her hand; the thought of him taking further liberties made her queasy.

Her glance flickered briefly to the man beside her. He smiled. "I believe there will be dancing later. Will you be my partner?"

"I think not. I'm sorry, my lord. Perhaps it is the rich food. My stomach feels rather out of sorts."

"There is an ailment of that nature going around I believe." His green gaze slithered over her, cold, reptilian. Astra stood, hastening to disguise the shiver of loathing the man aroused in her. She had to get away. As much as she longed to see Richard, to reassure herself that he was really well, she could endure Lord Faucomberg's company no longer.

As soon as she was out of the hall, Astra lifted her skirts and raced across the courtyard to the main palace. She slowed as she reached the narrow but elegantly wainscoted hallway. She should go back, she thought abruptly. She should not be such a dismal coward. Better a coward than a fool, she decided as she hastened up the stairs to the tiny bedchamber. She needed time to think things out.

She entered the bedchamber and clutched her hands to her head. Sweet Mary, she had a headache. She had not lied to Guy; she truly did feel ill. All this turmoil, this worry, was undoing her.

She struggled out of her gown, then washed and lay down upon the small pallet. She had almost begun to relax when she heard voices in the hallway outside the door. One of the voices belonged to Isabel. Its shrill unnatural tone floated clearly through the heavy door.

"It was so nice of you to escort me to bed, Richard."

"As I said, it was on my way, and I wanted to see to Lady Astra. She departed the hall quite abruptly, and Lady Marguerite said she'd taken ill."

"I'll tell you a secret," Isabel murmured seductively. Astra sat up, straining to hear.

"Astra isn't ill at all. That was only a ruse to get out of the hall and meet Lord Rathstowe alone later."

"Rathstowe? She's seeing him alone?" Astra could hear the outrage in Richard's voice. She threw the blanket aside, ready to open the door and show herself. Then she realized that she wore only her chemise. She could hardly burst into the hallway half-dressed. She fumbled for her clothes, gritting her teeth as she heard Isabel's lying response:

"Of course. Astra has been busy while you were away. She thinks she has Guy wrapped around her little finger. Of course, we both know that's not so." Isabel sniffed loudly. "A high-born knight like Lord Rathstowe would never wed a poor little country mouse like her. Still, if Astra's too stupid to see through him, she deserves whatever she gets. She must be a wanton anyway; she's so free with her favors."

Silence. Astra heard Richard's harsh breathing, could almost feel his fury. "So, Lady Astra is not the sweet angel I guessed she was."

Isabel laughed shrilly. "Angel? Surely you can see

through Astra's false ways. Just because she was raised in a convent doesn't mean she's some guileless saint. I assure you, Richard, Lady Astra knows exactly what she is about. Have you not noticed the tight dresses she wears, the disgusting way she flaunts her body? She means to marry well, and she'll do whatever is necessary to reach her goal."

Isabel's voice trailed off, and Astra imagined her leaning close, bringing her pale, insipid face close to Richard's so he would kiss her. The image spurred her into furious action. She dug frantically in the big chest, trying to find her discarded bliaut by the dim light from the tiny window. She found it too late; she could already hear Richard's words of farewell.

"Goodnight, Lady Isabel. I'll leave you now. Perhaps I'll see you on the morrow."

Astra threw the garment down, shaking with rage. She wanted to attack Isabel, to knock her down and pummel her ugly face. She stood for a moment and stared at the unopened door, waiting for her deceitful roommate to enter. At the last minute, Astra changed her mind. She stuffed the bliaut back in the trunk and scrambled for her pallet. When Isabel entered, Astra was feigning sleep. She watched Isabel undress and crawl into the big bed. Astra's eyes glared daggers into the darkness. She'd never before felt this way; her whole being seethed with hatred. She wouldn't vent it openly, though, she decided. She'd be clever and tricky, like that wicked Isabel. Why, the woman had made her sound like a strumpet!

Astra shifted subtly on the lumpy pallet, her muscles tight with anger. It wasn't only Isabel's lies which enraged her, but the thought of Richard kissing the witch. She could almost see Richard's beautiful mouth covering Isabel's thin, hungry lips. It made her ill!

She wrapped her arms around her shoulders and tried to calm herself. She had to sleep. In the morning she would talk to Marguerite; her friend would help her. Somehow they would think of a way to deal with Isabel!

"Marguerite!" Astra whispered, leaning over the curtained bed. "Wait till Isabel leaves to get dressed. I have to talk to you."

Marguerite nodded sleepily, then returned to her slumbers. When she woke again, Isabel was gone, and Astra sat unmoving on the bed, her mouth drawn into a grim line.

"Ma belle, what is it?"

"It's Isabel," Astra answered in a strained voice. "Last night after I left the hall, she convinced Richard to escort her to bed. She told him lies about me. I heard her through the door. She implied I was offering my favors to Lord Faucomberg. Oh, Marguerite, she all but called me a whore!"

Marguerite made a disgusted sound. "I'm not surprised. I suspected that scheming wench was up to something."

"I don't know what to do," Astra continued in a worried voice. "Richard sounded angry, and then he . . . he . . . I think he kissed Isabel." Astra clutched her arms around herself, feeling sick again.

"Mmmmmm. So, that's Isabel's plan. She means to make Richard think you were using him, then offer to console him with her own scrawny little body."

"She wouldn't! She wouldn't dare! Not after taunting

me for letting him have his way with me. How could she be such a hypocrite?"

"Apparently it is quite easy for someone like Isabel," Marguerite noted dryly. "She hates you, and likely sees Richard as a way to hurt you. Then again, she might really want him for herself. Richard is a handsome young gallant, a good catch, for all that he is poor. I'm surprised no woman at court has trapped him into marriage yet."

"Marriage! You can't mean that! You said yourself Richard was a fortune hunter. Why would he marry someone like Isabel?"

"She is cousin to the Queen, and I'm sure it's not lost on Richard that the royal family is very generous to their relatives."

"She can't have him! She doesn't deserve him!"

"Really, Astra. Why do you care? Are you in love with Richard?"

Astra paled. "Of course not. Richard is a deceitful knave, a wicked rascal. How could I possibly love someone like that?"

"How, indeed? Tell me then why you feel impelled to rescue Richard from Isabel's clutches?"

"Because I . . . I . . . I hate her!" Astra's eyes widened as she heard her own words. "Mother of God, that makes me just as sinful and wicked as Isabel!"

"Hardly. Hate is a normal emotion, Astra, no matter what you've been taught."

"But I . . ." Astra paused, her delicate features distraught and confused. "Perhaps I should go back to Stafford, Marguerite. I'm not strong enough to guard my thoughts and feelings anymore. I fear I am becoming a terrible person."

"Certainly. Go back to Stafford. Life will go on at court

as it always has. Isabel will probably marry Richard, but that will be no concern of yours . . ."

"No! She can't have him!"

"You must fight then. You must make sure that Richard knows what Isabel is up to."

Astra nodded. "The Scriptures teach that it is right and good to fight evil, and I believe that Isabel's intentions are evil. I will do it! I will make sure Richard knows exactly what kind of person she is."

"Good. Let's see then, how will we go about this. I can get a message to Richard's squire that you want to meet with Richard alone. But where . . . ?" Marguerite glanced doubtfully at the small room. "Not here. It would cause a scandal if you were found alone together. The Queen's garden perhaps. It is surrounded by people and guards, but quiet enough for private conversation. Wipe your tears, Astra," Marguerite ordered sternly. "And change into your new blue gown—the one with the silver embroidery on the bodice. If you mean to fight, we must use all the weapons at our disposal."

Fifteen

It was odd, Richard thought as he walked toward the Queen's garden. He had been on the verge of sending a message to Lady Astra, asking her to meet him, when a page had arrived from her requesting the same thing. His grievance with her he knew of, but hers with him, he could hardly guess.

He saw her among the flowers, back turned. He hesitated. His anger was still fierce, and he wondered if he could trust himself to be civil. If what Isabel said was true, he had been fooled by Astra, duped by her guileless demeanor into believing she was different from the rest of the female vipers at court. It had been a long time since he had been taken in by a woman, and the thought that Astra had deceived him made him feel like a callow boy. Still, he had decided he must go through with the assignation. Someone needed to warn Astra what kind of man Guy Faucomberg really was. Even if she was as calculating as Isabel said, Astra was no match for the likes of Rathstowe. He stepped forward briskly.

"So, *demoiselle*—you wished to speak with me?"

The sound of Richard's cold, sarcastic voice made Astra jump. She'd been watching the garden path intently, not thinking that he might approach from the rear. Once again, Richard Reivers had managed to unsettle her.

"Aye, my lord," she answered as he pushed brusquely through a hedge and stood before her.

"Speak then. Convince me that I'm not wasting my time."

Astra's heart pounded. She had not expected Richard to be so angry, so abrupt. He obviously believed Isabel's sly words. Surely as soon as she explained, he'd be himself again, her smiling, charming Richard.

She took a deep breath and began. "I heard Isabel talking to you outside the bedchamber door last night. What she said was untrue. I'm not trying to find a rich husband. Lord Rathstowe means nothing to me. Isabel just made that up so you would hate me, and you would . . . you would kiss her."

She saw the surprise in his eyes. They swept her face—as if he could read the truthfulness of her words by perusing her features.

"You listened at the door?"

"It is my bedchamber, too. Isabel's voice was loud enough that I could not help overhearing."

"And you claim it is all lies?"

Astra nodded. "Isabel mislikes me for some reason. Every word she said was false. Lord Rathstowe has been very attentive to me, but I have not encouraged him. I swear it!"

Richard's eyes were still narrowed. "You sat with him at the banquet last night . . . and the night before."

"That was Marguerite's doing. She is friends with Lord Darley, and the Baron asked Faucomberg to join us."

"He means nothing to you?"

Astra shook her head. "I cannot think he is seriously interested in me, and even if he were, I would not encourage his attentions. The way he looks at me makes me decidedly uncomfortable."

Richard took her hands and held them in his own. "I am relieved you recognize Faucomberg's sly charm for the sinister manipulation it is. I cannot advise you strongly enough against the man. Please stay away from him."

The warning sent a shiver down Astra's spine, but she was too distracted to worry on it. She was consumed with watching the expression on Richard's face; he looked grave and concerned, almost tender. The softness on his features was a dramatic change from his usual ironic countenance.

"I wonder, Astra—how do you know I kissed Isabel?"

She blushed. "I . . . I guessed."

Richard moved closer. His tanned face was unnervingly near. Astra felt her breath catch in her throat.

"You took the trouble to meet me here, to make sure I understood your feelings," he whispered. "Could it be, *demoiselle,* could it be that you care for me?"

She struggled to find her voice. Things were not turning out as she'd planned. She had intended to warn Richard about Isabel, and also make it clear that she knew about his skillful manipulation of her feelings and assure him it could not happen again. Now, somehow, she could not make herself say the words.

"Admit it, Astra. Admit that you want me to kiss you."

His voice was so soft. His eyes were hot, burning pools of blackness. Astra felt herself sliding into the dark mystery there. In another minute, she would be utterly lost.

"I . . . I want you to kiss me."

His breath was warm and distracting, and she could smell him—the vague, not displeasing odors of leather and sweat. His body seemed to beckon to hers, making her feel weak and trembly. She remembered how smooth and silken the skin of his chest had felt under her fingers.

She stretched her arms around his back and felt the thick muscles beneath his tunic. His warm, gentle lips entranced her. She allowed him to coax her mouth open and slide his tongue inside. The feel of it shocked and thrilled her at the same time. She knew he mimicked the movement of a man's part inside a woman, and she could not help wondering what it was like to have a man inside you the other way—if it would feel so tantalizing, so right.

It almost hurt when Richard ended the kiss and leaned slowly away from her. She could hear his quickened breathing, see the warm flush spread over his dusky skin. His eyes were bright, dazzlingly dark and alluring. She wondered why he had stopped.

"Did you like that Astra? Do you want more?"

She looked away, too embarrassed to answer, and stared fixedly at a bee alighting on the pale yellow roses that grew nearby.

"You'd best be careful." Richard's fingers reached out to touch the neck of her gown. "The bees will mistake you for a flower as well."

He said no more, but she felt his hand tracing the design on the bodice of her blue samite bliaut, leisurely outlining the shape of the silver flowers embroidered there. His fingers glided over the smooth fabric and came to rest on the folds of the linen chemise that filled in the low neckline. She held her breath as he teased with the ribbon that laced up her gown. Half-expectant, half-horrified, Astra waited for him to undo it. Then his fingers danced away, lightly brushing the curve of her breast as he withdrew his hand.

"A gown like that, Astra, it invites a man to undo the

laces, to see what treasures are hidden beneath. Is that why you wore it—to tempt me?"

She felt her face blaze. She wouldn't answer him.

He took her hand. His calloused fingers clutched hers tightly; his voice was a low, seductive murmur. "I want you, Astra. I want you desperately. But there is no privacy here. We must find a place where we can be alone."

Astra sucked in her breath. She wanted him as badly as he did her, but she dare not give in to her sinful urges.

"I was wrong to meet you here." She backed away. "It seems you are still mistaken about me, if you think I would agree to a casual dalliance."

He followed her, his body edging closer and closer to hers. She was intensely aware of his sleek, hard muscles, the sheen of his tanned skin and long dark hair. "No, I don't think I'm mistaken at all. I think you want what I can offer you."

"Stop!" Astra gasped. She reached out her hands to push him away. "You're too clever for me, my lord. Perhaps you should find someone else to play your games with, someone . . ."

". . . someone like Isabel?"

Astra felt her heart grow chill. No. She didn't want him to end up with Isabel.

"So that displeases you? Good. I want you to want me, Astra. For whatever reason, I have a burning need to have you desire me as fiercely as I do you."

He pulled her to him, widening his stance so she stood between his thighs. His fingers reached under her veil and glided along her neck. He lifted her face and looked deeply into her eyes. She could feel his male part—hard and hot—through his tunic and her gown. It probed into her belly. At the same time, his mouth met hers.

There were too many sensations: the tantalizing thrusting of his tongue, the rippling fire his fingers aroused as he fondled her neck, the sheer male hardness of him pressed against her like some burning, implacable force. She wanted to be away from him and yet be closer, so much closer.

"Astra." Richard interrupted their kiss to moan her name, and Astra seized her chance. She leaned away and grasped his big hands in her trembling fingers.

"Richard, please. You said yourself, this is not the place; there is no privacy here."

He nodded, his eyes wild and dreamy, his chest heaving. After a moment, he released her. Astra's eyes darted around. She wondered if anyone had seen them from the palace. What had possessed her to suggest this meeting? Then she remembered—Isabel. She had met with him to make sure he knew what a conniving witch Isabel was.

"Richard, you must not trust Isabel. She gossips horribly."

He looked startled. "Do you think I need protection, Astra?"

She hesitated. It sounded foolish that she should worry about someone like Richard. "I'm sure you know exactly what sort of woman Isabel is. I was only afraid you would believe her lies about me. You don't, do you?"

Richard's face was serious; his eyes hauntingly intense. "I don't know what to believe, Astra. When I'm with you, my thoughts run all topsy-turvy and cock-eyed. I begin to doubt things I've believed all my life."

He stared at her a moment, then moved close again, his mouth near her ear. She felt his warm breath tickling her neck, then his lips on her earlobe, nibbling. Her strength drained out of her. She leaned helplessly against him as his tongue found the inside of her ear.

Pleasure shot through her, harsh, blinding. She forgot the lack of privacy in the garden, the danger of his seductive words. She was limp, faint, aware only of the delicious tremors that raced down her body and shattered her senses, threatening to engulf her in terrifying ecstasy. Only when Richard removed his tongue and spoke did she come to herself.

"That's only the beginning, Astra," he whispered, his lips still close. "I haven't begun to make you feel the things I could."

Astra shivered and pulled away. She was mad to play this dangerous game. Where would it all lead? Richard had said nothing about marriage. She could hardly allow him to bed her without making some commitment to her.

"I have to go," she mumbled. "Marguerite is waiting for me." She adjusted her clothing, then hurried from the garden, fleeing as if the devil himself were after her.

Richard watched her leave, then closed his eyes. What was she? Part angel, part enchantress? When he was with her, his thoughts grew jumbled and confused. He forgot that she was poor, that he could never marry her. When he held her in his arms, he was willing to say anything, promise anything in order to possess her. She made him dare to dream that love and kindness might prevail. She transformed him, made him yearn for that magic, enchanted world she believed in.

He blinked and felt the spell fading. He couldn't let a woman blind him to his lifelong ambitions. It was wealth and power that would make him happy, not fancies of love. The kind of lust Astra inspired was a powerful thing, but it was still lust. He was not about to let his body control his life. He adjusted his clothes, trying to subdue the ache in his groin. He could go to Ruby, but he knew she wouldn't satisfy him. It was Astra he wanted. Astra—with her skin like fresh cream and eyes as innocently blue as a child's. She made him want to protect her, to wrap her in his arms and keep her safe from the horror and ugliness of the world.

He made a face. God help him. He was becoming a sentimental fool. Astra could not really be as pure and sweet and kindhearted as she appeared. She had already shown she was not immune to the failings of her sex, that she could be as greedy and vain as other women. Her attitude toward Isabel revealed her jealousy. She might never give herself to him, but she did not want Isabel to have him either.

Did that make his angel as corrupt as all the other women he had known? He could not decide. Nor could he shake the deep longing Astra aroused. She befuddled him, bewitched him. It was dangerous. He could not afford to give up his ruthlessness, the armor of savagery he had constructed to survive his harsh upbringing. He could not afford to let himself feel tender and gentle toward a woman. To do so was to risk becoming soft and weak and ineffective. That was exactly what had happened to old Henry. The man was a king, but he acted like a lovesick boy. He had no balls. He let his wife run his life, his kingdom. The worst of it was that it was destroying the country, allowing England to rot from within from greed and lawlessness, while the rest of Europe laughed at them as a bunch of inept and uncouth dullards.

Richard felt the bile rise in his throat. God forbid he should be in thrall to a mere woman the way Henry was to Queen Eleanor. That would never happen to him. No woman was going to manipulate and weaken him, not even an angel-faced beauty like Lady Astra.

Sixteen

"Where have you been?" Marguerite asked sleepily.

Astra removed her cloak and sat down on the edge of the bed where her friend lay. "The chapel. I've been praying."

Marguerite yawned. "At this hour? I thought one of the advantages of leaving Stafford was not having to rise early for prayers."

"I was troubled. I thought some time alone in meditation would help untangle my thoughts."

Marguerite sat up and pulled the furs and blankets around her bare shoulders. "What have you decided?"

Astra exhaled a shaky breath. "It's clear that Richard is a danger to me."

Marguerite gave her an amused smirk. Astra ignored her and continued. "When I'm alone with him, I am unable to control my fleshly desires, and he is no better." She picked at a loose thread on the rose satin coverlet. "Richard has said nothing of marriage, and I fear he does not mean to offer it. I must avoid being alone with him again at all costs."

"What about Isabel? I thought you were determined to thwart her plans."

Astra gave a strangled sigh. "I have done what I can, Marguerite. I have warned Richard about Isabel. The rest is up to him. If he decides to take a wife for the sake of her dowry, I cannot stop him."

"Poor little sweeting," Marguerite murmured. She patted Astra's hand. "We'll find you another suitor, I promise." A sly smile twitched her lips. "Rest now. I have an adventure planned for tonight that will make you forget all about the maddening Richard Reivers."

Astra nodded vaguely. She did not think even one of Marguerite's escapades could lift her gloomy mood. She had made up her mind to avoid Richard, but having done so, she felt as if she had killed some part of herself. He enchanted her, and it was not just his thrilling kisses or handsome face that drew her to him. She sensed a boyish, wistful longing beneath Richard's glib charm and cynical words. She suspected he had been hurt very deeply in his past, and she longed to soothe him, to ease his unhappiness. For all the aura of danger that surrounded Richard, there was a vulnerability about him as well. He aroused her tenderness almost as much as he aroused her passion.

Stop, she admonished herself. Richard was a dangerous man, one whose extraordinary allure had the power to threaten her immortal soul. She recalled the sensation of his tongue probing her ear. The ecstasy of it had seemed to plumb the very depths of her. It was obscene, shocking, and it had felt so wonderful she had well-nigh let down her guard completely. If he hadn't stopped . . . Sweet heaven! How far would she have let things go?

Astra removed her overtunic and lay down on the bed. Marguerite had finally risen and left the room, and everything was quiet. Astra's thoughts spun in wild circles, then gradually calmed. There was no doubt of it, she decided. She had to tell Richard she could not see him again, except in the company of others. It would be difficult, but she dare not weaken. The sake of her future depended on her resisting the glorious temptation he offered.

"Where are we going?" Astra asked breathlessly as she met Marguerite in the half-deserted courtyard outside the palace.

"Shhhhh! It's a secret."

"I don't like this," Astra murmured, glancing around uneasily. "We should be dining with the Queen this very minute. What will we tell her if we are missed?"

"I've already explained to Her Majesty that we have accepted an invitation from Lord Darley. His London house is not far, and we will be properly escorted there by my father's knights." Marguerite reached out to adjust the hood of Astra's cloak so it better concealed her face.

"But we're not going there, are we?" Astra accused. "That was merely a lie you told the Queen so she wouldn't be suspicious."

Marguerite gave Astra a sharp glance. "We did indeed have an invitation from Lord Darley. I understand that Guy Faucomberg and Adam Ferreres will be joining him this evening. Perhaps you would like to go after all?"

Astra thought of Richard's jealous anger in the garden and shook her head. Even if things were finished with Richard, she did not want him to think she had lied to him. Besides, Richard had warned her that Faucomberg was a dangerous man, and she believed him. It seemed wise to avoid Rathstowe as much as possible.

Marguerite took Astra's arm and began to lead her toward the knights' quarters. "I am pleased you see that gathering for what it is—a stuffy meal among pompous, boring men who will likely discuss politics all night. What

I have planned for tonight will be much more entertaining."

Astra glanced uneasily at her friend. After some of the scrapes she had been in with Marguerite, it seemed unwise to follow blindly wherever she led. Astra hesitated, forcing Marguerite to halt. "Do you promise we will be escorted at all times? Do you swear it upon your psalter?"

"What's this? Don't you trust me?" Marguerite asked in a hurt voice. "You are my dearest friend—how could you think that I would ever allow you to be unprotected?"

"Swear it," Astra continued persistently. "Swear that we will be escorted at all times."

Marguerite heaved a sigh. "Oh, all right, I swear it—on my prayer book or the holy rood or whatever you wish."

Astra nodded, somewhat satisfied. Even Marguerite would not break a holy vow.

They continued walking; their footsteps echoed sharply on the flagstones of the quiet courtyard. They reached the low, dark building that served as barracks for the King's soldiers, and Marguerite gestured for Astra to wait while she went inside. A few moments later she returned, followed by two well-armed knights.

"De Saer, Weyland, this is Lady Astra."

The two men bowed slightly. Astra noted they did not look particularly pleased. She guessed they had as many doubts about the night's excursion as she did.

"Where are we going?" Astra again asked as they reached Kingsbridge Wharf, and one of the knights beckoned for a wherry. "I'd like to have some idea of what's ahead of us."

"London Bridge," Marguerite answered firmly. She removed her hood and shook her ebony curls until they billowed out from beneath her sheer rose-colored veil. "What would a visit to London be without exploring its famous bridge?"

"My lady, I do not think . . ." one of the knights began.

Marguerite silenced him with a glare. "Nonsense. It's still well before sunset, and the city is overrun by sergeants and beadles whose duty is to keep the peace. We'll be perfectly safe."

Astra felt a prickle of warning in her belly. She had seen for herself that London could be a dangerous place, even in the daytime. How much more so would it be after dark? She glanced at the two knights who walked behind them. The men were armed to the teeth, and Marguerite had promised to remain in sight of their escort at all times. Astra wondered if her naivete made her exaggerate the dangers of the city. Besides, she really did want to see the famous bridge. She joined Marguerite and the two knights in the wherry.

The river was swift but relatively calm this night. Still, Astra was relieved when they disembarked at a wharf near Billingsgate, and Marguerite announced they would walk the rest of the way. It was a lovely evening. Behind them, the sky glowed with the dazzling orange and violet of a summer sunset.

They passed the Tower and came out on Walbrook Street at the entrance to the bridge. Astra gasped in amazement. There were houses and shops crowding the narrow causeway across the Thames. "Sweet heaven—it's almost a town unto itself," she murmured.

"Think of it, Astra; there are likely more people living on the bridge than there are in the whole village of Stafford."

Astra nodded, feeling awed. Watching the waning sunlight reflect from the jumble of buildings covering almost every inch of space on the bridge, she realized that this was a sight she might well tell her children about someday.

They passed through the massive gatehouse and began to traverse the bridge. Astra's pleasure turned quickly to apprehension. Houses and shops loomed over the passageway across the river, almost blocking out the sky. The street itself was so narrow two horsemen could scarcely pass. The bridge stank unrelievedly of excrement and garbage. Astra felt a sense of suffocating enclosure, and she was greatly relieved when they finally reached the other side of the bridge and progressed into open space.

"You've seen the bridge then, Lady Marguerite," the older of the Fitz Hugh knights said sharply. "It's time to return to Westminster."

"But we haven't eaten yet, and I'm starved. Aren't you Astra?"

Marguerite looked to Astra for confirmation. Astra didn't know what to do. She heartily agreed with the knight that they should go back, but the thought of immediately returning along the airless, almost subterranean route they had just passed through filled her with dread. "I suppose we could rest awhile."

Marguerite smiled delightedly. "Well, then, now to find a place to dine." She set off briskly down the quay.

"This is Southwark, my lady," the younger knight called after her. "There are no eating establishments in this part of the city that are fit for gentlewomen."

"Of course there are, de Saer." Marguerite cast a wicked grin backwards. "I've heard you say that a man can find anything he wishes in Southwark."

De Saer flushed at Marguerite's teasing. The older knight, Weland, flashed Marguerite a resentful look, then shrugged at de Saer. "It seems Lady Marguerite must learn for herself."

Astra felt her stomach do a little flip-flop. It was obvious their escort had doubts about their destination but were not willing to do anything to deter Marguerite. With utmost reluctance, she joined the knights and followed after her friend. She felt relatively safe with de Saer and Weland on either side of her. It was Marguerite—walking far ahead—she worried about.

De Saer had not been exaggerating, Astra thought glumly. Even compared to the rest of London, the filth of Southwark was appalling. Manure and refuse were piled everywhere. Shabby dwellings crowded almost to the river, and down the runnel-like streets ran hordes of naked, dirty, emaciated children. As they turned off the quay, beggars immediately accosted them. Marguerite had one of the knights scatter a handful of coins from the purse he carried for her. The wretched souls scrabbled and fought over the money. Astra shuddered. She remembered a similar depressing scene in the courtyard of St. Paul's, and Richard's remarks about only the strong surviving.

They walked among the low-slung alehouses huddled along the narrow streets, and Astra saw with surprise that there were well-dressed knights mingling with the ruffians. As they turned the corner, she caught a glimpse of a broad-shouldered, dark-haired soldier a few paces ahead of them. Almost immediately the man turned and spoke to his companion, and Astra realized it was not Richard. Even so, her heart pounded, and a hot ache throbbed inside her. Suddenly, in her mind, she was in the garden by the Tower again, watching Richard take off his tunic. She had not been able to look away from his gleaming brown skin and thick corded muscles. When he had leaned down to kiss her, his mouth rose-brown and wet, she had reached out and touched him. She could still recall kneading her fingers into his naked, silky skin, how she had lost herself in his scent and feel and taste.

Marguerite, now walking next to Astra, leaned over and whispered in her ear, "What deep thoughts are you thinking?"

Astra blushed. Marguerite saw the flush on her cheeks and smiled. "Ah, let me guess; you were thinking about Richard."

Astra started to protest. Marguerite chuckled and patted her arm. "It is all right, sweeting. I know you have not forgotten him. Indeed, he is not an easy man to forget. I still say he has the most splendid shoulders in Christendom."

"Have a care for my feelings, Marguerite. The mere mention of Richard distresses me."

"Oh, I am well content that it does. It takes only a tiny reminder of Sir Richard to make your cheeks go pink and your eyes sparkle. I imagine the thought of him produces other interesting changes in your person as well. Perhaps your heart beats faster, your gown grows suddenly hot and tight . . ."

"Marguerite! Your words are most unseemly!"

Her friend chuckled again. "I am right or you would not protest . . . nor would your face turn such a flaming shade of red. You are still in love with him. I would wager my last silver penny on it."

"For the thousandth time, Marguerite! It was not love, but lust! The man arouses my most base, vile . . ."

"Hush, sweeting. Our escort might overhear."

Astra clapped her hand over her mouth, utterly mortified. In her frustration she had been talking loudly, virtually announcing to the Fitz Hugh knights that she lusted for a man! She glared at Marguerite, who nearly collapsed in a fit of giggling.

"Find a place to eat, Marguerite," Astra said coldly. "Otherwise I shall take our escort and leave you."

Marguerite gestured to a nearby tavern. "At last. This place will do perfectly."

Astra looked doubtful. The gloomy alehouse called the Black Swan appeared no better than the rest of the Southwark establishments they had passed. Their escort led the way into the place, and Astra saw that it was filled with grim-faced knights and villainous-looking sailors. De Saer and Weland exchanged an uneasy glance, and both touched the swords they wore at their belts.

Marguerite selected a table in the far corner, and a blowzy serving wench wearing a startlingly bright shade of lip rouge sauntered over to them and demanded to know what they wanted. Marguerite ignored the wench's impertinence and ordered a trencher of food. The knights did likewise, and Astra also nodded her assent to the woman's questioning look. As the woman cleared the table of used ale mugs, Astra could scarcely tear her eyes away. The bar maid wore a gown so thin and loose that her large, pendulous breasts were nearly visible beneath it. The thought occurred to Astra that the woman likely sold more than food to her customers.

As they waited for their meal, Astra perused the rest of the establishment's occupants more closely. A mangy pack of men diced at the other end, casting furtive looks at Marguerite's party. In one corner a drunk slumped over a table, snoring loudly, while from a table of hard-eyed soldiers came guffaws of laughter. One of them stood up and stretched his long, lean form. Astra's eyes widened in shock as she gazed across the dim tavern. Now that the tall knight had moved aside, she could see a dark-haired girl sitting on a bench between two other knights. Her gown was down to her waist, her plump, round breasts fully exposed.

"Marguerite!" Astra gasped. "This is not a tavern, it's a bawdy house. We must leave at once!"

Marguerite glanced at the half-naked girl, then set her jaw. "We came to eat and so we shall. I won't be driven off by a pack of ruffians who don't have the decency to find a bedchamber in which to indulge their crude entertainments."

"Lady Astra is right," de Saer interjected angrily. "This is no place for highborn females. If there should be trouble . . ." his jaw clenched. "There are only two of us, *demoiselle.* We would not have a chance against a group like that."

"Aye," his older companion muttered. "If you were not paying us so well, Lady Marguerite—above and beyond what your father offers us—we would not have given in to this mad folly of yours at all. This place is a cesspool. No decent woman should allow herself to be seen here."

"Are you implying that Lady Astra and I are not decent women?"

Sir Weland flushed, and Astra guessed that Marguerite's clever tongue was too much for these simple fighting men. By the time they finished arguing, the food would have arrived, and Marguerite would see that they stayed to finish it.

She stood. "Marguerite, I insist we leave. If you don't allow these men to escort us home immediately, I will no longer call you my friend."

Marguerite gave a hurt little sigh. "I must say, you can be a tyrant at times." She rose and leaned close to whisper in Astra's ear. "We can't leave yet. I promised someone I would meet them here. You wouldn't want me to go back on my word—would you?"

Astra made a strangled sound. It was all clear to her now. Marguerite had an assignation with a man, a man she dare not meet with at the palace. "Dear Lord, Marguerite," she whispered back, "who is he? What have you done?"

Marguerite gave her a sly smile. "There's no harm in it. He's a nobleman, a very respectable man. He'll see to it that we are safe."

Astra opened her mouth to express her exasperation but had no chance. The tall soldier from the other table had risen and walked toward them. "Leaving so soon?" he leered.

Sir Weland stood and grabbed Marguerite's arm, steering her firmly toward the door. De Saer was on his feet a second later. He put his hand on Astra's sleeve and urged her after their companions.

The tall knight moved directly into their path. His face twisted into an evil grin. "I was addressing the lady."

Without answering, Weland drew his sword. The sound of other weapons being drawn hissed through the room.

The tall knight jerked his head. "We only want the dells, mate. Leave them here, and you can be on your way." He smiled genially, displaying an assortment of black and broken teeth.

Astra held her breath as she sensed their escort's hesitation. *Mary, Mother of God!*, she prayed. *Please don't leave us to these brutes!*

A bare heartbeat passed before the Fitz Hugh knights

lunged forward and the tavern erupted into a turmoil of flashing knives and thrashing bodies.

The dark-haired girl at the other table screamed, the sound echoing horribly in the low-ceilinged room. Astra and Marguerite clutched each other, watching hopelessly as their defenders groped and struggled directly in their pathway.

"The back way!" Marguerite gasped. Astra nodded and joined her friend's frantic race across the slippery, sawdust-strewn floor. The red-rouged serving wench loomed in front of them, gaping at the confusion. Astra shoved her aside.

They sped through the narrow, smoke-filled kitchen. As the back door came in sight, a tall form appeared in their pathway.

Seventeen

"Astra! Marguerite! What's happened?"

Astra threw herself into Richard's arms. "Help us, Richard! Help us! Those horrible men are after us, and they're killing the Fitz Hugh knights!"

"What? Where are they?"

Astra and Marguerite pointed breathlessly. Richard drew his dagger and tore through the kitchen.

The two women hugged each other in relief. Then, after a moment, Marguerite announced: "I'm going back. Those are my father's men. I'm responsible for them."

Astra nodded. "I'll . . . I'll go with you."

The two women crept cautiously back toward the main room of the tavern. The sounds of fighting had abated, but they could hear angry shouting. They peeked around the doorway. The serving wench blocked their way, but Richard's smooth, taunting voice came to them clearly.

"Even your cowardly lord, Faucomberg, won't be able to get you out of this blunder, Fitz Warren. Those women aren't cheap doxies you can abuse for your pleasure. They're gentlewomen, the Queen's own ladies."

"A likely story, Reivers," Richard's opponent sneered. "I hardly think any of the Queen's ladies would be wandering around Southwark after dark."

"It's true." One of the Fitz Hugh knights spoke; Astra

was not sure if it were de Saer or Weland, but she recognized his slight northern accent. "Lady Marguerite is the daughter of Lord Reginald Fitz Hugh. He won't take kindly to having his daughter frightened and mistreated."

"Lady Marguerite, is it?" the man named Fitz Warren gloated. "The word is that Fitz Hugh's daughter is a light skirt. That she'll lift her linen for any man who wields a shaft big enough for her tastes. And the little pudding-pie doll with her—she looks like a fine piece as well."

"Shut your filthy mouth!" The rage in Richard's voice made Astra tremble. She pushed forward, trying to see past the serving woman. She caught a glimpse of Richard's back, but still could not see his antagonist.

"What's it to you, Reivers?" the man named Fitz Warren snickered. "You're only a low-born bastard. But then, it's rather appropriate for you to defend these whores. After all your mother was one herself."

Astra could see the muscles in Richard's back tremble, and she guessed he raised his knife to attack. She gasped in terror and forced her way into the room. Richard's opponent's sword glittered in the dim light.

The sword flashed. Richard jumped back, then a moment later, sprang to meet his enemy. There was a terrible anguished cry. Richard's opponent collapsed to the floor, moaning and clutching his face.

"No!" Astra called out. Richard turned. His face went pale as he recognized her. "Get away, Astra. Don't look!"

It was too late. Her gaze was compulsively drawn to the wounded man who thrashed and twisted on the floor. The man held his hands to his face, helpless to remove the dagger that protruded from his bloody, ruined eye.

Astra swallowed convulsively. The room began to sway.

Her legs turned to water beneath her, and she crumpled soundlessly.

Richard was halfway across the room when Astra collapsed. Two steps more, and he knelt beside her. He reached out to touch her waxen face, then hesitated. Astra despised violence and bloodshed. Would she ever forgive him for what he had done today?

"My God, is she all right?"

Richard looked up to see Marguerite's shocked, pale countenance. His fury broke loose again. "Why did you bring her here? What madness possessed you to subject Astra to the scum of Southwark?"

"I . . . I . . ." Marguerite stammered. She glanced uneasily at the tall, blond-haired knight who had just entered the tavern.

Richard's eyes flickered to the man, then back to Marguerite. "You were meeting Christian, weren't you?" he accused. "You brought Astra here to disguise the fact that you were meeting your lover."

Marguerite's fine features darkened with resentment. "We were guarded by my father's men the entire time. I never imagined anything would happen to Astra. Indeed, nothing did. I'm sure she fainted only because she was so appalled by your savagery."

"My savagery! Would you rather I hadn't come to your aid? Would you rather I let that sick bastard ravish you and Astra?"

"It wouldn't have come to that," Marguerite said coldly. "De Saer and Weland could have dealt with him."

Richard frowned in disgust, then glanced again at Astra. She stirred slightly. He gave her a stricken look, then stood and addressed Marguerite's companion. "Get Astra back to Westminster, Christian. Make sure nothing else happens to her."

The knight nodded. "Of course, Richard. I'm happy to do whatever I can. I only wish I'd arrived sooner. Perhaps then you wouldn't have been forced to take on Fitz Warren by yourself." He cast an apprehensive look toward the wounded man, who was now surrounded by his rough companions. "I hate to think what Faucomberg's going to make of this. He'll likely go to the King and denounce you."

Richard shrugged. "It was worth it." He gave Astra one last look, then began to push through the crowd of knights and ruffians. On the way out the door, Ruby caught his arm.

"You were magnificent, love, simply magnificent."

He shrugged her hand away. "Not now, Ruby."

"Which green do you prefer, Astra?" the Queen asked thoughtfully. "This one seems too bright, the other too drab."

"It would depend upon where you are going to hang it." Astra fingered the lush velvet cloth laying across the table. "If it is a dark room, the brighter shade would not seem so vivid. The light you view it in will make a great deal of difference."

Queen Eleanor nodded. "I'll have to take both bolts to Woodstock and examine them in the bedchamber there. Then I must also consider the paint and the design for the wainscoting." She sighed. "There is so much to do. I am glad you are coming along to help me, Astra. I truly value your opinion. For all that you were raised in a nunnery, you have reliably good taste."

"Thank you, Your Grace. I'm pleased I can be of assistance."

"Your Highness, there is a Lord de Lacy outside asking to see Lady Astra," a servant interrupted.

"De Lacy?" Eleanor cocked her head in surprise. "Isn't he keeping Lady Marguerite's company these days?"

"Aye, Your Grace," Astra answered. "Perhaps he seeks my advice in some matter regarding her."

"Go then." Eleanor waved her hand in dismissal. "I've bored you long enough with my plans for the manor at Woodstock. I don't mean to keep you from indulging in the little intrigues the young men and ladies of the court are wont to pursue."

Astra bowed and hurried from the room. By the time she reached the gilded-ceilinged antechamber, she was breathless with worry. Why did Will want to see her? Was it to warn her? Had the news of the disastrous events at the Black Swan begun circulating among the palace gossips already?

She clasped her sweaty palms together and approached Will. "Lord de Lacy." She curtsied.

"He's gone," Will announced, not even bothering to bow or kiss her hand. "Richard's gone to Wales. The King sent him there; Henry all but banished him from the court."

Astra said nothing. A sick ache started in her belly.

"I cannot help blaming you and Marguerite for your part in this. If you hadn't been wandering around Southwark like a pair of brainless infants, Richard wouldn't have been forced to defend you. The man Richard maimed is in the employ of one of Richard's worst enemies, Guy Faucomberg, the Earl of Rathstowe. Rathstowe went immediately to the King and told Henry about Richard Reivers's uncontrollable temper and unchivalrous fighting methods. The King was very aggrieved. He ordered Richard off to Wales and threatened to do even worse."

Astra swallowed. She had caused trouble for Richard, grave trouble. Somehow she must remedy it.

"I will go to the Queen," she announced. "I will explain my part in Richard's downfall. I will make her understand that he was only doing his duty in defending me."

Will's eyes widened. "What of your own reputation, *demoiselle?* The Queen will be extremely angered to learn of your adventure in Southwark. She might even send you away."

"I . . . I must risk it," Astra answered in a shaky voice. "I cannot allow Richard to suffer for my mistake."

"And what of Marguerite? You will damage her reputation as well—a reputation that, I might add, is already in tatters. No, Astra, bringing disgrace upon yourself will not improve things for Richard. He is already anxious that you will not forgive him for again shedding blood in your presence. If he learns that your prospects at court have been damaged because of his actions, he will be even more distraught."

Astra clenched her hands in frustration. "What am I to do then? I cannot let Richard pay for what was Marguerite's and my mistake."

Will's face softened, and he reached out to touch Astra's arm reassuringly. "I am sorry, *demoiselle.* It was wrong of me to come to you in anger. I know you did not mean to hurt Richard, and you likely went to Southwark in all innocence of the consequences of your venture. It is Marguerite who should bear the blame for Richard's misfortune." His mouth quirked. "Of course, she will have a thousand excuses if she has one."

He sighed. "I think it would be best if you did nothing,

Astra. Continue to be dutiful and to cultivate the Queen. In all likelihood, Henry will get over his anger. If Richard serves him well in Wales, we can hope the King will forget the incident."

If Richard died in Wales, it would be her fault.

A tear trickled down Astra's face, but she did not release her hold on her rosary to wipe it away. More tears blurred her vision, making the chapel candles merge into a glittering tapestry of light. She closed her eyes and imagined Richard dead on some lonely battlefield, his beautiful body maimed and ruined, his dazzling dark eyes closed forever. A new wave of grief washed over her. What if Richard died and she had never had a chance to tell him that she loved him, that even though she had tried, she could not forget him? How would she live with herself then?

For a moment, Astra allowed herself to sink deep into the mire of her misery, then she impatiently brushed her tears away. She must stop this foolish crying and concentrate on praying. It was the one thing she could do to help Richard. The one way to make up for the pain she had inflicted upon him. She would pray for him; with all her heart she would pray.

She had to be somewhere, Marguerite thought irritably. Astra wouldn't run off to Wales by herself. She had more sense than that. More sense than most people. Certainly more than that fool Will. Why had he told Astra about Richard's troubles in the hallway outside the Queen's private chambers? He should have broken the news more gently and certainly chosen a more private setting.

Now she had to find Astra and allay her fears about Richard's situation. After all, Henry lost his temper all the time—and got over it by the next day. Why should it be any different with Richard? Especially if he fought well for the King in Wales. If Richard could make a difference there, the King would forgive anything.

Marguerite wondered if Astra would believe her. She'd likely think she'd ruined Richard's life and be beside herself with worry. Marguerite quickened her pace, trying to think. If she were Astra, where would she go? The thought of the chapel sprang to mind as she turned the corner.

Candles glowed along the walls, filling the small nave with an unearthly, flickering light. Marguerite stepped forward slowly and saw Astra near the altar. She was praying so intently she did not appear to hear Marguerite's footsteps.

Marguerite paused a few paces away from her friend's kneeling form. Astra was very pale; her delicate features might have been carved out of ivory. Her eyes were closed, the long auburn lashes perfectly still. A tendril of golden hair had escaped from her blue veil and curled against her cheek. It seemed as if a nimbus of light surrounded her. Marguerite caught her breath. Astra looked like a vision—a blessed angel or the incarnation of the Holy Mother herself.

Astra's lips began to move, breaking the spell. Marguerite stepped forward and called her friend's name.

Astra rose stiffly. "You've heard?"

Marguerite nodded.

"Oh, Marguerite, I don't know what to do. I've very nearly destroyed Richard's life! If the King doesn't forgive him or any harm befalls him in Wales . . ."

"It's not your fault! Don't even listen to Will. He can

be such a dolt sometimes. It was Richard's own temper that got him into this predicament. He was defending us, aye, but he didn't need to put out a man's eye to do it. There were plenty of other knights in the tavern that night who would have come to our aid. No, Richard simply lost control. He has a violent temper, and when Fitz Warren taunted him about his mother, he turned into an animal."

Astra shuddered. There was truth in Marguerite's words. Sometimes Richard terrified her. There was a side of him which was untamed and wholly wild. He reminded her of the deadly beasts imprisoned in King Henry's menagerie. "Surely Richard has been taunted before," she remarked in a troubled voice. "I've heard it is a common ploy in battle to use insults to distract your opponent into letting down his guard."

Marguerite's face was thoughtful. "The difference is, with Richard, the scurrilous remark has validity. Christian told me himself—Richard's mother really was a whore."

Astra's eyes went wide. "His mother was . . . was one of those women?"

Marguerite nodded. "I don't know the details, but Christian says it's true. Fitz Warren obviously knew about it as well and deliberately goaded Richard. In truth, I cannot feel sorry for Fitz Warren, despite the pain he must have suffered. Taunting a man like Richard was a stupid thing to do."

Astra groped her way to the rail at the altar and leaned heavily against it. "Dear God. Poor Richard. No wonder he is so bitter about women."

"Well, now you know," Marguerite said casually. "Richard has obviously known a lifetime of adversity; a short campaign in Wales isn't likely to do him in. Come along,

Astra. You must have something to eat. The Queen said you had not yet broken your fast today."

"As if I could eat!" Astra moaned. "My stomach is rolling around like butter in a churn. No matter what you say, I cannot help worrying about Richard. It is not true that I am not to blame for his problems. I asked him to help us. He would not have gone to face Fitz Warren if I had not requested his aid."

"Oh, bother, Astra, he was only doing his duty. A knight is supposed to rescue helpless women."

Astra clutched her prayer necklace tightly. "Perhaps it is more than that which troubles me. I worry that Richard will die without ever knowing how I feel about him."

"How do you feel about him?"

"I believe I am in love with him. It is not merely lust which makes him occupy my thoughts so constantly. I care deeply for Richard. When I found out he was in trouble with the King, I realized I would do anything I could to help him."

"Well now, that complicates things, doesn't it?" Marguerite gave a sudden sigh. "Why is it that women always fall in love with men who can never marry them?"

Astra looked at her sharply. Marguerite shrugged and continued. "It's true. Will said that Richard was determined to marry a rich woman. Of course, that was some time ago. Perhaps Richard has changed his mind by now." She darted Astra a swift, calculated glance. "There are ways to encourage a man to marry you. If you were to allow him favors and get with child . . ."

Astra stared at her friend, utterly aghast. "No! I would never agree to such an abhorrent scheme. To trick a man into marrying you—it is beneath contempt."

"Of course I do not mean you should trick him. Merely give him a *petite* nudge."

"I could never do something so dishonest. If Richard does not offer for my hand of his own accord, it was not meant to be!"

"Perhaps he will. After a few weeks moping in the Welsh Marches, dreaming of you every hour of the day, Richard may finally face the fact that he loves you too. Once he admits that, the rest will fall into place. There is really no impediment to your marriage except Richard's obstinance."

Astra nodded. Her eyes grew misty as she dared to hope, to dream of a future with her enchanting Richard. With an abrupt shake of her head, she sought to dispel the impractical thoughts from her mind. "What a coil it all is. I wish I could tell Richard how I feel. If only he were not in Wales!"

Marguerite wrinkled her brow in thought, then her face lit up. "The Queen expects you to accompany her when the court moves to Woodstock for a fortnight of hunting, and Woodstock is much closer to Wales than London. It is likely that there will be couriers sending news to the King about the war. Why not ask one of them to take a message?"

"I cannot do it. My feelings are much too personal to entrust to a messenger."

"I will have to think on it more, but there must be another way. I wish I could go with you to Woodstock."

"Why can you not go?"

"Because the Queen hasn't asked me," Marguerite answered with a twitch of her dark brows. "She's very fond of you, and she's heard enough rumors to guess I haven't been the best influence for you. I suspect she thinks a few weeks away from me will do you good."

Astra glanced at her friend, wondering if it were true.

Eighteen

Damn Wales—and damn its miserable weather. Richard pulled up the hood of his cloak and gazed dismally into the sodden, gray twilight. It was going to rain again—for about the thousandth time since they'd arrived.

"Any sign of them?" asked Tom Stroket, the stout knight who shared guard duty with him.

Richard shook his head. "They're likely in hiding, waiting to ambush us as soon as we move out. It's the way of the Welsh bastards."

Stroket nodded glumly. A drop of rain fell on his big Norman nose and dribbled off the tip. "It's a demonic form of warfare. They refuse to meet us in pitched battle, then cut us down one by one. You never hear a sound, then all at once there is a dagger buried in your throat or a gray goose-feathered shaft quivering from your belly." He shifted his broad shoulders uneasily. "I've heard some of the men are refusing to do guard duty. They say it's too risky. But you, you volunteered for it. Are you really that fearless?"

Richard cleared his throat and spat. "I've fought in Wales before. If you can stand the miserable weather and the vile diet of fatty mutton and coarse porridge, it's not so bad."

"When were you here?"

"A few years ago. It was a wasted effort, like this one. Since Henry failed in the twenties, there hasn't been much chance for the English."

"Henry lost then, didn't he?"

"I don't know that he'd say he lost. Having no taste for the misery of a Welsh campaign, Henry went off to fight in France instead. But, aye, in effect, he gave up most of what John gained in Wales during his reign. The truth is, Henry's not cut out for fighting wars like this one." Richard shifted restlessly. "He's too soft. To win you'd have to go in and burn and slaughter and kill until you brought them to their knees. Henry doesn't have the stomach for it."

"Henry doesn't have the stomach for a lot of things," Stroket commented softly.

In the dim light, blue eyes met black ones warily. "Have you thought about it?" Stroket asked after a moment. "Have you thought about hiring yourself out, maybe even to the French?"

"Christ, of course I've thought about it," Richard growled. "Who wouldn't, in my situation? I've fought for Henry for years, and all I've ever gotten for my trouble is a set of armor and a new warhorse every few years. I'm not getting any younger."

"They say King Louis is very generous with his soldiers. Some of the better born knights he's made his vassals, put them in charge of fine estates, even castles."

"Still," Richard mused. "It means betraying your homeland, your king. Henry and Louis aren't at war now, but sooner or later it could happen. Then it would mean facing your old comrades across a battlefield."

Stroket nodded. "If only there were some way to know what the situation is in France. It could all be talk. I have half a mind to go over there and see for myself how the wind blows."

"If you find out anything, let me know. I'm not fit for court life, of that I'm sure. I'm going to have to make my fortune by other means."

"You sound bitter. Did something happen in London to sour you on Henry?"

"You might say that. I went to the King directly and asked him for a grant. He treated me like an errant lapdog."

"Perhaps it is time to turn mercenary."

Richard nodded. He could not help thinking about Astra. How would she react if he betrayed Henry and hired himself out as a soldier?

"There's something else bothering you, isn't there, Reivers?" Stroket mused shrewdly. "I've never known you to be so morose and moody on campaign before."

Richard met Stroket's squinty, blue eyes briefly. "I guess you could say I finally succumbed. There's this woman in London . . ."

"A woman!" Stroket guffawed, appearing startled. "Mary's tits, Reivers! What did it take to win your heart—a gold-plated pussy?"

Richard grimaced at Stroket's crude words. "Not exactly. Although if beauty were wealth, she would be a great heiress."

"She's the most beauteous creature to grace this fair earth, eh?"

Richard smiled stiffly. "Of course."

"But you haven't wed her yet—why not?"

Richard's eyes darkened for a moment as he considered telling his friend the truth, that Astra didn't want him, that she was too refined and gentle a woman to be attracted to a crude, violent soldier. Then he shrugged. "She's poor. I can't see clear to making her my wife until I know I can take care of her. You know how it is; after the wedding comes a passel of brats you have to feed. I've always been a soldier, Tom, just my sword, my armor and my warhorse. How can I hope to look after a family?"

"Plenty of men do it. The woman stays home and takes care of the brats, while you go off fighting, earning their bread with your blood and sweat."

"And if I'm killed—what future do they have? No thanks. My mother got caught in that trap, and I saw what became of her. I'm not leaving any wife of mine to such a fate."

"Then look to France, comrade," Stroket said with a wink. "There's no wealth to be had in England unless your name is Berenger or Lusignan. Come to think of it, by the time the King's clan of scavenging relatives is done, there may not even be an England."

Tom got up and walked off to piss. Richard slumped more gloomily into his oiled leather cape, then spat on the ground, trying to rid his mouth of the taste of the horrible sour wine they were given in their rations.

France sounded wonderful—sunshine, fragrant meadows, crusty bread, good wine. A virtual paradise, and if Strocket could be trusted, still up for grabs. Aye, it was something to consider. He'd never thought to betray his King, but that was before Henry had shown himself to be such a weak bastard. Any king who let an idiot like Faucomberg dictate to him wasn't much of a king at all.

Richard ran his hand over his face, rubbing away the wetness. There really wasn't anything to keep him in England now. Astra didn't want him. He'd never forget the horror on her face as she watched Fitz Warren writhing in his own blood. No, she'd never forgive him. She considered him a monster, a beast. A painful pang of longing swept through him. He had never wanted a woman as much as he wanted Astra. This time it was more than a mere hardness in his loins or an itch in his blood. He wanted something more than merely to take his angel to bed. He wanted to possess her, to meld her soul with his own, to capture some of her purity and sweetness forever.

Richard clenched his fists until the cold metal of his lance ate into his flesh. He couldn't give up yet—that would mean letting Faucomberg and his kind finally win. His mind drifted back, remembering the taunts: "Bastard, whoreson, beggar." Even now the words retained their power to wound. It seemed only yesterday that he had been a ragged, unwanted, unloved boy. A boy who wondered daily if it would not have been better if he had not been born, if his filthy slut of a mother should not have murdered him in her womb.

No, he would not give up. He must keep trying to win Henry over. If he could lead a successful encounter with the Welsh, the King would have to reward him. Beating the Welsh was not impossible; you merely had to think like they did.

He glanced out into the gathering darkness, an idea forming gradually in his mind. The Welsh had always defeated the English by stealth and cunning. What if the same tactics were used against them? The Welsh would not expect a small body of English to sneak up upon them in the night. If he could find out where their camp was, have the men in his command forgo their splendid armor and don rough garments, use daggers and cunning instead of numbers . . .

Richard's heart raced. It was a daring plan, and he was not sure some of the men would agree to it. But still, it was better than doing nothing, better than sitting here, waiting to be attacked. And if he succeeded, the rewards would be well worth the risk. If he could report to Henry that at least one band of marauding Welshmen had been wiped out by his forces, the King might accept him back into his good graces, mayhaps even reward him royally.

Hope and exhilaration filled him, easing away the stiffness the rain and cold brought to his muscles and joints.

"Tom!" he called out softly to his companion. "Come here. I just had this thought."

With all the royal family's retinue and baggage, it took five days of traveling to reach Woodstock. Astra immediately decided the journey was well worth it. Compared to the squalor of London, the luxuriant countryside of the Midlands was near heaven. The air was pristine and fresh, the manor itself stately and cool. Even the grounds around the estate seemed washed clean by the frequent rains. Still, like the palace at Westminster, the manor was filled to bursting with people. Astra found herself assigned to sleeping on a pallet outside the Queen's chamber, crowded in with a dozen other unmarried women.

Astra washed the dust of the road from her face and changed into a fresh gown, then joined the rest of the royal entourage in the King's Hall. It was a luxurious room, with a high-vaulted timber ceiling and a floor of dark red tiles. Except for the light that shone in the large trefoil window on one wall, the room was dim. Velvet draperies along the walls kept out the cold, and the heat of summer. The royal couple arrived to sit at the large oaken table on the dais, and the rest of the court guests took their places at the rows of trestle tables.

Halfway through the meal, a group of mud-spattered soldiers entered the hall and walked to the dais. Astra observed the King lean forward to talk with one of the men who had just arrived. Something about the knight caught Astra's eye. His shoulders were unusually broad, and despite his disheveled appearance, there was a graceful elegance in his stance.

Astra's breathing quickened. Was it possible? Could it really be?

The man gestured. The King listened, his drooping eye giving him the appearance of being half-asleep, even though it was obvious he paid close attention to what the man was saying. The soldier turned, still gesturing, and Astra's heart seemed to leap into her throat. It was Richard! He was there, at Woodstock, in the very room!

Astra clasped her hands together and tried to calm herself. If the men were there to report on the war in Wales, it seemed likely that the King would ask them to stay for the banquet. Afterwards there would be entertainment, and, while everyone lingered in the hall, she would have a chance to speak to Richard. It seemed almost too wonderful, too fortuitous to be true.

As Astra watched, the King nodded curtly to the group of soldiers, then turned his attention to the food set before him. Obviously dismissed, the bedraggled delegation bowed to the King and Queen, then left the dais and began to make their way across the hall. Astra stared in desperation after Richard's departing form and prayed he was only leaving to wash and would rejoin the banquet later.

Servants brought in steaming platters of roast coney, sturgeon in sauce, capon in crust, fresh onions, leeks, and fruit tarts and pies. Astra took tiny portions and absent-mindedly pushed the food around on her trencher. She had no appetite for anything except the sight of the man she loved.

As the meal progressed, and Richard did not reappear, Astra began to worry that the King had ordered the soldiers back to Wales immediately. She cursed herself for not following Richard the moment he left the hall. He had been so close—not more than two dozen paces away—and she had let him slip away. The frustration built inside her. She began to squirm and shift in her seat until several people cast her reproving glances. Unable to bear it a moment longer, she excused herself from the table and left the hall.

Astra's heart sank when she saw the nearly-deserted courtyard. It seemed all too likely that the party of soldiers had left. Her only hope was that they had been forced to rest their horses before setting out again. After questioning a servant, Astra made her way through the maze of alleyways and outbuildings behind the manor and found the stables. There she encountered plenty of horses, but no soldiers. She asked one of the King's grooms, and he shook his head. He had seen no knights recently in this part of the royal complex.

It was almost twilight, and Astra was growing desperate. Retracing her steps, she made her way back to the entrance of the manor. She had intended to ask the guard at the gate if he had seen the knights from Wales, but when she glanced out toward the darkening forest, she guessed where Richard was. A veritable army camp had been set up on the strip of parkland between the manor and the woods. The soldiers who accompanied the King had prepared to bed down for the night outside the gates of the manor. It was likely that Richard and the other men from Wales had made camp there as well.

Wistfully, Astra stared out at the tents and glowing

campfires. There was no way to go to Richard now. It was growing dark, and she could not leave the manor without attracting notice. Besides, if she stayed away from the hall much longer, the gossip would begin.

Astra returned to the hall and reluctantly took her seat. There were a few curious glances sent her way, but nothing truly ominous.

The royal gathering was being entertained by a jongleur. The Queen favored traditional love stories from her native land, and this evening the ballad was about Tristan and Isolde. Astra usually found herself unaffected by tales of love and woe, but tonight the singer's words had special poignancy. She near wept when he reached the part where the lovers were separated. It seemed so much like her own fate. Richard was here, living, breathing—and likely sleeping now—in a tent not a stone's throw away from where she sat, but he might as well have been in the Holy Land. Worse yet, he would likely return to Wales and the dangers of battle without ever knowing that she cared.

The performance ended, and the King and Queen rose to go to their private quarters. As the mass of courtiers and ladies began to depart the hall, a sudden thought came to Astra. The manor was exceptionally crowded, especially the sleeping apartments. If she could manage to slip out during the night, she would never be missed. Still, how would she find her away around the manor? How would she get through the gates? She wished Marguerite were here, but somehow she would have to manage by herself.

As the crowd of Queen's ladies filed from the hall, Astra knew abruptly what her plan must be.

"Lady Alyce," she called out pleasantly to a small dark-haired girl who lingered behind the other women. "Wait for me; I would have a word with you."

Nineteen

"What is it, Astra?" Lady Alyce's large brown eyes were both interested and wary as Astra hurried up to her. Astra held a finger to her lips and drew the other woman aside. "I have a favor to ask of you," she whispered. "Can you keep a secret?"

Lady Alyce shrugged. Astra took a deep breath, weighing the risk she was taking. Alyce was quiet and kept to herself, but it was rumored that she regularly left the palace to meet lovers. It might be only gossip, but Astra did not think so. When any knights were around, Alyce's simpering smile always seemed to grow brighter, and her melting brown eyes danced around like little birds seeking a branch to alight on. Of all the ladies who served the Queen, Alyce seemed the one most likely to be willing and able to plan a nighttime excursion outside the manor.

"There is someone I must meet with privately tonight," Astra began. "He is camped outside the manor with the other knights. Can you help me?"

Alyce's eyes perused Astra's face shrewdly. A slight smile touched her lips as she answered. " 'Tis easily done. Most of the guards will help you—if you explain what you're about. The few who are stubborn can usually be bribed."

Bribed? Astra's heart sank. She'd not thought of that. She had no money, not a penny.

Alyce saw her look and smirked. "Not with coin, you ninny. A quick feel, a long hot kiss—that's all those sort are after."

Astra felt decidedly sick.

"I'll go with you if you like," Alyce offered. "There's a big Saxon I've had my eye on. I'm afraid he'll be marching for Wales soon."

At the mention of Wales, Astra's determination intensified. She couldn't let Richard go back to that horrible war without telling him how she felt.

"What time?" she asked grimly.

"Listen for the bells of matins. I'll be awake. We'll wait for the watch to go by, then slip out."

It wasn't cold at all, but Astra couldn't help shivering as they crept out of bed and slipped past the rows of sleeping women. Alyce went ahead of her, moving with the confident stealth of one accustomed to night errands. Astra followed her uneasily. Their hair was covered and both wore drab, old clothes meant to disguise them from curious eyes. Astra knew that Marguerite would be appalled that she was meeting her lover in a simple brown bliaut and ragged cloak, but it couldn't be helped. If they were stopped, Alyce said the ruse was to say they were kitchen maids.

The manor was quiet. The only noises were the soft snores floating from the sleeping chambers and the scuffle of rats and other creatures among the floor rushes. They left the royal family's private quarters and stole breathlessly through the Great Hall—it was still, eerie. Rushlights burned along the walls, illuminating the large cavernous room. Alyce led Astra into the kitchen. In the huge fireplace a fire was left burning. A dozing page kept watch nearby. The leftover smells of food stirred Astra's senses and made her hungry. Alyce carefully opened the creaking door, and out the back way they went, scurrying like mice.

The damp night air washed over Astra's face. She was alert now, intensely aware of everything around her. There was a bright full moon—the Corn Moon the peasants called it. It lit the manor courtyard with a blaze of whiteness. Alyce glanced up at it and shook her head.

"There's no hope we won't be seen. We must find a guard to help us."

Astra nodded; the anxiety in her belly tightened. They circled the yard and passed the buttery, the granary, the mews. As they neared the gate, they heard a low growl. Astra stiffened, expecting the dog to attack.

"Hullo, boy, what is it?" a voice muttered.

Alyce stepped out of the shadows to face a lean, wraith-like soldier.

"It is us, sir," she said calmly. "My friend and I are scullery girls in the kitchen. We have an errand in the camp. Will you let us pass?"

Even by moonlight, the man's leering smile was obvious. "An errand, have you now? And what errand might that be?"

Alyce's voice was suddenly seductive. "One of the knights has asked for . . . ah . . . entertainments. You would not want to disappoint the Black Leopard, would you now?"

Astra drew in her breath sharply. She had made no mention to Alyce of who she was meeting!

The soldier was almost as surprised. He guffawed low,

then grabbed Astra, pulling her out of the shadows. He stared hard at her face, and Astra's stomach seemed to fall into her legs.

"Aye, he might be wanting you, for all that," he said in a thoughtful voice. "You're right comely wenches. But it seems unfair that he should get both of you. There are other of us soldiers who get lonely, too."

"He asked for us both," Alyce said coldly. "Would you dare to disregard the Black Leopard's wishes?"

Astra couldn't be sure, but she thought she saw the man's eyes widen in fear. Then his face again twisted into a crude smile. "I've heard of the Leopard's voracious appetites. No doubt he'll take you both at the same time—the greedy, gluttonous bastard!"

Astra stared, unable to believe what she'd heard. It couldn't be true—surely Richard didn't indulge in such depravity. The man was simply jealous and eager to disparage his betters.

"Will you help us?" Alyce coaxed, "There might be a reward in it for you."

"Aye, I'll help," the man growled. "Take you right to his tent I will. I just hope the Leopard thinks it's worth his while. If he don't . . ." his eyes glittered. "I'll expect to get my reward anyway."

Alyce nodded, and the man turned and led them to the gate. He spoke low to the sentry, then stepped aside so the guard could see them more clearly. Astra resisted the urge to pull up her hood. The guard appeared to be inspecting her to see if she was alluring enough to interest a famed knight like the Leopard.

After a moment he grunted. "I guess Reivers is up to his old tricks. Been a long while since I've known him to take two wenches to bed."

Astra frowned. She really must speak to Richard about his shocking reputation.

The soldiers' camp was much noisier than the manor. Despite the lateness, many of the men were still up, dicing and talking around the fires. As their escort led them unobtrusively through the rows of tents, Astra could hear snores, grunts, sighs and occasional feminine laughter. She was glad she had asked Alyce for assistance. Even if she had been able to get through the gate unnoticed, she would never have found Richard's tent, and the thought of wandering around alone at night among all these soldiers unnerved her.

After a while the man guiding them stopped and rubbed his chin thoughtfully.

"What's wrong?" Astra whispered.

"Can't find it. Thought he'd have his banner up to mark his tent, but he don't."

She wanted to scream with frustration. The man had no idea where he was going. All this time he'd probably been leading them in circles!

"Might as well ask someone," he added. "Wait here."

Astra closed her eyes, trying to calm herself. The whole night was absolute folly. By the time they found Richard, it would be almost morning, and she'd have little time to talk to him. She should never have attempted such a foolish thing. Marguerite was good at intrigue, but she was not. When she tried it, everything ended up so bungled it was almost comical.

Behind her, Alyce yawned. Astra turned, regarding the sleepy-eyed woman curiously. "This sort of thing—do you do it often?"

Alyce shrugged. "Often enough. It's easier at the palace. I know the guards there, and they aren't such bumbling dullards. I tell them who I want to meet, and they take me there, for a price, of course."

Astra nodded, feeling a familiar queasiness in her belly. For all that she dressed in fine clothes and put on airs for the Queen, Alyce was little better than a strumpet.

"Why . . . why do you do it?"

Alyce made a vulgar sound. "What think you?—I like it. My father's plans are to marry me off to some filthy rich old geezer. Why shouldn't I enjoy myself with lusty young men while I can?"

"Are you in love with any of them?"

The moonlight was bright enough for Astra to see Alyce's face quite clearly. Her delicate features contorted into a sneer. "Love is for ninnies." Her brown eyes fixed coldly on Astra. "You think your precious Richard truly cares for you? Hah! You're only his latest challenge. As soon as he has you, his interest will wane quickly enough." Alyce's brittle smile returned. "Perhaps then he'll seek me to warm his bed. Or we could even pleasure him together—what the French call a *menage a trois.*"

Astra's eyes widened. "You can't really think that Richard would agree to that!"

"I have heard that the Black Leopard's tastes are quite varied," Alyce purred. "And that he is not easily satisfied by the commonplace or ordinary." Her eyes ran over Astra assessingly. "Which makes me wonder what use he has for you. The gossip is that you were raised in a convent and know absolutely nothing about men."

Astra was too stunned to respond. She had no chance anyway. The soldier had returned and was motioning for them to follow him. They walked back through the camp, seemingly taking the same route they had just traveled. The man finally paused in front of an unmarked tent.

"Here in dwells the Black Leopard. I suggest you wake him and ask for my fee."

Astra stared at the shadowy tent uneasily. What if the man were wrong and it were not Richard's tent? What if Richard did not greet her eagerly? Worst of all—what if he were not the man she knew at all but a corrupt stranger with bestial habits?

She glanced at her two companions and realized her doubts were irrelevant. Alyce and the soldier expected her to go into the tent and face the Leopard alone, and they would not abide a long delay.

Slowly, anxiously, Astra pulled aside the tent flap and went in.

At first, it was too dark to see anything, but gradually her eyes adjusted to the dim light that filtered through the tent opening. The place was a frightful mess. Weapons and clothes lay everywhere. A huge chest sat in the corner by the entrance, a chessboard on the top. Finely carved game pieces were strewn across it like discarded children's toys. She took a step into the tent and stumbled on an empty wineskin.

"Who goes there?"

She righted herself, looking toward the bedplace. She could make out Richard's form. The shape of his bare chest was visible, his face still shrouded in shadows. She took a deep breath and answered.

"It is I, Astra de Mortain."

She could hear his indrawn breath. Moments passed. "Astra?" he finally asked. "Is it truly you?"

She nodded, then felt a fool. He couldn't see her.

"I've come to talk to you."

There was a rustling sound as he threw the blankets

aside. The tent was too low for him to stand up. He approached her awkwardly, his head bent down.

"Astra? What are you doing here?"

She sighed in consternation. She'd just told him what she was doing—was he witless?

He moved within a few feet of her, then stopped. She still could not see his face. She glanced at his body, then regretted it. Richard appeared to be completely naked.

Astra averted her eyes. "A man helped me find you. He expects a reward."

"A reward?"

Astra gritted her teeth at Richard's denseness. "Aye. He helped me sneak out of the manor yard, and then led me to your tent. I must give him something."

Richard nodded slowly, then went to the large chest, and upending the chessboard and pieces, opened it and dug inside. He stumbled over to Astra, swearing as he stepped on something, and handed her a cold, hard object. Astra did not look at it, but ducked through the tent opening.

The soldier was waiting a few paces away. She thrust the object at him, seeing now that it was a polished dagger.

"The Leopard wants you to have this for your trouble."

The man nodded and turned away. Astra started back toward the tent. Alyce put a restraining hand on her arm.

"Here now, what about me?"

Astra sighed, then entered the tent again. Richard appeared to be fumbling around by the bedplace. She could hear scuffling noises in the corner.

"Richard, I m sorry. There was a woman too—one of the Queen's ladies. Without her, I would never have known what to do. I'm afraid she expects a reward, too."

"All right, let me find a lamp." Richard's voice sounded sleepy, distant.

A light flared, revealing Richard's nakedness. Astra closed her eyes. There was the sound of more fumbling, and then Richard's breathing close by.

"Here," he said, taking her hand and pressing another metal object into it.

Astra turned to the tent flap, finally opening her eyes. Outside, Alyce was waiting. Her eyes grew wide when she saw the brooch.

"Holy Mother! He gave you this?" She glanced at Astra, her face speculative. "Mayhaps I was wrong. It seems you mean more to Sir Reivers than I thought."

Astra resisted the urge to say something cutting. She didn't want to get in an argument with Alyce. She just wanted her to leave.

"The blond knight?" she questioned Alyce. "Do you think you can find him?"

" 'Tis no matter," Alyce answered, still looking at the ebony brooch. "If I can't, I will go back to the manor." She raised her head to scan the night sky. "It's growing near to morning anyway. There is no time to dawdle, Astra. Go to your lover and seek to please him well. If you are fortunate, perhaps he will make you his mistress."

There was an unexpected wistfulness in Alyce's voice that made Astra's throat grow tight as she turned away.

Twenty

Richard met Astra at the tent entrance and immediately pulled her into his arms. He tried to kiss her, but found it awkward in the low tent. Slipping to his knees, he wrapped his arms around her hips and pressed his face into her breasts. Astra squirmed.

"Please, Richard. I came to talk."

"Talk," he said huskily, trying to pull her down beside him. She resisted him, her heart pounding. Richard had seen fit to put on his hose, but his chest and shoulders were still bare. She could not think with all that sleek, warm skin exposed.

"Please, Richard, dress yourself and come outside with me."

Slowly he released her. She watched him fumble by the bed again, searching for the rest of his clothes. Then he sat down on his bedroll and began to dress. It was strange to watch him clothe himself, strange and somehow intimate. As he slipped his tunic over his head and managed his cross-garters and boots, Astra imagined watching him dress in the morning, as if he were her husband.

When Richard was done, he ran his fingers through his sleep-tousled hair and faced her.

"I am ready."

Outside the tent, Astra glanced to the east nervously,

searching for the tell-tale glow of dawn. The sky seemed very dark, the moon still high and bright.

Richard appeared beside her and took her arm, then leaned over and kissed her. The kiss banished the night chill completely and left her hot and breathless. Encouraged, Richard slid his fingers into her hair and fastened his mouth upon hers. Astra's whole body caught fire, the flames sucking the air from her lungs and making her so dizzy she could hardly stand.

"Richard, we have not talked yet," she broke away to protest.

Reluctantly, he released his hold. "Lovely, Astra," he murmured. "I can't believe you are really here. When I woke and heard your voice, I thought it was a dream. Or mayhap a holy vision. You look more like an angel than ever."

His fingers raked her disheveled braids, deftly undoing the tangled plaits until Astra's hair fell in loose waves over her shoulders. He buried his hands in it and pulled her close so he could press his mouth to her neck. "Now you are as I first saw you—your hair wild and golden in the sun. You are my goddess, my Venus, my angel. Let me worship you, Astra. Let me worship you as I wanted to then."

He whispered the words almost in her ear, and the vibrations sent a hot thrill down her body. His hands tore at the loose neckline of her gown until it gave way. Finding the bare soft skin at the top of her breasts, he nuzzled, then nibbled, his rough mouth sending sharp, almost painful sensations down Astra's body. Her knees wobbled. Richard held her up, his hands firmly cupping her buttocks.

Astra moaned, then managed to come to her senses enough to push him away. "Have you no decency, Richard?" she said sternly, "We are in the midst of an army camp. If I am seen, it will go hard with us. Have a care and find us someplace private to talk."

"Aye," Richard mumbled. "You are right. I will take you somewhere no one will find us."

She gasped as Richard swept her off her feet. She'd never had a man carry her before. It felt strange and exhilarating. She worried she was too heavy. For all that his arms felt strong and secure around her, she could hear him panting.

"Pray, don't overexert yourself. I can easily walk."

Richard laughed. "Do you think for one moment that I will agree to release you? Hah! I have thought of nothing but this for weeks, nay months. I have half a mind to carry you off into the woods and keep you to myself forever."

Astra felt a stirring of unease. For all that he was jesting, there was something unsettling about Richard's words. She could half imagine him abducting her and keeping her as his prisoner. The thought aroused her oddly. Her heart was already his captive; what would it be like for him to enslave her body as well?

She had no idea where they were, but it was surely in the woods somewhere. Ahead was a clearing in the trees where the moon shone as bright as day. He carried her there and put her down. His arms still encircled her tightly.

"Astra, my love." Richard rained kisses on her face and neck. Astra tilted up her mouth, searching for the warm wetness of his lips. He found her mouth and sucked greedily at her lips, then thrust his his hot tongue between them. His hands roamed over her breasts, her belly, her hips, then tore demandingly at the neck of her gown. His urgency seemed to make Astra's reason reassert itself. She struggled to push his hands away.

"Nay, Richard, we have not talked yet."

"Talked of what?" he murmured, his lips still busy torturing her.

"I wanted to tell you—I am sorry for what happened in Southwark. I did not mean to involve you in a conflict on my behalf. If you would wish it, I would be willing to go to the King and explain you were only doing your duty."

"Ah, Astra, there is no need," Richard sighed. "I would gladly endure Henry's wrath for your sake anytime. I was only afraid you would hate me for using violence to defend you."

"I wish you could have ended the trouble another way, but I could never hate you, Richard." She reached up and gently touched his face. "I . . . I love you."

She felt Richard's body tremble. He crushed her against him desperately and gave a low moan. "Oh, Astra, if you knew what your words meant to me. If you only knew."

His hands caressed her, impatient, almost frantic. She gave into the breathless, urgent need his touch evoked, and allowed him to work down the neck of her gown so her breasts sprang free. He cupped them roughly, then stepped back, staring.

"God in heaven, you're beautiful," he groaned. "You're even more beautiful than I remembered."

Astra felt a sense of horror mingling with her desire. Her breasts were completely bare. It was night, but the moonlight was very bright. It was almost as bad as when he had seen her swimming in the pond in the forest. The very thought of it made her feel weak and shaky.

"Richard . . . I . . ."

"Hush," he whispered. "I only want to look, to drink my fill of you."

"But Richard," Astra protested, suddenly frightened,

"we cannot do this. It is not right. Someone could come upon us. Someone could . . . oh!"

Richard's leg had somehow entangled with hers. Astra lost her balance and went down with a soft crumpling sound. She was not hurt, only dazed. Richard's arms had cushioned the impact, but it startled her to change position so quickly.

Richard let go of her arms, then reached up to pull off his tunic, tossing it aside. He knelt on her skirt and forced a knee between her thighs, urging them apart. Astra panicked.

"What . . . what are you doing?"

"Hush. I only want to look at you."

His voice was low, vibrant, tender. Astra felt herself giving in. Her doubts seemed to float away, and she suddenly was aware of nothing except the man who loomed over her. His shoulders were like dark wings; his handsome features glowed silver in the moonlight. At this moment he seemed as wild, as beautiful as his leopard namesake. She reached out to caress him. The skin of his chest was warm, smooth, alive, as luxurious as velvet under her fingertips. She closed her eyes and gave in to the sensation, floating down a river of pleasure and contentment.

"I dreamed of touching you like this," she whispered. "When you went off to Wales, I was so afraid. I was terrified you would be hurt, or killed . . ." Her voice broke off with a quiver of emotion.

Richard's hands slipped over her breasts, stroking in slow, rhythmic circles. "And I thought of you, every moment. I dreamed of loving you, touching you. I thought perhaps I wanted to die. I imagined heaven was filled with angels like you."

She clutched his hands to her heart. "Do not say such

things. It is sinful to wish for death. If you had died, a piece of me would have died also."

"But I have found heaven here," he said. He leaned forward to press his face in the hollow between her breasts. "Such sweetness . . ."

Astra shuddered. In her fantasies she had imagined Richard resting his head on her chest, his dark hair soft against her skin. Now it was happening, and the thought of it made her nipples tighten until they ached. Longing shot through her, and a sigh escaped her lips. As if in response, Richard twisted his head and brought his mouth down on her throbbing nipple. He suckled her deeply. His hand stroked her other breast, teasing the nipple with his fingers.

Astra moaned and arched her back, giving in to the shimmering pleasure. Richard's mouth was everywhere. He laved hot kisses on her nipples, then traced the swelling curves of her breasts with his tongue. His fingers followed, fondling, squeezing and stroking her as if he could not be satisfied. Astra found it a kind of exquisite torture to be touched so many places at once. Her mouth felt wet and hungry, and the place between her legs had grown so swollen and hot she could barely lie still.

Richard gave a ravaged sigh. "Oh, Astra, I cannot endure it—I must know the rest of you as well!"

She felt his searing mouth desert her, leaving the night air cool on her wet, sensitive skin. Frustrated, she tried to sit up. Richard forced her down with one hand, while his other hand fumbled with the folds of her bliaut. She cried out as his fingers found her bare leg and moved upward. In seconds, her skirts were pushed to her waist, her legs and hips exposed to the luminous moonlight.

Astra went rigid. She might as well be naked—her

breasts and hips were completely uncovered and only a narrow strip of cloth shielded her belly. It was like it had been in the forest, only he was much closer now, his fingertips mere inches from her most private parts. She felt his eyes upon her, and the blood rushed to her face, making her feel hot and fevered. She was ready to swoon. If she had known what he meant to do next, perhaps she would have.

Soft hair tickled her thigh. Astra drew in her breath and tried to squirm away. Richard's hand on her belly held her down. His lips brushed her thigh and moved upward. She clenched her legs together and whimpered. His breath was hot. It started an itch deep inside her, a quivering, irresistible itch. She could not escape the tormenting heat of it.

Her chest heaved. His mouth came down on the soft cleft between her thighs, but she did not shatter into pieces as she expected. She made a soft, animal-like sound, and her legs slid apart.

The slightly rough skin of his face pressed against her tenderest parts, sending spasms of heartstopping pleasure through her body. His lips devoured her; his tongue alternately soothed and tormented. The sensations expanded and grew, rippling within her like the current of a river. She reached down blindly and buried her fingers in his hair, bracing herself against the raging tide that threatened to consume her. Darkness spilled over her. Darkness lit with vague pinpoints of light, like stars. The stars grew and swelled, filling the night.

She trembled, shivering convulsively. Richard stroked her softly. His face rested on her thigh. She reached down and pulled him up to her, desperate to have his strong arms around her. He kissed her, his lips still musky with her scent. She felt light and boneless, as if she might float away. Every inch of her tingled, and she still could feel the imprint of Richard's mouth on the throbbing flesh between her legs. He had possessed her, claimed her, and the fever his touch had aroused could not be easily quenched.

He began to kiss her roughly, and she realized that he had not found satisfaction yet, that there was more to lovemaking than what she had just experienced. The knowledge frightened her and intrigued her. She let her fingers explore his bare torso, wondering if she could hope to offer him the same pleasure he had given her. Richard grabbed her hand and pressed it against the front of his hose. She felt something rigid and warm—and startlingly alive.

"Touch me here, Astra," he begged. "Please."

She moved her fingers slowly, tenderly, then tensed as the sound of voices cut through the darkness.

"It came from over here," a man called sharply. "I don't think it was an animal; it sounded like a woman's voice."

"Jesu, Rob, it's probably just a couple of lovers enjoying the moonlight. Why can't we leave them be?"

"Because we don't know for certain what it was. It might be poachers, brigands, even an assassin targeting the King."

Astra held her breath and clutched at Richard's arm. If they were found, she would be disgraced. The Queen would banish her from court. She started to rise. Richard restrained her with an iron-like grip.

"An assassin!—does Henry think some disgruntled baron is out to murder him?"

"In truth, I think he fears madmen more than his barons. The King seems blissfully unaware of the real trouble lurking in his kingdom. . . . What ho! Did you hear something?"

The sound the men had heard was Astra's chemise tearing. Richard had ripped it off and was struggling to fasten it over her hair and the top part of her face. Having managed that, he pulled her beneath him and pressed his lips noisily to hers.

Astra gasped, fighting the kiss. What did Richard mean to do—rape her in the few short moments before the King's men found them? She struggled as he threw up her skirts and thrust his heated groin against hers. Then, despite herself, Astra groaned.

"Shit, Geoffrey, I told you it was just a pair making the two-backed beast. Stand up, man, let me see your face."

Slowly, carefully Richard stood. He moved in front of Astra and blocked the men's view of her.

"Sir Reivers! We did not think to find you fucking in the woods. Silk coverlets and soft beds are more in keeping with your reputation."

"The wench is well-born, and she wishes to keep her identity secret," Richard answered. "I thought we'd be safer here than among the prying eyes of the camp."

Astra pulled the torn cloth against her face, wondering how much of the rest of her the men had seen. Richard had jerked down her bliaut before he stood, but she guessed they had gotten a good eyeful anyway.

"Sorry to trouble you in the middle of that, Reivers. She looks like an exceptional piece."

"Oh, she is," Richard agreed coolly. "She's well worth risking my life and limbs prowling around the forest at night."

"Married?" one of the men asked, trying to peer around Richard.

"She might be," Richard answered in a low, threatening voice. "As I said, it is essential that her identity be concealed."

"We'll leave you to your pleasure then, Reivers," one of the soldiers said nervously, beginning to walk away. "But I would advise you to see your ladylove back to her bed. The King's household is already stirring."

The other man turned away with reluctance and followed his companion into the woods. Astra stood up, wondering if her shaky legs would hold her. Despite her fear, her body throbbed with longing and incompletion. Richard turned to her. Perhaps it was growing light after all, for Astra could see his features clearly. His mouth was harsh, his eyes tense and brooding.

"That was close," he muttered. "Too close."

His face softened and he reached out and pulled her to him, burying his hands in her hair as he kissed her. It was a desperate kiss, so full of hunger and longing it brought tears to Astra's eyes.

Richard leaned away, his hands still caressing her neck. His gaze locked with hers. Slowly, his fingers trailed down her body. They lingered over her breasts and belly, then reached her hips and fumbled with the folds of her skirt. As Richard's hand pressed against the heated, aching flesh between her legs, he brought his mouth close to her ear.

"You are mine, Astra," he whispered. "I claim you now and forever. I will not wed you until I can provide for you, but never doubt that you belong to me, and me alone."

Twenty-one

By the time they reached the manor, the eastern sky glowed with the pale colors of dawn. Astra held the torn piece of her shift around her face and kept her head bowed while Richard exchanged a few words with the man at the gate. The sleepy-eyed guard let them pass without even glancing at Astra.

They moved unnoticed through the courtyard and found the kitchen entrance. To Astra's surprise, Richard followed her in.

"You must not come with me. What if you are seen?"

"Damn the risk. I want to see you safely to bed."

Astra shook her head, but allowed him to follow her stealthily through the hall. At the corridor leading to the wing where the women slept, she paused and again motioned for him to leave her. Reluctantly, Richard nodded. He gave her a tender kiss, then his dark eyes swept over her with an intensity that made Astra tremble. Fearing he would pull her into his arms again, she turned and ran down the hall.

Richard stretched out stiffly on his bedroll. The damp morning air, the night spent rolling around on the grass, the ache of unrequited lust—they all contributed to the discomfort of his body. But his heart—ah, that was another matter. He felt absurdly, deliriously happy. Astra loved him!

The thought made him smile, then laugh out loud. He grinned into darkness. He had not known until this night how much he loved Astra, how intensely he needed her. The feel of her body in his arms filled him with strength and joy; with Astra beside him, it seemed possible he could do anything.

A sense of awe filled him as he recalled Astra's hips and thighs trembling as he pleasured her. Never had he known such delight in satisfying a woman. What would it be like when their bodies were joined, and he awakened the rest of Astra's virginal passions? He closed his eyes and contemplated consummating their love. Surely the ground would shudder and the stars whirl madly in the heavens in the exquisite moment when he entered her.

But when would that be? He had used his success in Wales to convince the King to let him return to London, but once there, he would have little opportunity to be alone with Astra. She deserved to experience lovemaking in a place of beauty and comfort. How was he to arrange that? He was used to satisfying himself with women who did not care where he took them or how. Astra was different. For Astra, he wanted a well-lit room where he could savor every inch of her spectacular beauty, a clean, sweet-scented bed with, aye, a silk coverlet. He wanted her to remember the magic of their first time forever; she would never forget him, her wild and passionate Black Leopard.

A twinge of conscience stabbed him. Once bedded, Astra would expect him to wed her. He was not yet ready for that. He feared marrying a poor woman, feared what the consequences would be if something happened to him before he had a chance to assure his fortune. Astra would be left alone. Widowed, without a rich dowry, she might not find a wealthy husband so easy to attract. If there were children, it would be worse. No, he could not marry her yet. He would not wed Astra until he could properly care for her.

"Astra! I've missed you dreadfully!"

Astra gave a cry of delight and joined her friend in an exuberant embrace.

"It has been so long, *ma petite,*" Marguerite exclaimed. "Let me look at you! Oh, you are more beautiful than ever."

"It has not been so long. We were gone less than a month."

"It seemed like an eternity, *ma belle.* You've no idea how dull London is without you."

"I cannot imagine that. It appears to me that London is always exciting."

"There *were* entertainments." Marguerite smiled enigmatically. "Without that nasty Isabel around to gossip about me, I managed to have a few adventures."

"I don't want to know," Astra demurred, rolling her eyes. "I'm relieved at least to see that the Tower of London still stands."

"What of you, Astra. Did you see Richard?"

"I . . . I did." Despite her intention to appear confident, Astra's words came out in a nervous, uncertain voice.

Marguerite's face brightened with excitement. "What did he say?"

"I don't want to speak of it here," Astra protested, looking around the crowded courtyard. Everything was chaos as the royal household and their baggage arrived at the palace. Squires and servants raced everywhere, carrying trunks, boxes, even the King and Queen's personal furniture.

"We must find a private place," Marguerite said. "I'm simply dying to know what transpired between the two of you."

Astra nodded and allowed Marguerite to lead her through the bustling courtyard. She hesitated when her friend attempted to guide her into the Queen's chapel. "Not here!" she protested. "We can't talk in a holy place!"

"Why ever not? It is the perfect location for a private rendezvous. Hardly anyone ever comes here."

"But it is sacred!" Astra could hardly imagine confiding what had happened with Richard here.

"Bother and nonsense! It's merely quiet and private." Marguerite grabbed Astra and pulled her into the chapel, leading her into a corner. "I'm not budging until you tell me about Richard."

"Sweet Jesu, Marguerite. I don't know if I can."

"Of course you can. You merely open your mouth and say it."

"But it is . . . so . . . so embarrassing."

"Embarrassing? How delightful!"

"Oh, Marguerite, if you knew what he did to me . . ."

Her friend gave her a worried look. "Dear Astra. I hope you didn't heed my earlier advice. I'm not sure it would be wise to let Richard get you with child. If he refused to claim the babe, it could get most unpleasant."

Astra shook her head impatiently. "I did not let him . . . that is . . . I'm sure there is no way I can be with child."

Marguerite nodded. "You are a maiden still. That is a relief. But what *did* happen?"

PHOEBE
CONN
BELOVED
BESTSELLING AUTHOR
SHANNON
DRAKE
PRINCESS
OF FIRE
BESTSELLING, AWARD-WINNING AUTHOR
GENTRY
Jo
Goodman
FOREVER
IN MY
HEART

Astra smoothed her traveling gown, trying to settle her nerves. "It did not go well in some ways. We had no chance to talk of marriage or our future. But he was very passionate, very possessive. He . . . he told me he loved me."

"Did you meet him alone?"

"Aye, I did. I slipped out of the manor one night and went to his tent."

"Saint Anne, Bridget and Holy Mary—you didn't!"

Astra nodded. "I had help. Lady Alyce went with me; she convinced a guard to help us find Richard's tent . . ."

"Lady Alyce? Oh, I know about her. She's a slut."

"Nevertheless, she helped me and told no one afterwards. I was very fortunate. It could have been disastrous when the King's guards found us in the wood . . ."

"The King's guard . . . ?" Marguerite interrupted, her eyes wide. "They saw you?"

Astra nodded. "It would have been terrible if they had recognized me, but Richard covered my face and then he pretended to . . ." She broke off, blushing furiously. She could not forget what it had felt like to have Richard's hot groin rubbing against her own.

"He pretended to . . . oh, my," Marguerite giggled. "Sir Reivers is rising in my estimation by leaps and bounds. He protected your honor with a most ingenious ruse . . . and of course it was at great sacrifice to himself."

Astra tried not to smile. Looking back on it, the situation had been rather comical. "His subterfuge appeared to work. Even when rumors began to circulate about the knight and the half-naked woman found in the woods by the King's personal guard, no one suspected me."

"Half-naked! Sweet Jesu, Astra, what *were* you and Richard doing?"

Astra's face flamed. She hadn't intended to say so much.

"Richard *had* to pull up my skirts to make it look convincing."

"Of course, he *had* to," Marguerite answered, nearly choking on her mirth. "He likely *had* to pull down his hose and stick it in, too. Otherwise, they might have thought he was just *pretending.*"

"Jesu, Marguerite! I told you we did not do that!"

"So you did. But you forget that I am much more experienced than you, and I know there is a great deal you can do with a man without him actually sowing his seed."

"I am still a maiden, Marguerite! I did not even see him naked!" Not unless you counted what she had seen of him in his tent, Astra thought guiltily. And then there was the fact that even if she hadn't seen his private parts, she had touched them through his hose.

Marguerite was silent, regarding her intently. "I know you well, Astra. Richard must have done something to you. When I look at you, I no longer see a shy, innocent maid. Whether or not he has accomplished it in fact, somehow he has made you into a woman."

"Is it so obvious then?" Astra asked anxiously. "No one else has noticed, not even the Queen."

Marguerite smiled. "It is a subtle thing. There is a glow about you, a lovely color in your cheeks. It is most becoming."

Astra let out a sigh of relief. "I have been so worried. I was afraid Alyce would say something, or the Queen would become suspicious. But no one said anything, and Richard and the other soldiers left for the Marches the next day."

"But nothing is settled between you?"

Astra shook her head. "Richard was very ardent and possessive, but we never discussed the future. I've been thinking ever since, Marguerite, and I've finally decided on a plan to convince him to wed me."

Her friend smiled. "Now you're beginning to plot and scheme like me!"

"I feel sure Richard would marry me if he were more confident of his future," Astra continued, ignoring Marguerite's remark. "He wants to be rich, to have his own *demesne* and castle. I intend to go to the Queen and ask her if she will help him achieve his ambitions."

"The Queen?"

Astra nodded. "Everyone says she is fond of me, and they also say she is the power behind Henry's throne. If she cannot convince the King to reward Richard for his loyalty, no one can."

Marguerite gave a most unladylike whistle. "It is brilliant, Astra. The Queen does dote on you, and she exerts a powerful influence on Henry's decisions. If Richard were confident of his future, he would not hesitate to marry you. Will has already told me as much."

Astra nodded, smiling radiantly. The thought of marrying her beloved Richard filled her with exquisite happiness. She could hardly wait to put her plan into action.

"Have you told Richard?"

"I have not spoken with him since that night in the forest."

"Perhaps you shouldn't tell him—perhaps you should speak to the Queen first and then, if she agrees, break the news to Richard later."

Astra frowned. For all Richard's ardent words and passionate lovemaking, he had never actually proposed to her.

"I cannot go to the Queen until I am confident of Richard's intentions," she pointed out. "I will not presume . . ."

"That is nonsense, Astra. Richard has obviously taken liberties with you. He *must* wed you."

"But he can be very stubborn. Richard would not like it if he felt I were making this decision for him."

"Really, Astra," Marguerite admonished. "Sometimes a woman must take these matters into her own hands. If you want Richard, you should be willing to do whatever is necessary to convince him to marry you. Unless, of course, you'd rather forget him and find a more compliant suitor."

"Forget him?" Astra shook her head vehemently. "It is too late for that. For better or worse, my destiny is with Richard."

"Well. Whatever he did to you in that darkened wood, it must have been extraordinary. I have never seen you like this—so determined and sure of yourself. The nuns of Stafford would never recognize you for the timid little novice they raised."

Astra smiled uncertainly. If Marguerite only knew.

"Everything is ready?"

The dark, beetle-browed man named Repke nodded. "Just as you asked for, sire. The room is prepared—fresh rushes on the floor, a clean soft bed, the best Gascony wine, real wax candles, even a silk coverlet." He regarded Richard with a twitching smile. "This one must really be something, to put the Leopard to such trouble. Usually you have no quarrel with tuppin' 'em on a dirty straw mattress."

"Aye, she is special," Richard answered absently. "Nothing is too good for my lady."

"A lady?" Repke's beady eyes glittered, and he moistened his lips greedily, all but salivating over this juicy bit of information.

Richard gave him a threatening look. "Aye, she is a lady. She deserves privacy and discretion. I expect you to keep your knowledge of this liaison to yourself. If not . . ."

He had no need to finish, for the man's lascivious look rapidly turned to fear. "Certainly, Sir Reivers. I am always discreet." He touched his lips. "Sealed they are. They'd have to kill me to make me talk."

Richard gave the man a cold look of disbelief, then handed him a bag of coins.

Repke walked away. Richard's eyes followed him with a brooding stare. This business was costing him a fortune. He'd had no idea that a clean room and a few luxuries were so hard to come by in Southwark.

He looked around the filthy street. On the corner, two bawds in gold wigs and scarlet dresses flaunted their bare breasts to passers-by, while a wizened little man wheeled by a stinking cart full of dung. Southwark was a cesspool, as depraved as the cities Sodom and Gomorrah. Here a man could buy anything he wanted—sex in all its perversions, virgins and young boys, poison, a knife in the throat of an enemy. It was a pesthole, a nightmare of poverty, disease, violence and despair. It was no place for a sweet innocent like Astra.

He sighed, feeling torn. It did not seem right to bring his gentle angel here, and yet, it was the only way they could be safely alone. In Southwark a man could discreetly indulge his vices and everyone would look the other way. It was their only chance to experience the night of rapture he had planned since Woodstock.

And then what? Richard frowned. He was no closer to being able to marry Astra than he'd been before. The King was well pleased with the daring ambush he had planned in Wales, but there was still no mention of a reward. Without a grant from the King, he could not hope to make Astra his wife. She deserved to be rich, to always dress like a fine lady, to have servants wait on her. He would not wed her until he could give her that.

He started to walk down the narrow street, so deep in thought he almost stepped into the foul, overflowing gutter that ran down the center. He swore and jumped to the side, glancing backwards uneasily. It was not like him to be so muddle-headed. That was one deleterious effect Astra had upon him. The mere thought of her made him turn into an addle-pated idiot. He couldn't afford to lose his edge; he needed to keep his wits about him at all times. That bastard Faucomberg might well be planning more trouble, and he must be ready for it.

That was another reason he must bed Astra. If he were finally able to release his tormenting lust, he wouldn't be so edgy and preoccupied. He could get back to the business of winning his fortune.

He paused, his back to a sturdy alehouse, and allowed himself to contemplate the fulfillment of his plans. Tonight, Astra would open her legs for him. She would sigh in her soft voice and stroke him with her tender fingers. In turn, he would make her swoon and sigh and quiver. He would give her unimaginable pleasure. All night he would love her. The sordid horror of Southwark would be forgotten. When the sun rose on the morrow he would awake to paradise and his angel beside him. Heart and soul and body—she would finally be his.

The image heartened him and called back his usual confidence. He was the Black Leopard, one of the most formidable warriors who had ever served King Henry. He would to be a great man some day—a baron, a man who influenced others. No one would laugh at him or spit in his face or call him a bastard ever again. He would win the fame, wealth and glory he deserved. And when he did, Astra would be beside him.

Twenty-two

Astra laced up the bodice of the pale violet gown, then glanced at her reflection in the borrowed mirror. Tonight she would have to be adamant. Richard could not touch her or kiss her until they had discussed their future together.

She straightened her shoulders and made a stern face in the mirror, trying to feign a confidence she didn't feel. She had agreed to meet Richard alone, and he no doubt assumed she was going to let him bed her. Somehow she must resist his attentions and force him to listen to her plan. Once he knew she meant to go to the Queen and ask for her aid, he might be confident enough of the future to propose to her. Astra took a shaky breath. It was a daring scheme, worthy even of Marguerite.

Perhaps that was what worried her. Marguerite's clever plans somehow always went awry at the last minute. Tonight was too important for that. She must settle her future with Richard. She could not go on like this. She ached for him and lived for the mere sight of him. She must have some assurance he would be her husband someday. Then she could give herself to him and let him take her to that breathless, rapturous paradise again.

A frown wrinkled her brow. That was it, the fatal flaw in her plan. She wanted Richard much too badly. If he began to kiss and caress her, she would be lost. She could not allow him to suborn her will. She must be firm, nay, obstinate. Until they spoke of their future, she could not allow him to touch her.

Astra leaned forward and gave herself one last look in the Queen's mirror. She looked alluring enough, if perhaps a little pale. She pinched her cheeks to give them color.

"No need for that. Merely think of Richard kissing you, and your cheeks will bloom like roses."

Astra nearly knocked over the mirror. "Marguerite! You startled me! Is it time already?"

"Aye. Will's men are waiting for you at the back entrance to the palace. They'll hire you a wherry to take you to Queenhithe."

"And the Queen?" Astra asked nervously.

"Your notion to pretend sickness was brilliant. She thinks you are in bed with the ague. I've let on that it is catching, and I'll see to your needs myself. Even the servants will avoid the chamber where you are presumed to be resting."

"If I can only depart the palace without being seen . . ."

"Wrap up in your cloak and walk slowly. No one will guess that such a tattered, old garment conceals a beautiful young *demoiselle.* They'll think you're one of the washerwomen."

Astra nodded and took a deep breath. She'd never done anything like this before. Even when she met Richard in his tent, she'd had Alyce to guide the way. The idea of venturing out alone to meet Richard terrified her.

As Marguerite had predicted, no one paid the slightest attention to Astra as she left by the back entrance. She saw two soldiers waiting there and pulled back the hood of her cloak so they would recognize her. They settled her between them to escort her to the Kingsbridge quay. They helped her into a wherry, said a few words to the oarsman, then bowed and sent the small boat on its way.

Astra had traveled the Thames several times before, but she had never found it as unnerving as she did tonight. The dark water swirling around the boat made her stomach dip and sway. The wherry seemed pitifully small compared to the rain-swollen river. She clutched the edge of the boat tightly and struggled to keep the gorge from rising in her throat.

She stared at the riverbank to distract herself, seeing the city from a new perspective. It was nearly twilight, but the shapes of houses and buildings were still visible through the mist. Huge ships were anchored along the docks. Their masts rose up in a ghostly forest. As they passed the bend of the river, Astra saw open fields and gardens beyond the city, then the river edge grew crowded again with great warehouses for storing goods arriving from French ports as well as Genoa, Venice and the Baltic.

London Bridge loomed ahead—nineteen stone arches spanning the river from Bridge Street to Southwark. The current of the river grew faster. Astra held her breath as they sped down the formidable causeway. Abruptly, the oarsman steered the wherry toward shore and guided the boat to dock at a large quay.

"Queenhithe," he announced in a bored voice.

Astra gathered herself together and climbed unsteadily onto land. She searched the nearly deserted wharf for Richard. Panic engulfed her as she realized how alone and vulnerable she was. A shadowy form loomed up behind her, and she opened her mouth to scream in terror.

"Astra, beloved."

Shaking with relief, she allowed Richard to embrace

her. He smelled warm, sweaty and wonderfully, reassuringly male. As his hot, plundering mouth found hers, she almost forgot her resolution to resist him until they talked. Then his hands slid beneath her cloak. Astra pulled his fingers from her bodice laces and stepped back.

"Richard . . . I . . . I must talk to you."

"In due time, my love. First, we must find a warm, dry place."

She nodded. The mist had thickened; it covered everything with a fine, bone-chilling dampness. Richard took her arm and began to lead the way down the quay. Astra had to walk rapidly to keep up with his long, powerful strides. Several times she attempted to begin the conversation she wished to have; he insisted it could wait until they reached their destination.

"Where are you taking me?" she finally asked.

"Southwark."

Astra stopped walking. Her memories of the crude settlement on south bank of the Thames were very unpleasant.

"What's amiss?" he asked.

"Southwark is a place of sin and abomination. I don't want to go there."

"Please, Astra. You will be with me. I will protect you."

"But why must we go *there?* Certainly you know of its disgusting reputation."

"Disgusting, aye, but also private. No one from court will think to look for us."

Astra sighed and allowed Richard to take her arm again. She didn't relish the long walk over the bridge and the feeling of suffocation that afflicted her as the houses crowded in above them, shutting out the sky.

"Why didn't you have me take a wherry to Southwark? I am tired of walking."

"Shush, love. I could not risk you arriving in Southwark before me. I shudder to think of you in such a place alone."

His voice was tender, soothing. Astra decided not to argue. It made her sound like a peevish fishwife. That was hardly the way to win a man's favor, to entice him to propose.

As much as she dreaded Southwark, Astra was relieved when they reached the massive gate at the end of the bridge. As they walked the narrow passageway over the bridge, her breath clawed in her chest, as if she were smothering. They reached the street and she took a deep breath, then grimaced as the rank odors of Southwark filled her nose.

"Only a little further," Richard coaxed. "Then I have a surprise for you."

Astra nodded. Her legs ached and her feet felt pinched in her elegant slippers. At this rate, she would be too exhausted and irritable to care if Richard took her to bed. She was not even sure she any longer had the energy to hold him off until she convinced him of her plan.

She shivered as Richard led her down a narrow alleyway. It was nearly night. The quarter moon shone feebly through the fog, offering little light to guide their way. A cat yowled in the distance, sounding for a moment like a child screaming in pain. In the shadows near their feet, Astra heard rustling sounds and what she fancied were the squeaks of rats. She clutched Richard's arm fiercely and dug her nails into his thick muscles.

"Ayez pitie. Ayez pitie."

Astra screamed as a wraithlike creature appeared out of the mist. Swathed from head to foot in rags, it extended a clawlike hand toward them and begged in a rasping, foreign voice.

"Ayez pitie. Demoiselle? Monsieur?"

Richard tried to lead her past the creature. Astra hesitated. The moon broke through the mist, and she caught a glimpse of the phantom's face. It was a woman, not old. Her nose was gone; it left a horrible scar in the middle of what must have once been a lovely face. Her blue eyes were wild, ravaged. She might be wasting away with fever, or merely starving.

Astra pulled at Richard's arm. "Please, Richard, give her something."

"God's wounds, Astra! I cannot feed every leper in Southwark!"

"She's not a leper," Astra whispered. "Her nose has been cut off."

"Probably a whore who set up her customers to be robbed," Richard grumbled. He reached for his coin bag. "A wound like that is the mark of a thief."

"We should help her anyway. If she was a whore, who would want her now?"

"You'd be surprised," Richard said grimly as he pulled out a handful of pennies. He gave them to Astra. She offered them to the woman coaxingly, as if tempting an animal to eat. The woman regarded her warily, then reached out and grabbed the coins. She disappeared immediately into the mist.

"Jesu, Astra, you're too soft-hearted. You're going to beggar me."

"Thank you," Astra whispered. She felt warmer, knowing she had done God's work. The squalid alleyway seemed less threatening. She began to relax.

The moon disappeared. Astra heard voices inside the

buildings they passed—curses, laughter. She guessed they were behind a row of alehouses and cookshops. The smells grew more nauseating. A man threw a pail of something out a doorway ahead of them. Richard swore as they reached the spot and had to step over a mess of reeking fishheads and entrails.

"Sweet Maria, what a stink," Astra gasped.

"Only a little further."

Ahead of them, the shadows seemed to move and moan. Richard pulled her closer and shielded her with his body. Pressed against him, Astra felt herself relax just as the moonlight caught the form of a couple embracing against a building. Pale silver light reflected on naked skin, and Astra saw what the couple were doing. The woman's skirts were up to her waist, the man's bare buttocks bunched and thrust—in and out, in and out.

They passed the couple within inches, the man's raspy breathing harsh in their ears. Astra clung to Richard, feeling strange. It was repulsive, yet there was that odd, aching feeling between her legs. There was an emptiness there, as if she needed to be filled—filled with Richard, with the hot, leaping warm thing she had felt beneath his hose.

Richard's breathing beside her seemed harsher, more labored. She realized he was aroused, tantalized as she was. Her heartbeat quickened. She had been mad to think she could be alone with this man and be able to resist him.

"Here it is."

Astra gazed dubiously at the gloomy two-story building. There were no windows, no sign of light or comfort. Richard guided her to a wooden ladder, placing her hands on the rough sides.

"The back entrance. The other way is locked. No one will know we are here."

She let Richard boost her up, and began to climb. It was a struggle in her long skirt. She felt Richard behind her, ready to catch her if she fell. She guessed that her wriggling bottom was directly in his face. The thought made her blush.

She was sweating when she reached the top, her silk gloves full of splinters. She climbed onto the small landing there and stared in dismay at the small, crooked doorway. She was ready to swear at Richard, to rail at him for making her endure such torture to reach this crude place. Then he opened the door to the room and made her gasp with surprise.

It was a very pleasing room. A brazier glowed in the corner, and tall, gleaming candles illuminated the rest of the cozy space. A table with a pitcher and two pewter cups stood in one corner, a bed in the other. The bed was not large, but it was covered with a sumptuous silk coverlet of vivid purple.

"Are you hungry, Astra? I can have them bring food up."

Astra shook her head. She was hungry, but much too nervous to eat.

"The room is . . ." She did not know what to say. He had done this all for her. It was a gift, a splendid, romantic gift.

Richard suddenly seemed shy. She could not credit it, but he was. He seemed stiff when he walked to the table, completely unlike his usual graceful self. His hand shook visibly when he poured the wine.

Astra's stomach was full of butterflies. When she took the goblet of wine, she had to hold it against her body so she wouldn't spill it. She took a sip. It was fine and sweet, much like the wine served at the King's banquet table. It went down slowly, burning a fire to her belly. The blaze suffused her limbs and warmed her. A flush crept over her skin.

Richard watched her from across the room, and she saw for the first time how elegantly dressed he was. Velvet hose, soft calfskin boots, a scarlet satin tunic that laced up his broad chest—he looked more like a prince than a knight. Only the jeweled misericord at his waist and the scar on his cheek gave him away as a fighting man. She studied his face, the dark, intense eyes, the smooth high cheekbones, the soft, slightly fleshy mouth. He was beautiful as only a man could be. Beautiful and dangerous. He reminded her of a gleaming gold dagger, the gracefulness of its lines unmarred by the deadliness of its function.

"Take off your cloak, Astra."

She went to the table and put down the wine, then slipped off the ragged, dowdy cloak and laid it carefully on a stool by the fire. Richard was only a few feet away. His eyes moved over her body. The gown she wore was tight. It skimmed her hips, nipped in tightly at her waist and molded closely to her breasts. She'd worn it relatively unadorned, with only a slim silver girdle at her waist, delicate black silk gloves and a simple purple veil over her hair, held in place with a circlet of silver. She'd perspired on the way up the ladder, and the sheen of moisture on her skin made the dress cling more tightly than ever.

Richard's eyes moved to her face. Her whole body felt heavy, as if she were underwater.

"Your hair, Astra. I want to see your hair."

She turned away to hide the ridiculous trembling of her fingers. The circlet was easy to undo, but it caught on her gloves. She took them off and lay them carefully on top of her cloak, then removed her veil. Her hair was still tightly bound in braids twisted around her head. She began to undo them.

It was a tedious process, and it seemed to take a long time to finish. She looked up once. Richard's face was rapt, intent. His chest heaved slightly, as if he could not breathe properly.

Her hair tumbled down. She fanned her fingers through it and smoothed out the twists and crimps. Her hair had grown since she'd left the priory. It was nearly to her waist now, and it felt heavy, uncomfortable. It swirled around her shoulders like the waves of a frothy golden sea.

"Sweet God in heaven. You're beautiful beyond belief."

Astra looked away, overcome. There was such intimacy between them. A current of emotion seemed to flow through the very air in the room. This man had glimpsed her naked, but he was acting as if he had never seen her before. She trembled to think what it would be like when he kissed her. The thought prompted Astra to remember her purpose. She would not succumb to him without some assurance of her future.

"Richard—I must speak with you."

He walked to her slowly, smiling faintly. She could see the faint sheen of sweat on his brow, the wetness of his teeth between his parted lips. She could smell him.

When he was very close, he grasped a handful of her hair and brought it to his lips.

"Talk," he said.

Twenty-three

His body was so close, throbbing, hungry. His eyes were like deep, dark pools of desire. She wanted to drown in them. Instead, she pulled away from the edge.

"I heard you were a hero in Wales."

There was surprise in his eyes, then a flicker of something else—anger, bitterness.

"Aye. If you consider bloodshed heroic."

She gave him a questioning look. Richard's mouth twitched, then spread into a grim smile. "Oh, the King is well pleased with my work. The rumor is that he finally means to reward me with something more than empty words."

Astra took a deep breath; this was her chance. If her plan succeeded, Richard would at last have the land and power he desired. Then he could marry her!

She met Richard's eyes, smiling tremulously. "It is said the Queen is fond of me, and I know she has great influence over her husband's decisions. Perhaps if I went to the Queen and asked for her help, she would speak to Henry on your behalf."

Richard's voice was soft. "You would do that? You would solicit the Queen for my sake?"

"Of course, Richard. I love you. I would do anything for you, anything so we could be together."

He reached out slowly and took her face in his hands. "My sweet, darling Astra. How generous you are . . . and how innocent. Think you the King hands out castles every day?"

"I . . . I've been told he does, to his relatives at least. Why not to one of his loyal knights?"

Richard removed his hands, and his face grew hard. "Why? Because I'm no one. I have no fine family behind me, nor does the royal blood of Henry III or Eleanor of Provence flow in my veins."

Astra stepped back, startled by the bitterness in his voice. "But you said . . . you said the rumors . . ."

"They are rumors, nothing more. I don't believe for a moment Henry really means to award me property. It could be years before he decides I've earned anything beyond a fond pat on the head."

"But if I went to the Queen . . ."

Richard shook his head. "No. It's very kind of you to offer, Astra, but I won't have you groveling to Eleanor."

"I don't mind, Richard. I would do anything I could to help you."

"No! I don't trust the Queen, and I won't be beholden to her as well as Henry." He gave Astra a sharp, probing look. "I don't want you to become involved in court politics. The things I've done are bad enough; I won't have you reduced to the level of the rest of the she-vipers who surround the Queen."

"But I want to help you," Astra said in a frustrated voice. "Why won't you let me?"

"Have you considered, Astra, that my pride might be involved? I don't want a woman, any woman, to go begging for favors in my name!"

Astra stared him. Richard was surely the most exasperating man she'd ever met. "Does your pride matter more than our future? You've told me you won't wed me until you have a *demesne* of your own, yet you refuse to do all that you could to reach your goal of possessing property!"

Richard's dark eyes met hers fiercely. "If you knew the things I have already done to win Henry's favor . . . if you only knew . . ."

"I care not what you have done in battle. I want to know what you mean to do now, here in London, to gain Henry's goodwill."

Richard spoke through gritted teeth. "I will bide my time and hope that Henry doesn't send me off somewhere else to fight for him."

"No," Astra breathed softly. She looked down at the fresh rushes strewn on the floor. A cold dread moved in her veins. The thought of Richard being sent off to war again was nearly unbearable.

"Astra, I don't want to fight with you. I brought you here so we could be alone . . . so we could enjoy each other." She looked up. The fierceness had left Richard's face. His expression was tender as he moved toward her.

Astra felt her body responding to his nearness. If he gathered her into his arms, she would be lost. She took a step back. "Will you wed me before Henry sends you away?"

Richard's face softened even more. "I would if I could, but it is not possible. I have no land, no money, no prospects. I spent nearly my last penny on this room."

"But surely you have *some* material wealth. I saw the chest in your tent, the chess set, the jewels and weapons."

"Booty, aye, I have some booty from the wars I fought. But it's not enough to buy a decent piece of land, let alone pay to build a manor."

"There is the manor Lord Fitz Hugh will give me," Astra whispered hopefully.

"It could not support us in anything but modest comfort. I want you to have much more than that, beloved. Therefore, I cannot wed you until I amass my fortune."

"Yet you refuse to do all that you could to win the land and property you covet. You refuse to let me go to the Queen for help!"

Richard's jaw set in a hard line. "I've told you, I don't want you begging to that bitch."

"She's not a bitch! Eleanor's been nothing but kind and sweet to me."

"She's using you, Astra," Richard said coldly. "You're simply too naive to see it."

"And you're too stubborn and pigheaded to believe the human heart is capable of true affection."

"Perhaps," Richard said softly. "Although you've done much to change my mind in that matter." There was an amused glint in his eyes, a half-smile on his lips. "Beloved." His hands sought her waist, drawing her to him. "We did not come here to fight. We can discuss this later."

His lips brushed her hair; his arms embraced her possessively. Tears welled in Astra's eyes. He felt so warm and strong and safe. She wanted so much to give herself to this man. But she could not, not yet.

"No!" she cried, pushing his hands away. "I won't let you touch me! Not until I know you mean to wed me."

"Of course I will wed you. I want no other woman."

"When?"

"I've told you, lovey, when . . ."

". . . when you think you are wealthy enough," Astra finished. "Aye, you *have* told me." Her eyes met his scornfully, then she glanced away.

She stared at the lovely room. Richard had brought her here for one purpose and one purpose only. He meant to seduce her, to take her maidenhead without offering her the security of marriage. He obviously believed that she was so in thrall to his kisses and caresses that he could manipulate her at will. His arrogance made her furious.

"You are mistaken, Richard. I am not some cheap slut you can have with your smug smile and a soft bed. I won't sell myself for such a mean price."

Richard reached out to soothe her. Astra jerked back and raised her chin defiantly. "You told me once all women are whores. So be it. If you want to bed me so badly, you must meet my price. It will be marriage or nothing, Richard. If you care more for your stupid, vainglorious ambitions than me, you will have to sleep in your fancy, silk-covered bed by yourself!"

Richard stared at her a moment, then chuckled.

"Good God, you're a surprising little wench! I never knew you had such fire. It must be the hint of red in your hair that makes you so enticingly passionate. It is near rose-colored between your legs. Such an exquisite fiery shade that makes me want to . . ."

"Stop! You're lewd! Disgusting! Vile!"

Richard laughed. "There's no need to call me names. You're no saint either, Astra. You do flaunt your body. You wear tight gowns and use your lovely blue eyes and sweet smile to make men sigh for you." Richard reached out and gently stroked her cheek. "I know you want me as much as I want you. When I touch you, your skin grows hot and your mouth gets wet."

His hand moved down to caress her neck. A shiver rippled through her as his fingers sought the sensitive skin beneath her hair. "You cannot deceive me, Astra. I've sucked your luscious nipples, and I've tasted your sweet, lovely cupid's nest, and I know that you ache for me as badly as I do you. You wouldn't have come here otherwise."

Astra forced herself to look away from his dark, hypnotic gaze. If she gave in to him now, she would prove him right about herself . . . about women . . . about everything.

She faced him with determination. "It's clear I was mistaken about you," she pronounced coldly. "They told me you were a knave, a cheat and a whoremonger, but I didn't listen. I let myself be aroused by your bold kisses and indecent talk. I was too foolish to see you for what you really are."

Richard's seductive mask seemed to slip. His dark eyes narrowed with anger, and he began to pull off his tunic. "Then see me for what I really am, Astra. I'm a hot-blooded man with a thunderous ache in my balls. And I have something you want, Astra. Something big and hot and hard." His hands went to his hose. He jerked them down.

Mother of God! He was naked except for his boots and the velvet hose around his ankles. She tried not to look but found it impossible. His man thing jutted out like a post. It was brownish red, almost purplish. The hair around the base of it was black and silky. It was the most shocking thing she'd ever seen in her life. She raised her eyes to his.

"Take me home, Richard."

She saw him almost visibly deflate. The burning hunger in his eyes faded, to be replaced by anger. "No."

"I want to go back to Westminster. Please escort me."

"You'll have to find your way by yourself. I've already troubled myself enough on your account tonight."

She watched him pull up his hose and put his thing away. Carefully, she noted. Men took such care with their man things, treated them like precious babies. It was odd, considering the way they abused the rest of their bodies.

They stared at each other. Finally, Astra realized she had no choice. He obviously wasn't going to escort her back to Westminster, and she couldn't stay there. If she did, he'd surely try again to bed her. His man thing was like a weapon; he'd put it away for now, but he could still use it to threaten her later.

Slowly, carefully, she put herself back together. She couldn't do her hair by herself, so she twisted it up in a roll on the back of her head and pinned it. Then she put on her veil, the circlet, her gloves, and finally, the cloak.

He hadn't budged. He was standing by the brazier, as if he were cold. His face looked rather sad and boyish. She started to feel sorry for him, then realized what he was making her do. She would have to find her way out of Southwark. At night. Alone.

Gritting her teeth in fury, she walked to the door. Without looking back, she opened it and went out.

The small landing was swathed in mist. For a moment, she couldn't see at all. Then she gradually made out the ladder and climbed down shakily. Icy fear gripped her as soon as she reached the ground. A dark alley in Southwark had to be in one of the most dangerous, horrifying places in England, mayhaps even the world. It was smelly, rank and so dark she could see no more than a few paces. She heard familiar scurrying noises near her feet. She couldn't decide what she was more afraid of—furry, sharp-toothed rodent vermin, or the human kind of vermin.

She had to get out of the alleyway. The street might have other dangers, but it was better lit. It was madness to think of finding her way to the wharf. The best plan she could think of was to seek sanctuary in a church. Even the most hardened cleric wouldn't turn her away. It was an ancient tradition that criminals could find comfort and safety within the sacred walls of the holy church. Surely there was room there for an errant young woman as well.

It was so dark; she sensed an opening in the alleyway instead of seeing it. She could hear voices, the clink of cups. She must be near one of the alehouses. If only she could find the front.

A tall figure walked out of the mist ahead of her and blocked the way. Astra shrank back and tried to decide whether to scream. It was too late. Cold fingers covered her mouth, while another hand grabbed her shoulder.

"Don't scream, Astra."

Her whole body seemed to turn to pudding and slither into a puddle on the street. "Richard!" she cried as his hand left her mouth.

"I decided I couldn't let you risk it. I don't have the heart to leave my worst enemy alone on these streets—let alone a pathetic little mouse like you."

Astra's fear had deserted her, leaving in its place a hot, fevered rage that almost made her sick. "Slimy toad," she hissed at him.

He took her arm, and they began to walk toward the quay.

Richard smiled into the darkness. Having gotten over his initial anger, he was beginning to enjoy himself. His demure little angel had surprised him with her determination and nerve, but he found he rather liked her that way. It made Astra even more appealing to know she was not a hypocrite or a tease. She sincerely believed he had no right to her body until he wed her. She had stood up to him as boldly as any man. To know that she took her ideals seriously fired his admiration for her all the more.

They neared the docks, and the path grew foul and slippery with dampness. Richard tightened his grip. When Astra stiffened in response, his smile deepened. Women were like horses—the spirited ones always gave you a better ride. They might throw you off a few times, but when you finally mastered them, it was almost always worth the wait. He savored the thought; it would help keep him warm on the long, chilly journey back to Westminster.

Twenty-four

They said nothing else to each other on the way back to Westminster. When they arrived at the palace, Richard bowed, bidding Astra adieu as if they were the most casual of acquaintances.

Shaking with fatigue and cold, Astra slipped in by the back way and made her way to the chamber where she was presumed by the rest of the court to be sleeping. No brazier or lamp had been lit, and the room was dark and frosty cold. Her numb fingers struggled with her ruined gloves, then the laces to her gown. At last, still wearing her chemise and stockings, she climbed into the bed and pulled up the blankets and fur throw.

She wondered if she would ever be warm again. Her limbs were like icicles, and the pile of bedcovers did little to ease her shivering. She worried that she was ill, then realized that at least part of her uncontrollable shuddering was a reaction to the strain she had endured. On this night she had risked her reputation and likely her life. Worse yet, she had done it all for a miserable, ungrateful, lecherous fiend who did not have the decency to wed her!

Her anger returned, warming her slightly. She'd been mad to ignore the stories about Sir Reivers. Her own experiences should have taught her what a rogue he was. What kind of man spied on young women bathing in the woods? Or for that matter, what kind of man took a young maid out alone in London and sought to debauch her in a stinking sewer like Southwark? Richard was everything people said he was: a scoundrel, a philanderer, a fortune hunter.

Astra nursed her anger and indignation. Wallowing in the heat of her outrage helped drive away the anguish that lingered in the pit of her belly. If she weren't so furious, she'd be able to remember how alone she was, how cold and miserable. Even more frightening, she'd have to face the fact she had tried once before to forget Richard and failed. The thought galled her, haunted her, threatened her. Richard Reivers was a total louse, but she seemed to love him anyway.

Despair stalked her, and she turned her face to the dark, featureless wall of the tiny chamber and willed herself not to cry. The night had been long, and she was dreadfully tired. Very slowly, her body warmed, and her fevered thoughts eased. As the misty night crept toward the milky dawn, she nestled deeper into the soft blankets and slept.

She did not awaken until very late, stirring only when there was a commotion in the room. She opened her eyes and beheld the Queen herself looking down on her.

"Astra, my dear, can you hear me?"

Astra sat up abruptly, shocked to find Her Highness stroking her forehead.

"Your Grace!"

"Thank the heavens you are better. Your skin is cool; the fever must have broken in the night."

"You should not be here!"

"Nonsense, I have no fear of contagion. I have nursed my children through many ailments. Besides, Lady Marguerite has been seeing to you, and she has not taken ill."

"I . . . I . . ." Astra stammered, utterly flabbergasted by the Queen's concern.

"Lie back. You are still very pale. I'll have some gruel brought. Perhaps I should have the court physician look in on you later. He might need to bleed you."

"No, please!" Astra gasped. "I am much improved. In fact, I feel quite well!"

She struggled to sit up, endeavoring to look like a paragon of health. The Queen frowned, but did not press her to lie down again.

"You do appear more hearty than I expected. Perhaps you will be well enough to join us in the Great Hall tonight. I have some charming entertainment planned."

"That would be lovely. I look forward to it."

The Queen left. Astra sank back on the bed, near faint with relief. She had an absolute terror of physicians, and the sight of blood affected her distressingly. She intended to look surpassingly healthy by tonight, even if she had to paint her cheeks with rouge to manage it.

Astra had risen and dressed when a faint knock sounded at the door. Marguerite entered, her eyes bright. She closed the door tightly, then sat down on the bed.

"You must tell me everything, simply everything! Did he propose? Did you let him bed you?"

Astra flushed. Considering the events of last evening by the cool reason of daylight did not make her feel any better. Nay, she felt worse.

"I'm afraid it did not go exactly as planned. Richard and I quarreled most intemperately."

"Quarreled? Whatever did you quarrel about?"

"He will not wed me. He has a dozen excuses if he has one."

"And so, you did not let him bed you?"

Astra shook her head. "He was quite angry; in fact, he threatened to abandon me in Southwark in a fit of peevish temper."

"Southwark! Surely he did not!"

"No, he capitulated and brought me back to Westminster, else I likely would have perished in some filthy alley."

"Jesu, Astra, what a disaster!" Marguerite exclaimed. "I count myself partly responsible. I felt sure that Richard was enchanted with you, that he only needed a little nudge to succumb completely."

"You were wrong. Richard Reivers is the most stubborn man I have ever met. He says he will not wed me until he is wealthy, and I believe he means to stick by his words."

Astra sighed. Marguerite reached out to touch her cheek. "Poor sweeting. You truly love him, don't you?"

Astra stared miserably at her friend, then nodded. As much as she wanted to deny Marguerite's words, she could not. No matter what Richard did, no matter how he angered her, she could not change how she felt about him. He had stolen her heart, nay, her very soul. Without him, the world was a gray and cheerless place; she could scarce think of life without him.

"If you are certain of your feelings, Astra, I know exactly what we must do."

"What?"

Marguerite smiled enigmatically. "We shall make Richard marry you."

Astra gave her a startled look. "I thought . . . even you said my getting with child would be unwise."

"I have abandoned that plan. I have another." Marguerite smoothed the fur throw on the bed thoughtfully. "Do you know the story of the King's sister, Lady Eleanor, and Simon de Montfort?"

"I know they are wed."

"They *had* to wed. The King caught them in a compromising situation and forced de Monfort to marry Lady Eleanor. Henry is quite pious, and even though there was no child yet conceived, he would not allow his sister's honor to be tarnished."

"But I've heard they are devoted to each other."

"They are, my dear. In fact, there are those who think that the incident was all a ruse to get Henry to allow them to marry. They gambled that Henry would insist on the marriage even though he opposed giving his sister to de Monfort."

"What does this have to do with Richard and me?"

Marguerite smiled triumphantly. "We will also use Henry's sense of propriety to force a marriage."

"How?"

"You and Richard will be found in an improper situation. Although you are not related to the King, I know he feels great fondness toward you, that he cares for you like a daughter, or a sister. He will not allow Richard to abandon you if he believes Richard has dishonored you. The King will order Sir Reivers to wed you."

Astra could only stare at her friend. Even the fearsome Black Leopard could not deny the command of his liege lord. If the King did make such request, Richard would be well and truly trapped.

"Richard loves you," Marguerite continued. "His refusal to wed is nothing more than pigheadedness. Once the marriage is inevitable, he will accept that having you as his wife is truly his heart's desire."

Astra nodded. Richard had said he meant to marry her. All they would be doing is forcing him to act upon his words. Still, the scheme made her very uneasy. "We should speak to Will," she suggested. "He seems to have much insight into Richard's heart."

"There is no time. Will is in Thornbury visiting his family, and we must act quickly—before the King sends Richard back to Wales or some other godforsaken battlefield."

A chill went down Astra's spine. Richard had spoken of the King sending him away. When might that be? Tomorrow? Next week? If Richard went away to war, she might never see him again. Astra chewed her lip doubtfully. "If I were to agree to your plan, Marguerite, what exactly would we do?"

"First, you send Richard a message expressing consternation at the rift between the two of you. Suggest that you meet to talk. Then, when you and Richard are alone together, the trap is sprung."

"How?"

"Don't be dense, Astra; you seduce him, of course!"

"Seduce him? Why would I want to . . ."

"Relax, sweeting. It will only be pretend. A few kisses and caresses, your bodice and headdress found in *deshabille.* That will be enough to suggest Richard's intentions." Marguerite's smile broadened. "Someone comes looking for you. They find you in Richard's arms. He is pawing you, as he is wont to do anyway. The story of the scandal is reported to the King. He is outraged, determined to see Richard do right by the young maiden he has so callously dishonored. *Voila!* You have yourself a husband."

Astra shook her head. "Richard would be furious if I did such a thing. He has a great deal of pride; I am not sure he would ever forgive me if I tricked him into marriage."

"I know Richard will be outraged, but in truth, it serves him fairly. For years he has toyed with the hearts of young maidens; he deserves to get his comeuppance. Besides, I have no doubt you could convince him to forgive you. Once the two of you are wed, he will be able to indulge all his desires in your bed." Marguerite raised her brows suggestively. "I should imagine you would win him over in a matter of nights."

Astra felt herself being swayed. It took her breath away to think of herself in bed with Richard, finally able to sample the delights he had oft tempted her with. Her head swam with feverish, erotic images. Richard's handsome, enticing face pressed against her body. His mouth and fingers teasing, torturing and then satisfying her. The aching hollowness inside her filled with Richard's stirring, magical flesh.

She forced the delicious thoughts away. If she went through with Marguerite's plan, she would be deceiving the man she loved. Their marriage would begin with a lie. It was not right; it simply was not an honorable thing to do.

"I cannot do it. I appreciate your offer of help, Marguerite, but it would violate my conscience to trap Richard into marriage."

Marguerite's eyes narrowed. "Astra de Mortain! I am surprised at you. Have you no backbone at all? This man has cozened you and manipulated you shamefully. He dragged you off alone to Southwark and threatened to abandon you there. Richard Reivers deserves to be forced to marry you. You must prove you are not some cheap doxy he can use and then toss aside. You must let him know that you are a lady, a well-born woman who deserves better treatment!"

Astra sighed. Richard had treated her poorly. Although he rescued her in the end, she could not forget the long minutes she had endured in the darkened alleyway, imagining herself as helpless prey for the brutal predators of Southwark. Part of her was angry enough to seek revenge for that humiliation, but her conscience held her back. "No. It would not be right. I must think of some other means to convince Richard to marry me."

Marguerite stood up abruptly. "Have it your way, Astra. Continue to mope around the palace, longing for a man you could easily have if you put your mind to it. Rest assured that if I were in your situation, I would do whatever I could to see to it that the man I loved married me. But if you are too much of a coward . . ." She gave Astra a pitying glance, then quit the room.

Astra stared after her friend, anger and doubt warring in her breast. Was Marguerite right? Was she a coward for not taking a firmer stance with Richard? After all, he had compromised her; by rights he should make her his wife.

She sat down on the bed and considered the man who so tantalized and infuriated her. She was sure Richard loved her. It was only his odd ideas about women and marriage that held him back from asking for her hand. He seemed to think that he must be wealthy before taking a wife. Perhaps if he knew how little fine gowns and jewels meant to her, how modest her needs really were—perhaps then he would change his mind.

A sense of resolution filled her as she stood and adjusted her bliaut. She would meet Richard and plead with him. This time she could not let anger muddle her thoughts and force childish ultimatums from her lips. She would explain how much she loved him. She would tell him that she wanted to give herself to him, but she loved him too much to demean them both by becoming his mistress. Richard might be cynical and worldly, but she did not think he was so hard-hearted that he would refuse her argument. She would appeal to his sense of honor, his passionate pride.

A soft smile curved her lips. Marguerite believed that seduction and trickery were the way to win a man's heart; how surprised she would be to find that persuasion and honest sentiments could work as well.

Twenty-five

He would never understand women, Richard decided as he attended to the heaping trencher in front of him. He could have sworn Astra was furious with him, so angry she would not speak to him for days, and then only if he coaxed her with fond words and wistful smiles. Then, this morning, she had sent him a message saying she regretted her harsh words and wished to meet him alone in the Queen's chapel after dinner.

He glanced around the hall, searching for a glimpse of her, then turned back to his food. The chapel—it was hardly a likely choice for a romantic tryst, although perhaps that was the point. Mayhap Astra had in mind a tearful reconciliation, followed by another discussion of their future together.

Richard grimaced. They were clearly at an impasse on the subject. He would not wed Astra, nay, could not, until he felt more secure in his future. And obviously, if he would not wed her, she would not bed him. Given that, there seemed little point in their meeting.

He almost dreaded seeing her again. Astra's very presence enflamed him so painfully he could not trust himself to be alone with her. He had been on the verge of losing control and ravishing her several times already. If he continued to see her alone, he was likely to stumble into the abyss of his passion and not come to himself again until he was buried deep between her virgin thighs.

He shifted uncomfortably on the bench, his body reacting instantly to the image in his mind. God's blood, he was in a sorry state if the mere thought of Astra gave him a stiff one! He could only hope that the peaceful, holy setting of the chapel would quell his lust so that he could keep his hands to himself.

The meal was finished by the time he spied Astra at a table near the doorway. She looked unaccountably pale, he thought, although perhaps it was her gown. It was a deeper color than she usually wore—almost blood red. He had a rapid vision of Astra's beautiful breasts spilling from the bodice, her fair skin contrasting dramatically with the deep color. He mopped at his forehead with his sleeve. If he did not get some satisfaction soon, he was likely to slip into madness.

The entertainment that evening was a troupe of brightly-dressed youths who performed daring feats with knives. As the court watched with bated breath, one man flung knife after knife at a winsome young woman, the deadly blades coming so close they impaled strands of her hair and the filmy costume she wore. Ordinarily Richard would be interested in such an amazing display of marksmanship, but tonight he had other things on his mind. He glanced at Astra repeatedly, waiting for her to rise and leave the hall. When she made no move to do so, he wondered if she were so enchanted by the knife throwers she had forgotten their assignation.

The entertainment continued. One man had himself bound to a circular board that rotated like a wheel. The board was raised upright, and as the bound man spun around, the other man flung knives at his whirling form.

There were gasps and exclamations of fear from those watching, but when the spinning board came to a stop, it was seen that the man was unhurt. The knives had all struck between his outstretched arms and legs.

Richard looked again for Astra. She was not there. He felt a twinge of embarrassment that his attention had been diverted by the knife thrower but also relief that she had finally left. He would wait a few moments and slip away himself.

The troupe prepared for their most impressive feat. The knives were dipped in pitch, then set aflame. The hall echoed with cheers of excitement as the young woman took her place against a battered wooden board and prepared to face the blazing implements. Richard rose slowly, his eyes scanning the enrapt crowd. They would never even see him leave. He padded stealthily from the hall, casting one backwards look to see the first flaming knife sail across the room and miss the woman's hair by inches.

The royal complex was quiet, the air still and ominous. Richard walked through the filmy darkness. The only sound was his own footsteps echoing on the stonework and the thud of his misericord against his hip. Ahead, the elegant shape of the tall stained glass windows in the Queen's chapel beckoned.

The chapel was quiet. Richard wondered if Astra had arrived yet. He expected to find her praying, kneeling at the rail before the altar. She was not there. He walked slowly into the dimly lit chamber. Candles flickered in recesses set along the wall.

"Richard?"

She stepped forward from the shadows. Her face was pale. He walked to her and took her ice cold hand.

"What is it that could not wait, *demoiselle?* Did you

fear I would disappear before you had a chance to torment me again?"

"Richard . . . I . . . I must apologize."

"For what, beloved? Calling me a slimy toad?"

"I did not mean that! I was angry."

"So you were," he agreed, his voice becoming more sober. "You were very angry at me."

He pulled her closer to a flickering candle so he could see her face. She looked tense, strained, but still surpassingly beautiful. His eyes lingered over the pure, delicate line of her cheeks, the wide-set blue eyes, the softness of her small mouth.

He wanted to kiss her. He restrained himself. Grasping her other hand, he twined his fingers with hers, using the distraction of her small, chilled fingers to keep his hands occupied.

"I'm sorry, beloved. Nothing has changed. Your anger has altered nothing. I still cannot wed you." His voice faltered slightly on the last words. He hated to hurt her, but he was unwilling to lie. He would not promise her marriage in order to gain her bed.

"Richard, please. Listen to me. Your plans to win a title and wealth—they are not necessary. I would marry you even if you were a beggar."

He sighed. They were back to this same tired argument. "Beloved, I don't question your convictions, only your lack of experience." He gripped her hands more tightly. "Sweet Astra. Don't you realize how cruel and bitter life can be? Beggars make poor husbands." He released one of her hands and reached up to touch her petal-soft cheek. "Even your extraordinary beauty would vanish in a year on the London streets."

"I don't care," she said stubbornly.

"I care. I won't see you ruined because of me."

"Ruined?" She drew away from him, and he saw the flash of anger in her eyes, the evidence of her charming fiery temper. "I am ruined already. You have seduced me, compromised me, cozened me shamelessly. And now you have the audacity to speak of marriage as being my ruin!"

"Astra, dearest, I did not mean . . ."

He saw her draw a deep breath, as if fighting to restrain her anger. When next she spoke, her voice was calm and deliberate. "Have you no sense of honor, Richard? Of common decency?"

He stared at her, longing near choking him. How could he explain his terror of marriage without burdening Astra with the misery of his past? It was hopeless. She would never begin to understand—unless he told her about his mother, his boyhood, the taunts. . . . He closed his eyes. No. He could not bear to shatter her pretty illusions about him, about the world they lived in.

"I don't want to fight with you, Astra," he said wearily. He opened his eyes and released her other hand. "There is no purpose to this conversation. I will not change my mind." He gave her a sad smile and turned to go.

"Wait!"

He hesitated. There was something desperate in the way Astra looked at him. She could not guess how fragile his control was. Once he went to her and held her warm flesh, his mastery of his lust would weaken, the ferocity of his need overtake him. "Astra, I am sorry." He turned away again.

"Please, Richard, don't leave me!"

He groaned aloud, then whirled and pulled her into his arms. She felt soft and warm, her mouth eager and wet. His hand traced the line of her slim neck, then eased down to undo the laces of her bodice. He sighed into her mouth as his hands found bare flesh. He rubbed his palms over her torrid, swollen nipples, enflamed by the evidence of her desire, then pressed his aching groin hard against her stomach.

Blind, raging hunger filled him. He maneuvered her to the wall and braced her against it. Astra moaned, a sound of both longing and fear. He pulled away and looked at her, drinking in her stark, dramatic eyes, her rosy, swollen mouth, her magnificent breasts glowing like alabaster in the pale light. Desire danced along his body like a shimmering flame, and he lunged forward, his body finding hers like an arrow meeting a target.

"Wait," Astra cried. He met her eyes. They were huge, wild. In their enigmatic depths he could see the flicker of the candles all around them. The flames seemed to dance, as if from a sudden draft. In the next instant, he heard sounds behind him. Startled, he released Astra and stepped back.

"Sir Reivers, I would have a word with you."

It was the voice of his monarch, his liege lord, the anointed King of England. Richard turned and dropped to his knees.

"I have heard of your reputation with women, Reivers, but I did not credit it. I thought it was a scurrilous exaggeration put forth by your jealous comrades. But it seems it is true. You are a lecher, a villain, a scoundrel."

"Aye, Your Grace," he muttered tonelessly.

"I won't abide it, Reivers." The King's voice was clipped, controlled. "I won't abide it—not even in one of my finest, bravest knights. You will mend your ways. You will leave the maids alone."

"Aye, Your Grace."

"From now on, Reivers, you will seek your satisfaction in your marriage bed. Forthwith, I command you to take Lady Astra as your wife. Since you have seen fit to sample her charms already, I see no reason to delay the wedding. You will both present yourselves in the Painted Chamber tomorrow, three hours past sext, to exchange vows."

Richard closed his eyes. He heard the King depart, and with him the whispering courtiers who had followed him to the chapel. There was another sound behind him, and he realized Astra still stood there, waiting.

He rose stiffly, his mind a jumble of thoughts and reactions. Then the truth came to him with agonizing clarity. Astra—she had enticed him to the chapel, had begged and pleaded with him to marry her. Then, to make sure she got her way, she had arranged this little scene for the King's benefit.

The numbness faded, and a violent, blazing rage filled him. He turned toward Astra, not daring to look at her. "Get out of here, damn you!" he muttered.

There was a scuffling sound as she raced out of the chapel. The last echoes of her footfalls died away, and he let out a deep breath. He turned and gazed at the spot where Astra had recently stood, her back pressed against the rough stonework, her eyes wide with longing and dread. And guilt—her face had been full of it.

His hands clenched into fists. He could hardly believe it. His sweet angel had deliberately tricked him. She had lured him to the chapel and seduced him. She had asked to meet him there alone, then tempted him with her irresistible body. When he had tried to escape her, she had called him back and urged him to incriminate himself even further.

He glanced down at his disheveled clothes, then pictured Astra with her bodice undone. No wonder the King had been so angry. He had been on the verge of deflowering a virgin, here, within the sacred walls of a chapel. The King could not know that Astra had plotted the whole thing; that she was as guilty as Eve.

Richard's lips curled into a snarl. He had thought Astra was an angel, and she had turned out to be a demon instead, a starry-eyed, sweet-faced succubus. She had stolen his soul, then sold it to that devil of a king. She had made him out a fool, a dupe, a witless pawn. And there was naught he could do about it. Henry had commanded that he wed, and unless he wished to flee the country instead, he would be forced to marry the woman who had done this to him.

Briefly, he toyed with the notion of going to Paris and offering himself to Louis, hiring himself out as a mercenary to the French King. He discarded the thought in disgust. If he went to France now, he would be considered a traitor, an outlaw. It would be *he* who was asking a boon of the French king, not the other way around. He had not yet sunk so low that he would put himself in such a humiliating position.

No, better to marry Astra, to placate Henry. It should not be so difficult. After all, until a few moments ago, he had wanted to wed her. God knew, he would likely still be able to muster some desire for her. His traitorous body continued to crave Astra's flesh even if his heart felt naught for her.

But that was not true. He did feel something—a searing hatred. All the love and tenderness had died, leaving a cold, black loathing. All the better to wed her. Then he would have the means to make her pay for what she had done. He would turn her passion against her. He would use it to shame her, to humiliate her.

Richard turned toward the doorway. A slow smile curled his lips while the rest of his features darkened with a look of cold-hearted vengeance.

Astra raced down the palace hallway. The blood pounded in her temples; her breath came in great heaving gasps. But even as she ran, she knew there was no escape. The horror of the scene in the chapel followed her.

She reached the door of her bedchamber and leaned against it heavily. Terrible visions danced before her eyes: King Henry staring at her exposed breasts, his face slack with shock, Richard kneeling as the King berated him, Richard standing, his hands clenched in anger as he ordered her away.

He blamed her; Richard thought she planned for the King to find them. He thought she had deliberately entrapped him. How could he think such a thing of her? Except . . . except, she had very nearly done it, hadn't she? She had considered tricking Richard into marriage, had contemplated it very seriously during her discussion with Marguerite. Who was to say that a part of her had not intended for it to happen? Why else had she called him back when he tried to leave her? Why else had she allowed him to undo her clothes and and all but consummate their passion against the chapel wall?

Astra rested her cheek on the cool wood of the door, feeling sick. She had destroyed things with Richard; he might marry her, but things would never be the same between them. He would always believe that she had tricked him, that she had humiliated him before the King.

The King? Astra straightened. How exactly had the King come to be there? Had Marguerite. . . . *Sweet Jesu,*

Marguerite must have brought the King to the chapel! For a moment, anger replaced Astra's despair. How could her friend have gone against her wishes so callously? How could Marguerite have been so cruel?

A noise from inside the room startled Astra from her thoughts. She opened the bedchamber door and went in. Marguerite was sitting on the bed, braiding her hair. For a moment Astra gazed at her; then she let loose with her fury.

"Dear God, Marguerite, how could you do such a thing?"

Marguerite gave her a baffled look. "Do what, Astra?"

"Bring the King to spy on us."

"The King? Spy on you? I don't know what you mean."

"Of course you do!" Astra advanced toward the bed. "You couldn't accept the fact that I didn't want to trick Richard, so you found out I was meeting him alone in the chapel and sent the King after us anyway. I have to congratulate you, Marguerite. Your plan worked exceedingly well. The King did order Richard to marry me. I now have the husband I always wanted—the only trouble is that he hates me!"

Saying the words out loud undid her. Astra began to cry. When Marguerite came to comfort her, Astra found that her grief was greater than her rage. She collapsed into her friend's arms.

"There, there," Marguerite soothed. "It can't be so bad as that. I don't know what happened—no matter what you think—but it is surely not so awful as you suggest. Sit down. Compose yourself and tell me everything."

Astra looked up through her tears. "You don't know what happened? Truly?"

Marguerite shook her head. "How could I? I've been in

this room all evening. My meal did not sit well on my stomach. I left the hall nearly as you did."

"Sweet Maria! That means . . ." Astra swallowed a sob. "Who could have done it? Why would the King come looking for us?"

"Really, Astra, you're speaking in riddles. Start at the beginning."

Astra took a deep breath. She related her plan to talk to Richard, her decision to meet in the chapel where she thought he would be less likely to become amorous. She described their conversation and how it became an argument, how Richard had started to walk away. . . . "And I called him back, Marguerite. That is the worst of it. I couldn't let well enough alone. I *wanted* him to kiss me, to hold me—even knowing what might happen!"

"And what did happen?"

Astra took another deep breath. "First he kissed me. Then he undid my bodice. He pushed me against the wall. I stood there, watching him. He pulled me into his arms. I could feel him." She closed her eyes at the memory. "He was actually going to . . . to . . ."

"And that's when the King found you?"

Astra nodded. "I saw him first. I called out. Richard pulled away just as the King spoke." She bit her lips, choking back another sob. "Henry was livid. He chastised Richard, then he ordered him to marry me."

Astra's desperate eyes met Marguerite's. "I was so shocked, I didn't say a thing. After Henry left, Richard shouted for me to go away. I knew then that he thought I had planned the whole thing."

"Well." Marguerite's voice was matter-of-fact. "I must say I am astounded. The scheme worked beautifully. Of course," she added as Astra's eyes again lit with accusation. "I did not urge the King to follow you to the chapel. That was a bit much. Whoever involved His Majesty likely had a different result in mind than what actually occurred."

"What do you mean?"

Marguerite gave her a thoughtful look. "Isabel. I overheard her a few days ago suggesting that the Queen might be interested in what Lady Astra and Richard Reivers did when they were alone together."

Astra leaned back against the bedpost. "She wanted to shame me."

"No doubt. Instead, she lost Richard forever. It's rather ironic, isn't it?"

"What about Richard?" Astra asked morosely. "He hates me. He believes I betrayed him, betrayed us."

Marguerite shrugged. "Tell him that it was all a mistake; that you never intended to entrap him."

"He'll never believe me," Astra breathed. "I'm not sure I even believe it myself. There was a moment there, when the King said we would wed immediately . . . I felt happy, relieved." She shook her head. "I was willing to sacrifice Richard for my own ends. I am guilty, Marguerite, nearly as guilty as he believes me to be."

Marguerite put her arm around Astra. "Don't fret, sweeting. Richard's temper is a fleeting thing. His mood will pass, and then he will remember that he loves you."

Astra sighed. "I think not. I have hurt him too badly."

"Hurt him? How have you hurt him? The King did not cast him into disgrace; his career is not ruined."

"I have proven him right about women, about me."

"Nonsense," Marguerite said briskly. "Deceit has always played a part in the pastime of love. We tell the men that we do not desire them, that we have no interest in their caresses. They tell us that they do not wish to wed, that they have no hearts to break. We both lie. It is a frolic, a game."

Astra shook her head morosely. She did not think Marguerite understood. If love were only a game, perhaps that was worse. For Richard, she knew, hated to lose at anything.

Twenty-six

The gown hanging from the wardrobe was beautiful. Cloth of gold shot with threads of silver—Astra had never seen the like. It amazed her that the Queen had offered it to her for a wedding dress. But then, everything the Queen had done today was amazing. She had hovered around Astra since the morn. She offered to loan her things, fussed over her hair and waited on her as if she were the maid and Astra the queen.

It was all for naught, Astra thought grimly. Even the Queen could not help her shake the despair that clung to her like a noxious mist. It made her eyes burn with tears, her throat feel so achy and full she could not eat or scarce talk. It was her wedding day, but she felt as if she were preparing for a funeral.

She had not seen Richard, nor heard anything from him. While Marguerite and the Queen assured her that tradition did not permit the groom to see his bride until the wedding, Astra knew what Richard's silence meant. He had not forgiven her. He hated her. She had seen the look on his face when he ordered her from the chapel. It was a look of shock, of betrayal, of utter loathing.

Astra sighed and reached out to stroke the lovely gown. She had been afraid to touch it before this, for fear she would stain it with her tears. It seemed as if she had cried the whole night through. Finally her tears were spent.

She turned as Marguerite entered the room. Marguerite's bright smile faded as she saw Astra's face. "Astra, you must lie down! There are only a few hours until the ceremony, and you look most fatigued."

Astra nodded numbly and allowed Marguerite to help her into the bed. They were in the bedchamber where she had feigned sickness. It felt familiar, safe. She wished she need never leave it.

"It's all arranged," Marguerite went on with a kind of frantic cheerfulness. "The Queen insists you must have a private bedchamber for your wedding night. I don't know which baron or earl she expelled from it, but the room she's chosen is exquisite. She's there now, seeing to all the little romantic details. You would think it was her wedding night, the way she carries on."

"The Queen has been most kind," Astra responded in a weak voice.

"Of course. She wants you to know that she does not blame you for what happened. She told me she feels guilty for not looking after you more. I think everyone realizes now exactly what sort of man Richard is. The very idea of ravishing a young woman in a chapel!"

"If you recall, Marguerite, you once encouraged me to seduce Richard."

"Well, I may have suggested something along those lines, but I never dreamed he'd go so far." Marguerite lowered her voice to a husky, conspiratorial whisper. "The gossip is that he had your gown down to your waist, his prick in his hand, and he was backing you up to the wall."

Astra shook her head wretchedly. "Jesu, Marguerite! How can you listen to such vile gossip?"

"Well, even you said the man was a beast! Of course," Marguerite continued, her eyes glittering. "That may not be such mischance tonight when he finally takes you to bed. You must tell me all about it, Astra, every naughty little detail!"

"He may not have the heart to touch me after what I've done to him. I will be surprised if he even speaks to me."

Marguerite shook her head. "Richard may punish you with silence, but he dare not fail to touch you. There must be proof of consummation on the morn. The bedsheet must be bloodied, or it will go worse than ever with Richard. If the King thinks Richard has taken your maidenhead already, he will truly be wroth."

"Dear God," Astra whispered. The disaster seemed to worsen minute by minute, her private shame becoming more public every passing hour. She had not thought that Richard would be duty-bound to consummate the marriage. The idea horrified her.

"There now, I'll let you rest. The bells have just rung for sext, so it will not be long now." Marguerite let herself quietly out of the room.

Astra lay back on the bed with a groan. She wondered if she could refuse to attend the wedding. Perhaps she could pretend the ague again, or simply die of shame in the next few hours. At the moment, death seemed a pleasant alternative.

She shuddered as she thought of facing Richard alone in a sumptuous bedchamber. A mere day ago she would have been aroused by the thought; now she was filled with dread. Would he rage at her? Threaten her? She did not think Richard would dare do her physical harm, but there were doubtedly other ways he could make her suffer. She gripped herself in fear, imagining what it would be like to be alone in the dark with the enraged Black Leopard, more beast than man. She imagined his eyes glowing black as midnight; his dusky skin flushed with the fever of his hatred.

Astra climbed out of bed, knelt beside it and began to pray.

An angel—curse his rotten mind for ever conceiving such a thing! She was an evil temptress in the guise of a goddess. Her radiant countenance masked a witch's soul. Her exquisite flesh overlay a heart as black as sin.

He had intended not even to glance at her, but how could he avoid it? She fair glowed like the sun in that miraculous gown. It matched her hair, almost. The fabric was a trifle less roseate than her long wavy tresses. Still, the effect was the same, a golden gown for a golden-haired wench. He thought of Stroket's remark about a gold-plated pussy and scowled. He would not think of her that way, not now. He would contain his lust until he could use it to humiliate her. It would not be long. Their vows would be over soon, and then the banquet. At last he would be alone with her, and he could punish her as he had fantasized all night of doing.

She guessed what he intended, at least part of it. Every time he looked at her, she trembled. The rest of the wedding party probably thought she had a touch of maidenly nerves. He knew better; she was quaking in fear at the thought of facing him.

Good. He wanted her afraid, wanted her to worry and agonize and suffer over what he intended to do. It would make her weak and pliable, meek and submissive. She would agree to anything; she would grovel; she would weep.

No, he wouldn't allow her to cry. Her tears distressed him and might actually weaken his resolve. It would be too easy to cause her that sort of pain. What he had in mind was a more exquisite form of torture. He would turn her passion against her. He would show her for the whore she was.

The witnesses and the King and Queen were arriving, the priest following after them. Without looking at Astra again, Richard took her hand. It was as cold and rigid as that of a corpse.

Black and silver—he'd worn naught but black and silver. It made him look like he was in mourning, but it suited him too. Her bridegroom looked like the Prince of Darkness in his plush black velvet hose and tunic ornamented with silver embroidery. It set off his sleek dark hair and eyes and made him seem even more like a lithe, graceful, dazzling beast of prey.

Astra could not help shivering as he took her hand. It was warm and hard, the palm ridged with calluses from holding reins and weapons. She could recall those rough, blunt fingers touching her, caressing her most tender parts. Now he gripped her firmly, impersonally.

He scarcely looked at her; the exquisite gown was wasted on him. He would never notice how perfectly it fitted her, how closely the color matched her hair. All the women had commented on it, oh'ing and ah'ing over how she looked as if she were dipped in liquid gold. She thought her face looked comely too. They had bathed her in rosewater, then rubbed her skin with silky cloths until the color came back to her cheeks. Her swollen eyes they had treated with hazel water and leeks, easing away the puffiness and redness until her blue eyes sparkled like sapphires.

She wore her hair long and loose, swirling over her shoulders in a silken veil just a shade lighter and more red than the fabric of the dress. Fastened only with a circlet of diamonds the Queen had loaned her, her unbound hair proclaimed her status as a virgin bride. The thought of it distressed her. She was a virgin, aye, but only barely. Richard had known much of her already. She had allowed this man scandalous intimacies. And yet, he was a stranger now, a grim, distant stranger. The teasing laughter in his eyes was gone; the dazzling smile had vanished. She was wedding a hardened warrior, a deadly, dangerous man.

The thought made her knees go weak. Without thinking, she grasped Richard's hand more tightly and leaned against him so she would not falter.

God's wounds! Was she going to faint? She was gripping his hand for dear life, and he moved closer to her when she swayed slightly. He could feel the heat of her body against his, the softness of it. She was a small woman, for all the voluptuousness of her form. Something about her made him feel protective, tender.

Damn! He would not allow her to make him feel sorry for her. She was a wicked, scheming bitch. If she could not stand, let her fall on her conniving little face.

He moved away from her, bracing his arm so she could not lean against him. She turned and gazed at him, her eyes full of sorrow. He met them with all the cold bitterness he felt, and she glanced away quickly, looking stricken.

Still, her shoulders straightened, her neck stiffened. She would not humiliate herself by swooning during the wedding ceremony.

The priest said his words, they answered. Astra's voice was clear and soft, his own virtually emotionless. It was time to kiss her. He turned toward her. She lifted her face up, looking like a lovely flower seeking the sun. He found her small lips and thrust his tongue in brutally, kissing her with a hungry savagery that drew shocked laughter from the people behind them and made the priest clear his throat.

There was a tap on his shoulder. Richard drew his mouth away from Astra's and turned to see the King staring at him ominously.

"There will be time for that, Reivers. I think you have scandalized the Court sufficiently as it is."

She could hardly keep from crying. There had been no hint of love in Richard's kiss, no affection or respect either. He had shown everyone watching that she was his chattel, his possession, the vessel for his seed. It made everything that had already passed between them seem disgusting and base.

It was so hard to smile, to accept the kisses and congratulations from the people gathered in the Painted Chamber. It was worse still after they went to the King's Hall for the wedding feast. She and Richard had been seated on the dais by the King and Queen. All eyes were upon them. She knew they were commenting on Richard's coldness, the almost vengeful way he heaped the food on her side of the trencher and, with a sneer, urged her to eat. She forced down some of the roast peacock and quail pie, then pushed the food away. Her head throbbed. She could not see how she would endure the rest of the evening—let alone the night.

"Richard!—you look devastating. I cannot tell you what a beautiful pair you and Astra make."

He looked up, smiling numbly at the next well-wisher. Then he saw who it was, and his smile turned slowly to a jeer.

"Beautiful pair indeed!" He glanced across the room to where his new wife was chatting with the Queen. "Astra and I are yoked together in eternal misery. I suspect I have you to thank for that, Lady Marguerite."

"Me?" she exclaimed innocently. "Whatever are you speaking of?"

Richard brought his face close to Marguerite's, as if he were going to kiss her. But his voice was menacing and bitter.

"I can't think that this scheme was all Astra's doing. She had to have help. Where else would she turn but her closest friend?"

"You know that you were destined to wed Astra," Marguerite answered, unperturbed. "If you could forget your foolish pride for a moment, you'd realize you've been blessed as few men ever are."

"Blessed? And why might that be, Marguerite? Because I've wed a woman as fair as an angel?"

"Aye, and as good-hearted and kind as well. Astra is a rare jewel, Richard. I've worried for a long time that you aren't good enough for her. I hope you prove me wrong."

"Good enough!" he snarled. "The lying slut is worth

no more than a quick tumble. She has no money, no dowry, nothing to make her worthy of being my wife."

"Nevertheless, she is your wife now," Marguerite answered coldly. "I advise you to treat her with respect."

"Or else what? What will you do to me?"

Marguerite shrugged and started to walk away.

"By the by," Richard called after her. "Will should be back soon, and I intend to tell him what you've done."

Marguerite stiffened. "Leave Will out of this. He and I are friends."

He laughed. "I thank God Will is immune to your fiendish charms. Imagine, not being susceptible to the wicked lure of women. It almost makes me envy him."

Marguerite gave him a long, cold stare and walked away.

He turned back to his wine cup. He seldom drank to excess, but tonight was different. The wine seemed to heighten his anger, honing it to a fine bitter edge. By the time he took Astra to bed, he would be well gone in his cups. No inhibitions or doubts would trouble him or swerve him from his intended purpose.

Astra returned to the table. He regarded her with appraising eyes. The color was back in her cheeks, warming her flawless creamy skin. He watched her breasts rise and fall rhythmically beneath the snug, bright gown. Then he turned to her and placed his hand on her lap beneath the table. He felt her tense as his fingers found the juncture of her thighs. He rested his hand there lightly. She did not move. He began to stroke and caress her. Her breathing quickened and the flush in her cheeks deepened.

He leaned over, forcing her eyes to meet his. Her bright blue eyes wavered and danced with shame, with hunger. He smiled. He was growing hard. He was ready.

* * *

She prayed silently in the quiet room. If she concentrated, she could almost forget the sensation of Richard's hand fondling her beneath the table at the banquet. There had been such threat in the way he touched her, such controlled hostility. She shuddered.

Thank heavens the women had finally come for her and led her away to prepare for the marriage bed. For all their giggling and sly remarks, there was something comforting in the way the women had cared for her. They had gently removed her bridal gown, then dressed her in a delicately embroidered nightdress. After brushing and carefully arranging her hair, they gave her another goblet of wine to drink—to steady her nerves, they said. Then they helped her into the massive canopied bed and left her to wait for her bridegroom.

It was a beautiful room. The walls were covered in finely carved wainscoting. Flowers, vines and scrolls danced in the soft light from the bronze candelabras. The upper walls were a fine, cool blue that matched the carpet on the floor. Around the large, square room, chests and aumbries had been placed for storage. The huge bed was a work of art. Each post was intricately carved into a design of writhing beasts. Lying under the ornate scarlet and blue canopy, Astra could make out the forms of dragons, wyverns, and serpents on the massive supports.

She moistened her lips, tasting the wine. It had helped to relax her. She felt almost sleepy. The terrible dread was gone, and she had at last gained some mastery over her emotions. Richard would punish her, she knew that, but perhaps when it was over, he would be able to forgive her. She could not help clinging to that frail hope. It did not seem possible that what Richard had felt for her could turn entirely into hate. There must be some faint ember of love left. She would find that spark and nurture it. She would endure whatever punishment he chose to mete out. She would be calm, patient, forbearing. She would wear down his hatred with the force of her love.

A sense of determination filled her. Christ had taught that it was blessed to turn the other cheek, to meet cruelty with kindness, hatred with love. She would follow the Blessed Savior's example. Her love for Richard was surely stronger than his anger. She would prove it to him. Closing her eyes, she willed the lingering tension in her limbs to ease.

She must have dozed. The candles had burned low; they flickered from an unseen draft. She was cold; the chill night air easily permeated her thin lawn gown. She sat up slowly and wondered if the brazier had gone out. She slid to the edge of the enormous bed and peered out from the curtained space.

Her husband sat in a high-backed chair across the room, watching her.

Twenty-seven

She froze. They stared at each other. His eyes seemed sleepy, languid. Even from across the room, she could smell the wine on his breath. She suspected he was drunk.

"Come here."

Nervously, she obeyed him. He still wore his wedding attire, but it looked rumpled and soiled. Up close, the warm smell of sweat mingled with the wine. He watched her coolly, eyeing the delicate white gown with a look of disgust. "Take it off," he ordered.

She hesitated. His eyes met hers. "I've seen you naked before. I wish to do so again."

She slipped the gown over her head and let it fall to the floor in a ripple of white.

"I'd rather you wore nothing to bed. Nay, let me amend that. I'd rather you wore nothing when you are in my presence. I want to enjoy what I've paid so dearly for."

His words were bitter. She looked away, waiting for him to broach the subject of her betrayal.

"Come closer."

She approached until she was merely an arm's length away. He was wearing gloves. Somehow that made her feel even more vulnerable. His eyes ran over her, inch by inch. They settled on the place where her thighs met her body and lingered there. She shivered, although she was no longer cold.

"Turn around."

She knew exactly where his eyes focused. The thought of it made her bottom itch. She flinched when he touched her. His leather-clad finger rubbed beneath her buttocks, then threatened to poke between her legs. She held her breath, feeling like a prize bull being inspected at market.

"Turn around again. Lift up your breasts. Show them to me."

Her fingers shook. His eyes watched, burning.

"Make your nipples hard."

"How . . ."

"Rub them. Pretend I'm sucking them."

She knew her face was red. It was a sin to touch yourself, to give yourself pleasure. Her hands were clumsy; she couldn't concentrate, but somehow knowing that he watched made her body respond. He reached out and stroked an erect nipple, teasing it with the very tip of his gloved finger. The sensation sent a sharp, almost painful tingle through her body. He stroked the other nipple delicately, flicking the abrasive glove across the sensitive tip. She winced.

"You have a very responsive body, Astra, so very sensitive. I imagine some things will be almost unendurable for you."

The threat in his voice nearly undid her. She closed her eyes and breathed deeply, trying to regain control over her jangled nerves.

"Lift up your hair."

She opened her eyes and obeyed, pulling her carefully arranged tresses back so that he could see her breasts better. He watched her, smiling slightly.

"Jiggle them."

A stab of resentment made her tense. She had gone from prize bull to performing bear. Surely he couldn't expect her to . . .

"I said, jiggle them! Make them bounce!" His voice was hard. She did as he bade, feeling awkward and foolish. Her breasts felt heavy. It was strange to feel them unbound and free, bobbing up and down. It made the nipples throb.

"I like that," he said, smiling. "Does it hurt?"

"A little," she whispered.

She stopped, panting. She looked at him. He was still smiling, but he looked pained somehow, as if his clothes were too tight. She felt a stir of hope. He was becoming aroused. Soon he would stop this strange, perverse loveplay and take her to bed.

"Go lie on the bed."

She obeyed him, relieved. He did not follow her immediately, but began dragging furniture across the room. He placed two chests at the side of the bed, then carried over two of the gleaming candelabras and placed them on top. He pulled the curtains on the bed as far back as they went, then walked to the chair and dragged it across the floor to place between the two chests. Then, seemingly satisfied that the bed was effectively illuminated, he again sat down in the chair.

Astra's throat went dry. Richard still hadn't undressed, and he obviously wasn't getting in bed with her. She had the horrible feeling that he planned further entertainment at her expense.

"Lie facing me and spread your legs."

She went rigid. It was one thing for him to see her naked. He'd done that before, and she knew what he saw. But this . . . it made her feel impossibly vulnerable, thoroughly embarrassed. She moved to face him, then eased her knees apart an inch or two.

"More."

"Richard, I . . ."

"Shut up! You're my whore, Astra. I'm going to make you earn your price."

Closing her eyes, she did as he said. It felt odd; the cool air in the room chilled her.

"Wider. Much wider."

She opened her eyes and met his glance.

"Do as I say," he whispered threateningly.

Her legs trembled and her stomach felt weak. She could feel the wetness between her legs, a strange burning sensation.

"Play with yourself."

"What?"

"You know what I mean—touch yourself."

"I . . . I can't."

"Of course you can."

"It's a sin."

He laughed mirthlessly. "Who told you that—the nuns?"

She nodded.

"They aren't here. I am. I want you to do it. I *demand* that you do it."

She tried. Her hands shook. The first vague stirrings of desire faded. She was too mortified to feel anything.

"You'll have to learn how to arouse yourself. I want you to be ready for me when I want you. I won't waste my time pleasuring you."

It hurt to have him talk that way, as if their lovemaking would always be for his pleasure, not hers. It was obvious he never intended to forgive her. Her hand fell away as the tears filled her eyes.

"You know, don't you?" he whispered. "You know I'm going to punish you. You know I'm going to make you pay."

She shivered, then pulled her legs beneath her and wrapped her arms around her bare body. Her throat hurt; her whole being ached with misery. She could feel his hatred. She had been wrong to imagine that things could ever be the same between them. She waited, expecting him to vent his anger, to shout at her, perhaps strike her.

He watched her mutely, suddenly uneasy. He had expected her to defend herself, to justify her deceit. He had also expected her to argue with him or refuse his demands. She had done none of those things. Instead, she had obeyed him. Her compliance robbed him of the satisfaction he sought. What point was there humiliating her if she endured it so bravely, so sweetly?

And yet, he was determined to make her suffer. He could not let her escape punishment; he could not let his vengeance be undermined by pity.

"You tricked me, Astra," he said slowly. "You forced me to wed you. I had intended to take you to wife, but that is no matter now. Now I know your true character, I wouldn't have you. But, of course, I have no choice. Your cleverness has seen to that. You are my wife now, until death do us part. Are you happy, Astra? Are you pleased?"

"I was wrong," she whispered. "I made a mistake. I should not have . . ."

He made a sound of disgust. "Now she repents. At least you have the decency to regret your treachery. You rise in my estimation minute by minute, Astra. But it is not enough. You made me out a fool. Do you truly expect me to forget that?"

"I'm sorry my lord. I did not mean . . ."

"Shut up!" he said bitterly. She edged away from him. "Your feelings do not matter to me. You have succeeded in gaining yourself a husband, Astra, but I don't think it will be to your liking. I told you once that I think all women are whores. Now you are not only a whore, you are a whore who has been bought and paid for. You have earned my name, my protection, my honor. In exchange I can do anything I want with you."

That frightened her, he could tell. She crouched back on the bed, acting as if she feared he would strike her. Let her expect the worst. She couldn't know that what he wanted most of all was to touch her, not with violence but passion. He dare not let her guess that he was so choked with desire that he could scarce keep up his pretense of hatred. He had to maintain his anger. As long he did not actually give into his longing to caress her, his will would remain stronger than his lust.

"Let us continue, Astra. I was enjoying what you were doing. Come to the edge of the bed."

She hesitated, then slid forward and moved her thighs stiffly apart.

"Begin again," he said huskily. "Arouse yourself while I watch."

He watched her struggle. She looked bewildered and resigned. After a few moments, he leaned forward and slid his hand up her thigh. "That's pathetic. You're not even wet."

"I'm not good at this. It makes me feel filthy, sinful. I feel like a . . . a"

"A whore," he finished. "You are a whore, you're my whore."

"No, I'm not! I'm your wife!" She sat up and moved into a more modest position, then glared at him.

He met her eyes evenly. "It's the same thing, Astra. I own you. I can beat you, abuse you, use you any way I wish. As long as I don't kill you, I can do anything I want."

"The King . . ."

". . . would probably shake his head and lecture me, but he wouldn't interfere. Start again. You make me impatient. I'm miserably hard already."

"Maybe if you took your clothes off," she coaxed. "Got into bed with me . . ."

"Do you want to touch me? Do you want to see my shaft?"

He pushed the chair away and began to undress rapidly, furiously. He finished tearing off his clothes and stood before her, watching her. He was gratified to see that she looked frightened. He climbed onto the bed, straddling her. "Do you like it Astra? Is it big enough for you?"

"It's too big," she choked.

"You'll learn to like it. I'll ride you often enough that you'll get used to it. Since it's your first time, it's bound to hurt. I won't try and spare you, so you'd best spare yourself. Try to make yourself wet. If it helps, you can touch me. If I wasn't so far gone already, I'd even let you take it in your mouth."

She gasped.

"Oh, you'll learn that too. I consider it essential training for my whore."

He watched her try to accept this information, then she met his eyes boldly.

"I think I will . . . touch you."

He watched as she fondled him. She was tentative at first, then her fingers stroked him in a way that could only be described as loving.

"Stop," he moaned. He closed his eyes tightly. This was not working. Her tender, tantalizing touch was stealing away every shred of his anger. He was already so on fire for her he could scarcely endure it. Watching her caress him in the candlelight, her hair burning golden, her delicate features gilded with rosy softness—it was too much.

He opened his eyes. "I won't be able to last. Is that what you want?"

She stared at him.

"Do you think if you use your hand to spill my seed, I'll leave you alone? It doesn't work that way, Astra. The marriage isn't valid until I take your maidenhead."

She gave his body a quick, cautious glance, then lay down stiffly. "I'm ready," she said in a determined voice.

He regarded her warily. What did she intend now? Did she want their lovemaking to be finished? The thought revived his anger. He leaned over her and nudged her legs apart. He couldn't resist touching her once, seeking her intriguing female softness. Tense, rigid flesh met his fingers.

"Jesu! You're as dry as the Jerusalem desert!"

"I'm sorry. I told you I wasn't good at this. Why can't you kiss me?"

"Because I can't be bothered," he snapped.

She turned away, her shoulders shook as if she stifled sobs. Unwanted pity filled him. He'd never bedded an unwilling woman before; he didn't relish the thought of beginning with Astra. Somehow he had to arouse her, and yet he'd swore to give no thought to pleasuring her.

He lay down next to her and let his hand glide between

her thighs. He pressed it firmly against her mound. She squirmed.

"Hold still," he whispered. "Let's find out what sort of words arouse you."

She looked at him, baffled. She had no idea of what he was about, but then, neither did he.

He leaned toward her, his mouth near her ear. "Do you like to think of me touching you, my hand down your gown, touching your nipples? Rubbing them, making them hard?"

He thought he saw her cheeks flush, and he could almost imagine that her body quivered slightly beneath his fingers. Ah, perhaps, this would work after all.

"Do you remember the day I first saw you, when you were swimming? Do you know how you looked to me? Your breasts were wet and glistening, the nipples pink in the sun. I wanted so badly to suck them, to spread you out on the bank and devour you until you begged me to stop."

He felt her shudder. "So you like dirty talk. That's useful to know. I don't have to touch you, I'll merely tempt you with words." Despite the threat, he could not resist stroking her slightly. As he felt Astra's immediate response, a smile spread across his face. "Such a wanton," he murmured, his voice husky with his own passion. "You have a vocation for this, Astra. You could be a very skillful whore."

He pressed down on her sensitive flesh. "Do you like to think of me inside you, Astra? How do you think it will feel? Do you think I will satisfy all your longings and desires when at last I fuck you?"

He felt her stiffen at the word. "What is it, Astra?" he asked in mock surprise. "Does that word offend you? Shall I use another? There are many ways to describe what a man does to a woman. He 'tups' her or 'bangs' her, 'futters' her, or 'toffs' her. He plays leapfrog with her, opens her lock with his key, rides her like a horse, cuts off a slice from her loaf, sits in her saddle and tumbles her. He puts his arrow in her quiver, finds safe harbor in her cinque port."

He paused, still smiling, aroused beyond bearing. "So many fanciful terms. But I prefer to call the thing what it is. What of this, Astra . . ." he whispered directly in her ear. "Tonight I will spread your legs wide and fill you to bursting. Then I shall ride you—long and hard, until you beg me for mercy."

She did not move or make a sound. So still she was, he wondered if she even breathed. He raised himself and leaned over her. His eyes traveled the length of her, taking in every alluring inch. He could scarce restrain his yearning to love her properly, to kiss and caress her, to explore her luscious beauty. His gaze alighted on her face. She watched him, her eyes deep liquid blue, filled with an expression of fear, longing, and some other emotion he could not name.

Frustration filled him. He had to finish this, to bury himself in her irresistible body and lose himself in the safety of his own lust. He covered her and guided himself to the opening between her legs. Her body would not seem to give way. He cursed and used his fingers to probe her woman's flesh. She was as dry and tight as ever.

"Damn you!" he muttered.

"It doesn't fit," she whispered.

"It will," he insisted.

He tried again. He was sweating, breathing hard. She cried out.

"Damn your miserable maidenhead!" he exclaimed.

He rolled off and lay beside her, breathing raggedly. Her voice was soft, beseeching. "Maybe if you would . . ."

"Touch you!" He turned to her. "Is that what you want? You want me to caress you? To kiss you? You've trapped me again, haven't you? Lady Astra *will* get her way, won't she?"

She began to cry. He leaned back and tried to summon the hate and anger he knew he felt for her. He conjured up the scene in the chapel, the King's angry, offended voice, the whispers of the courtiers, the hardness of the floor as he knelt like a shamed boy. His rage rekindled, but not enough to block out the sound of Astra's tears. He had to make her stop, to somehow finish this thing between them. He would forget his vow for now. Once the marriage was consummated, he would be at his leisure to torment her.

She jerked when she felt his hand between her legs. She was sore, battered. Did he truly expect her to endure any more?

But somehow it was different this time. He was touching her softly, skillfully. She told herself that he didn't care, that there was no feeling guiding his caress. It didn't seem to matter. Gradually the exquisite ache in her lower abdomen returned. Her body weakened; she slid slowly into the hot, throbbing abyss.

She thrashed and moaned, trembling as he slid a finger inside her. The rhythm he used was slow, agonizingly gentle. In and out, in and out. Her thoughts unraveled; her breathing grew frantic. His other hand moved to her buttocks. He fingered, squeezed and traced the cleft of her bottom. She moaned and moved against his hand. His fingers caressed her mound, searching for the sweet sensitive spot she longed for him to find. He nudged it at the same time he eased a second finger inside her.

She began to shake and cry out. He held her close, coaxing her with soft words in her ear. The wetness seemed to pour from her. He brought her to the peak of passion again, and yet again.

All at once, he pulled his hand away and covered her. She could feel the burning hardness probing her again. This time her body yielded. He entered her, pushing, pushing. She cried out as he penetrated the final barrier. The pain swallowed her, then ebbed. Inside her, he thrust and pounded, as if searching the inner boundaries of her body. She held on tightly, breathless with the wonder of being so close to him.

He attained release with a great gasp and cry, then collapsed on top of her. He was sweaty and heavy, but she did not care. She stroked his hair until he jerked away.

The candles had almost gutted out, but there was still light to see. Their eyes met, and Astra saw his narrow and grow wary.

"Are you sated, Astra?" he whispered.

She nodded, watching him uneasily.

His hand found the swollen, battered place between her legs, teasing it again to life.

"Do you think we have finished, wife? Think again. We have just barely begun. Next time, I will last longer, much longer."

Twenty-eight

The candles were all spent when she awoke, the brazier burned down to ashes. A pale, wan light filtered in from the round, glazed window in the corner of the room.

She was cold, her legs only halfway beneath the blankets. The scarlet silk coverlet and the rest of the bedcovers were wedged beneath Richard's body. He slept on his back, one arm covering his face, the other stretched out to the side. Despite the chill in the room, he seemed warm. Heat radiated from his chest and limbs. Astra had the urge to snuggle up to him, to warm her cold body against his. She discarded the thought quickly. He would obviously wake, and even if he were not angered, he might well decide he was not sated yet.

Sated—what would it take to make Richard pronounce himself satisfied? She could scarcely imagine. He had not let her sleep until almost dawn. Her body felt bruised, utterly pounded. She had not dreamed that lovemaking would be like that. With dogs and other animals she had seen, coupling lasted a few moments. She knew it took longer with a man and women, but still she had not imagined it lasting all night.

Shivering with cold, she moved toward the side of the bed and sought to recover her discarded nightgown for warmth. Her legs were stiff and aching, and she seemed to have to pull them along after her. When she reached the edge, she glanced down and saw the streaks of blood on her thighs. The sight hardly surprised her; in fact, she wondered that there was not more. It still amazed her that Richard had fit inside her. His man part, his shaft, was huge. Surely there was not that much space within her. Indeed, she had never really known that such a place existed inside her, let alone that it could stretch to accommodate such a monstrous thing.

She closed her eyes, remembering. At first it had hurt, then the pain had gradually dulled. That was early on in the night. Later, as he continued to move and thrust within her, she had transcended the soreness and begun to feel something else—a throbbing hungry need that made her buck and writhe against him. She knew then what men meant by "riding" a woman. His thighs had clenched around her while he drove into her like a horse galloping. Then he had made her wrap her legs around his hips while he rocked and writhed some more.

She opened her eyes and rubbed her arms to stop her shivering, then walked gingerly across the floor to where the nightgown lay. She groaned as she bent to pick it up. She straightened and slipped the gown over her head, then stood numbly in the center of the lovely bedchamber. She was not sure what she felt. Her emotions felt as wracked and drained as her body did. It was too much, to feel such anxiety, such desire, such ecstasy, all in such a short span of time.

Across the room, Richard stirred and muttered in his sleep. She watched him warily. She had no illusions that things were right between them. She knew that he would still hate her when he woke. Richard's anger had nothing to do with his lust. No matter the passion shared between them, he was still capable of hating her. In fact, she wondered if his lust did not make him hate her all the more. She knew he had intended to avoid giving her any pleasure last night, and he had failed. He could not satisfy himself without pleasuring her. She suspected that he found that fact infuriating.

She sighed. What a coil it was. She had never intended to hurt Richard, to make him so angry. She loved him. His bitter, mocking words were not enough to kill her love, for she knew from where his fury came. She had trapped him, and like a wild beast imprisoned in a cage, he merely struggled and raged to gain his freedom. Thinking of it that way made her hurt for him. She wanted to soothe him.

She approached the bed slowly, gazing beneath the silken canopy. Tears stung her eyes. He was so beautiful, his sprawling legs graceful and lithe, his broad chest so sleek and solid. She wanted to lay her head there, to cuddle beneath his arm, to smell the intoxicating male musk of his skin.

She glanced at his male parts, and her mind was drawn back to the memory of touching him the night before. His shaft had been hot and silken, and despite its solidity, the skin there was supple and velvety. She recalled that it more than filled her hand, and she had had to keep forcing away the thought that it would soon be inside her. Still, it had been pleasurable to explore the various textures—the harsh, curly hair at the base, the long smooth shaft, the sweetly-soft tip.

A smile curled her lips as she gazed upon him. There was nothing there to frighten her this morn. His man part was now only a meek, dangling thing resting on a thatch of wavy black hair, the soft, wrinkled pouches where he carried his seed nestling below it.

Then a thought came to her, and her smile faded. He had planted his seed deep within her last night. There had been so much of it, oozing out of her, dripping down her thighs. Surely he had put enough inside her to make a baby grow. That was another thing to worry over. Would he love a babe if she had one?

She sighed and eased herself onto the bed, trying not to wake her husband. He mumbled and pulled his arm away from his face. His hair fell back and exposed the thick, corded muscles in his neck, the curve of his powerful shoulders. She stared at him, admiring the clean, smooth lines of his masculine features. His mouth was slightly open. She wanted to kiss him, to taste his breath, even if it was stale and sour with wine. He had not kissed her last night. A kiss was too intimate, too tender. He might stroke her and fondle her and put himself deep inside her, but he would not kiss her.

Her heart pounded in her chest as she squeezed her eyes shut tight and leaned over him. She brought her lips to his. His mouth moved beneath hers.

"Astra."

He kissed her back for a moment, a mere heartbeat. Then she felt his body stiffen. She opened her eyes. He was staring at her; his face was cold and hostile.

She retreated to the other side of the bed, tears stinging her eyelids. Richard sat up and stretched. Then he turned to her; his eyes scanned her slowly, impassively. He reached over and lifted up the hem of the nightgown, jerking it to her hips. Fearing his cold silence, Astra edged her legs apart. He briefly touched one blood streaked thigh, then fumbled with the bedclothes beneath her. He pushed the bloodstained coverlet to the floor, then got out of bed and began to dress.

Astra covered herself with the remaining blankets. She burrowed into them, trying to bury her hurt and misery. Richard dressed quickly in his rumpled wedding clothes, then went to the door and called for a servant. When the gray-haired maid entered the room, he pointed to the coverlet and told her to take it to the King. Then he left—without even a backwards glance toward the bed.

The servant retrieved the coverlet and hesitated by the door. "My lady, may I get you anything?'

"My clothes," Astra mumbled. "A fresh gown and water to wash with. The Queen or Lady Marguerite can tell you where my things are."

"Of course, my lady."

The servant left. Astra sighed and sank deeper into the soft bed. She had been right to expect the worst. Richard still hated her. Despite all the passion they had shared, he was a stranger, a menacing, angry stranger.

She sighed again and allowed herself to escape into sleep.

When she woke, she sensed it was late. The room was colder than ever, but she could see that it had been tidied. The furniture had been pushed back in place, the candelabras refreshed with tall, gleaming candles. Her blue gown and a clean chemise lay across the chair.

Reluctantly, Astra left the warm bed and washed her face, hands and sticky thighs with the now tepid water the servant had left. Then she slowly dressed.

She dreaded the thought of facing the other women. She was a virgin no longer, and everyone knew it. She couldn't help flinching as she thought of the servant carrying the bloodied evidence to the King. It was obviously Richard's way of getting back at both of them for forcing him to wed.

After donning her gown, she combed her hair, then braided it neatly and coiled it on top of her head. She fastened it in place under a veil. There was nothing else to do, no excuse to delay. She squared her shoulders and went out the door. She approached the Queen's private chambers and listened for voices. It was quiet for once, no gossiping murmurs. All eyes turned to her as she entered; Isabel's face was scornful, but the rest of the women looked mostly curious.

"She's very pale," one of the younger women whispered.

" 'Tis no wonder," another woman whispered back. "They say the Leopard is an animal in bed, as well as on the battlefield."

A few women giggled, but they stifled almost immediately as the Queen entered.

"Good morrow, Astra. You look quite refreshed."

Astra forced a smile. "I slept well, Your Highness, if very late. I am sorry to be so tardy."

"No excuse is necessary. You are a married woman now with a husband to look after. I do not expect you to wait upon me every moment of the day."

Astra nodded graciously and went to a chest in the corner to retrieve the embroidery she had been working on before the wedding. She took a seat and pretended to examine the half-finished banner with great interest. She had once been excited by the project. The royal banner featured the device adopted by the Plantagenet kings before Henry III was born and consisted of three gold leopards rampant on a field of scarlet. Astra had imagined someday designing a similar device for Richard. It would feature one black leopard of course, but she had not decided on the color for the background, nor what flowers or foliage to use for decoration.

Of course, it was a fruitless pursuit now. Richard would likely never accept such a gift. A small sigh escaped Astra's lips. When she looked up, Lady Alyce was regarding her intently. The Queen got up to go to the nursery, and Alyce leaned forward.

"What's wrong, Astra? I thought you and Richard were truly in love—did you quarrel already?"

Astra shook her head, not knowing what to say.

"Astra, *ma belle!*" Marguerite entered the room with an elegant flourish of her green and rose satin skirts. "I did not expect to find you here. I had imagined that you would still be abed." She winked devilishly. "Surely you did not get much sleep last night!"

Astra smiled and tried desperately to hide her misery. It was impossible. Sharp-eyed Marguerite frowned, then motioned her to follow her into the hallway.

"What is it, Astra?" she asked when they were alone. "Is there some trouble with Richard?"

"You know there is! Richard believes I forced him into marriage, and he has not forgiven me."

"Has he hurt you? Was he cruel to you during the bedding?"

Astra looked away. How could she explain what Richard had done to her? There was not a mark upon her, and she could truly say she had never known such ecstasy, but still, things were far from right between them.

"It was not like that. He was odd and threatening . . . but he did not actually hurt me."

"What of pleasure, Astra? Did he not see fit to pleasure you?"

"Of course he pleasured me. It is not Richard's way to force a woman against her will. He made me want him."

"What then?"

"He does not love me anymore," Astra said in a quavering voice. "Indeed, I think he hates me!"

"Oh, that. Give him time, Astra. When Richard gets over his anger, he will be as enraptured with you as ever."

Astra shook her head. She could not explain her foreboding. Inconstant Marguerite could never understand a man like Richard. Beneath his charming, playful exterior, there was a hard, unforgiving core. Thinking about it made Astra shiver.

"We'd better go back," she said nervously. "The gossip will be worse if we remain in the hallway."

Their appearance in the ladies' chamber was greeted with giggles and sly, knowing looks.

"Are you getting advice from the little bride, Lady Marguerite?" Isabel asked mockingly. "I should imagine that it would be the other way around. The rumors suggest that you are already well acquainted with the mysteries of the marital chamber."

Marguerite flushed and said nothing. Astra gave her friend a sharp look. It was not like Marguerite to let a barb from Isabel pass without a retort. As Astra watched, Marguerite went to the sewing chest and took out a piece of embroidery. Astra frowned. It was odd for Marguerite to spend time sewing; everyone knew she detested the task. Astra watched in puzzlement a moment, then turned back to her own work.

Thud! Richard's lance hit the quintain square in the center of the red target. At the same time the counterweight of the device swung around; he ducked deftly and the heavy arm whizzed by, missing him by a good margin. He turned his horse and started back for another pass. His body might ache with fatigue, but his brain still hummed like a drawn bowstring. He must relieve some of the tension or go mad.

His glance focused for a moment on the palace, visible across the training field and the low, dark shape of the barracks. He grimaced as he thought of the extravagant bedchamber he had left a few hours before. His wedding night had not gone as planned, not at all. The harder he tried to hurt Astra and humiliate her, the more poignantly aware he had been of how beautiful she was and how much he wanted her. The cold harshness he had shown her was a lie, a defense to keep her from guessing how deeply she affected him. And she had accepted even that.

He shook his head, trying to banish thoughts of his wife from his mind. The destrier increased his speed rapidly as they neared the target. Richard flexed his muscles until they grew as tight as coiled springs. With all his strength, he thrust the lance in the red "x" again. The force of his blow knocked the device from its supporting base. The quintain and counterweight fell sideways.

Richard eased the destrier around the field, trying to find calm for himself as well as his mount. He was breathing heavily and his muscles trembled. The exertion had finally begun to purge some of the restlessness that gnawed at his innards. He allowed the horse to slow to a walk and approached the group of young soldiers waiting at the end of the field. He could hear their awed whispers as he neared them.

"Sweet Jesu, did you see that? He broke it!"

"Damnedest thing I ever saw. Can you imagine facing him on the battlefield?"

"I told you he was the best." The voice of Nicholas, Richard's squire, came low and proud. "There's no one else like the Leopard."

Richard almost smiled. It was pleasing to know he inspired such admiration. Still, the youths' awe would not serve them on the battlefield. They needed to keep practicing and learn the trick of it themselves. It might well save their lives someday.

He made his face stern as he neared the group, intent on instilling some discipline. A mocking voice to his right diverted his attention.

"Very nice, Reivers. It's well that you keep practicing your warrior skills. With Henry's mood these days, you have little hope of ever rising above a knight."

The muscles in Richard's face and jaw went rigid. Curse Rathstowe! Of all times for him to visit the training field.

Richard's eyes flicked sideways, and he caught a glimpse of his enemy. Faucomberg's face was flushed with amusement, his wide pink mouth stretched into a gloating grin. Richard resisted the urge to smash his fist into his tormentor's mocking countenance. He would not sink so low as to attack his foe in such a cowardly fashion.

He turned. "If you wish to do battle, Faucomberg, say the word. The choice of weapons is yours."

The red-haired man laughed, a startlingly shrill and effeminate sound. "Fight you, Reivers? I think not. I have better things to do with my time. In a few days I intend to announce my betrothal to a very wealthy young woman." His smile widened. "It's a shame you couldn't have found an heiress yourself, Reivers. It's obviously the only hope you ever had of being anything more than a common knight. I hear your wife is utterly penniless. Funny, I would never have taken you for such a dolt that you would marry for love."

The rage pounded in Richard's head. His vision faded, usurped by a red tide of hatred. When he could see again, Faucomberg was walking away. His unprotected back taunted Richard. It would be so easy to pull out his misericord and end the puling bastard's life! His fingers twitched; his tired muscles screamed with the effort of holding back.

Faucomberg disappeared beyond the barracks. Richard took a deep breath and started toward his destrier. He heard a sound behind him and remembered Nicholas and the other squires. Anger filled him anew. They had all heard Rathstowe taunt him; even now they were likely laughing at him. It was obvious the whole court knew how Astra had tricked him.

Richard walked toward his horse and grabbed the fallen reins. He began leading the animal the long way across the field. He stopped at the broken quintain, pulled his dagger and viciously attacked the sack of sand that had weighted the device.

By the time he finished, the sack was torn to ribbons and sand poured from a dozen gaping holes. He stared at the ruined object a moment, his lip curling in satisfaction. It was pleasing to think of ramming his knife into Faucomberg's pallid, sneering face.

Then his thoughts shifted, and he gave the sack another poke. This time he envisioned Astra's lush body, and the weapon became his own fleshly shaft. He frowned. For all her primness, Astra was so damned sensual it was near impossible not to want to pleasure her, even when he intended to hurt her. Now that they were married, he didn't have to coax her or trick her into loveplay. She was willing, indeed she obviously thought it was her duty to do whatever he wished. Even when he called her a whore and spoke cruelly to her, she had not fought back or resisted him. How did you confound that absurd sort of compliance?

And yet, her body had not been willing at first. He had had to gentle her, to coax her body into accepting his. Of course, he could have raped her. Perhaps if he had, she would not have been so tender and forgiving this morning. Then she would know what it was like to be trapped, cornered, humiliated.

He winced. It was the perfect revenge, but he hadn't been able to go through with it. If he had taken her then, dry and unready, she would have likely hated bedding from then on, not to mention him. Somehow he did not have the heart to make her suffer physical pain. Some stupid part of him still admired her, still hungered after her sweetness. It was a shameful thing, and he was going to have to get over it somehow. He couldn't let it interfere with his plan to punish her. Astra would have to pay the price for her treachery. He must make her realize that no one humiliated the Black Leopard without regretting it the rest of their life.

He gave the sack one last savage thrust and turned and walked toward the palace.

Astra glanced nervously at the knights surrounding her at the banquet table. It had been Richard's idea that she sit with his "friends" as he called them. As soon as she reached the Great Hall for the evening meal, her husband had beckoned her over to join the group of rather disreputable-looking soldiers. Richard had greeted her civilly enough. He kissed her cheek, introduced her as his "lady wife," even helped her to sit beside him. But for all his courtesy, she had no hope that he had undergone any change in his feelings. Although he smiled, his eyes were cold and hard; there was a mocking edge to his voice when he addressed her.

The group of knights looked as ill at ease with her presence as she was with theirs. Their talk was subdued, and she sensed they resented having to curb their rough language for her sake. Richard appeared oblivious to the tension at the table. He talked animatedly and encouraged the other men to join in the conversation. Astra flushed as the talk turned to plans for later in the evening and the "stews" of Southwark, the most notorious district of brothels in the city.

"Remember the lady," one man cautioned, with a nod toward Astra.

"Astra does not care," Richard assured them. "She's a married woman now. She's well acquainted with what goes on between a man and his mistress."

Astra said nothing, only ducked her head. She knew Richard was playing some sadistic game with her, and she shuddered to think where it was leading.

"There must be quite a few women in London who will be disappointed that the Black Leopard has married," one of the younger knights said with a guffaw. "What do we tell them, Reivers? Is there no hope you will join us tonight?"

"Not tonight," Richard said nonchalantly. "For now I am content to keep to my wife's bed. My intention is to teach her all the tricks of a whore; then I will not have to go in search of my pleasure elsewhere."

There was nervous laughter around the table. Astra put down the bite of coney she had been on the verge of eating. She now had a glimpse of Richard's intentions, and it made her feel ill.

"I know of one whore who will be furious that Richard Reivers is a faithfully wedded man," someone suggested. "What of Ruby, Richard? Do you mean to give her up, too?"

"Ah, Ruby," Richard answered, smiling gleefully. "She's a fine piece. I once thought that she had the most beautiful tits in Christendom. Now I know that that honor goes to my lovely wife."

There were gasps of surprise, then muffled laughter. Astra fought the urge to crawl beneath the table.

"Aye," Richard said loudly. "My wife is the perfect woman—obedient, passionate and endowed like Venus herself."

"We envy you, Reivers," one of the men said. "For all that the King forced you to wed Lady Astra, it seems that you have gotten the best of the bargain."

Richard's scar twitched, and Astra held her breath, wondering if the reminder of her betrayal would throw her husband into a rage. His voice was smooth and unruffled when he spoke: "You are correct, Roderick. I've decided to make the best of the situation. I did not want a wife, but now that I have one, I can see the advantages. Certainly she will require less coin than the famous Ruby. While many whores have special talents and techniques, you have to pay for them. My wife is already paid for, so it's only a matter of training her to please me. And of course, she is very eager to learn."

Astra had had enough. She rose, intending to leave the

table. Richard restrained her with an iron-like grip on her arm.

"My wife has only one fault," he said with a cold smile as he still held her arm. "She was raised in a convent, and she can be maddeningly shy and demure when it comes to matters of lovemaking. I intend to change that. When I am done with her, she will have no shame, no shame at all."

Richard's grip loosened, and Astra finally broke away. She struggled to free her skirts and finally managed to scramble ungracefully over the trestle bench and dart for the doorway.

Twenty-nine

It was cold in the courtyard, and she had left her cloak behind. Astra shivered in her velvet gown as she hurried down the darkened stone walkway outside the palace. She could not return to the wedding bedchamber or even to the Queen's gallery, for Richard would surely find her. But there was one place she hoped he wouldn't think to look.

The chapel was lit with candles along the walls, and the familiar soft, flickering illumination comforted Astra. She knelt for a time before the altar, praying for strength and God's help in turning Richard's anger to love. It seemed to ease her heart. She felt calmer when she rose, more able to deal with Richard and his mocking cruelty.

Still, she was reluctant to go back to the main palace and risk facing him again. She had a faint hope that if he continued to drink wine with his boisterous companions, he would eventually forget his vengeful plans for her. He might even be enticed to join them for a night of whoring in the "stews" and leave her alone.

That thought reassured Astra and disturbed her simultaneously. It might be safer for her if Richard vented his lust with a harlot, but it still made her jealous. She did not like to think of her husband in the arms of another woman.

She was well and truly mad, she decided, to care at all. Richard had humiliated her publicly and privately. He had mocked her and taunted her and treated her with utmost coldness. And yet, she still loved him, still had hope that some day he would get over his bitterness and love her again. She clung to that hope. Her reason was powerless against her feelings for Richard. No matter how blind and crazed it was, she cared for him, worried about him, desired him.

Astra sighed softly and stood. Perhaps her love for Richard was God's punishment for leaving the priory, for failing to dedicate her life to the Lord. She had wanted a husband, a lover. She had wanted romance and passion. And she had received everything she'd wished. She had no right to complain, to be bitter.

She wrapped her cold arms around her body and tried to find the strength to return to the palace. There was a sound behind her. She turned and saw a familiar form among the shadows.

"Are you returning to the scene of your triumph, Astra? Does it thrill you to think of how beautifully your plan worked? How well you succeeded in making me into a groveling ass before the King?"

She shook her head and tried to quell the shuddering in her body so she could answer him. "It was not like that, Richard. I never meant to hurt you." Her voice choked. "I love you so much I was willing to do almost anything to have you, but I did not mean for things to turn out the way they did. I know you feel you cannot trust me. In truth, I do not blame you for being angry."

"You do not blame me! How noble of you, Astra. How fucking noble!"

She flinched. Any attempt to explain would be hopeless. Richard could only see it one way. He believed she had humiliated him for her own ends.

He moved toward her, into the light. She saw his face—so hard, so cold, so angry. The fear rose up in her, choking her. Her body seemed to freeze to the spot. He reached out and grasped her arms, then ran his warm fingers along her chilled flesh. She began to tremble even more violently. He brought his mouth down on hers for a rough, possessive kiss. She was so hungry for his affection, some little hint of intimacy. She gave in to him easily.

He kissed her until she felt breathless, lightheaded. Then he released her, and she knew the terrible pain all over again. There was still no warmth in his eyes, for all that his face was flushed with passion. His lust seemed to feed his anger, for his hand grasped her arm with a grip as cold-blooded as his eyes.

"Come to bed, wife. The night is early."

With each step he took, he forced himself to remember the pain and humiliation she had caused him. It was well she had gone to the chapel. There the bitter memory was clear. She had enticed him, betrayed him. He clenched his jaw. It had sickened him to see Astra's cheeks flame with shame as he taunted her before the other soldiers, but even so, it was not enough. His vengeance was not satisfied.

They walked down the wainscoted hallways of the palace. The place was quiet, faintly-lit with cresset torches on the wall. They neared the bedchamber where they had spent their wedding night. He saw Astra hesitate. He turned and pushed her against the wall, then fumbled with her bodice. After undoing the laces, he tore the chemise beneath it down the middle, freeing her breasts.

She tried to push him away. "There was no need for

that! We are almost to the bedchamber. I will undress for you there. Can you not wait?"

"No," he answered coldly. "I cannot wait. I want you here, against this wall."

She struggled to push his hands away, but he maintained his possessive hold upon her breasts. "I don't wish you to wear undergarments anymore, Astra. I want to be able to unlace your gown and fondle you whenever I wish."

"That is indecent!"

"And yet, you did not protest when I undid your bodice in the chapel. If you were willing to flaunt yourself then, why not now?"

"I did not flaunt myself," she argued. "I was fully dressed until you near-ravished me!"

"But you knew it would happen. You planned it, and you did not care who saw. Tell me, Astra, was it thrilling to display yourself to the King of England?"

Her eyes widened; she did not answer.

"I'm afraid it was all for naught, Astra. For all that he was likely stirred by the sight, Henry is a pious, self-righteous old fart. He'll never make you his mistress."

She pushed him away and struggled to be free of his grasp. "How dare you say such a thing? I could not even imagine doing something so despicable. The King is married; Eleanor is my friend!"

"They say it begins with little things, Astra, small lies, small betrayals. Gradually it becomes possible to undertake schemes of greater and greater evil. Before you know it, actions you once considered despicable come to seem quite acceptable."

"It was not like that, Richard," she protested weakly. "I never meant to hurt you. I thought I could make you happy."

"You lie," he muttered. "You wanted me. Your lust for me was as strong as mine for you, but your selfish, scheming female heart would not let you give in until you made sure you trapped me into marriage. You're naught but a devious little slut. You pretended to be a pure and virtuous lady, but the truth is that you are ruled by that sweet, warm piece of flesh between your legs. You made me wed you because you wanted me to bed you and that was the only way your precious conscience would allow it!"

He felt her slump against the wall, anguished by his words. All at once, he pitied her—and himself. He had planned to force her to fight him by ravishing her in the hallway. Now, feeling her small, soft body sag with despair, he wondered if he could bear to do it.

No. He would not weaken. He wanted her, and he would have her.

He reached out tentatively and began to stroke Astra's breasts. He played lazily with her nipples, watching the rosy tips tighten to hard, enticing points. Overcome, he began to pull up her skirts.

Astra gave a little shriek of surprise. He silenced her with a kiss and pushed her more closely against the wall. His right hand found its way between her thighs.

Astra managed to pull her mouth away. "What are you doing?" she entreated.

"Making you wet. I don't want a struggle like last night."

"Please . . . let's go to the bedchamber. I'll take my clothes off . . . I'll do anything."

"I like it here. Admit it. You like it too."

"Someone could come along at any time . . . a servant . . . anyone . . ."

"If you don't want it, why are you so wet?"

"I . . . I don't know!"

"Because you can't resist me. You're made for me, Astra. For my hands, my mouth, my . . ."

"No!"

"Go ahead, Astra, cry rape. I'm your husband. I can take you here, right now if I wish."

"No!"

Her panic did not distress him. It was only her false modesty which made her cry out. Already he could feel her body welcoming him. "Jesu, you're nothing like last night. You're so wet and slippery. My finger goes inside you easily. Mmmmm."

"Oh! Please!" She leaned against him, moaning low in her throat. Her whole body shuddered. Then, suddenly, she pushed against him, throwing her weight into his chest. Surprised, he staggered backwards, pulling her with him.

Astra let out a shriek as he crashed into the wall behind him with a thudding sound and they both went down. "Damn bitch!" he muttered. "I ought to beat you for this."

Astra got up as swiftly as she could, smoothing her skirts. Insanely, she felt a surge of relief that Richard hadn't been knocked unconscious. He lay there, regarding her with narrowed eyes.

"If you promise to wait until we get to the bedchamber, I'll help you up," she whispered.

"What if my ardor has cooled? What if I don't even want you anymore?"

She stared at him, saying nothing. She had never known such a baffling, changeable man.

He started to rise, stiffly, as if something hurt him.

"Are you well?"

"Well enough." He glared at her with a sulky, offended look.

That was all she needed to hear. She turned and scooted into the nearby bedchamber. For a moment she considered trying to bar the door, then discarded the notion. It would be best if she did not provoke him further.

He loomed in the doorway. She took one look at his hostile face and backed away.

"Please, Richard . . ."

He smiled leeringly. "Do you fear me, little wife?"

"No," she whispered. She must be brave. She must make him see reason. "Why should I fear you? You are my husband."

"Nay, Astra, I am not your husband. I am your unwilling husband."

She could feel his bitterness, the raw wound she had dealt to his pride. Once again, the image of a trapped animal flashed into her mind, unnerving her. She could not help edging away. She moved backwards until her legs were pressed into one of the large chests that edged the room. He followed her, moving with the slow, easy grace of a cat stalking its prey.

She held her breath as he loomed over her. He stared intently at her ruined bodice and half-exposed breasts.

"I want to touch you." He said it flatly, as if it was something that surprised him. "I can't seem to rid myself of the urge for your flesh. I want to take you and take you, again and again, until I am weary of the sight and feel of you."

His eyes moved to her face. "What think you, Astra? How many times must I have you tonight before I am satisfied? Five? Six?"

Mutely, she shook her head. She did not know what was

wrong with him. He seemed to hate her and yet lust for her at the same time.

He moved toward her and pinned her against the chest with his thighs. She had the sense that he meant to finish what he had begun in the hall; she glanced anxiously toward the open door.

"My lord, please, cannot we ensure our privacy?"

He smiled. "Are you afraid the King's guard will come along and see us? Perhaps I should invite them in? It might be entertaining to see you whore for them."

His pressed his hard groin deeper into her belly.

"I could tie you to the bed and let them each have a turn . . . or would you rather have them watch us?"

"You would not . . . surely you would not!"

"I don't know, Astra," he murmured, stroking her cheek with a calloused finger. "Truly, I am torn between showing you for the whore you are or keeping you to myself."

She closed her eyes, praying. Richard was only trying to frighten her. Surely he would not really do something so bestial.

His finger still stroked her face, moving down to trace the line of her jaw.

"I think for now, I will keep you for myself. Perhaps later, when I am tired of you, we will have to resort to more unusual entertainments."

Astra breathed a sigh of relief, but she was still reluctant to open her eyes. She cried out in surprise when he lifted her up onto the chest. A candelabra crashed to the floor. Fortunately it was not burning, or the beautiful carpet would have been ruined. Richard jerked up her skirts; his hands found her bare hips.

"Open your eyes, Astra . . . and your legs."

She did as she was told, watching him with expectation

and sudden desire. It was horrifying to think that he would use her like this, but strangely arousing as well. He pulled down his hose, and she felt his shaft warm and teasing against her nether lips. He pushed her legs further apart and pulled her toward him at the same time. Her mouth widened into a silent "o" as he entered her.

She groaned, somewhere between delirious pleasure and agony. It was too much—surely a woman was not meant to accommodate a man like this. Richard moaned too, and sweat glistened on his face.

"Sweet heaven! I cannot move."

Silently, Astra praised the heavens herself that Richard was forced into immobility. If he moved, she was sure her body would break into pieces.

"You are too tight," he muttered.

Astra felt a stab of irritation that she was once again being blamed for her body's unyieldingness. What was he complaining of anyway? She was the one being impaled by his enormous thing.

His hand slid up her thigh, searching for the juncture of their bodies. His fingers found her taut, aching outer lips where they surrounded him and began to stroke.

"Oh, please," she moaned. "Do not do that!"

"Why not?" he asked silkily. "Don't you like it?"

"Oh! I . . . I . . . it is near unbearable!"

"It makes you wet. It makes your sweet slit open wider for me."

"Oh! Ohhhh!" she moaned as he touched the exquisitely tender spot buried in her cleft.

"Have a care how loud you moan, lovey. The door is still open."

She looked behind him, staring in horror at the open

door. It did not matter. She could not move, could scarce think enough to breathe.

"Oh, Richard, please stop!"

"I have only begun."

He began to thrust into her, and everything dissolved into a throbbing, blinding miasma of feeling. Her breasts bounced, the sweat dripped from Richard's brow, and her body screamed with pleasure. Richard's hands held her hips and braced her body as he drove into her, harder and faster. She struggled to find a grip on his shoulders. She wanted to be closer to him, to have him hold her, to kiss her. He was too intent to care, his face brutal with passion, his eyes closed in concentration. She screamed as he drove into her with a final convulsive lunge of his hips.

He collapsed against her, panting. She was overwhelmed with tenderness for him. She wanted to clasp him to her breasts, to stroke his dark, sweat-stained hair. But fear made her hesitate. Lovemaking did not seem to evoke the same feeling in him as it did for her. She wondered, now that he was satiated, would he be angrier still?

He disengaged himself from her, an odd smile quirking his lips.

"That was once, Astra. How many more times will there be tonight?"

She pulled her skirts down and regarded him warily, then slipped from the chest. Her legs quivered and wobbled beneath her, but she made it to the door. She shut it tightly, then turned back toward her husband.

"Come to bed," she pleaded softly.

He leaned against the chest, his face sleepy, but still mocking. "I would have you again before I sleep."

"My lord, I think . . ."

"I said I would have you again."

She bit her lips, wondering if he really meant it. How could he want more? She had heard that men needed time to recover after lovemaking. Was he such an animal that he could perform again immediately?

"I . . . can we at least undress first?"

"Undress." He shrugged.

She felt awkward again. It was maddening. He had just done the most intimate thing to her that a man could do to a woman, and yet she still felt shy around him. Would he ever stop making her feel like this—as if his hot eyes upon her had the power to stop her heart from beating?

She slipped out of her clothes. Her breath quickened as more and more of her body was bared. She was keenly aware of the wetness dribbling down her leg, the smell of him upon her.

"Now, undress me."

She walked toward him uneasily. She did not know where to begin. She knew nothing about undressing a man; his clothes baffled her.

"My boots," he prompted.

She knelt down. He obediently held out his foot. She pulled. The boot came off easily. The other one she had to tug. She was perspiring by the time she moved on to his hose.

She reached beneath his long tunic, and her hands touched his waist, feeling his taut, warm belly. His hose hung around his hips. She pulled them down, her hands gliding over the hard, rough, hairy skin of his legs. Her face was near his crotch, but the tunic covered him. She could not help wondering if he was aroused again.

She stood up and began to undo the laces at the neck of his tunic. Her fingers were shaking, although she was not sure why. She reached around to work the tunic up over his back. He made no move to help her, only stood there, his arms dead weights as she tried to pull the sleeves loose. She had to stand on tip-toe to ease the tunic over his head. It caught on his massive shoulders. She paused and rested from her exertions. For a moment, she had the urge to pull the tunic over his face and leave it there. Instead, she stretched up again and gave a final tug, freeing him from the last of his clothes.

Their faces were only inches apart. Richard was watching her with an amused grin. It made him seem boyish. She wanted to kiss him.

"Touch me."

She took a deep breath. His skin was warm and tantalizingly smooth. Her fingers skimmed over his hard flesh as she savored the strength and maleness of him. She found each scar, each imperfection in his fine, brown skin, and caressed it. He shifted impatiently, then his hands grabbed hers and jerked them to his groin.

"Touch me there."

He was not as she had known him before. His shaft was not hard, but neither was it soft. She touched him gingerly, wondering what he wanted. She looked up and met his eyes. They were cold and bitter again.

"Arouse me."

She began to stroke him, slowly, uncertainly. She tried to remember the rhythm he had used when he was inside her. She felt inept, clumsy. She envisioned another woman doing this to him—a whore. How did she know what to do?

"Faster, rougher. You won't hurt me."

She tried to be more vigorous. His shaft seemed to grow harder as she rubbed it. He leaned back against the chest, closing his eyes. Her arm grew tired. She went back to fondling him again.

"Take it in your mouth."

She hesitated.

"It won't hurt you. Whores do it all the time."

All the time. She closed her eyes, imagining him with another woman.

"Do it, Astra. I insist."

It was not as awful as she thought it would be. His flesh there tasted much like the rest of him—warm and slightly sweet. His shaft came to life in her mouth, swelling, stiffening. She panicked. It was hard to breath when he pushed against her throat, and he was beginning to thrust into her mouth.

She pushed him away, panting for breath.

"What's wrong?"

"I'm afraid I will choke."

"Or are you afraid I will spill my seed in your mouth?"

Her eyes widened. She had not thought of that.

"Surely it is a sin to waste your seed that way."

"A sin?" He laughed incredulously. "If you counted that a sin, then every man in Christendom is doomed to hell."

"They all do this?" Her eyes widened even more. She had not known. She had assumed this was some scandalous perversion he demanded of her.

"No, all men do not do this—but they would like to."

"Why then . . ."

His eyes were cruel. "I suspect that many men would never ask this of their wives. It is not a skill a lady needs to know. But of course, you are not a lady—you're my whore."

Something seemed to snap inside her. She no longer

cared if she aroused his anger further. She would not endure his mocking, contemptuous words any longer.

She jerked her shoulders up, standing as tall as she could. Her eyes met his unflinchingly. "You're wrong, Richard. I am a lady, your lady wife. I demand that you treat me with a little respect!"

He looked startled, then his face flushed with rage; his eyes grew dark and wild.

"Respect! You will not speak to me of respect! All my life I have struggled to win it. I've risked my life, swallowed my pride, had my face ground into the dirt by dozens of men who thought themselves better than me." He paused and his mouth worked, as if the words he spoke strangled him. Gradually he gained control and continued. "And now, after all my efforts, I find myself made a laughingstock before Henry and the arrogant, scheming men around him." His face contorted with anguish. "Do you not see what you have done, Astra? You have humiliated me before my liege lord, before the entire English court!"

Astra stared at him. The look of abject suffering in his eyes made her ache with pity. She had no doubt she was seeing the real Richard Reivers at last. Not the ferocious, frightening Leopard or the charming, glib suitor, but the desperate, tortured boy beneath. It was like a knife in her heart to know she had contributed to his terrible pain.

She reached out her hand, imploring. "Richard, please forgive me. I never meant to . . ."

"No!" He lunged toward her, his features still harsh with agony. "You will pay, Astra. *I will make you pay!*"

She could not help herself. She kneeled down upon the beautiful carpet and sobbed.

Thirty

Richard gritted his teeth at the sight of Astra weeping at his feet. He had to stop her wretched crying, but how? He dare not allow her to think he cared for her pain. He wanted her to feel trapped and helpless. It was a fitting punishment for the woman who had connived to entrap and humiliate him.

God, it was hard to maintain his anger when she wept like that. If only she would get angry and rage at him instead. Then he would be able to keep taunting her, to hurt her as he planned.

He closed his eyes, trying to block out the sound of her sobs. Why wouldn't she fight him, attack him as he had her? How had she managed to remain tender and contrite, her body warm and willing? He recalled her moan of pleasure as he penetrated her. In that moment, the passion of her response had completely undone him. He had forgotten his anger and vengeance and given in to the ecstasy of possessing her, the rapture of melding their flesh.

He suppressed a shudder. It was not supposed to be like that. No woman had ever affected him this way before. He had always kept his distance, used their bodies, manipulated their childish moods for his own ends. Women were meant to be seduced, to be taken, to be enjoyed. You were not supposed to care for them. If you did, you ended up like old Henry—weak, contemptible.

She was still crying. She looked pitiful. She wasn't very big anyway, and now she was curled into a little ball on the blue carpet. Her long braids fell forward over her knees, veiling her creamy skin. It was just as well. He didn't want to see her beauty. He had to make her cease crying. His own throat was burning. Watching her made him want to weep himself.

"Stop it, Astra." He forced his voice to be cold and commanding. She did not look up. If anything, she wept harder.

"I won't abide this. If you don't quit mewling, I'll beat you senseless."

There was no answer. He felt like a fool. He was incapable of beating her. He knew it, and she likely did too. Maybe that was why, up to now, she had remained so calm, so yielding. She knew his weakness. The thought unnerved him. How would he ever punish her, ever wreak his vengeance against her, if she had the power to unman him with her tears, her gentleness?

He took a step away from the woman crouched at his feet. Astra was dangerous. He had let her see too much of himself, of the anguish and desperation that drove him. Now she would use that knowledge to weaken his resolve, to manipulate him. She would reduce him to a spineless buffoon. He had to get away.

He found his clothes and dressed hurriedly. Astra wept softly, unceasingly. He refused to look at her.

He struggled into his boots and quit the room, slamming the door behind him. Out in the hallway, he felt better. He would find the other knights and drown his fears in an alepot and the warm comfort of a whore's slick thighs. He grimaced. He had no taste for a sloppy, smelly trull after Astra, and he had no heart for a joyless night of debauchery with a pack of crude soldiers he hardly knew.

God's teeth, how he missed Will!

She was freezing. It was the cold that finally made her get up and stumble over to the bed. No matter her problems, there was no point getting chilled to death.

She shivered in the soft blankets for a while, trying to warm herself. It was no use. Her heart felt cold and empty, as if it were full of ice. She would never forget the haunted, hopeless look on Richard's face. There was no way to block out the knowledge that she had contributed to his suffering, to the bleak, soul-rending pain that was destroying him.

Astra clutched a fist to her mouth, suppressing a gasp at the almost physical distress her thoughts evoked. There had to be some way to reach Richard, to make him realize how much she loved him, how desperately she wanted to heal his wounds, not worsen them. If only he would let go of his anger for a moment, if only if he would listen to her.

She shook her head. Perhaps it was too soon. It had only been two days since the scene in the chapel. Only time could ease the intensity of the bitterness Richard bore in his heart. Or perhaps nothing could. Astra's body stiffened as she considered that her husband might never forgive her, that he might go to his grave hating her.

No. She could not think like that. Richard had loved her once, and she had to believe he still cared for her a little. If nothing else, she was certain his desire for her had not waned. She touched herself, remembering the sensation of Richard's body inside her own, the splendor of their joining. It had been much more than an expression of lust. Something bound them, flesh-to-flesh, spirit-to-spirit. No matter what Richard thought, there was some deep tie between them, some closeness so profound and intense that nothing less than death could destroy it.

Hope, fragile but enduring, suffused Astra's heart, and she slept.

Someone was poking him. Richard woke slowly, trying to sort out the irritation of the hand jabbing in his ribs from the vexations of his dreams.

"It's morning, Richard. You must have spent a rough one last night to be such a slug today. I could have cut your throat twice over in the time it's taken you to rouse."

"Will! What are you doing here?" Richard asked sleepily as he sat up on the bench in the knights' quarters.

"I might ask you the same question. The first thing I learn upon returning to London is that you have wed. The second thing is that you've quarreled with your new wife and are sleeping off your temper in the barracks."

"Good God, Will." Richard passed a hand over his eyes. "Don't sound so bloody cheerful. My life's a ruination. I'm wedded to that bitch Astra, and the King is furious with me."

"What's that? You aren't happy with Astra? I thought you were besotted with the woman."

"Besotted, bewitched, befooled—they are only different words for the pathetic state of being so blinded by a woman's charms that you fall into her trap like a despicable ass. I've been had, Will. The King made me marry Astra."

"Why?"

"Trickery. Astra lured me into the Queen's chapel and enticed me with her charms. In came the King—prim old Henry got a good eyeful of my wife in luscious *deshabille.* He saw me with Astra backed up against the wall and rape on my mind and didn't waste time asking questions. We were wed the next day at his royal command."

"Jesu, it sounds rather sordid."

"Oh, it was. Now you know what appalling baseness the pure and innocent Lady Astra was willing to stoop to in order to have her way. But I have turned the tables on her," Richard added, his mouth twitching. "Astra may be my wife now, but I'm determined to treat her like the whore she is. I've already had two nights' entertainment at her expense, and by the time I'm through, she'll wish she'd never met me. She'll be ready to put out a shingle and sell herself to any man rather than share my bed."

Will de Lacy regarded his friend coldly. "Is that why you're sleeping here, mumbling and moaning in your wretched slumbers as if you had the ague? You look like hell itself, Richard, and I'm not convinced you're enjoying this plot to humiliate Astra. I think you still care for her. You're just too stubborn and vengeful to admit it."

"I still lust for her, aye, but that's different. Eventually I'll get my fill of Astra and stop wanting her. It's only a matter of time."

"You scratch the itch and it goes away, is that it?"

"Or something like it. Now that I know Astra's true nature, I should be able to cure myself of my passion for her after only a few more nights."

"What a miserable goal, Richard. You should be happy to find love. You shouldn't seek to extinguish what many men search a lifetime to find."

"I don't want it," Richard said stubbornly. "I don't want

to care for a woman. It's dangerous, inconvenient, absolutely foolhardy."

Will shook his head and made as if about to leave. Richard stopped him.

"Don't go, Will. You haven't even told me about your visit to Thornbury."

Will sighed. "Nothing has changed. My father insists I wed and see to the business of getting an heir."

"Find one then, Will. London is crawling with women hungry for a rich husband."

"It's not so simple. If I wed a woman I am fond of, I will feel guilty that I cannot offer her more than brotherly affection, and if I wed someone I have no feelings for, what sort of marriage is that?"

"It's the sort of marriage most men have. Look at Gloucester—the King's brother endured a loveless marriage for years. He got the son he wanted and a fortune as well. You'd be wise to follow his example."

"I'm not likely to get a son," Will said bitterly. "And I don't covet land enough to ruin some young woman's life by marrying her."

"Then marry a poor woman. Offer her enough rich gowns and baubles and she'll not care a whit if you ever share her bed."

"I don't fancy such an arrangement. Unlike you, Richard, I have my conscience to think of."

"You're too bloody sensitive!"

"And you're too much of a bloody bastard!" retorted Will, stomping away.

Richard stared after him, his mouth twitching irritably. How had he come to be quarreling with Will? It must be Astra's fault. Ever since he had met her, things had gone wrong. There had been the disastrous tournament in Tudbury, the fruitless journey to London to seek the King's favor, and now the galling punishment of having to wed a woman he didn't want. He had lost his luck, the aura of invincibility and glory that made him the fierce and deadly Black Leopard. What was wrong with him?

"The Queen observes that you are troubled. She's bound to question you," Marguerite warned.

"I can't imagine what I shall tell her." Astra sighed and rolled up her needlework. "If I even hint at the truth, she's likely to have Richard publicly flogged. Yet I don't lie well enough to convince her that nothing is wrong."

"Perhaps you could turn her concern to Richard's advantage. If she thought that he was disgruntled because you have no real dowry, she might agree to go to the King and ask him to help Richard."

"No. I told you that Richard does not wish me to beg a boon of the Queen on his behalf. If I were to do something like that now, when he is already so wroth with me . . ." Astra shivered. She couldn't bear to think of the consequences if Richard suspected her of more intrigue and manipulation.

"It is a coil," Marguerite agreed, looking grimly at her own needlework. She sighed. "Nothing is going as planned."

Astra regarded her friend uneasily. It was unlike her to be so melancholy. "What's wrong, Marguerite? I have guessed that you are troubled, but I have been too distracted by my own cares to delve into the matter."

Marguerite continued to stare at the linen chemise she was embroidering. "It is a grave thing, Astra, and one that no one else must know of, especially the Queen."

"What, Marguerite? What is it?"

Her friend looked up; a bitter smile twisted her lips. "I've done exactly what I warned you against. I am *enceinte.*"

Astra gasped. "How far gone are you?"

"By my reckoning the babe should be born near St. George Day."

"Holy Mary! That does not give you much time!"

"Time for what, Astra?"

"Why, to wed the father before anyone guesses, of course."

Marguerite's mouth quirked bitterly again. "That is part of the dilemma. You see, the father is already married."

Astra's mouth fell open. She stared at her friend, too shocked to speak.

"Do you hate me, Astra?" Marguerite asked softly, her eyes lowered.

"Of course not. It is only that I don't know what to do, how to help you. It would seem you must marry someone though—and quickly."

"Don't you want to know who the father is?"

"Not unless you wish to tell me."

Marguerite sighed, her dark eyes shimmering with tears. "It was Christian de Hasting, the man I was meeting that night we went to Southwark. You know how seldom it is that I find noblemen to my liking. Christian is different. He is robust and handsome for all that he is well-born. He speaks graciously and has fine manners, but he is not above a wicked jest or a venturesome frolic. We could not be seen together in public often, but we met alone whenever we could. It was paradise for a time, but I'm afraid my feelings got the best of me. Oh, Astra," Marguerite moaned. "What can I do? I always said that if this happened, I would get rid of the babe, but somehow . . ." She patted her still-flat stomach tenderly. "I cannot seem to make myself do it; this is all I have left of Christian, all I will ever have."

"Blessed Jesu! Don't even speak of such things. To make yourself lose the babe would be a terrible sin!"

"Better to burn in hell than face my father's wrath," Marguerite muttered.

"Your father loves you; once he knows of your trouble, I am sure he will move heaven and earth to find you a husband."

"No, he won't—because I'm not going to tell him."

"Not tell him? What do you mean? You must tell him. Only with your father's help can you possibly hope to find a husband in time. If you do not wed soon your reputation will be ruined."

"It doesn't matter," Marguerite said stonily. "I intend to tell my father that I have decided to return to Stafford and take vows. Stafford is a poor abbey; I suspect it will take only a small portion of my dowry to persuade the good sisters to take me in. Perhaps they can even find a home for a child—someplace close by where I could visit occasionally."

For a moment, Astra could only gape at her friend. The idea of Marguerite living out her life in a priory was utterly preposterous. "You can't be serious. You hated Stafford, and you have absolutely no vocation for the holy life. There has to be some other alternative. If you won't go to your father, we must somehow find you a husband ourselves."

"How?" Marguerite arched her dark brows.

"What of Will?" Astra asked, her face brightening. "You said he would not wed because he cannot father children, but perhaps you could strike a bargain with him. He forgives you the babe, and you give him an heir. It seems the perfect solution."

"I'd rather be a nun."

"Why?"

Marguerite's shoulders stiffened. "I cannot explain it. Suffice to say that a marriage between William de Lacy and I would be a very troubled one."

Astra gazed at her friend in bafflement, then reached out to embrace the taller woman. "I'm sorry," she whispered. "If I could do anything for you, Marguerite, you know I would."

"There is nothing," Marguerite whispered. Tears stained her smooth cheeks. "There is nothing anyone can do."

No, Astra decided. She would not accept Marguerite's despair. If there was life; there was hope. She had to believe that. She would pray—for both of them; surely the answer would come to her.

Thirty-one

Astra clutched her cloak tightly about her and shivered in the freezing autumn wind. The leering knight at the barracks said that William de Lacy had gone to check on one of his horses—a mare who had a bad leg and was always going lame. Astra hurried across the offal-strewn courtyard to the stables. It was the perfect opportunity to speak to Will alone.

The idea had come to her that afternoon while she was pondering Marguerite's predicament. For all that her friend dismissed the idea out of hand, Astra felt sure that Will would be willing to wed Marguerite once he knew the disaster she faced. Will was a kind-hearted and loyal man. Astra could not forget how distressed he had been when he found out Richard had gone to fight in Wales. Few men ever showed such concern for the fate of another, and Astra did not doubt that he would show similar compassion for Marguerite.

She slowed as she reached the stables. It smelled strongly of horses and manure and was warmer than the wind-wracked courtyard, but it was also huge and dark. Astra could hardly imagine how she would find one man in such a place. She moved slowly down the dim rows of stalls, searching. If he was going to tend to a horse, Will would have taken a light of some kind. She would look for the glow of a horn lantern or torch from one of the stalls.

It was not light that drew her finally, but the sound of voices. They were softly-pitched, faint but enough to guide her down another corridor. She paused. Ahead of her she could make out the forms of two men facing each other, illuminated by the faint glow of a lantern. They were so close they were almost touching, and their voices were low and indistinct. Something about the scene disquieted her. There was a strange intimacy in the way the two men stood next each other. Astra could not help wondering if they were conspiring something.

"Lord de Lacy?" Her voice rang out in the stillness of the stables. The two men froze. Astra felt a stab of fear. What if these men were ruffians, plotting something sinister? She was alone, defenseless, and no one had any idea where she was.

"Who's there? Who goes?"

Astra did not recognize the voice of the man who queried her, but he sounded cultured, refined. She relaxed slightly and answered. "It is Lady Reivers. I have come looking for Lord de Lacy. I was told he was here, seeing to an injured mare."

"Astra, is that you?"

To Astra's relief, Will stepped forward, into the weak light of the lantern.

"My lord, I am sorry to interrupt, but I would have a word with you. It is regarding Marguerite."

"Marguerite?" Will's voice sounded strained, confused.

"Aye. I can return later if you wish. But I would speak to you tonight. It is urgent."

"Of course, Astra. My friend and I were on the verge

of returning to the palace ourselves. I will escort you there in a moment."

"If you please, Will, it might be better if we talked here. Marguerite does not know I come to speak to you, and I'd rather she did not learn of it."

There was silence for a moment, then Will nodded. "I will be with you in a moment." He exchanged a few whispered words to his companion, then the man called farewell and disappeared down the corridor. Astra felt a pang of disappointment that she hadn't had a chance to see his face. She was exceedingly curious about what the unseen man and Will were discussing.

"My lady, what is this? What has distressed you so much that you would seek me out in this rude place?"

Astra took a deep breath. Now that she was alone with Will, she was not sure quite how to begin.

"I've come to ask your aid, my lord. Not for myself but for Lady Marguerite. It appears you are quite fond of her, and she has need of help right now."

"Marguerite? What's happened?" Will reached out and grasped Astra's hands. She could see his face clearly now; he looked alarmed. She had been right to come to him, to ask for his help.

"She is . . . going to have a baby." It was very embarrassing, not the sort of thing one spoke about to a man at all. She guessed from Will's strained silence that he was embarrassed as well.

"The father?" Will asked softly. "What of him?"

"He is already wed," Astra answered, wincing as she realized how she betrayed her friend's secret. For a moment she had the gloomy thought that she was meddling in another's life. Would this turn out as wretchedly as things had with Richard?

Will said nothing.

"Marguerite must wed someone, and soon, or there will be a terrible scandal."

"Her father—surely with his wealth and influence, Lord Fitz Hugh can find Lady Marguerite a husband."

Astra sighed. "She doesn't want to tell her father. She has this absurd idea to enter a convent and have the babe in secret."

"A convent?" Will looked aghast.

"I know it is madness—that's why I've come to you."

"How can I help?"

Astra took a deep breath. "You could wed her yourself."

Only a heartbeat passed before Will answered. "That is not possible."

"Why not? You're fond of her, you admire her, and you do not appear to seek the company of any other woman as much as hers." Astra paused, considering. Perhaps Will wasn't free to wed. "Are you promised elsewhere? Has a betrothal been made for you by your family?"

Will shook his head. "No. There was a betrothal once, but I broke it and paid the woman's family off. The truth is, it would not be fair for me to wed any woman. I fear I would not be much of a husband."

"Oh, your infirmity," Astra said, nodding. "I had forgotten."

"My infirmity?"

"Aye, the sickness or defect that makes you unable to father children. I cannot think the problem would matter much to Marguerite. She is not overly fond of little ones, and she will have the babe she now carries. I would think that would be enough to content her."

"Content her? My dear Astra, I don't think I am the kind of man who would content Lady Marguerite at all!"

Astra folded her arms over her chest stubbornly. "It is true Marguerite usually prefers bigger, more robust men—and cruder ones too, for that matter. But she can hardly afford to be particular now. The important thing is that she weds someone soon."

Will looked taken aback. Astra suddenly realized how ungracious her words had sounded. "My lord, I did not mean to imply that any man would do. I would not be here if I did not admire you greatly. I think you are an exceedingly kind and considerate man. Any woman would be a fool not to want to wed you."

"You flatter me, Lady Astra," Will answered with a wistful, bitter smile. "If you only knew how most people view one such as me. I worry that even someone as gentle and sweet as you would be repulsed if you knew what I really was."

Astra frowned and laid a tender hand upon his arm. "Richard chose you as a friend; he cares deeply for you. You are my friend too, and I'm sure that whatever grieves you would not make me feel differently toward you, if I knew of it."

Will's eyes met hers; the anguish in them startled Astra. "I have denounced Richard as a fool because he will not see your innocence and purity of heart. I believe in that, and because of it I will risk sharing my secret with you. But you must make me a promise in return. You can tell no one what you know about me, for my enemies would use the truth to destroy me."

"Of course, my lord. I swear it."

Will turned away and stared pensively into the flickering shadows the lamp cast upon the stable wall. "Have you heard, Astra, of men who love other men instead of women?"

"Men who love men? Surely the Scriptures teach that it is our Christian duty to love others as we would our brothers."

"Nay, Astra, I do not speak of that kind of love, but the kind of love a man feels for a woman, the hunger, the desire, the burning that is known as lust."

"Lust? You lust for other men? How can that be?"

Will sighed. "I know not, but I have felt it since I was a boy. When I was of an age to feel the first stirrings of the flesh, they were directed not toward women, but toward other boys. A man such as me is counted as damned by the Church. For a man to lie with another man is considered a great sin, an abomination. And yet . . ." his voice shook. ". . . I cannot help myself."

Astra nodded. That much she understood, for it had always been that way between her and Richard. They could not help themselves either.

"Tell me, Will, is it a passion that afflicts your heart as well as your body? Have you known love such as I feel for Richard?"

"Aye, I have known that, too, although it often seems futile. My trysts need always be quick and furtive. There is little time for true love to grow."

Astra thought a moment, then quickly made up her mind. For all that she knew Will was condemned by the Holy Church, she would not adjudge him.

"Nay, I cannot denounce you, Will, for I am a sinner too. I do not see clearly, though, what this has to do with Marguerite. Do you think she would mislike wedding you because of your . . . ?"

Will nodded. "Marguerite is a lusty woman with a taste for men of hearty sexual appetite. Wedded to me, she would be condemned to celibacy, for I have naught to give her except the fond tenderness of a brother."

She had not thought of that, Astra realized with a sinking heart. No wonder Marguerite had so quickly dismissed the notion that she wed Will. It would mean facing life with a man with whom there was no hope of passion. For someone like Marguerite, being a nun might seem easier to bear.

Astra sighed heavily. "I thank you for your honesty, Will, although I cannot say you have eased my mind." She glanced in the direction Will's companion had disappeared. "That man you were with—is he . . . ?"

"My lover? Aye, he is. Now you see how we must meet, the stealth with which we must plan."

"I am sorry, Will. If I could ever aid you, know that I would. You have been a good friend to Richard, and for that I thank you."

"Are things still strained between you and Richard?"

Astra nodded. "I did not mean to hurt him, Will. Although it was in my mind to force Richard to marry me, I never meant for the King to see him disgraced. I begin to wonder if he will ever forgive me. His anger seems to have no end."

"Richard is a proud man. It will take time for his wounded dignity to heal."

"It does not aid me that I bring so little to the marriage. I know that Richard feels that I have not only humiliated him, but thwarted his ambition as well."

"I have no words of consolation to offer you, Lady Astra. He is an odd one, the man they call the Leopard. Because of his past, his heart is filled with bitterness. I can only hope that the love of a good woman will eventually heal his wounds."

"Please, Will . . ." Astra's voice was imploring. "Tell me about Richard. Tell me why he is so terribly unhappy."

"You know naught of Richard's birth and upbringing?" Will asked.

"Not really. I had heard that his mother . . . that she was a harlot."

"It is true, although it is wise to consider the woman's reasons for doing what she did—something Richard will not do."

Will took Astra's arm and began to lead her through the stables. "Richard's sire was a nobleman who abandoned Richard and his mother soon after he was born. His mother was disgraced and desperate. I'm sure she had exhausted every other hope before she decided to sell her body. By serving as mistress to a succession of well-born men, she was able to secure Richard a position as a page in a noble house. I believe she loved her son and wanted to make some sort of life for him. She gave Richard the best chance she could."

"Richard has never forgiven her, has he?"

Will shook his head. "No, he fails to see that she did the only thing she could have. He won't face the fact that her sacrifice enabled him to survive and finally prosper. He sees only the shame she brought down upon him. Richard is a man torn between love for the woman who bore him and a fierce hatred of her for peddling her own flesh—even if it was done to keep him alive."

"Oh, what a grievous decision for a mother to make," Astra murmured. "My heart aches for the poor woman. Is she still living?"

"Nay, the shame and sinfulness of what she did eventually stole away her will to live. She died when Richard was still young."

"Did she never tell him who his father was?"

Will shook his head as they paused at the entrance to the stables. "She said he was born of a wealthy and powerful lineage but gave no name. As a boy, Richard used to peruse the face of every nobleman he met, searching for a glimpse of his sire. He has long since given up the quest. I suspect that Richard favors his mother anywise. It was said that she was a great beauty, with tawny hair, skin like silk and great dark eyes like burning coals."

Astra nodded solemnly. "I thank you, Will de Lacy, for telling me of my husband's past. Knowing what Richard has endured makes me love him all the more dearly." She gave a deep, wracking sigh. "Would that I could somehow heal the wound that festers in his heart. Instead, I fear that what he sees as my betrayal has made it all the worse."

Thirty-two

"What say you, Will? Are you up for a night of revel at the Black Swan?"

Will looked up from fastening his cross-garters as the two men dressed in the barracks to go to the King's Hall. "You are but three days wed. Your place is with your wife."

Richard smirked. "Do you suggest we take her with us? What an amusing thought. I could introduce my wife to Ruby. The red-haired wench could teach her a thing or two."

"You're jesting."

"I thought the distractions of Southwark might ease my black mood, and we could celebrate your return to London."

"Richard, I don't think . . ."

"I'll say goodbye to my lovely wife, then meet you by the Kingsbridge quay." Richard patted his friend on the shoulder and was gone.

Will grimaced as he imagined Richard bidding farewell to Astra. The Leopard was in a strange mood tonight, and his wife would bear the brunt of his nefarious temper. How much could she bear? If Richard continued to abuse her, would Astra eventually learn to hate her husband?

It was a damned shame, Will thought morosely. Astra certainly deserved better. She was a rare jewel, a woman both beautiful and kind-hearted, one fair to look upon and fair-minded. She had not flinched or turned away in revulsion when he told her of his aberration, but been compassionate and nonjudgmental. That she saw fit to call him "friend" after his shocking confession revealed exactly how generous a soul she really was.

But Richard could not see her goodness; his anger made him blind. It was clear he still despised Astra for tricking him into marriage. Why had she done it?—Will wondered. Astra was not one to do things lightly or without believing that good would be served by her actions. Even if she had entrapped Richard into marriage, he could not help but believe she was innocent of any malicious intent. If she had forced Richard to wed her, she had likely had good reasons. It was obvious that she loved her husband, that she wished only for his happiness. If Richard could not see her for what she was, he was a short-sighted fool!

Will got up slowly. As much as he hated following Richard on this perverse journey to Southwark, it seemed best to go along. Mayhaps after his friend had consumed a few pitchers of ale, Will could talk some sense into him.

"Do you want me, wife?" Richard purred.

Astra leaned mutely against the bed. She had been afraid of this. She had not seen Richard all day, and she suspected he was working himself into another temper. He was smiling, a smug, wicked smile. It told her that he had more torment in mind for her.

She watched him, trying to summon up the patience to deal with his endless hostility. After their last confrontation, she had decided to avoid him for a few days, even accepting Marguerite's offer to sleep in their old bedchamber. Then the Queen had stopped her in King's Hall and asked her how things were with Richard. Astra had been too startled and tongue-tied to do anything but mumble that she was on her way to meet him at that very moment.

What a quandary she was in. If she loitered around the other women, the Queen was sure to find out about Richard's mistreatment and punish him. But if she allowed Richard to get her alone, he would continue to harass her. Observing him tonight, she decided he had prepared for this confrontation by drinking heavily. His gait was unsteady, the whites of his eyes were laced with red, and he carried an open wineskin in his hand.

Astra took a step back, trying to think. What did he want from her? Her tears seemed to enrage him, while her compliance aroused him to greater cruelty. What was she to do?

He moved closer, then took a great gulp from the wineskin and wiped his mouth on his dirty black velvet wedding tunic. He smiled again. "Take your clothes off, wife. I wish to pleasure you before I go."

Sighing, she struggled to undo her gown. As he had requested, she wore no chemise beneath. It felt odd to have only her gown against her bare skin, and it was uncomfortably cold in the drafty palace. Still it was convenient when you were constantly baring yourself for a man's enjoyment. Astra had no doubt that harlots did without undergarments completely.

"Come here."

She eased herself forward on the bed, tense with both expectation and dread. She felt a little better that he had not put the wineskin down—what could he do with one hand?

He leaned over and kissed her. She inhaled his wine-stained breath, gasping. It was a practiced kiss, one much like those he used to seduce her with when they first met. His tongue dallied in her mouth, languidly, leisurely. Predictably, her body responded. She began to tremble, feeling both hot with fever and cold with shivers. She had no will to resist as he knelt between her thighs, then grabbed her arm near her shoulder and jerked her, one-handed, farther up on the bed.

She closed her eyes as he touched her. What madness was this—that he should be able to arouse her so easily? In seconds, her nipples had hardened, her legs gone weak. He kissed her again, and she smothered a moan in his mouth.

His touch was deliberate, cold, but devastatingly sure. His fingers made circles around her breasts, teased her tight nipples, then dipped to stroke her belly. She arched her back as he neared the juncture of her thighs. His fingers teased, toyed, tempted. She lifted her hips as he fondled the curve of her lower buttocks, lingering near, so near to the damp, hungry cleft between. She trembled with longing.

"What is it, Astra? What is it you wish?"

"I . . . I . . . I want . . . you."

Richard touched his hand to her mouth. "Nay, wife. I will not be yours tonight." He smiled again, slyly, enigmatically. "I have made you greedy and impatient for more, and it was shockingly easy. I think you missed your vocation, Astra. A woman as shamelessly responsive as you was not meant to be a nun. What do suppose you were meant to be, Astra?"

"A wife," she dared to whisper. "Your wife."

Richard's face hardened. He pushed her down against the bed, then splashed the contents of the wineskin over her belly and thighs. Astra cried out at the coldness of it, then raised herself up to stare at the crimson mess that streaked her lower body and dripped onto the bedcovers.

"What are you doing?" she gasped.

"I'm finishing my wine, before I go."

She shrieked as she felt his warm mouth on her, his tongue licking her skin. He started at her belly and moved downward. Slippery, sensuous sensations rippled over her skin. His tongue was hot, scalding, and yet, where it touched, her body shivered as if cold. He stuck his tongue deep into her navel, drawing another startled cry from her. He looked up and met her eyes, smiling slightly, then his mouth moved lower, gliding between her hipbones.

Slow, silkily, he licked her, making her body hum and vibrate like a tightly-laced tambour. As he trailed his fiery tongue through the hair of her mound, her mind went empty, her thoughts stretching out into nothingness. He sucked the drops of wine from the insides of her thighs, licking closer and closer to the yearning, melting center of her. Finally his tongue slipped inside her, and she sighed in gratification. The pressure increased, insistent, burning. She moaned and thrashed. His hands clutched her bottom tightly, while his mouth coaxed her closer and closer to some elusive shattering triumph.

Then, all at once, the tempting, bedeviling mouth slipped away. She groaned and looked up. An excruciating pang of incompletion wracked her body from one end to the other.

"Please, Richard . . ."

"Please what? Satisfy you? Why should I?"

She sighed in frustration. "Why do you torture me?"

"Because you deserve it." He smiled and reached for

her hand, pressing it against his groin. "See, you are not the only one unsatisfied."

"Then why not . . . love me?" She rubbed him slowly, as seductively as possible.

Richard pulled away. "Because it pleases me to deny you. Thinking upon all the times you lured and tempted me, then thwarted my passion, I realize there is no punishment as just, as righteous as this one."

"You're leaving me?" Astra whispered. The full extent of his abandonment shocked her. She had not imagined this. "Where would you go?"

"To my mistress. A woman who is honest, who does not betray me to the King."

Astra's heart sank. He meant to bed another woman tonight. The thought overwhelmed her with jealousy. "Please don't," she begged. "I will do anything you ask. I will even . . ." she bit off the words. Groveling would only increase his resolve to hurt her.

"Anything, Astra?" He loomed over her, all taunting eyes and tantalizing maleness. "Of course you would; you're my whore."

Astra closed her eyes. "I am not a whore, Richard," she said vehemently. "I am your wife."

"But you are not a *lady*. You forfeited that title when you contrived that sleazy entrapment in the chapel. A lady does not bare her breasts to entice a man in a holy place. For that matter, a lady does not sneak into a knight's tent while he is sleeping. Nor does she meet a man at night alone along the wharves of London."

Astra gritted her teeth. She would not listen to his absurd insults. She had done those things out of love for him, not because she was unchaste. She opened her mouth to argue with him, but had no chance.

"For that matter, Astra, a lady does not beg her husband to bed her. She is pleased that he satisfies his vile needs elsewhere. She spreads her legs only to beget him heirs, and even then she is reluctant. But you, Astra, are a wanton. Your legs fly open at my touch, you moan and quiver at a mere kiss."

As he spoke, Richard moved close again. His hand pressed against her aching mound, arousing a low moan from her throat.

"You are wet for me, always wet." His caressing hand moved away. "Once you maddened me with lust, but now . . ."

Astra heard the sound of Richard getting up from the bed. She opened her eyes and saw him leave the room, shutting the door softly behind him. She sat up, and clutched her arms around herself. It was true. She could not resist him. Never, ever. No matter what her resolve, her body betrayed her.

But perhaps that was because her body knew the truth that Richard, in his anger, sought to deny. They were meant to be together, to be joined as one.

"Watch where you're going, you wretched scum!" Richard shouted at the drunkard who staggered into him, near knocking him down.

"Peace, Richard," Will implored. "Your path is not much steadier than his. We'd best hurry before you fall into the gutter."

They walked on. Will glanced apprehensively at the eerie, mist-shrouded street ahead of them. It was ill chance to be out on a night like this. The fog provided the perfect concealment for thieves, marauders and murderers. Richard and he would be lucky to have only their purses cut instead of their throats.

Will breathed a sigh of relief as they reached the Black Swan. He was pleased to see that the place was near-empty this night. There were few here to pick a fight with Richard or to see him go upstairs with his whore. It would be a fine thing, Will thought, if Lady Astra should hear of this. What lady would not be dismayed to find that her husband of three days was already off to visit his mistress?

Will had hoped that Ruby would not be there, that she might have left with some other customer already, or disappeared into the dark maw of Southwark, never to be heard from again. But there she was, serving some ruffians at the other end of the tavern. Watching her lean over the table, her ample breasts jiggling beneath her thin gown, Will felt a wave of disgust. How could Richard desire a woman like that? One who flaunted her body to every man who passed through the tavern? One who sold herself to anyone with enough silver to pay for her pleasure and the cold, dirty room upstairs?

Will shook his head and wondered at Richard's madness, his stubborn blindness to the beautiful, gracious woman he had wed. Somehow he had to jolt his friend out of this trough of bitterness and self-pity and make him see reason again.

Ruby saw them almost as soon as they were seated. She turned from her rough customers and sauntered over, her hips swaying provocatively.

"Well, well. Look what the dog dragged in. I thought perhaps you'd found another lair, Reivers." Her lips twitched lasciviously as her black-rimmed eyes sank to his crotch. "I've missed my pet. Not another man in London has a blade that fits my notch so deliciously." She leaned forward over the table. The flimsy gown gaped open, displaying her breasts. "The upstairs room is open, love. Would you meet me there now or have a drink first?"

"He'll have a drink," Will answered quickly. Richard nodded sullenly. Ruby gave Will a contemptuous look and went to fetch the ale.

Will leaned close to his friend. "I cannot think that you would want *that* tonight. Ruby cannot hold a candle to the beauteous creature waiting in your bed."

"Expert on women are you now, Will?" Richard observed acidly.

"Nay, but I do have eyes in my head, and ears, too, for that matter. Ruby's naught but a nasty trull who'll spread her legs for any man."

Richard's dark eyes drooped sleepily. "They all do that, Will. She's just more honest about it than some women. I like that. I like her honesty."

"Honesty?" Will snorted. "She'd rob you while you slept if you had anything to steal. Don't flatter yourself to think you hold Ruby's heart—women like that don't have one."

Richard said nothing, merely took a sip from the nearly empty wineskin he carried. If he kept up at this pace, Will shuddered to think how ill his friend would be on the morrow. At least Astra would have a reprieve while Richard slept off his aching head.

Ruby returned and plunked down a tankard of ale before each of them. Then she stood by expectantly, as if waiting for Richard to gulp it down and follow her upstairs. Richard gave her a hostile look, then stood up. "I've got to piss," he muttered.

Ruby watched him walk unsteadily to the door. "You need any help, love, just call me," she taunted softly.

Ruby turned to go, but Will grabbed her wrist and jerked her down on the bench beside him. "While he's gone, you and I are going talk."

"We've nothing to talk about, you filthy jack!"

"Yea, we do have something to speak of," Will hissed, reinforcing his words with a sharp nudge from his misericord. "We will speak of Richard. I don't want him contaminated by your vileness; I'm willing to pay you to turn your attentions elsewhere."

"But he hasn't even bobbed me yet!" Ruby protested in outrage. "You think I don't look forward to my nights with him? He's a far cry from the usual rubbish that comes here. Oh my, Richard is good. The best I've ever had. Why should I give that up?"

"I said I'd pay you, bitch. I've got gold."

"Now, why would you do that?" Ruby's hazel eyes narrowed in suspicion. "You've never cared if the Leopard quiffed me the nightlong afore this. What ails you, de Lacy?"

"Richard was married just three days ago. I'd not have him break his vows so soon."

"Married? The Leopard?"

Will nodded stiffly. He hadn't wanted to tell her, but she'd not grabbed for the money as quickly as he'd expected. Maybe there was a chance of deterring her some other way.

Ruby smiled. "Got a rich one, did he? Tush, tush, Willy Boy. I don't give a fart if Richard's wed some ugly, rich countess. It's all the more reason for him to come back to me. I intend to give him a right proper welcome, remind him of exactly what he's been missing. And I don't want none of your ill-gotten purse," she added defiantly. "You'd probably call the beadles after me and say I pinched it. What would the likes of me be doing with gold anyway?"

"I should call them," Will said coolly. "Turn you in for the cheap strumpet you are. You'd look a fine sight with your head shaved, being carted off to the stocks at Smithfield." He fingered one of Ruby's coppery curls. "I don't think Richard would find you so much to his liking without your pretty hair."

For a moment, Ruby paled, and Will knew she was considering the punishment for prostitution. They shaved the woman's head, then dragged her through the streets while the crowd pelted her with offal and called out dirty names.

Ruby jerked her head away from Will's fingers and gave him a cold, malevolent stare. "The price of being a bawd ain't near so high as that for what you are. I've heard that men who buggar boys are sentenced to be boiled alive. You might think of that before you threaten me."

Will met her eyes with a steady gaze, but deep down he knew she was right. He was not a man who could use the influence and wealth of his title to threaten others; he was too vulnerable himself. Still, there must be some way to get Ruby to quit Richard. It seemed she genuinely desired him. Perhaps the way to wipe the sneer off her painted face was to make her jealous.

"By the by," Will began, leaning back casually. "You're wrong about Richard's wife. She's not rich at all, and she's a far cry from being old and repulsive. She's as fair to look upon as any woman alive."

Ruby snorted contemptuously. "I don't believe you. If Richard's wife wasn't a plain, scrawny bitch, he'd not be here so soon after his wedding."

Will shrugged. "Ask him. Richard'll tell you that his

wife has the face of an angel—and the form to make a man think he has died and gone to heaven."

"How would you know? You're hardly fit to judge a woman's looks."

"I'm only repeating things Richard has said. He can scarcely restrain himself when it comes to describing his wife's beauty. I heard he told a table of knights that his wife had the best tits in Christendom."

"He couldn't have!" Ruby screeched. "That's what he always said about mine!"

Will gave Ruby's bosom a disdainful glance. "I think you're beginning to sag, Ruby. In another year or two, you'll look like naught but an old bossy cow."

Ruby shot him a look that implied she would gladly scratch his eyes out. Her own eyes narrowed to shrewd slits.

"I don't believe a word you say, Will de Lacy. If Richard's wife is a beauty, why doesn't he want to lie with her?"

"A lover's tiff. He'll forgive her by tomorrow, and return to her bed. He wedded her for love, you know. She didn't even have a dowry."

Ruby's mouth fell open. "She can't be poor. Richard had no reason to take a wife except for land and property."

"Believe me, she doesn't have a silver penny to her name."

Will struggled to repress a smile. Ruby's face was unpleasantly flushed with jealousy, her painted lips twisted into an ugly grimace of hatred. Let Richard see her like this—it might well cool his ardor, especially if he recalled Astra's sweet, tranquil countenance.

"Where is he?" Ruby asked suddenly. She looked around. "He should be back by now."

"Why don't you go find him? Ask him about his new wife."

"I will." Ruby rose haughtily from the bench. "I'll do just that."

As she walked away, Will let his grin break free. Richard was very sensitive on the subject of his marriage, and Ruby was too stupid and jealous to leave the matter alone. It should be an ugly fight.

Thirty-three

"Jesu, you startled me! I thought you were some fiend out to slit my throat."

"It's only me, love. Why are you out here alone? It's so much warmer inside." Ruby's fingers edged up Richard's arm.

"I'm thinking." He leaned away from her. He was so tired; the wine was already giving him a headache.

"Will told me you've wed."

"Bloody bastard can't keep his mouth shut."

"What's she like?"

"God's teeth, Ruby, I don't want to talk about it!"

"Why not?"

He glared at her.

"Is it true she's poor?"

"Damnation! I said I don't want to speak . . ."

"Is she beautiful?" Ruby interrupted. "Does she truly have a pleasing form?"

Richard regarded the woman beside him resentfully. Will was right, he'd been a fool to come here. Ruby was an ill-mannered squall, worse even than Astra. At least Astra didn't nag at him like this.

"Aye, she's fair. What of it, Ruby?"

"How fair? What's she got that I don't?"

"You don't want to know."

"Aye, I do," Ruby said petulantly. "I've a right to know. I had you afore she did."

Richard closed his eyes, fighting his weariness. His head seemed to be spinning. "You never had me, Ruby. You were merely a pleasant lay, that's all."

Ruby reached out and put her arms around him. "Tush, love, we had more than that. I never even charged you after the first time. I lay for you because I wanted to. You were always the best, the sweetest, the fiercest . . . my darling Leopard."

He pushed her away in disgust. He could smell her, and she was none too clean. It had never mattered before, but now it did. Astra's pretty flower scent still clung to his hair and skin. He could not believe he had left her for this.

"God in heaven," Ruby muttered, struggling to regain her balance. "It's true, isn't it? You're in love with her!"

He clenched his teeth, saying nothing.

"I can't believe you'd be such a dense-pated fool, to fall for a fancy lady bitch. They're all mewling, white-faced little sticks that don't know the first thing about pleasing a man . . ."

"Shut up, Ruby. I told you I don't want to talk about it."

"Why? Because you're on the outs with her? Not three days wed and already you're fighting." Ruby's lips pulled into a delighted sneer.

"I told you to shut your nasty, painted slit!"

"You never had trouble with my mouth afore this," she taunted. "You always liked what I did with it, swallowing your sweet pet almost whole."

"Jesu, Ruby, what does it take? You keep up with this, and I'll shut your mouth with my fist!"

"Try it," she taunted. "I have naught to fear from a

henpecked fool like yourself. Next you'll be wearing the horns for your lady wife. Now that she's wed, she has no reason to keep her legs together. As soon as you leave London, she'll be lifting her linen for some well-hung gallant."

The rage rose in him, blotting out the dizziness. He lunged forward and aimed for Ruby's provoking mouth. Before he could land the blow, strong arms grabbed him from behind.

"Christ, Richard. She's not worth it!"

Will's words sank in slowly. His friend was right. It was stupidity to let Ruby taunt him. He didn't want to be here, in this filthy alley. He didn't want to be anywhere near this place.

He sagged back against Will. His stomach was roiling dangerously. "We've got to leave," he muttered. "Got to get back to Westminster."

"Sure, sure. Go back to your royal slut," Ruby called out. She turned and went into the tavern, hips still swaying outrageously.

Richard rubbed his hand over his sweaty face. When he opened his eyes, Will was standing there, watching him coldly.

"You're jealous."

"And you're imagining things."

"I think not. I heard what Ruby said to you, how she provoked you to strike her. The thought of Astra with another man is what made you lose control."

Richard shook his head, trying to clear away his confusion. Will had a point. Why should he care? Why should the thought of Astra being unfaithful anger him?

"You love her, Richard. You're sick with it, out of your head."

"That's the wine."

"You're no better sober. Admit it. Admit that you love Astra."

Richard leaned back against the rough wood of the backside of the tavern. Could Will's words be true? Could he still love Astra—even after what she had done? He was sure he hated her, but maybe he was wrong. His plan to punish Astra had not worked out at all; every taunt and piece of nastiness he used against her had cut into his heart as deeply as it had hers. Even now he felt as if he was bleeding to death from a dozen wounds. He would never forget the anguish in her eyes on their wedding night, the tenderness on her face when she kissed him the morning afterwards, the despair that made her weep at his feet. Every cruelty he aimed at her came back to haunt him. Was that love?

"Let's go back," Will coaxed.

Slowly, he nodded.

She was asleep. The beautiful room was dark, the curtains on the bed pulled closed. His stiff cold fingers fumbled to undo his clothes. He could not forget how he had left her. Astra had offered herself to him, begged him for love, and he had turned away, mocking her. The image pained him. Dear God, how he could possibly keep up this pretense of hatred!

He pulled back the curtains, searching for a glimpse of her. It was too dark to see, but he could hear her even breathing and smell her faint, female perfume. She lay there in her splendid beauty, offering him everything he wanted, and yet he must reject her, again and again. It was growing harder and harder to keep his caresses cold and impersonal, to incite her lust and reject her love. Her tears had tormented him, but no more than her placid, wide-eyed tolerance of his anger. When she gazed at him with that aching look of love that promised acceptance and forgiveness of anything, he was undone. How could he fight an angel?

He eased slowly into the bed. It would be better if he did not wake her. She was a slippery, bedeviling foe, and he could not understand her. Any woman he had ever known would have begun to fight back by now, to wound him with words if naught else. They would have long since complained to the Queen and begged for release from their torment. It was evidence of Astra's amazing forbearance and selflessness that she had not done so. Her love made her protect him from the Queen's wrath. It was an amazing thing, and he had not known the like in his lifetime. Men could be loyal unto death, but women were weak, fickle creatures—or so he thought before he met Astra. Now he wondered.

He shook off the mood with a shudder. Next he would be thinking of children and planning for a future with Astra. He was not ready for that. He had no way to keep a family, and no instinct for fatherhood. It would not be fair to curse a child as he had been cursed. He had been lucky so far, but he could not predict that he would not be killed in his next battle. Then how would Astra fare? She was as poor as him. She might be so stupid and naive as to trust to the future and benevolence of her friends, but he was not.

The winds of fortune swept across England every few years, making paupers of lords and destroying great families. There was no security, no future at all. It was madness to bring children into such a world. Born to toil and woe—the Scriptures said man was destined to such.

Richard closed his eyes and let the images come to him until his throat was choked with despair: the men in his mother's bedchamber, the grunts and moans, the vacant look in his mother's dark eyes, the bruises that sometimes marred her creamy skin.

At first he had been afraid, but then he grew older and knew shame, the taunts of the other boys, the condescending look on the faces of the knights he served. They marked him for what he was: a bastard, a whore's son. Gradually the shame had turned to rage. He lashed out—and was beaten. He had vowed that day to become so strong and fierce no man would ever defeat him again. He trained to be an awesome, intimidating knight, but even as he neared his goal, he learned that strength and battle prowess were not enough. Only land and wealth gave true power, protection from the cruel words and mockery of others.

It was then he set his sights on being rich. It did not seem like such an unreasonable dream. Plenty of men had risen high by winning battles for their king, plenty others had married well and found fortune that way. But always the goal eluded him. Henry was too dissolute and wavering to raise a lowly knight; the heiresses he sought mistrusted his handsome face and winning smile. He came away empty-handed.

Now his dream seemed further away than ever. He was saddled with a penniless, helpless wife who foolishly believed in rainbows and the Holy Church and the goodness of her fellow man. A woman so naive she actually imagined that love could survive in marriage, that loyalty and faithfulness were the natural way of things between a man and his wife. She likely expected him to never go to whores—even when he was away from her.

It was preposterous, and he knew he would fail her eventually. Perhaps, more than anything, that was why he hadn't wanted this marriage. He didn't want to fail Astra, to destroy her fair, enchanted dreams. It would be better if he abused her so much that she asked for an annulment. Let some other man try to live up to her fantasy of wedded life; it was not for him.

But so far, he realized ruefully, he had not had much success in driving Astra away. Here she was, lying beside him, sleeping peacefully, waiting for him to come back to her. If he pulled aside the bedcovers, he would likely find her naked, as he had asked her to be for him.

The thought made his throat go dry, and he hardened almost instantly. How could he resist such damnable temptation—even if he knew it would only lead to more suffering in the end?

He sighed and turned toward her. In the morning, he would be cold and cruel again. In the morning he would be sober and rested and sated. He would be better able to deal with her. His thoughts wouldn't be so muddled, twisting and turning in hopeless circles.

He reached out and touched a silken shoulder. She sighed softly as she turned toward him.

It was a dream. She was in Richard's arms, and there was no anger and bitterness between them. His hands were tender, poignant in their gentleness. His body was hot and alive, scalding her. She wanted him with a great surging need that robbed her of fear and wariness, and it was the most natural thing in the world to open her legs for him.

He slid inside her without the slightest difficulty or hesitation. The fire sprang between them, burning them both as they writhed and twisted.

The bed danced, the night danced. She escaped the tangled cord that bound her to pain, to thought, to the boundaries of her soul, and sailed in a long corridor of light, panting and gasping at the bliss of it.

Richard was with her, above her, within her, as one. He let her cup his face and cry out his name, and in the wordless darkness she even sensed he smiled. It is a dream, she thought. It must be, to be so close, so safe, so happy. And yet there was a raw edge to it, a slippery, savory fierceness, a quickening in the blood, a brutal merging of the flesh.

She shed her hazy contentment and sought the fury of it, the white-hot ecstasy of their joining. It came upon her like a vast, heaving storm, tearing her to bits, rending her asunder with a bucking, pitching crescendo that wrenched an anguished cry from her lips. She had reached it, some place far away and only half-known, and she was not alone there.

The storm subsided, and they were only tangled limbs and sticky bodies, hot skin and chests heaving like bellows. The division between their bodies renewed itself. It was dark and late, and Astra realized that she knew the man panting beside her only by his scent and the feel of his skin. He was a stranger still, and when the darkness lifted on the morn, his eyes might well be full of hate.

The thought made her draw away. She remembered how he had left her, unsatisfied, humiliated, miserable. He had gone to a whore, to a common, filthy, unchaste woman, but one he liked better than her.

Tears burned the corners of her eyes. Why had he come back? Why?

He must have known she despaired, for he reached for her and gave her a vague, familiar pat on her flank, such as one might give a dog. Still it soothed her, kept her tears from falling. This time there were no mocking words, only the companionable sound of his breathing. This time he had not taunted her, but took her with a profound possessiveness that left her shuddering. Something seemed changed between them, but she could not be sure what it was.

She longed to look into his eyes, to search his harshly handsome face for the answer she needed. She heard his soft, rhythmic breathing and sighed.

It was too late; already he slept.

Thirty-four

"Papa! You've come!"

"My dear Marguerite," Lord Fitz Hugh responded, giving her a fond kiss as they met in the entrance to the Queen's gallery. "Is something wrong, sweeting? Your summons was unexpected. I'd not intended to return to court until Candlemas."

"Nothing is wrong," Marguerite reassured him blithely. "But now that my friend Astra has wed, you must see to bequeathing her the manor near the Thames."

"Oh, the manor. I'd near forgotten. Well, that is no great matter. With the help of the King's clerks, it will be an easy enough transaction to complete. Tell me, Marguerite, whom did she marry? I hope he is a man worthy of her."

"Very worthy. The King himself gave his blessing to the marriage. Lady Astra has wedded Sir Reivers, one of the fine young knights who rescued us near Tudbury."

Fitz Hugh nodded. "I remember him now. He was without land himself, if I recall. No wonder they need the manor."

"Richard may be poor, but Astra loves him dearly. Oh, Papa, is it not like a jongleur's tale, a handsome, courageous knight and a fair damsel wedding for love?"

"Love?" Fitz Hugh barked, his thick brows pulling into

a frown. "Well now, that is a dubious reason to marry. I hope you don't have any silly notions of a love match."

"Of course not, Papa. Indeed, these months at court have taught me that there is a much deeper purpose to life than I ever dreamed. In fact, that it is part of why I have called you here—to discuss my future."

"Your future, aye," Fitz Hugh nodded emphatically. "Indeed, that is the very thing I wish to speak about. I am on the verge of negotiating a marriage contract for you that will be the envy of every man at court."

Marguerite's eyes lit up. "A marriage contract? Truly?"

"I'm sure the man will meet with your satisfaction, Marguerite," her father answered smugly. "He is young, lusty and well-favored in looks. I had surmised that that was what you were aiming for."

Marguerite blushed. "Who is he, Papa?"

"Guy Faucomberg—heir of one of the finest families in England."

Marguerite's mouth gaped open.

"You know him, don't you?" her father prompted. "I thought so. His father said he was at court this summer. So, then, Marguerite, what do you think of him?"

Her mind whirled. Faucomberg. Will and Richard despised him. Astra said he gave her the shivers. Still, he was indecently rich, and if there was a way to convince him the babe was his. . . .

"Are you pleased, Marguerite?" her father asked impatiently. "I've worked hard on this match. It means enlarging the Fitz Hugh estates most favorably, and you will be a wealthy woman in your own right. Should Faucomberg be killed in war, you never need marry again, except of course, where the King commanded."

"Of course, I am delighted, Papa." She bent slightly to

plant a kiss on his broad cheek. "Do you have any idea when the wedding will take place?"

Her father shrugged. "I have no idea. Your mother will be seeing to that end of the venture."

Marguerite gave him her most radiant smile. "I hope it can be soon, Papa. Very soon."

"Guy Faucomberg!"

Astra nodded. "I know you are not fond of the man, but still, it is a fortuitous turn of events. Marguerite has given up her absurd notion of taking holy vows, and I am very much relieved."

Astra and Will de Lacy were walking in the Queen's garden. It was a fine fair day, and while Astra noted wistfully that all the flowers were already dead or dying, the warm sunny air belied the fact that summer was over.

"Well, I am not relieved," Will muttered. "Poor Marguerite—she would be better off having the child without a husband than cursing the babe to a sire like that."

"Really, Will—you mislike the man that much?"

"Aye, I do. He's a cruel devil who treats women like the dirt beneath his feet. What do you think will happen when Faucomberg learns Marguerite was *enceinte* when they wed? I can only hope he doesn't beat her and make her lose the babe!"

"He won't find out," Astra answered confidently. "Marguerite is pressing her father to have the wedding take place right away, and when the babe is born, she means to bribe the midwife to say it was simply born before its time."

"Jesu, it's obvious you grew up in a convent, Astra. Faucomberg may be pigheaded in some ways, but he's not utterly stupid. He'll know something is amiss when a summer babe comes in the spring and is born full-grown and healthy."

"Perhaps he won't care. Perhaps by then he'll be in love with Marguerite."

Will's blue eyes narrowed coldly. "Believe me, Astra, Rathstowe isn't going to fall in love with anyone, leastwise his wife. Marguerite will be lucky if he doesn't kill her for her deceit."

"Surely you're wrong," Astra responded in a shaken voice. "You know how angry Richard was with me, but he never abused me physically and even now he seems to be getting over his wrath."

"I'm pleased Richard has come to his senses, but I do not think you can compare him to Rathstowe. Richard was blinded by his anger, but underneath he is good man—as loyal and decent as anyone. Rathstowe is not cut of the same cloth."

Astra sighed. "I hope you're wrong, for I doubt I can persuade Marguerite from the marriage. She feels it is the only way to avoid telling her father the truth, and she is determined to do that at all costs."

"Why? I cannot think that Fitz Hugh is such a monster he would not forgive his daughter her predicament."

"Of course he would forgive her. But Marguerite worships her father, and she is loath to disappoint him once again. To avoid that, she is willing to do anything—even waste away in a convent the rest of her life."

Will shook his head. "The convent will seem like heaven after the hell Rathstowe will put Marguerite through if he learns the truth. If you cannot persuade her to give up this madness, I must see to it."

He turned to leave the garden; Astra touched his arm

softly. "I appreciate your concern for Marguerite, Will, but in truth, I did not ask you here to discuss Marguerite's predicament, but my own."

Will glanced at her in alarm. "Astra, what is it? You said things were better with Richard."

"Aye, they are. He is calmer these days, much less angry, but still he worries me."

"Why?"

Astra leaned down to pick a slightly wilted aster from among the dried weeds, searching for the words to explain her problem. Richard was no longer cold and mocking, but he was not the man she had fallen in love with either. "I should not complain, but I cannot help it, Will. I think something is wrong with Richard. He speaks to me seldom, comes to me only for lovemaking. Sometimes I find him looking at me in a way that makes me afraid."

"Afraid? How so?"

She straightened. "It is as if he pitied me. As if he knew what was to happen to me, and it grieved him somehow."

"Does he still seek to . . . to punish you?" Will asked hesitantly.

Astra blushed. "Nay, he is not so harsh a lover these days, nor does he taunt me and mock me unto tears. But that is the thing that worries me, Will. He says almost nothing to me at all. Richard—who once dazzled me with his witty jests and enchanting words, who once we were wed regularly tormented me with his vulgar talk and base gibes—he is nearly silent these days."

"I have marked it, too, and I know not what to make of it. It seems as if some ill-humor has befallen the Leopard, some burden that he cannot or will not speak of."

Seeing Astra's worried face, Will hurried to soothe her. "I'm sure his melancholy will be fleeting. Richard has always been one for strange moods, but in the end, he returns to his usual light-hearted, charming self."

"I hope you are right," Astra murmured. "I cannot shake this cold dread that clutches my heart. But perhaps some of my worry is for Marguerite. Go, Will, and talk to her. Try to stop her from wedding Faucomberg, before it's too late."

Will nodded and hurried from the garden.

The courtyard of Westminster bustled with activity as the dozens of grooms, squires and servants prepared for the King's hunt. Will dodged the mayhem of horses, hounds and retainers and hurried toward the tall elegant woman dressed in a stunning black velvet riding costume, her sleeves slashed with scarlet sarcenet, her black veil studded with rubies.

"Lady Marguerite!"

She turned and gave him a dazzling smile. "Will, come and greet my father. He just arrived at court this morn."

"Lord Fitz Hugh." Will bowed deeply.

"Ah, de Lacy. I must congratulate you. I charged you with the onerous task of looking after my daughter while she was in London, and I must say you have done well. I have just spoken to the Queen, and other than one little escapade in Southwark, Marguerite has avoided trouble for the longest stretch I can recall."

"It was my pleasure, your lordship," Will offered stiffly.

"Nonsense. I know exactly what my daughter is like, and I anticipated that the temptations of a King's court would prove even worse than those of an isolated country priory. It impresses me that you have managed to prevent her from tarnishing her reputation beyond what a decent man can allow."

Will's eyes met Marguerite's. He saw defiance etched in their gleaming depths, and he gave her a sad smile. "I would speak to you later," he murmured as he bent to kiss her hand.

"De Lacy, I won't have you thinking I mean to let your efforts to protect my daughter's virtue go unremarked," Fitz Hugh was saying in his bluff, hearty voice. "If you would but ask a boon of me, I would be delighted to reward you in some fashion."

"No reward is necessary, your lordship. I did what I did out of fondness for your daughter."

Fitz Hugh frowned. "That simply won't do, de Lacy. I intend to repay you, and so I shall. If you cannot think of anything this moment, give the matter some thought over the next few days." He smiled broadly, and his dark eyes twinkled. "You'd be a fool not to take advantage of me. I vow I am so pleased with myself these days, I'd agree to almost anything you might ask."

Will felt his heart sinking as he responded to Fitz Hugh's prompt. "And why is it that you are pleased, my lord?"

Lord Fitz Hugh puffed out his chest. "A few days hence, I expect to announce a brilliant match for my daughter's hand. I can't mention the man's name yet, because the final negotiations aren't complete, but suffice it to say that it will be the wedding of the season."

"That is good news, your lordship. When will the happy event take place?"

Lord Fitz Hugh frowned. "Her mother fancied a Yuletide wedding at Ravensmore, but my Marguerite is impatient for the deed to be done."

"That's right, Papa," Marguerite said sweetly. "I really don't want to wait."

Will gave Marguerite a swift, knowing look. "I wouldn't rush things, Lord Fitz Hugh. A few weeks is hardly enough time to plan for a wedding. The contracts must be signed, and there is all that folderol of gowns and food and entertainment to be arranged."

Marguerite gave Will a hostile look. "If I mean to be wed, I'd rather not waste time about it, Papa."

Fitz Hugh shrugged. "Of course, if the wedding can be moved up, I will see to it. 'Twould be a relief to me to dispense with all the foolish frivolity women seem to insist on."

Marguerite rewarded her father with a spellbinding smile. Will swallowed uneasily. He had to speak to Marguerite as soon as possible. As far as he was concerned, she was about to entangle herself in an arrangement that would bind her for life to a man as cold-hearted and cruel as the devil himself.

The autumn air rang out with the clatter of hoofs, the anxious bark of the hunting dogs and jingle of the noblemen's spurs. At the head of the brightly-garbed procession of the King's hunting party, the scarlet and gold royal banners snapped and whipped in the breeze. High ranking noblemen, knights and ladies in a brilliant procession of saffron and purple samite, gold and black diapered silk, crimson, green and deep blue velvet rode in a long line down the dusty road. Bringing up the rear were the royal servants: dog handlers, falconers, personal retainers, as well as carts carrying food and other provisions.

Astra cast a glance sideways at her husband as they rode

in the middle of the caravan. Her heartbeat, as always, quickened at the sight of him. Unlike the rest of the splendid company, he wore a rather ragged-looking leather tunic and worn green chausses tied with cross-garters. He looked more like a huntsman than a knight, but the old clothes became him, their roughness contrasting appealingly with his gleaming dark hair and velvety brown skin. Astra thought he had never looked more handsome, and her breath caught each time she remembered that he had actually asked her to go along on the royal hunt.

Distracted, Astra forgot to guide her horse, and the rather plodding black gelding stumbled slightly. She clutched the horse's mane nervously and worried that she would suffer the indignity of falling from her mount before the hunt even began. For all that her charming green velvet riding costume made her look like a fine lady, her lack of skill on a horse reminded her that she was naught but a simple country girl.

In contrast, Richard sat his horse with the easy grace with which he did everything. His spirited chestnut mare pranced and jerked at the reins as if she could not wait to run. She had long delicate legs, an aristocratic, almost dainty head and an elegant, curved neck. To Astra, she seemed too fine and lovely a thing to have much speed or endurance, but Richard vowed that she was likely the fastest horse in the field today. He proudly told Astra that he had won the mare in the tournament at Tudbury, that she had been brought back from the Holy Land by a crusading nobleman.

They rode north from London, journeying to the Royal forest. The day was surprisingly warm for October, the sky blue and clear, the sunshine bathing them in mellow golden light. Astra felt a great contentment in riding beside

Richard, even though he said little and seldom glanced her way.

Ahead of them, Marguerite struggled to control her frolicsome white palfrey. Her face was flushed from laughing and she paused frequently beside some knight or lady to exchange teasing comments with them. Watching her, Astra knew that Will had not yet told her his worries about Lord Faucomberg. Even blithe, carefree Marguerite could not be oblivious to such a horrendous warning.

Astra tensed as she recalled her conversation with Will about Marguerite's prospective husband. His ominous words made her appreciate Richard all the more. Her husband had vented his anger at her in humiliating ways, but he had never struck her. Then too, the pleasure he had given her more than made up for the pain.

She glanced at Richard shyly, recalling the wonder of his silent, passionate lovemaking the night before. He caught her looking at him and gave her a hard, probing stare in return. Her body responded instantly. Her breasts felt warm and heavy beneath her clothes, and the familiar ache started between her legs. She met her husband's lustful eyes with surprise. It was hours from nightfall and miles from their bedchamber. Did he mean her to endure this agony of desire all day? Was this some new form of punishment?

She had little time to dwell on it, for they reached the edge of the forest and the formal procession ended. Ladies and knights dismounted to take quick refreshment before the hunt began. Falcons were unhooded, dogs unleashed and supply carts unharnessed. The noise and confusion made Astra uneasy. She had never been on a hunt before and she had no idea what to do. She worried that if she left her horse she would have to ask for assistance to mount again. Marguerite had no such concerns. She had dismounted and now stood with her cunning little russet and gray gyrfalcon on her wrist. She was showing off her bird to some dark, immensely tall knight that Astra had not seen before.

Astra rode toward her friend, then paused as she saw that Will had the same destination. She worried that he would not be able to get Marguerite away from the knight and warn her about her intended husband. Astra hesitated, biting her lower lip and wondering what to do. She had almost made up her mind to go to Marguerite and see if she could help Will when she felt a hand upon her knee. She looked down into Richard's intense black-brown eyes.

"You will ride with me, lady," he said in the lazy, husky voice she knew so well. She nodded slightly, forgetting for a moment her worries about Marguerite.

"Should I dismount?" she asked him.

Richard shook his head. "We'll be setting off soon. Stay on your horse and follow me."

Astra nodded, wondering if that would not be difficult enough. She'd never ridden in the woods before. On the journey to London they had stayed to the roads and trackways, and even at Ravensmore they had done most of their riding in open country. She watched her husband as he exchanged words with some other knights. She was afraid to trust this change in his attitude toward her. Only days ago, he had been cold and harsh, taunting her with his plans to go whoring. Now he was acting much like the Richard she'd once known, seductive and possessive. What did it mean? And why was he so quiet, almost brooding?

The hunting horns sounded with a harsh, melodic blast, and the confusion in the field intensified. Astra gripped her reins with sweaty palms as she contemplated the ride to come.

"Astra, are you thirsty? Do you wish some wine?"

Richard had appeared beside her again. She reached down and took the wineskin from him.

"Don't be so nervous, lovey." Richard smiled. "I'll ride slowly; I promise I won't leave you behind."

"Who else will be riding with us?"

Richard shrugged. "I don't think anyone else will want to lag back. Most of this band takes their hunting seriously. They wouldn't want to miss seeing the kill."

"And you?"

"I've been on hunts before—but never with you." Again he gave her that look. It seemed to make her heart cease beating in her chest.

The horns sounded again and Richard mounted his horse, guiding the mare ahead of her. In a flurry of dust and bright color, the main portion of the hunters set off into the woods. Small groups of knights and ladies followed after them, until the trampled field was empty except for the provision carts and servants. Richard and Astra were the last to ride out after the horses and bellowing hounds.

Astra felt the throb of excitement pulsing in her veins. The mild wind in her face, the sharp scent of fallen leaves and dying vegetation, the thrilling cry of dogs and horns in the distance—it was like nothing she had ever experienced before. Ahead of her, Richard's mare flashed dark and lithe through the underbrush, and the molten gold sunlight trickled down through the half-bare trees. She forgot her fear in her enjoyment of the fine day and the pleasure of being away from the stink and crowds of London. She had missed the woods, the soft call of thrush and plover from the upper branches, the whispering sound of small animals scurrying along the forest floor, the scent of fresh air and foliage.

The autumn woods seemed peaceful and quiet. A few stray leaves floated down upon her hair, and beneath the horses' hooves she could hear the crunch of dead leaves and grasses. The green of summer was gone, but here and there among the drabber browns and grays of the fading forest could be seen small patches of fiery red berries, sparkling yellow birch and orangish maple leaves. It had rained the night before, and the very air seemed to sparkle, as if the autumn shower had washed away the dust and left the forest one last day of glory.

In the distance, the sounds of the hunt receded until Astra could almost forget their purpose in riding out. She followed Richard dutifully, trying to keep up with the mare's swift walking pace even as she longed to stop and savor the sights around them. She was very aware that they had fallen hopelessly behind the rest of the hunters. The thought made her vaguely anxious, but could not quell her enjoyment of the forest's autumn splendor.

Richard reined the mare to a halt and waited for her to pull alongside him. "Shall we stop here?" he asked, a faint smile on his face.

She frowned in puzzlement. "But the others . . . we're already behind. We'll never catch up if we pause now."

He leaned very close; his mouth quirked slightly. "Do you care? Do you really want to watch some helpless animal die?"

"No, of course not."

He dismounted and tied the skittish mare to a tree, then came back to help her off her horse. He reached up and put his arms out for her. She hesitated only a moment before sliding into his waiting embrace. His hands were iron-like around her waist, and he did not release her immediately. They stood face-to-face, chest-to-chest. She looked up at him, feeling the sudden excitement flutter through her.

"We're alone."

She nodded. His dark eyes were opaque, unreadable. The faint smile was gone, and that odd look again touched his features. His hands moved over her possessively, gliding from her waist up her back, then resting against either side of her neck. His fingers fanned out along her nape, then reached forward to stroke the hollow of her throat. She could feel their calloused tips against her throbbing pulse.

"Do you know what I'm going to do now, Astra?"

"What, my lord?" she whispered back.

Thirty-five

Richard's dark eyes glowed. "I'm going to do exactly as I wanted to do that first time I saw you in the woods. I'm going to lay you down upon the forest floor and pleasure you as you've never been pleasured before."

"Here, my lord?"

Richard nodded. "What better place?"

She frowned, still puzzled. Why would he choose a forest glen over their beautiful bedchamber at the palace?

The riddle lost her interest as his fingers crept lower, gliding over her shoulders, her arms and down to her waist. He drew her forward slowly, then dipped his head and slanted his lips to hers.

It was a tender, lingering kiss. Astra slid her hands along his back and leaned her body into his. She felt safe, utterly secure. She wanted to melt into him, to bury herself in the sharp, male scent of his body. He cradled her in his arms for a moment, then his hands went to her neck again, sliding beneath her veil and braids to fondle her nape. There was something very gentle in the way he touched her. His fingers were soothing, skimming over her flesh almost delicately. He fingered her hair, then kneaded her scalp until Astra's whole body went limp.

His mouth moved over hers, savoring, nuzzling. Astra kissed him back with breathless wonder. It had never been like this between them before. There was no hurry, no urgency. Time stood still as he explored her mouth with lazy enjoyment. Astra dared to meet his probing tongue with her own, to taste her lover's mouth with an eagerness that matched his.

He was so different than her. Everything about him was bigger, harsher, rougher. She reveled in the contrast between them, his hard mouth devouring her delicate lips and tongue, his strength crushing her softness, his massive arms and chest enfolding her smaller form. She imagined the contrast of their naked bodies, his so dark and lean and angular against her milky, rounded fairness.

She ran her hands along his back and felt him shudder with desire. She was enthralled with his powerful, male physique, delighting in the feel of the thick, firm muscles along his back and shoulders. Boldly she sought the taut, tempting flesh of his buttocks. He did not resist her caressing fingers, but his muscles seemed to tighten as she stroked them. Intent upon her exploration of her lover's body, Astra scarce realized how passionate and greedy her fondling had become until Richard reached down and grasped her hands.

"Nay, lovey," he whispered. "You must not hurry me."

Astra looked up at him, probing his dark, mysterious eyes. They held her, ensnaring her hopelessly. His hands slid to her waist, and she arched her back and thrust her breasts up, offering herself to him. She saw his breath catch, and his eyes grew darker and wilder, glistening with desire.

He lowered her slowly to the ground as he slid to his knees, then stretched out beside her. His hands trembled as they searched for an opening in her bodice. Her riding costume was modestly cut and unlike most of her gowns, laced not up the front, but under her arms. She drew his hands there, and then giggled as his fingers tickled. Her laughter seemed to ease his passion, for he smiled and abandoned her laces.

"You thwart me, lady, but it is all to the good. I would have you uncover your hair before I see you naked."

She nodded, and sat up so she might undo her coiffure. It would be a pleasure to discard her veil and let down her heavy braids. He watched her. A faint smile lingered on his lips and softened the passionate look in his eyes. Astra felt so dreamy and content, she did not worry how she would ever repin her hair by herself. She had no sense of any world outside this one. The sun would always shine, the soft breeze was never ending. They had all eternity for their lovemaking.

Finishing her hair, she lay back and closed her eyes. She heard Richard's deep, regular breathing as he leaned over her. His fingers fumbled with her laces once again. She lay limp and passive, feeling the warmth of the dappled sunlight upon her face.

He pulled the loosened gown down as far as it would go and cupped one bare breast in his palm. A hungry, insistent tide surged through his loins, but he ignored it. He wanted this time to last. He wanted to remember every blissful moment of it, to savor every exquisite inch of this woman.

The liquid softness of her breast stirred slightly against his hand. He stroked her deliberately, watching the pale pink areola of her nipple stiffen and swell. He fingered the engorged tip until she began to pant. Had anything more lovely, more enticing ever been created to tempt a man? The perfection of her still made his throat go dry. He had seen her naked a dozen times now, but each time she stirred him almost painfully. He reached for her other breast, teasing the nipple to turgid readiness. Then he dipped his head to taste her. The honey-sweet lushness of her skin made his head swim. He sucked her nipples and lapped her skin, surrendering to some ancient longing to nourish his soul in the soft rapture of a woman's flesh.

Beneath him, she moaned and stirred. He pulled away, aware that her passion grew too intense for his languid purposes. He eased himself down beside her and turned so his eyes rested on her delicious, tempting form. Then he used his hands to soothe her, pressing his palm against each inflamed nipple until she lay still. Finally he leaned over and began to kiss her again.

He wanted to memorize the shape of her mouth, the way her lips opened for him like a flower unfolding its nectar-laden petals in the warmth of the sun. He wondered at the mystery of her sensual, voluptuous mouth, why it beckoned his tongue to taste and delve and fill it until neither of them could be satisfied with anything but further joining. He wanted to love this woman one last time, to sate himself with her opulent beauty, to pleasure her until he had naught else to give her.

His body began to tremble with need as she arched her hips frantically beneath his. It was time to satisfy her violent craving, but not with the completion she sought. He shifted off of her so he could raise her skirts. Again, he was awestruck, wondering. The nest of rosy hair between the curving hips, the rounded silken thighs, the daintiness of her ankles and feet—had ever a woman been formed with such an extravagant promise of pleasure incarnate?

She was a Venus, her nether parts as finely wrought as the master work of the greatest craftsmen. From the red gold jewel-work of her mound to the alabaster perfection of her skin, she was as divinely lovely as the rarest *objet d'art* ever designed.

He nudged her thighs apart, and for a moment all reason seemed to flee from his mind. He nearly surrendered to raw instinct, the agonizing need to fill the silken, pink sheath that awaited him. He held back. It was not time yet. He would arouse her further and satisfy the first heat of her longing before he offered her the final consummate pleasure.

He smiled at her, trying to reassure her. Astra's eyes were wide, the black pupils dilated until they near swallowed the gentian blue of her irises. Her face was flushed a deep pink, her lips rose-colored and deliciously swollen. He kissed her softly, delighting in the yearning heat of her plush mouth. Then his trembling fingers glided slowly down her body.

She gasped as his hand found her mound. He let his fingers rest there for a moment, enjoying the heat of her. Then he began a leisurely, teasing rhythm, one finger dancing against the quickening nub at the tip of her cleft while the rest of his hand pressed hard against her swollen nether lips. Her body seemed to shimmer with excitement, her breasts bouncing slightly as she worked her hips against his hand. Her head fell back, eyes closed, lips parted in ecstasy. Her thighs fell apart, exposing the slippery pink folds between them. She was wet and glistening, a delicate, blushing pink that distracted him from his deliberate rhythm.

Unable to resist, he pushed two fingers inside her and heard her frantic moan. Then he resumed pleasuring her with his thumb. Her body arched, her fingers clawing desperately at her velvet skirts as the ravaging force of her peak surged through her. He stilled his fingers, feeling the vibrations inside her swell and then subside.

Slowly he pulled his hand away and let her rest as he feasted his eyes on her glowing, dewy beauty. Her legs shifted together, her eyes opened lazily. She saw him staring at her and seemed to flush even more.

"Lovely Astra," he murmured.

She gazed back at him, seemingly uneasy. He recalled that he had done this to her before, coaxed her to lose control, to abandon herself to the fiery passion of her body. And always before he had mocked her afterwards, or threatened her. A stab of guilt stung him. No wonder she watched him with such wary, anxious eyes. Even now she waited for him to shame her for finding pleasure in his lovemaking.

"Wish you there was more, Astra?"

Her eyes widened, as though in dread, and he cursed himself for not choosing his words more carefully.

"I would pleasure you more, should you wish it."

She said nothing. He fumbled with his chausses, pulling them down to bare his rigid shaft. Her eyes leapt there, and he saw her longing. He drew her hand to him, finally indulging himself in his own passion. Bit by bit his self-control vanished with each stroke of her caressing fingers. Sweat broke out on his forehead, and the muscles in his legs went rigid with tension. When he could tolerate no more, he gently pulled her hand away and rolled sideways to cover her. His shaft slid within her newly-primed sheath with slippery perfection.

* * *

She felt complete, utterly content. Their bodies were joined, her being enveloped in the dark, lovely warmth of his embrace. But between her legs, the greedy, insatiable throb had already started again. She felt him move deep inside her, finding her limit, pushing her to accept more and more of him. Her body responded, stretching and swelling to draw him to the very threshold of her womb. She wanted him like this, so far inside her there was no memory of them ever being separate beings.

The journey began with a slow, smooth rhythm that rocked her to higher and higher peaks of pure pleasure. She clutched him desperately, holding on as tightly as she could to his sweaty skin. He growled and thrust deeper, touching some place so sensitive it immediately sent her to the shattering heights of paradise. And then there was only darkness and roaring red fire burning a pathway across her very soul. As her lover plunged and pounded and thrust she dreamed she died and shot across the heavens like a dazzling cascade of stars.

Breathless. Her lungs felt too big for her chest, and her body lay heavy beneath his hot, slick-skinned weight. But for all she fought for breath, she did not want him to leave her. Ever. She could die like this, in Richard's arms. She wondered if perhaps she had. Could a mortal soul endure such stark, fantastic pleasure and not float away into the heavens forever?

A leaf blew down on her face, tickling her. She felt a moment of disappointment to realize that she was still alive, crushed in the arms of a flesh and blood man. To console herself, she stroked him, savoring the scent and feel of the exhausted male creature who sprawled over her. He had a right to be tired. No warrior had ever fought a battle with more grace and skill and passion. He was a heroic, divinely-inspired lover, a dark, muscular angel come to earth.

He stirred beneath her caress and finally lifted his weight from hers. She watched him, wondering if he had felt even a tiny bit of the soul-capturing awesomeness that she had known.

He looked very weary, and for the first time, she was aware of faint lines etched in the tanned skin around his dark, compelling eyes. His gaze was unreadable, mysterious, but there was naught in it of anger or contempt. She relaxed slightly and leaned back upon her pillow of fallen leaves. He continued to watch her, his gaze burning over her body. She had the sense that he was trying to memorize how she looked.

Slowly, he eased himself up to a sitting position. He leaned over her and gently patted her between her thighs, as if he could not resist touching her there one last time, then pulled her skirts down. He helped her sit up, his fingers brushing over her breasts almost wistfully as he straightened her bodice. Then he patiently redid her laces, and retrieved her veil and hair pins from the ground.

He stood up and adjusted his worn chausses, then helped her stand. To Astra's surprise, he did not appear ready to leave yet. Instead, he led her over to a large oak tree. He sat down beneath it, pulling her down at the same time, then leaned back against the tree. He adjusted her body so her hips rested between his thighs, and her head and shoulders leaned against his chest. He sighed contentedly, and Astra nestled herself against his warmth, giving in to her own lazy, satiated lethargy.

He sighed softly, smelling the faint fragrance of the woman in his arms. It was the aroma of contentment and security, the soft, safe sanctuary of childhood that beckoned unnervingly to a man the rest of his life. He had thought he was beyond the longing, but he was not. For years he had kept up his defenses against it. He had used the harsh excitement of battle, the thrill of danger and death to distract himself from his need to be loved. He had tried for years to be strong and tough and uncaring, to struggle and rage against the deadly mire of domesticity and weakness.

Now he was torn, tormented. Every fiber of his being longed to lose himself in his love for Astra, to bury himself in the velvety, fragrant warmth of her. It was a longing beyond the fever to press his shaft into her body, a hunger greater than the burning hum of lust in his veins. It was a deep ache unto his soul, a passionate craving for some elusive dream of tenderness and hope.

But he could not give into it. To do so would be to risk the shame and despair of his childhood. If he had learned one thing at his mother's knee, it was that it was dangerous to love. The world had no place for love; the harsh brutality of life always conspired to destroy it. Astra did not know that yet, and he did not want her to learn it. To protect her, he must leave her. The thought choked him, filling him with the burning sickness of despair. Desperate, he clutched Astra more tightly against his chest. He would not leave her yet. Just a few moments of holding her, feeling her heart beat so close to his.

She stirred slightly, and he realized he was likely crushing her. He released his grip, and exhaled his grief in a long, drawn-out sigh.

Thirty-six

"It is unlike you to lead a lady off by herself, Will," Marguerite said seductively. "Dare I hope that you've finally come to your senses and seek a favor of me?"

Will shook his head and guided his horse deeper into a grove of blazing maples. He was far too distracted to respond to her teasing.

When he felt certain that they had eluded the rest of the hunting party, he dismounted and waited for Marguerite to join him. She gave him her usual bright, vivacious smile, then drew her dark brows together thoughtfully. *"Mon Dieu,* but you are serious today. What's wrong? Has something happened between Astra and Richard?"

"Nay, it is not worry for Lady Astra which troubles me," he answered impatiently. "But for you, lady."

Marguerite gave him a startled look, then laughed. "Has my father been burning up your ears with tales of my adventures?"

Will shook his head. "Astra told me you are with child, and the father cannot marry you because he is already wed."

"Oh, that. That is yesterday's gossip, Will."

"And yet it is true."

Marguerite gave him a piercing look, her mouth quirking slightly. "I am surprised Astra told you of my indiscretion. Usually she has better sense."

"She came to me because she wanted me to wed you."

"Wed me!" Marguerite laughed. "Oh, what an innocent she is! Of course she would ask you to aid me that way. She has entertained hopes of marrying us off ever since the day we visited the city with her and Richard. What did you tell her?"

"The truth."

Marguerite arched a dark brow. "What did she say?"

"She has too kind a heart to condemn anyone, even an unnatural man such as myself. But she did agree that such a marriage would likely satisfy neither of us."

Marguerite nodded. "Astra is a saint, but not a complete fool."

There was silence between them for a moment, then Marguerite recovered her usual nonchalance. "It does not matter anyway, for my father has already found a husband for me."

"I know."

"Jesu! What has become of the quiet little Astra I once knew? I swear being in love has set her tongue to flapping like a Cheapside vendor."

"Don't be angry with her. It is fortunate she told me. This way I have a chance to warn you." Will grasped her arm. "I fear for you, lady. The man your father has arranged for you to marry is a cold, selfish brute."

Marguerite regarded him with a steady ebony gaze. "Most men have flaws, Will. And gossiping tongues tend to exaggerate the worst of those who are rich and powerful."

"This isn't gossip. I know the man, Marguerite. He deserves his reputation. He's the sort who seeks out the weak and defenseless and delights in torturing them."

"I am not exactly weak and defenseless."

"You will be his wife, and you well know how most noblemen consider their women. Even your father cannot gainsay him if he abuses you." Will took a deep breath and continued. "Faucomberg is an arrogant man, as full of his own self-importance as some puffed-up barnyard cock. When he discovers you carry another man's child, he will be enraged that you have duped him. Any hope that he might treat you with respect and consideration will be gone. He will regard you as no better than a whore, and he will feel no need for restraint in his cruelty."

Marguerite tilted her head thoughtfully. "I had my doubts once I learned that my husband-to-be was young and proud. It might have been better if my father had found me a dottering old fool who would be pleased to have a healthy young wife and an heir of some kind on the way. But I have not met the man—young or old—that I have not been able to bend to my wishes eventually."

"You must not wed him!"

"My father is very pleased with this match. Moreover, I must marry someone." She touched her midsection tenderly. "I am two months gone with child, and I would not inflict such shame upon my family. I have brought them enough trouble and worry already. I would not do that to them."

"Two months, that is not so long. There is still time to . . ."

Marguerite gave him a look of horror. "You suggest I should get rid of it?"

"It is done."

"No!" She clutched her stomach. "The babe is all I have left of Christian. I will not give that up too!"

"If you love the father . . ." Will began solemnly, "if you care for his child, consider this: if Faucomberg guesses the truth before the babe is born, he well might do something to make you lose it."

Marguerite's dusky skin paled slightly. "I can't believe he would abuse a pregnant woman. Is the man really so great a fiend?"

"I believe he is, and you dare not gamble that I accuse him wrongly. If he beats you until you miscarry, there is a grave risk you will die as well as the babe. By the rood, Marguerite, it could mean your life if you marry him!"

"You're as bad as the Queen's gossiping women, Will. I'm a great heiress, and Faucomberg is not going to murder me and risk losing my lands. Besides, he is not such a fool that he expects me to be a virgin. If I have to, I'll tell him the truth about the babe. He'll simply have to accept it. As long I do not make him a cuckold after we are wed, he has nothing to complain of."

"Can you do that, Marguerite?" Will asked abruptly. "Can you promise you will never bed another man but your husband? What if this man, Christian, what if both of you attend court again? Can you promise that you will not give in to the temptation to see him alone?"

Marguerite's dark eyes flashed. "Jesu, do you think me such a whore that I would stoop to that?"

"I don't mean to hurt you, Marguerite, only warn you. You are merely human, and once tempted it is easy to give in again. Faucomberg might kill you if he found out you betrayed him, or lock you away in a nunnery as old King Henry did with Eleanor of Aquitaine. It would be better if you married a more tolerant man—one who perhaps had a soul," Will added in a bitter gibe.

"I can hardly refuse my father without a good reason. Would you have me tell him I am with child?"

"It would be better to anger him now, rather than cause him despair later. I know enough of Lord Fitz Hugh to guess that he would hate himself if he found out he had wed you to a brutal, vengeful man."

Marguerite thought a moment, then gave Will an icy look. "It is time to rejoin the others. If we dally here any longer, there will be gossip."

Will nodded reluctantly. He could see that he had not swayed Marguerite, but he consoled himself that he had done his best. What else could a man do?

"You missed the kill," Marguerite announced accusingly as soon as she saw Astra. Seeing her friend's flushed, dreamy face, she added: "Or did you subdue another quarry, perhaps a dark, dangerous beast you have been pursuing for some months?"

"Oh, Marguerite," Astra whispered, unable to keep her happiness from her friend. "I think Richard has begun to forgive me."

"It would seem so. You look as contented as a cat full of cream. I am pleased for you, *ma petite.* Did I not tell you that your tender love and loyalty would win his heart?"

"You were right. I am so happy. . . . Oh, I near forgot." Astra gave Marguerite a sudden guilty look. "I do not mean to gloat. I know your circumstances are not nearly so blessed as mine. Did Will talk to you?"

Marguerite said nothing as she led Astra from the press of steaming horses, bloody-muzzled hounds and harassed servants. The King's party had returned to open country to rest and refresh themselves before riding back to Westminster. A veritable banquet was being set up on the trampled field, complete with pewter tableware, a huge spread of cold food, benches and even a dazzling white linen cloth on the trestle table being set for the King and his most honored guests.

Marguerite searched the crowd for her father and discovered him some distance away, talking to one of the King's councillers. She turned back to Astra.

"Aye. He warned me that my soon-to-be-betrothed is a vicious sort. He advised me to tell my father so he can halt the wedding negotiations."

Astra gave a relieved sigh. "Mother of God be praised. I was worried that you would not listen to him."

"I have not said that I will do anything of the sort," Marguerite retorted sharply. "I am still considering it."

"What's to consider? You cannot wed a monster like that!"

"Would you rather I shame the Fitz Hugh name by bearing a bastard child?"

"Oh, Marguerite, I did not mean that. Surely your father can find you another husband, one who will deal with your predicament in a reasonable and compassionate manner."

"Ah, but there's the rub—I must tell my father that I am *enceinte* or he will not understand my reasons for refusing the match with Faucomberg." Marguerite bowed her head, her voice trembling slightly. "Can you not see how badly the truth will hurt him? He is so delighted with the match he has made, and for once we have not been quarreling over everything. I had hoped that I could finally do something to make him proud of me instead of causing him heartache and embarrassment!"

Tears gathered in Astra's eyes. Poor Marguerite. It seemed her friend had finally plunged herself into a dilemma that even her nimble wits could not remedy. The two women walked back to where the others were eating. Astra saw Richard lounging against a tree with a capon drumstick in his hand. He smiled at her, and for a moment she considered asking him for his advice on Marguerite's problem. No, that would not do, she decided. The intimacy they shared was still new and fragile, and she also worried that her husband would not be sympathetic to Marguerite's plight. Instead she would talk to Will again. Surely if they put their minds to it they could find some solution for poor Marguerite.

She meant to go to Will immediately, but Richard gestured her over to eat with him. She walked toward her husband, feeling the familiar fluttering in her chest. Would she ever grow accustomed to the thought that this magnificent knight belonged to her?

The King was watching him, Richard noted uncomfortably. It was well that Astra was behaving as if they were the most happy of couples. No one at court had guessed at the abuse he had heaped upon his lady wife in the first few days they were wed. The dull ache of guilt pressed upon his chest. Now he was about to hurt her again. It was painful to contemplate. The only way he could bear to think of his departure the next day was to remind himself that it was all for Astra's good. He would go away to France, and the King would declare him a traitor and a criminal. With the Queen's help, Astra could easily get the marriage annulled and be free to wed another man.

He gave Astra a quick glance, noting for the thousandth

time how very fair she was when she smiled; her eyes were blue and tranquil as the clearest sky and her pink mouth unfurled like a blooming rosebud. He gritted his teeth, suppressing the longing that swept through him. He had one more night, one more night to love her.

Then he must forget her, drive her from his thoughts forever. There was no place in his life for a guileless innocent like her. If she stayed wedded to him, she would likely come to a bad end, much as his mother had. He must break the tie now, while she was still young and lovely. She would find better prospects elsewhere. He had once disdained the thought of her wedded to a clerk, but now it reassured him. She needed a man who would be there for her, who would not always be going off to war, threatening to make her a widow and their children helpless orphans.

The pain of loss burned in his throat, and he closed his eyes to stall the tears that threatened. When he opened them, he saw Will walking toward him. He had thought once to tell his friend his plans, but now he knew he could not. Will would argue and plead and do anything to delay his leaving. It would only make what he had to do all the harder to bear.

"What think you, Will?" he called with a sardonic smile. "Was it a good hunt? Was there enough blood to satisfy the gentlemen and ladies of the court?"

How was she ever going to get a chance to talk to Will alone?—Astra wondered nervously as she perused the crowded banquet hall. De Lacy was seated next to Marguerite's father, while she was placed far down the table between Richard and another knight. Across from them sat Marguerite, flirting as outrageously as ever. Astra took a distracted bite of the strong-tasting heron on her trencher and frowned. It was imperative that she speak to Will tonight; Lord Fitz Hugh would not wait long in announcing Marguerite's betrothal. Once he did, it would be too late to stop the marriage without causing great embarrassment to everyone.

She glanced quickly at her husband. Richard smiled at her and touched her knee beneath the table. Astra smiled back, thinking how odd and unsettling it was to have him acting so fondly after the anger and hostility he had shown her following their wedding. She could not help wondering what had made him change his sentiments toward her. Had he really forgiven her? Would he finally accept her love for him?

Their eyes met briefly, and again she saw that look in them, that flicker of wistful sadness she had observed during their languid coupling in the forest. It made her uneasy, although she could not say why. It gave her the urge to comfort Richard, to have him lay his head against her breast so she could stroke his hair as one would a child.

She forced her thoughts away from her own marriage and focused on Marguerite's problems. She was not quite sure what she would say to Will, although she meant to once again ask him to wed her friend. It seemed the only solution, the only way to save Marguerite's honor without dooming her to a bitterly unhappy marriage. Seeing Faucomberg after the hunt had decided it; she could not forget the image of Lord Rathstowe holding up a bloodied fox carcass in triumph. The man was a brute, a cruel and vile man who enjoyed watching other creatures suffer. Will knew that too; if he cared for Marguerite at all, he would simply have to marry her.

"You are quiet tonight, love." Astra started as Richard whispered in her ear. "Is something troubling you?" His hand played with her fingers, testing her delicate nails against his hardened palm.

"Nay, I could not be happier," she told him brightly. Their eyes met again, and a heavy lump formed in her throat. Oh, how she loved this man. And to think that he cared for her too. The thought filled her with aching wonder.

Servants and pages cleared the trestle tables and the musicians came in and began taking out their instruments. Since the Queen had not been able to attend the hunt because of the child she carried, Henry had ordered music and dancing this evening for her special entertainment. The soft sounds of lute, tambour and flute soon floated above the murmur of conversation filling the hall.

"I would meet you in the bedchamber anon," Richard whispered, his hand stroking Astra's thigh provocatively.

"May I stay a little longer and enjoy a dance or two?" Astra asked. She held her breath, worrying that she had angered him. His dark eyes studied her face, then he smiled.

"Dancing is naught but damn foolishness invented by women, but I suppose it does no harm to indulge their whims occasionally. Would you have me be your partner?"

Astra shook her head. "You have no fondness for the pastime, and I would not force you to join in to humor me. Perhaps I will ask Will to oblige me for a turn." Richard looked surprised, but did not protest. Astra stood and hurried over to de Lacy.

"I must speak with you," she whispered. "Would you pretend to dance with me?"

"One can hardly pretend to dance," Will noted wryly

as they joined the other couples on the hall's dark red tiled floor. "What would you speak to me of?" he asked as he took her hands to begin the carol.

"Marguerite."

Will sighed, the jovial look disappearing from his face. "I tried, Astra, truly I did. I told her exactly what sort of man she is contracted to wed. I don't think she will heed my warning."

Astra and Will backed away from each other and bowed, then met again in the center. "She dreads telling her father the predicament she is in," Will said. "Without his help she feels she chooses between Faucomberg and disgrace."

Astra nodded and moved on to her next partner. It took some time before she again found herself facing Will. "There is another way, Will," Astra whispered. "If you would marry her, no one would be the wiser."

Will looked distraught. "Surely you understand why that is not possible." He backed away.

Astra gave him a stubborn look and bowed. "Nay, I do not understand. Why could you not wed her for the sake of the child, then both continue living as you have been?"

Will gave her a startled look, then moved on to his next partner.

Astra nearly held her breath as she progressed down the line, bowing and turning gracefully. The dance would soon be over, then what excuse would she have to speak to Will?

Her body tensed as she neared him. "What think you?" she whispered.

"You would advise us to make this mockery of a marriage—knowing that we would both seek other lovers?"

Astra nodded as they drew apart. "Most marriages are contracted for other reasons than love," she pointed out as she neared him. "If you both agreed to the arrangement,

I do not see that it would be more difficult than the life you already lead. Indeed, it might be easier. You would legitimize Marguerite's child, even as she quelled the rumors about your peculiarity."

The carol ended. Will and Astra bowed to each other a final time, then he took her arm to escort her from the dance floor. "Can you really mean this, Astra? Does it not shock you that we would be breaking our sacred marital vows?"

"Oh, surely God would understand, Will. I think of the child. He or she needs a father, a family name. As for you and Marguerite, I cannot believe you were not meant to have any happiness at all."

"I can scarce imagine that you would countenance this, Astra."

Her blue eyes burned bright. "Everyone deserves to know love, Will. Without love we are no better than the beasts."

Will nodded, a strange lightness floating in his chest. There was something about Lady Astra; her warmth and goodness seemed to lift from him the pall of loneliness and despair that always hung over him. In matters of the heart, she was very wise. Perhaps her plan, outrageous as it was, had merit.

Abruptly, he released Astra's hand. She gave him a warm encouraging look, then nodded. He nodded back and hurried toward Lord Fitz Hugh.

Will bowed to the Queen, then to Fitz Hugh.

"My lord, if I might have a word with you?"

Fitz Hugh joined him quickly. His broad face was flushed with wine, a ready smile on his lips. "De Lacy."

"I have decided on what I wish for a reward, sir."

"A reward? Oh, aye, the reward I had promised you. What is it, Will?"

"I wish to wed your daughter."

Fitz Hugh's dark eyes bulged in amazement. "Marguerite? You wish to wed Marguerite? Even knowing what a defiant, troublesome little vixen she is?"

Will nodded.

"Well. This is a surprise. As I told you before, I have already arranged marriage plans for my daughter. Indeed, many of the negotiations have already been completed. I was on the verge of telling His Majesty this evening."

"But you have not made the announcement yet," Will said anxiously. "The betrothal is not public knowledge, is it?"

Fitz Hugh shook his head, thinking rapidly. The de Lacy family was well nigh as rich and powerful as the Faucombergs. Will seemed a quiet, unprepossessing sort, but he might make a better husband than hot-tempered Guy. "Tell me, de Lacy, have you spoken to Marguerite? Does she know of your suit?"

"No, my lord, she does not."

The older man frowned. "I'll have you know I won't wed Marguerite where she does not wish it. If she does not agree to take you, I won't force her."

"I will speak to her," Will answered, wondering when he would get a chance and worrying even more what the unpredictable Marguerite would say.

"But if she has no objections . . ." Fitz Hugh's ruddy face brightened even more. "Your wish is granted, de Lacy. Now that I think on it, I am amazed I did not come upon the plan myself. What better husband could there be for my daughter than one who is both protective and indulgent? It will be a challenge, Will, but I can see you are man enough for the task. My Marguerite needs a bit of taming. Still, I imagine the pleasures will be great for the man who can bring her to heel." Fitz Hugh gave his prospective son-in-law a suggestive wink.

Will could only smile numbly in response.

"You've asked my father for my hand?"

Marguerite looked so aghast, Will felt his confidence ebbing as rapidly as the tidewaters of the Thames.

"Astra suggested it. She convinced me it was worth doing anything to save you from Faucomberg."

"I'm afraid you are mistaken, Will," Marguerite responded with narrowed eyes. "I am content with the match, and I have every confidence I can manage my prospective husband."

"You don't know the man as I do. He is a beast, a craven, evil brute!"

Marguerite tossed her black curls with studied nonchalance. "I like a man with a little spirit, the lusty, restless sort. I am sure we will get along well."

"Nay, you will not," Will protested, feeling utterly frustrated. "He will beat and abuse you until he crushes you. You were blessed to have been raised in a warm and loving home, Marguerite, which is why you cannot imagine what such a man is capable of. He will have no concern for your wishes. He will go off hunting and whoring and living his life as he pleases, and if you dare protest, he will make you sorry."

"Then he will go his way, and I will go mine. Such an arrangement suits me well."

"You still do not understand! It will not be like that. Adultery is no crime for a man, but for a woman it is considered a grave sin. If Faucomberg discovers you have cuckolded him, you will be lucky if he does not kill you."

"You forget, Will," Marguerite responded, favoring him with a seductive smile. "I have not yet found a man I cannot bend to my will. Save you, of course, and that is because you are proof against all women's charms," she added nastily.

"That is it, isn't it?" Will muttered through clenched teeth. "You will not wed me because you cannot manipulate me. You do not accept your husband as your equal, you must have a man you have power over!"

"You have always been clever, Will. I am delighted you finally see the matter as I do." Marguerite all but purred.

Will sighed. He had known Marguerite was stubborn, but he had not guessed what an obstinate wench she really was. She was as arrogant as a man. She insisted on controlling everything. What could he do?—except tell Astra he had tried, and failed.

Thirty-seven

As soon as she woke, Astra knew she was alone. It was the first time she had slept later than Richard, but she had not thought he would leave her without wishing her good morning, not after the extraordinary intimacy they had shared the night before.

She sat up stiffly and felt the aching wonder of completion fill her limbs. Her skin still tingled from the rapture of Richard's touch, her womb still throbbed with the rhythms of their lovemaking. It had been a night of magic. Richard had loved her in every manner that a man could love a woman. Fast, slow, violent, tender—he had pleasured her a thousand ways, and left not an inch of her skin unexplored or unsatisfied. Astra could not imagine that any woman had ever been more thoroughly, exuberantly pleasured.

Still, she had not had her fill of him. For all his passion, his burning energy, Richard had not allowed her to caress him, to explore his body. She longed for the chance to hold her husband in quiet tenderness, to stroke him with not lust, but maternal sweetness. To soothe the tension from his thick muscles and love away the turmoil in his haunted eyes. But each time she had sought to succor him, he had turned her affection to arousal. Each time she thought to lull him to sleep, his shaft had risen, thick and rigid, pulsing with sexual need. It was almost as if he feared her tenderness and thought to thrust it away with his insatiable lust.

A vague unease filled her. For all that Richard seemed to care for her, she wondered if he trusted her—or if he ever would. She had broken through the barrier of his ironic, charming mask, but she could not penetrate the troubled tumult she found beneath. She was uncomfortably aware that Richard did not want her to understand him. He seemed to love her at last, but he had not accepted her love yet, not in the way she wished to give it.

For not the first time, she thought about Richard's past, about what had made him the man he was. Since Will had told her about Richard's mother, her love for him had grown even deeper and more poignant. Now that she could see the tormented, struggling boy he had been, her husband was much more comprehensible. She knew that despite his cocksure manner, his easy arrogance, Richard was afraid to love, afraid to trust. It might take her years to break through the wall of bitterness and mistrust he had built around his heart, but break through she would. She had only to love him enough, and someday those ancient wounds would heal.

She rose slowly. This morning the bawdy jokes of her wedding night had new meaning, for verily she was so sore from lovemaking she scarce could walk straight. She washed, dressed and arranged her hair, then left the bedchamber to hunt for Marguerite. Her friend's dilemma was never far from her mind. She was determined to try one last time to convince Marguerite to refuse the marriage with Guy Faucomberg.

When she reached the corridor leading to the Queen's chambers, Astra was surprised to find Will de Lacy waiting for her. His face was grim, his elegant mouth set in a stubborn line.

"Marguerite won't listen to a thing I say, but I've come upon a plan to make her wed me anyway. What say you, Astra? Will you aid me?"

"She won't listen to you?"

Will shook his head. "Marguerite is wretchedly stubborn; the woman is near as bad as Richard. She's convinced that she can handle any man, even a devil like Faucomberg."

"What do you mean to do?"

Will smiled grimly. "I intend to go to Fitz Hugh and tell him Marguerite is carrying my child."

"Your child . . . but why?"

"It's the only remedy for the mess Marguerite is in. If Fitz Hugh thinks the child is mine, he'll insist Marguerite wed me even if she doesn't want to."

Astra's eyes widened. "What if she denies it? What if she tells her father that you . . . that you can't father children because of your . . . your affliction?"

"It's a risk I'm willing to take. Marguerite promised me she would keep my secret, and I believe she will, no matter how angry she is."

"She will be hopping mad, you can be sure of that." Astra chewed her lips nervously. "Marguerite hates to be forced into anything. If you coax or wheedle her to do something, she goes along good-naturedly, but if you try to force her . . ." Astra winced. "She can be as nasty and vindictive as Richard when she's crossed."

"Aye, I know that. But that is part of the reason I must do this. Although I don't approve of the way you tricked Richard into wedding you, Astra, I do not doubt now that things have turned out for the best. You belong with Richard."

"As you belong with Marguerite?"

Will shrugged. "It is not the same, although I do think we are well-matched as companions, if not lovers. I am prepared to indulge Marguerite's whims as few men would. As long as she is discreet, I don't care if she has a dozen lovers."

"And you, Will, what will you gain from this marriage?"

"My family will be pleased, and it will help quiet the rumors about my unnatural inclinations."

"It seems there are advantages for everyone. What do you wish me to do?"

"You must confirm my story with Lord Fitz Hugh. I have every reason to think Marguerite will deny that I am the father of the child she carries. If she does, you are the only person who can convince Fitz Hugh that his daughter lies."

A chill of foreboding chased down Astra's spine. She was being drawn into a deception, perpetuating a blatant mistruth. She would be manipulating her closest friend, much as she had thought of manipulating Richard. Richard appeared to have at last forgiven her, but that did not mean Marguerite would.

"I'm not sure, Will. I have always believed that lying inevitably leads to greater evil. Who are we to make these decisions for Marguerite, to trap her into marrying you?"

"It is for the best, Astra. It is!"

"Perhaps. Still, I cannot promise you I will baldly lie to Lord Fitz Hugh if he asks for the truth."

Will's jaw tightened in anger. "I will do it anyway. If

Fitz Hugh refuses to take my word over Marguerite's, I will think up some other ruse."

"I wish you well." Astra grasped his hands in hers. "I will pray that things turn out for the best."

Will strode off purposefully to find Lord Fitz Hugh. Astra remained in the hallway, filled with lingering uneasiness. It wasn't only Will's plan that troubled her, but something else, some nameless anxiety that haunted her. She had an urge to see Richard, to reassure herself that things were well with him. She turned abruptly from the door to the Queen's solar and hurried down the hallway.

She approached the knights' barracks gingerly. She had never gone looking for Richard there before, and she felt uncomfortable entering the male world in which he spent much of his time. She told herself that she had a perfect right to look for her husband and walked determinedly into the low wooden building. Crude odors immediately assailed her nose—sweat, leather, horses. Their smell on one man was not displeasing, but multiplied by the several dozen soldiers who slept here, the reek was enough to make Astra's nose wrinkle in disgust.

The place was dimly lit by smoky rushlights, the floor filthy. From the darkened corners she could hear the sound of snoring. Despite the fact that it was near midday, some men appeared to be sleeping off the ale and wine they had imbibed too freely of the night before. She stood uncertainly, beginning to doubt that Richard would be found here. Certainly if she were him, she would spend no more time in this rank place than absolutely necessary. She was about to turn away when a grubby soldier who had been polishing armor in the corner rose and approached her.

"Lady, what can I do for you?"

Astra's heart sank as the man neared. She recognized

him from the night Richard had surrounded her with crude soldiers and taunted her before them. She could only hope that he did not remember her.

"Lady Astra." Something glinted in the man's bloodshot eyes, then they trailed over her body appraisingly. Astra flushed and looked away. He obviously recalled the incident. Even now he was probably wondering if she really had the "best tits in Christendom" concealed beneath her gown.

Forcing herself to ignore the wave of humiliation that washed over her, Astra looked up and steeled her features into what she hoped was a mask of calm.

"I'm looking for my husband. Do you know where he is?"

The glitter in the man's eyes faded, and his response was soft, almost kindly given. "No, my lady. I saw him leave earlier this morn with his squire. He wore armor and carried his weapons, so I might surmise he went to the practice field." He gestured. "The Leopard spends hours in practice; it's how he keeps from growing soft between campaigns."

Astra nodded, intrigued by this information about her husband. She had always wondered what he did during his days at court. It did not reassure her to think that he spent his time training for war.

Astra turned to go, but the man stopped her with a dirty hand on her arm. She froze, dreading what he might say to her.

"My lady, if you'd permit me, I would escort you there. It rained last night, and there's mud and muck everywhere. I can show you the best way, so you won't get your gown dirty."

Astra examined the knight warily. She expected to find

the crude glow of lust on his features, and she was surprised by his respectful, almost awed expression.

She nodded. She did not really know the way there, and it would help to have some kind of escort. She allowed the man to lead her through the courtyard and down a path past storerooms and other outbuildings of the palace complex.

"Is your business with Sir Reivers urgent?" the man asked.

"Nay, it is nothing really," Astra admitted sheepishly. "Perhaps I should not disturb him." She hesitated. The man took her arm again to urge her on.

"He's been at it since early this morn, so he'll likely welcome a break. Anyway, he's a fool if he's not glad to see you." The man grinned. "It's a wonder you still seek him out after that nasty business he put you through when you were first wed. It was not fitting for him to treat you so."

Astra stiffened, but said nothing. She did not like to think of that awful night. She had convinced herself that Richard had not really meant to abuse her the way he had; it had been his terrible anger which had made him so cruel.

"If you were my lady, I'd keep you away from other men altogether," the man continued. "Guess the Leopard is very sure of you. He must believe that if you put up with his meanness, you really love him."

They were almost to the practice field. Astra could see the rows of quintains along one end, but there was no sign of Richard or his squire.

"Huh! They're not here," the soldier mused, coming to a halt. "I could have sworn they would be. Where else would they go carrying all of their gear?"

Astra shook her head. The vague uneasy feeling was

worsening, but she refused to give in to it. "Mayhaps we missed them. They might have gone to the kitchen for some food or the armory for weapons or . . . something."

The soldier shrugged and began to lead her back down the dung-strewn pathway. "I hope you find him, lady. It seems a shame for you to ruin your slippers for nothing."

Astra nodded. Despite the man's help in negotiating the worst spots, her shoes were soaked and filthy. "It serves me right," she told him with a slight smile. "I was just being silly to look for him. I should have waited. I'm bound to see him in the Hall tonight."

The man nodded. When they reached the barracks, he dropped her arm.

"Thank you," she murmured.

"It's been my pleasure, lady."

Astra started to walk back to the palace. She heard the man's voice, low and sincere, behind her: "Don't despair, Lady Astra. The Leopard loves you. All of us have commented on it. He'd be a fool to forsake you."

Astra turned at the man's words, but he'd already entered the barracks. She paused there a moment, gazing at the crudely-built structure. What had the man meant? Why should the other soldiers think Richard might forsake her? She shrugged her shoulders and continued on. Obviously the man didn't know that Richard had forgiven her. Good tidings never traveled as quickly as bad.

"I cannot believe you would be party to such a wicked deception!"

"Marguerite, truly, I did nothing. I have not even talked to your father today." Astra clutched her cold hands together, trying to take deep breaths. Marguerite's anger was almost as unnerving as Richard's. At least Marguerite had waited until they were alone to confront her.

"Nothing! May I remind you, Astra, that this whole disaster began with your meddling? If you had not betrayed my secret to Will, he would never have come up with this appalling plot to make me wed him."

"He's only trying to help," Astra argued. "He wants to protect you."

"Protect me! He seeks to protect me by going to my father and telling him about my condition? God save me from my saviors! I thought you both understood that the last thing I wanted was for my father to know."

"It seemed the better course. Your father will get over his disappointment, while Faucomberg could make you suffer the rest of your life."

"It was my decision," Marguerite said coldly. "Not yours and Will's!"

Astra sighed. She was getting a headache. She had been through a week of Richard's unreasonableness and now she was going to have to endure Marguerite's.

"Pathetic, effeminate fool! I have half a mind to tell my father exactly what Will is. I doubt my father would be so happy to see me wedded to him then!"

"Really, Marguerite, that would be cruel. You promised Will you would keep his secret."

"That was when I thought he was an honorable man, when I thought he would keep my secrets as well!"

"What . . . what did your father say when he learned of the babe?" Astra asked hesitantly.

"Papa said very little, but he made it clear that I would wed Will as soon as the King gives his approval."

"Is that so bad?" Astra coaxed. "I know Will will try and be a good husband to you."

"Oh, indeed," Marguerite said sarcastically. "He will no doubt seek to satisfy my every longing. Trouble is, there is one longing that Will cannot sate. I sought a lusty, virile husband who would please me in bed, but now I am to wed a man who is as worthless to me as a eunuch!"

"You could take a lover," Astra suggested in a voice little over a whisper.

Marguerite's eyes narrowed, and her lips curled into a mocking grimace. "A lover! Astra, I am scandalized! Richard has truly corrupted you."

"But you said yourself . . ." Astra hesitated, confused by her friend's scornful words. "You have always told me that most marriages are little more than business arrangements, and that most wives sought out lovers to satisfy their other needs. I thought that you . . . that you might seek such an arrangement yourself."

"Perhaps I would have," Marguerite answered coldly. "But now I have no choice. In truth, it is not so much Will I object to as his reckless meddling in my life. How would you like to have your fate decided by others? To have the reins of your future rudely stripped from your hands? Now I know how Richard felt when you so callously tricked him into wedding you."

"When I tricked him . . ." Astra gasped. "Surely you recall that I refused any part of the deception. It was you who urged me to entrap Richard, in fact, you well nigh insisted upon it!"

"Perhaps I suggested the ploy, but you were the one who enticed him in the chapel. And now you've had a hand in plotting my marriage as well. It is conceit, Astra, wicked conceit to think that you have the right to rule others' lives."

Astra gaped at her friend. It was obvious that Marguerite was beside herself, that she was not thinking clearly at all.

"I beg your pardon for my meddling," Astra said in a quiet voice. "If you will excuse me, I'd like to lie down. I have a terrible headache."

Marguerite gave her a cold, disdainful look, then stalked haughtily out of the room.

Thirty-eight

"Richard's gone!" Will burst into the bedchamber as soon as Astra opened the door. "I've looked everywhere, and I can't find him. Worse yet, his squire, his weapons and horses have also disappeared!"

Astra backed toward the bed and sank down on it, a sick, cold dread washing over her. She'd known something was amiss but had refused to face it. Now she could no longer deny the truth. Richard had left her. His extravagant lovemaking had been his way of saying goodbye.

"I can't imagine where he has gone, or why," Will continued. "I was so hopeful that he had finally resolved his conflicts, that he was at last willing to accept your love for him." He approached Astra, his eyes full of tender concern. "To leave you like this—it is madness. He is throwing away happiness by the fistful."

"Perhaps that is what Richard wishes. Mayhaps he cannot allow himself to be happy, nor to be loved."

Will's eyes widened. "What do you know of it, Astra? Did you expect him to leave you?"

She sighed. "I have known, aye, that there was something wrong. Richard has been most attentive and loving the last few days, but there was an oddness about his affections, and I could sense great turmoil in his heart."

"Oh, Astra, I am sorry," Will said, sinking down beside

her on the bed. "I never guessed that he would leave you. Do you . . . do you want me to go after him?"

Astra shook her head. "Your wedding with Marguerite is set to take place in a few days, and I would not have you postpone it. Besides, if Richard has fixed his mind to this, you will not be able to sway him from his course."

"But, my lady, what will you do?"

Astra clenched her hands together. What, indeed, was she going to do? Her husband had abandoned her, and there was no assurance that he would ever return. The cold horror of it clutched at her heart.

"I will pray, Will," she said softly.

Will nodded, then turned and left the room.

Wearily, Richard wiped the sweat from his brow. They would never make it to the English port of Dover today. His voyage across the channel would have to wait. He glanced behind him. His squire, Nicholas, was still struggling with the mare. She was an obstinate animal, for all her delicate beauty, and she did not like the way Nicholas sat her. She had been prancing and tossing her head since they set out. Richard considered trading horses with his squire, but he knew that would mean Nicholas exchanging one discomfort for another. The huge destrier was not meant for ordinary travel. Sultan had a plodding, bone-jarring gait that was surely worse than the mare's balky ride.

He leaned forward to idly pat the horse's sweaty neck. Reasonably, he should sell both animals and purchase new ones in France, but he knew he would not be able to bring himself to do it. Sultan had served him well in too many battles to abandon him now, and the mare, called Kismet, was a prize not to be forsaken. Richard knew few nobles, no matter their title or wealth, who could boast of owning such an animal. Kismet was a mount fit for a prince, and he was not willing to part with her.

He shifted restlessly on the destrier's broad back, trying to find a comfortable position. The saddlebags were loaded down with the few possessions he had seen fit to bring and they crowded his legs. He could have carried them better on a sumpter pony, but that seemed unnecessary. He had taken only what he needed to barter for supplies until Gascony, and he had enough to buy food until he reached Paris. He hoped to be hired on long before that. He had heard that the French countryside was preyed upon by bands of ruffians, and he did not like the thought of traveling alone with Nicholas, the two of them guarding his dwindling store of booty.

The rest of his treasure he had left with Will's squire, with the directions that it should go to Astra. He could not help worrying what would happen to her. He had no doubt that the King and Queen would help her, but an annulment took time. Even then she would need gowns and jewels if she was to find another husband. He winced, thinking of the message he had left her. The knight who wrote it for him was not the most learned sort, but he had agreed to keep it secret until Richard was well on his way. That was important. Richard did not want to risk Will coming after him until he was across the channel and it was too late to turn back.

Still, it was worrisome to think that the message did not adequately convey what he felt. How could he convince Astra that she was better off without him? That he left her not because his love was lacking, but because he loved her too much? He sighed and rubbed his chest, as if that would ease the dull ache that lingered there. He had not known it would hurt so much. He was doing what was best for Astra, but it seemed to be wrenching his heart out. His body was fatigued and sated from their lovemaking, but still he hungered for her. He was not yet three days from London and already he was starved for the sight of her.

He dare not think about Astra, he admonished himself. If he drove himself to exhaustion, plunged himself into the raw, immediate battle of survival, he could trick his mind into forgetting about her. Then, eventually, the pain would ease. Someday Astra would be only a beautiful memory, an enchanted fantasy he could seek out when his spirit needed soothing. For now she was a torment, an ache that gnawed his heart.

He turned and shouted over his shoulder: "Nicholas—I see an inn up ahead. We'll stop there tonight."

The banquet hall was abuzz. Those who weren't whispering over the sudden announcement that Marguerite Fitz Hugh and Will de Lacy were to be wed were gossiping about the even more shocking news that Richard Reivers had disappeared, leaving behind his wife of less than a fortnight.

Astra sat stiffly beside the Queen, who had rallied to Astra's side as soon as the news reached her. In truth, Astra was too miserable to care about the whispers swirling around the room. Her worst fears had been confirmed. Will had questioned the other knights and finally found a man who admitted he had inscribed a message from Richard to his wife. The message was not to be delivered to Astra until two days hence, but Will had convinced the man, by rather brutal means in fact, that she should have it immediately.

Even now Astra's fingers clutched blindly at her skirts, as if they still held the precious parchment that sealed her fate. The note had been terse, but pointed. Richard had left her, and he had no intention of returning. He wanted her to seek an annulment, to forget she had ever known him. He wanted her to marry another, to begin her life anew. He loved her, but he could never bring her the happiness she deserved. It would be best for everyone if she forgot they had ever met.

Astra leaned over her heaping trencher, the tears threatening again. Hours had passed, but still the awful words retained their ability to reduce her to despair. Forget him? How could she? Richard had filled her heart and soul to bursting. Without him she was naught but a ruined, empty shell.

"Astra, my dear, if you wish to leave . . . seek the privacy of the bedchamber . . ."

Astra shook her head. She would not hide away and act like a grieving abandoned wife. To do so would imply that she had lost hope, that she did not believe her husband would return. Besides, she owed it to Marguerite to attend the banquet honoring her betrothal. For all that her friend had not spoken to her since their angry encounter earlier and even now regarded her with cold, hostile eyes, Astra would not dream of leaving the banquet. Will needed her. He seemed nervous, almost bewildered, and Astra knew his mind was on Richard as well as his worries that Marguerite would not forgive him for his machinations with her father.

Astra took a deep breath, and forced herself to down a

bite of her food. They would endure, she told herself silently. They would all endure.

The meal was almost over. Soon she would be able to leave the hall and lie down, Astra thought with relief. There was a tap on her shoulder. She looked up in surprise to see Lord Fitz Hugh regarding her with a kindly smile.

"Dear Lady Astra, how are you faring in all of this?"

"I . . . I am as well as can be expected, my lord."

He patted her shoulder soothingly. "My new son-by-marriage assures me that your husband will come back. That he loves you too much to stay away."

"I must believe it is true."

Lord Fitz Hugh did not leave her, so Astra rose to face him. "Are you troubled by something, my lord?"

Lord Fitz Hugh nodded and led her away from the King's table. He paused when they reached a quiet corner between the tables and the braziers brought in to heat the chilly hall.

"What think you, Lady Astra, of my daughter's wedding plans?"

"Will is a fine man. I'm sure she will be happy."

Fitz Hugh's broad forehead wrinkled. "It is strange. I have heard rumors about de Lacy . . ." He averted his eyes from Astra. "They say the man is afflicted, that because of some impairment he can never marry or father children. For all that Will claims the child Marguerite carries is his, I do not believe him."

Fitz Hugh's dark eyes probed Astra's face. "You are Marguerite's closest friend. I'm sure you know the truth of it. Will you tell me who begat my grandchild?"

Astra's throat felt dry, her tongue suddenly too big for

her mouth. Sweet Jesu, what was she to say? She knew Will wished her to lie and say the child was his, while Marguerite . . . what did Marguerite want? She licked her lips and faced the older man steadily.

"The truth, my lord . . . the truth is that Will will love the child and care for it as no other man can. He will also cherish Marguerite and seek to make her happy. I ask you, Lord Fitz Hugh, what more could you wish for your daughter and your grandchild?"

Fitz Hugh stared at her a moment, then nodded briskly. "You are very wise, Lady Astra. It was foolish of me to listen to gossip. The babe is de Lacy's, there is no doubt of it."

He turned to leave her, then stopped and slapped his forehead suddenly.

"Hellfire! I near forgot—the manor!" He grabbed her hand and began to drag her toward the King. "It's all been arranged, the papers were drawn up by Henry's clerks yesterday. I'm giving you Riversmere as a wedding present. We merely need the King's blessing and the matter will be settled."

"Your Grace." Lord Fitz Hugh bowed before the King. Astra curtsied beside him.

The King nodded. Fitz Hugh straightened and spoke. "Lady Astra has been like a daughter to me, Your Highness, and I could not let her marriage to Sir Reivers go unremarked. I am giving her Riversmere, one of my manors near Wallingford along the Thames. The grant will be held in her name, but I will expect Reivers to see to its defense."

King Henry's right eye drooped deeply, giving him the look of a sleepy feline. "What if Sir Reivers doesn't return? What if he is gone for good?"

"Of course he will return," Fitz Hugh asserted loudly. "He loves Lady Astra, and he will do his duty by her, I can assure you of that. If all else fails, I will track him down and drag him back to England myself!"

Henry nodded. Astra expected the King to dismiss her. Instead, he reached out and took her hand. "And you, Lady Astra, do you expect your husband to return?"

Astra met the King's eyes and opened her mouth to assure Henry that Richard would indeed be back. A harsh laugh sounded in her ear before she could speak.

"Reivers is a faithless bastard. He'll never return. The lady is well rid of him . . . as you are as well, my liege."

The King released her hand, and Astra turned to see Guy Faucomberg standing next to Lord Fitz Hugh, smiling mockingly. Astra's dislike of the man abruptly congealed to hatred, and she searched her mind for a properly cutting remark. The King's voice rang out before she could respond.

"Once again, Rathstowe, you meddle where your opinion is unwished for. To attack a man behind his back is low and cowardly; to do so before his wife is an even greater affront. I will not have you speak so before Lady Astra."

Faucomberg flushed, and his green eyes glittered all the brighter in his florid face. "My words are true, Your Grace. I'm doing a kindness in informing Lady Astra of her misplaced loyalty."

"I find it hard to believe you are truly concerned for my welfare," Astra said coldly.

"Of course I am." Faucomberg's thick fingers reached out and grasped her hand. "I thought it a pity when you wed the man. Your beauty is utterly wasted on such a vulgar lecher." He raised Astra's fingers to his fleshy lips.

"I had considered offering for you myself . . . then I found out your exquisite charms had been besmirched by Reivers's pawing lust." He released Astra's hand with a look of distaste. "It is a pity, a grave pity."

Despite her fury, Astra managed to meet his gaze with a slow, sweet smile. Even as Lord Rathstowe mocked her, a marvelous, vengeful scheme had come to her mind. Someone needed to put this man in his place, and she knew the exact person, the very one. The plan was utterly perfect!

"Really, my lord," she said calmly. "I had no idea you were seeking a wife. Perhaps you are too bashful to pursue the more desirable maidens effectively." She gave him a sly smile. "I will speak to the Queen about the matter immediately. I'm sure she will be pleased to arrange a suitable alliance for you."

Astra curtsied and walked away, glancing back only once to savor Faucomberg's puzzled frown.

"Christ's balls, you did not!" Marguerite gave a delighted shriek and hugged Astra. "It's marvelous, Astra, simply marvelous. Even I could not think of such a wicked revenge."

Astra smiled rather wanly. "Are you sure it is not too cruel? You don't think he will actually hurt her, do you?"

"Oh, no! Mark my words, Isabel Vipoint will more than hold her own in the marriage. Besides, she has only to complain to the Queen, and Her Highness will see to it that Guy is put in his proper place. So, tell me," she added. "How hard was it to convince the Queen that Lord Rathstowe should marry her cousin?"

"Oh, not hard at all. I played upon Eleanor's pity. I told

her that Faucomberg's family had been negotiating with the Fitz Hughs for your hand, but that he had lost out to Lord de Lacy. Then I mentioned that he had pursued me as well, but of course I ended up wedded to Richard. I made a case that the man was hopelessly shy. He clearly needed the King's assistance in obtaining a royal wife."

"And Isabel—how did she come into the conversation?"

Astra gave a sweetly innocent smile. "I merely mentioned that she seemed distressed at my wedding; the Queen assized the rest."

Marguerite gave a whoop of laughter, then sobered suddenly. "You certainly nailed Rathstowe's balls to the floor. What about Isabel—are you sure she's not happy about this turn of events?"

Astra shrugged. "Oh, she's happy. Rathstowe serves her purposes better than Richard. She would rather have a rich husband than a handsome, valiant one."

"Doesn't that bother you? Don't you want to see Isabel suffer as much as Rathstowe?"

Astra shook her head. "I don't believe Isabel is deliberately cruel, merely misguided. Besides, she played her part in getting Richard and me together. If she had not aroused my jealousy, I might not have realized as soon as I did how much Richard meant to me."

"No regrets then, Astra?"

"No. No regrets."

Thirty-nine

God's blood! As if he was not miserable enough, now it had to rain. The sunny, southern lands of Gascony were behind them, and they were riding wearily through the barren brown countryside of the heart of France. The nearer they came to Paris, the colder it grew.

A gust of wind blew rain into his face. Richard swore. It was obvious his luck had left him. From the moment he had fled London, nothing had gone right. The channel crossing had been miserable. He was not normally afflicted by seasickness, but when the storm blew up and turned the sea into a wicked gray maelstrom, he had been almost as useless as Nicholas. The courage had drained out of him even as the nausea had reduced him to a quivering, retching mess. He had spent the night sweating and puking in the foul-smelling hold, praying he wouldn't die before he reached France.

Shaky and weak, he and Nicholas had disembarked at Calais and began their long journey to de Monfort's headquarters at Bearn. It had taken several weeks of traveling to reach the English forces, and their luck had not improved there. At first, the man Henry had appointed as the seneschal of Gascony had refused to see him. Then, when de Monfort finally relented and granted him an audience, things had not gone as Richard expected. Instead of welcoming him to join his force, the Earl of Leicester had rudely interrogated him. Why was he in Gascony? Did he have orders from the King? Why had he left England?

Arrogant bastard!—Richard thought bitterly. He could still see de Monfort's cold, haughty face, his jutting jaw set stubbornly, his keen gray eyes narrowed in suspicion. He had treated Richard like an errant page rather than an acclaimed knight, and in the end he had announced he had no use for him. He needed men of tact and diplomacy, de Monfort said, not a knight famed for his ruthlessness and savagery.

Richard's own jaw clenched, remembering. He had not been dismissed so rudely since his days as an unwanted bastard, and the insult rankled sorely. He consoled himself by recalling the contemptuous gossip he had heard at court about the dour nobleman who was the King's brother by marriage. De Monfort was a grim, humorless man who had angered Henry on numerous occasions with his priggish self-righteousness. Few at court liked him, and the men took wagers on when the King would finally see fit to crush de Monfort's intolerable conceit.

Scant comfort he could take in that, Richard realized morosely. He had been in France nearly a month, and he still had not found anyone to hire him. It did not help that he had no letter of introduction, no title or troops. As a lone, unknown knight, he inspired no trust or confidence in the few noblemen he had met, and he was vulnerable in a way he had never been before. He tensed each time they had to pass through a forest or other sheltered ground, half expecting ambush. In the open fields it was worse. He watched the other travelers they encountered with gnawing dread, fearing they would be thieves or bandits.

As in England, the roads were dangerous and most people traveled in groups for protection.

At least he had Nicholas. Richard glanced backwards through the side-ways slanting rain and smiled at the misery on his squire's face. Nicholas was an awkward, quiet sort. He wasn't much of a horseman and his mastery of swordplay left something to be desired, but he never complained and his loyalty was unquestioning. The awe with which Nicholas regarded his master helped soothe Richard's wounded pride over the confrontation with de Monfort.

It was also good simply to have the younger man's company. As it was, there were times when Richard thought he might go mad with loneliness. He was used to the noisy camaraderie of an army camp or soldiers' barracks, and out in the open country, the silence was deafening. His thoughts strayed constantly to Astra, and sometimes he so ached with longing he wanted to weep. Her memory was a constant throbbing agony. He could not seem to rid his mind of her sweet mysterious scent, the exact shade of blue of her eyes, the feel of her flesh melding with his. The more he thought of her, the more he wanted her, until he felt he was starving, wasting away without the sustenance of her being.

It was an apt description, Richard thought grimly, rubbing at the dirty stubble of his whiskers. He no longer resembled the proud, sleek Black Leopard. He had turned into a gaunt, disheveled wraith, furtively crossing the bleak, sodden landscape.

"Sir Richard!"

He turned in the saddle, then cursed. While he was musing on his misery, a troop of men had been riding up behind them. Even from a distance, Richard could guess they meant no good. Their clothes were ragged, their mounts inferior and underfed. They had no reason to ride so close except treachery.

He urged his horse into a gallop, then glanced back for another look. They were about fifty paces back. If he had not let them get so near, the destrier and mare could likely have outrun them. Now he would be forced to fight. Richard reached for his sword, deciding his course of action in a second. He turned backwards on his racing horse.

"Nicholas! Leave me! Take the mare and run!"

The young squire's startled blue eyes met Richard's, then years of obeying orders made Nicholas dig his heels into the mare's sides. The horse took off like an arrow released from a bow. Richard saw his pursuers hesitate, thinking to follow. Then they spurred their ragged mounts straight for him.

Richard jerked the destrier to a halt so sharply the men shot past him, swearing. They turned their horses and hurried back, surrounding him. There were five of them. Richard met their wary glances with the most ferocious battle glare he could manage. They hesitated, then threw off their fear and charged him from all sides.

The red raging fury of battle lust was upon him. For a few moments, Richard was aware of nothing but the throbbing feel of his sword in his hand and the flash of bodies around him. His sword found the soft target of his attackers' flesh more than once, but he could not tell how much damage he had done.

They attacked, retreated, attacked again. Each time, Richard fought them off. Like a pack of wolves, they came at him, snapping and snarling, sapping his strength. The sweat poured down his face, his muscles screamed in agony. There were only two men down, he had three left to go. Despair gripped Richard. He was going to die like this, alone, brought down by a pack of slavering jackals. Astra would never know what had become of him.

The thought enraged him. He summoned up the last of his strength and charged the two nearest men. The well-trained destrier caught Richard's mood of desperation and reared, lashing out with its huge hooves. The hooves came down, crippling one man's mount. As the man slid from the sagging horse, Richard's sword cut through the air, neatly decapitating him. But the move left Richard's back vulnerable. Before he could twist away, he felt a sword pierce his hauberk. A burning sensation seared through his chest. The intensity of the pain nearly made him faint, but his sword arm was already lifted. As he sliced down with it, another man slumped to the ground, mortally wounded.

Now there was just one enemy left. Richard faced him dizzily. Sweat dripped into his eyes, and his whole body was a mass of quaking agony. The man's eyes glittered with triumph before he lunged.

Richard did not see the man's grip on his weapon loosen nor his eyes roll back into his head as the knife found his heart. Even as his enemy fell dead with Nicholas's knife buried between his shoulder blades, Richard was swooning. His shoulders slumped, his head drooped. He slid off the destrier with a graceless tumbling motion.

"I don't understand why you're doing it? Why you are going there now? Wouldn't it be better to wait at court, to see if Richard comes back?"

Astra smoothed the satin banner that lay across her lap. She was pleased with it, finally. Deciding on the black leopard on crimson had been easy. It had been much harder to settle upon a design for the border. She had finally chosen buttercups, a border of gold flowers encircling the lunging leopard.

"And why you trouble with *that,"* Marguerite added disgustedly when Astra didn't answer. "Richard abandoned you, left you like an unwanted mistress. Why go to the bother of sewing him a silly banner?"

"Because I want to," Astra answered calmly. "Just as I want to go to the manor. Riversmere is mine now. I intend to make it my home."

"I told Will you were mad, utterly mad. The Queen is perfectly content to have you stay at court. You'd be waited on like a princess, mingle with all the nobility of Europe, wear the latest fashions . . ."

"You don't understand, Marguerite. I'm tired of court. I miss the countryside, the forest and open fields, the fresh breezes. London is exciting, but I would not want to live here forever."

"But what if Richard doesn't come back? What will you do then? It's not fitting for a young woman to live alone and undefended in the wilds of England."

Astra had to stop herself from laughing in disbelief. Since when had Marguerite worried about what was "fitting?" "I won't be alone. There will be servants. Your father assures me that the steward of the place is a very competent and loyal man."

"You won't find another husband at Riversmere," Marguerite said, making a face. "It's a complete backwater; there's probably not a knight under fifty living within twenty miles!"

"Sweet Mary in heaven, I don't want another husband!"

"It's the annulment, isn't it? That's what's holding you back."

"Marguerite, we've discussed this. You know how I feel."

"It's done all the time, Astra. I know the Queen will help you. Her uncles have risen quite high in the Church."

"An annulment is always granted for a reason. What one do you propose I use? Richard and I aren't related, the wedding ceremony was performed properly—and I certainly can't use the excuse that the marriage was never consummated!"

"Why not?"

"Is your mind addled, Marguerite? No one would ever believe that Richard never bedded me. Why, most of the court thinks he took me in the chapel ere we were even wed!"

"No one has to believe it. It has nothing to do with the truth anyway. It's an excuse, a logical reason that the marriage should be dissolved. You pay the Church some money, and *voila,* you're no longer wed."

Astra sighed. "You don't understand, Marguerite. I don't want to dissolve my marriage. In my eyes, Richard will always be my husband. I want no other man."

"Mayhaps you should go back to Stafford," Marguerite suggested in an irritated voice. "Maybe you are meant to be a nun after all."

"I've thought of that," Astra answered calmly, ignoring her friend's sulky mood. "In my first despair, I wondered if Richard's leaving was God's way of punishing me for abandoning my life at Stafford. I considered going back and devoting my life to the Lord. But I've since realized that I had already given my heart to Richard, and it would be a cowardly, foolish thing to hide from my true feelings."

Astra looked down at the banner on her lap and again smoothed the silken material. "I believe Richard will come back. I can't tell you why, but I feel it in my heart." She looked up at Marguerite's skeptical face. "Perhaps I have listened to too many romantic tales of the jongleurs, but I believe that love can be so strong that it binds a man and woman together for life."

"What if Richard dies?"

The serene look on Astra's face shattered, and tears glistened in her eyes. "I pray every day that he still lives. I remind myself of what a brave, strong knight he is, how many battles he has already survived. I tell myself that if he were dead, I would know it, because a part of me would die, too."

"Jesu," Marguerite muttered, clutching herself. "Sometimes you give me the shivers, Astra. If what you and Richard have is true love, I want no part of it. It seems to me that it entails altogether too much suffering!"

Astra blinked back her tears and laughed. "Oh, Marguerite, you have ever been good for me. With you by my side, I will never be able to be too serious."

The two women shared a warm and intimate smile. Astra's part in arranging her friend's marriage had been quickly forgotten. As Astra had suspected, Marguerite was too inconstant to stay angry about anything. They were once again inseparable companions.

"If I am good for you, then perhaps you should come to Thornbury with Will and I. I'm planning to have my lying-in there, so that the de Lacys can welcome their new heir immediately." Marguerite rolled her eyes, making Astra laugh again.

"I'd like to, Marguerite, but as I've said, I feel I should go to Riversmere. If Richard comes back, that is, *when* he comes back, I want him to have some kind of home waiting for him. He's never had that, a real home. I think it would mean a great deal to him."

"Bah! You're just like my mother. You probably like all that chatelaine nonsense—cleaning, seeing to meals, making soap. You're going to waste all your beauty, working so hard, Astra. In a year, you will be naught but a red-faced, scrawny old hag, while I will still be elegant and beautiful."

Astra laughed again, then went to pack the banner with the rest of the things she was taking to Riversmere.

God in heaven, what was he to do? Nicholas de Ferres stood gaping at the carnage all around him. Five men lay dead, the rain washing their blood into frothy pools. A sixth man, his hero and employer, was crumpled at his feet. From the amount of blood seeping from the gash in his back, it seemed likely Sir Richard would be dead soon too.

Nicholas wiped his shaking, bloody hands on his leather jerkin, then forced himself to some semblance of calm. He sought out the winded destrier and dug in the saddlebags until his hands found dry cloth. He jerked out a velvet tunic and ran to Richard. Skillfully, he tore the tunic into strips and used it to stem the bleeding. Next, he dragged the wounded man over to the destrier and tried to heave him onto the horse.

It was impossible. The horse's back seemed to be miles off the ground, and the dead weight of Reivers's muscular body was too much for Nicholas. After three tries he gave up. Panicking, he realized that if he did not get Sir Richard to someplace where his wounds could be tended, he would die.

The mare whinnied, and Nicholas realized there might be another means of transporting the wounded man. Nicholas ran to the mare, and for once she did not shy away from him. He grabbed her bridle and dragged her over to where Reivers lay, praying she would stand still long enough for him to get the unconscious knight onto her back. The mare sniffed at Richard's prone body as if recognizing him. The smell of blood spooked her, but Nicholas spoke calmly to her and smoothed her neck the way he had seen Richard do.

When the horse had stilled, Nicholas tried again. Straining every muscle in his body, he heaved Richard up, then braced the unconscious man's body between his and the mare's. She trembled and rolled her eyes, but did not move. With a final excruciating effort, he hoisted Richard up and shoved him across the horse's withers.

For a moment, Nicholas just stood there, sagging against the horse, trying to get his breath. He told himself that the hardest part was over; now he had only to ride for help. He adjusted Reivers's position on the mare—using leather strips he found in the saddlebag to tie the man's limp arms and legs to the stirrups so he could not fall off. Then he led the mare over to the destrier and attempted to mount the warhorse.

It took him three tries, and by the time he managed it, he was so dizzy with fatigue and nerves he nearly toppled over the other side. Again he rested, trying to clear his thoughts, to banish the black terror that hovered over him. He did not want Sir Richard to die. His whole future depended on the man he served surviving and someday sponsoring him to be a knight. Besides, he liked Sir Richard, and near-worshiped his skill in battle. Four men killed by one! Jesu, if Reivers lived, what a tale he would have to tell!

If he lived. The thought jolted Nicholas back to his responsibilities. He scanned the bleak landscape, trying to decide which direction to go. Glimpsing a dark shape on the horizon to his right, he urged the destrier forward.

Forty

He had died and gone to hell. One of the torments there was to have burning hot pokers jabbed into his chest. The devils had found one particularly sensitive spot and were continually abusing it. His body was burning, his thirst was unbearable. He wanted to die, but that was foolish. He was already dead.

"Give him some more water."

Soft hands lifted him, and he had a moment of confusion. There were no angels in hell, and yet this was surely one. Astra?

It was not Astra. The woman's eyes were light brown, not blue, and her face was unfamiliar. Yet she held him tenderly and let him drink as much of the blessed water as he wanted. He could not make out anything else before he floated down in the darkness again.

The second time he awoke, he knew he was alive. Smells came to him—cooking meat, the dry, acrid scent of smoke. He was near a fire. Perhaps that accounted for the heat of his body, the fever that seemed to rage inside him. He tried to lift his head to look around the dwelling. He could make out shadows at the edges of his vision. They moved and talked, but he could not understand them.

* * *

He opened his eyes, and the world jerked into focus as if he had never left it. Nicholas was kneeling beside him, smiling his gap-toothed smile.

"You're going to live, Sir Richard. Paulina says that if you have survived this long you must be too stubborn and rotten to die."

Richard turned his head and saw the woman who must be Paulina. It was the angel of mercy who had given him water. She was every bit as fair as he remembered, and she was smiling so brightly there were tears in her eyes.

"I . . . I was wounded?"

Nicholas nodded. "You took a sword thrust clean through your mail, but not before you killed four men yourself. Oh, it was a thing to see, it was."

Vaguely, Richard recalled the battle. He could remember the first two men falling, then charging the remaining three. Three? "What happened to the fifth man?"

Nicholas shrugged, looking almost sheepish. "I got him in the back with my knife. It's a trick I learned from the knife throwers who performed at the palace. I've been practicing."

"You saved my life."

Nicholas smiled even more radiantly. "Killing the last attacker wasn't the half of it. Then I had to get you on the horse and carry you here. God's wounds, but you're heavy, sire."

"Where is *here?*" He tried again to lift his head and look around.

"The farmhouse of William and Margary de Say. This is their daughter, Paulina. It is her you should truly thank. She is the one who stitched you up and tended to you.

Without her, you would have bled to death. The wound got your lung. It should have killed you."

Richard leaned back and closed his eyes. He should be dead, but he was not. It was hardly the first time he had narrowly escaped death, but somehow it was different. He realized suddenly what a gift life was. He hadn't died, unknown, unmourned, in some muddy field in France. He had another chance.

"He needs to rest." The woman had a subtle accent, quite different from the Norman French of the English court.

Richard raised his head. "No, don't leave me. I . . . I want to thank you." He searched for the woman's face among the shadows. She leaned toward him.

"I want to repay you for what you've done. Have Nicholas get my saddlebags. I have jewelry, weapons, other valuables. I'll see that your family is generously rewarded."

"You see?" Nicholas broke in. "Did I not tell you that he was a rich knight, that he would more than make up for your trouble?"

The woman shook her head. "You do not need to pay me. Healing is a gift. I do it because it is blessed to help others."

"Is Paulina not wonderful?" Nicholas murmured proudly. "She knew exactly what to do. She stitched you up, then gave you medicine to help you mend and to ease your fever. I'll wager you would not have had better care if I had taken you to the court of Louis himself."

Richard closed his eyes again. What were the odds that he would be near mortally wounded within walking distance of a skilled healer? He was not a pious man, but even he could not ignore such a blatant sign from God.

He had been saved for some reason. For some reason his time had not come yet.

"Truly, Nicky, he needs to rest."

He felt a familiar, soothing touch. Richard opened his eyes to glimpse the woman leaning over him. No wonder he had thought she was an angel. Paulina was a rare beauty—serene golden-brown eyes, perfect skin, lush coral lips. Richard glanced quickly at Nicholas. He was gazing at Paulina with a look of complete adoration,

"I will rest now," Richard told them, smiling slightly. For a brief moment before he fell asleep, he wondered how he was ever going to be able to convince Nicholas to leave.

Riversmere was everything she had expected and more. Located on a quiet grassy knoll above the river, the manor reminded her of a place time had forgotten. Ivy curled up the walls of the ancient manor house and the crooked stone wall around the garden looked as if it had been there since the days of King Arthur. But for all that the manor was old and unelaborate, everything was in good repair. The steward, Hereward, was indeed an honest and responsible man. The granary and cellars were filled with wheat, rye, salted meat, cabbages, apples and leeks—more than enough food to sustain them through the winter. The stew pond was stocked with fish, the manor house furnished with whitewashed walls and fresh rushes on the floors.

Hereward and his wife, Lettia, had greeted Astra warmly, and told her that Lord Fitz Hugh had sent word to expect her arrival. They had already moved to a small cottage near the river and left the manor for her and

"Lord Reivers." Indeed, that was their only question—when was her husband, their master, due to arrive?

Astra had answered vaguely, telling them that her husband was on business for the King in France, and she hoped he would be back soon. They nodded eagerly, obviously delighted to be serving such an important man. Astra wondered what they would think if Richard never returned.

The manor was a large but simple two-story building, with a hall suitable for dining and entertaining on the first floor. The second floor was made up of two large rooms that Astra immediately envisioned as the master bedchamber and a nursery. She set about furnishing them as best she could. There was little furniture, and she had no idea about how to see to having some made, but Marguerite had sent bolts of fabric as a wedding gift and she immediately began sewing wall coverings to brighten the bare white walls.

She hung the Leopard banner in the center of the hall ceiling and surrounded it with alternating blocks of crimson and gold samite. Upstairs, she used deep green fabric to drape the walls and add warmth to the room. She fashioned a bedcover of crimson for the one narrow bed in the dwelling, and began embroidering it with a swirling pattern of flowers, vines and leaves around one regal leopard.

It was almost winter, and there was very little she could do with the garden. The part where vegetables and herbs were grown had been recently cultivated, but it looked as if what flowers there were had been allowed to go wild, spreading and climbing up the stone wall. Everything was brown and dead now, and it was difficult for Astra to identify plants, but she could see there were roses, chervil, rosemary and gillieflowers.

Astra's other chief frustration was that she had so little to furnish the place with. There was one big trestle table in the hall, and a number of benches and stools, but otherwise the big room was almost bare. Astra thought with longing of the beautiful things she had seen at the Cheapside market. The chests and ambries for storing things, the candlesticks and candelabras, the pewter cups and linen tablecloths. If she had known, she would have used the treasure Richard had left her to buy some things before she left London. Now it was too late. She would have to wait for spring to travel to Wallingford, or perhaps even Oxford, to find what she needed.

She wished now she had worried about such things instead of fussing with gowns and slippers and veils as she had at court. How foolish and frivolous she had been in London. She had been concerned with looking alluring and being entertained. It was a vain, empty existence that had little to do with her life now. Her beautiful gowns were stored away in a chest; she had nowhere to wear them, no one to see them.

Perhaps that was the part that was hardest of all. She was lonely, dreadfully so. Lettia had found her a girl in the village to serve as her maid, but the round-eyed, rosy-cheeked woman was not the kind of company Marguerite had been. Besides, it was not the days which were hard, but the nights. Astra wondered how she would survive the long, cold winter eves in the narrow bed with heated rocks to warm her feet, but no Richard to warm her heart.

She thought of him constantly, and her memories of him were so intense, so magical, sometimes she wondered if they could be real. Had he actually been that big, that handsome, that dazzlingly male? Had he truly touched her the way she remembered—his hands and mouth and body sending violent pleasure throughout every fiber of her being? It hardly seemed possible she had known such wonder. She had no proof of it, no reassurance it was not merely a dream. She had his name and the jewels and valuables he had left her, but little else except memories. She had hoped for a time that she might be with child, but then her courses had come with their usual regularity.

It did not seem fair. Marguerite had conceived near the first time she had known a man, or so she said, while even the dozens of times Richard had loved Astra had not started a babe growing inside her. She dearly longed for a child, a living, breathing remembrance of her and Richard's love.

Sometimes the loneliness and longing were so great Astra could not help weeping. Alone at night, she would clutch the one ragged tunic Richard had left behind, inhaling the tantalizing scent of him that clung to the wool, and crying. Could she have done something different, found some way to keep him from leaving her? Had he left her because of her treachery, her selfishness? Or was there some other wrong that haunted him? She thought of his mother, and the grief he must have borne because of who she was, and she wondered if Richard was afraid to love, afraid to be hurt again.

At times like that she knew despair, and she considered going back to Stafford and seeing if the nuns would still have her. If Richard did not return, it seemed her only recourse. She could not live here, alone, at Riversmere forever, and she had no heart for returning to court.

But somehow her despair always passed. The sun rose in the morning, banishing the gloom and loneliness of night. She found ways to keep busy. There was always cleaning to be done, meals to be prepared. She met weekly with Hereward to go over the accounts. He had been pleased and awed by her ability to read and write and do sums, and Astra was grateful she had learned such skills at Stafford.

There was a pleasure in helping things run smoothly at Riversmere. It gave purpose to her life and helped ease the sting of her unhappiness. At night, she sat before the fire and embroidered the coverlet, pouring all her love into the tiny stitches that formed the elaborate pattern. It would be a masterpiece, and when she slept beneath it, she would remember that she was the wife of the Black Leopard, and that he had once loved her with a passion and fury she would never forget.

Winter arrived. Astra reminded herself that storms across the channel were common, and that even if Richard decided to return to England, days and even weeks might pass before he was able to make the voyage. Then he would have to find her, for although she had left word of her whereabouts with people in London, Riversmere was a journey of several days.

She counted the days until Christmas and then the days afterwards. And still, he did not come.

"It is not forever, Paulina. I will be back."

Richard smiled as Nicholas said his goodbyes to the lovely French girl. He did not envy his squire, for he well knew what it was to ride off and leave your heart behind.

Richard himself took time to clasp Paulina's small brown hands in his, to kiss her sweetly on the cheek. He owed her his life, and even the jewelry and plate and other costly items he had insisted on leaving with her family could not begin to pay for what she had done. Her parents, a brown, drab couple who scarce spoke in Richard's presence, stood behind Paulina, politely nodding their farewells.

They rode north, away from Paris. The land was still bare and brown, but here and there they could see peasants spreading dung upon the fields, preparing them for the spring planting. Richard felt a vague homesickness for England, for the rolling hills and thick forests he had grown up with and always taken for granted. It seemed to him that he had never appreciated many things before—the comforting odor of cooking food, the sound of birds welcoming the day, the music of the wind in the trees and grasses, the scent of rain and earth. Although the wound in his back ached and his wasted legs were stiff and awkward on his horse, he had never felt so wondrously, gloriously alive. He wanted to shout with the mad exhilaration he felt, to urge the mare into a wild canter over the open fields. He felt reborn.

How many men, he wondered, were ever given this, a second chance at life? Most men died without really living, without ever pausing to appreciate the beauty that was everywhere. They fought and loved and lusted. They raged and coveted and hated, never stopping to think how blessed they were. But he knew. He was a walking, breathing miracle. He was young and healthy and his strength returned a little more with each passing day. And this time, he meant to use it differently. He would not waste his energies on seeking wealth or land, he would not squander his gifts in the pursuit of glory and adulation.

Richard shook his head, marveling at the change he felt in himself. The bitterness that had weighted him down for so long had vanished, and a fierce energy throbbed in his veins, making his heart sing with gratitude. All his doubts about committing himself to a woman had disappeared.

He no longer doubted that he had something to offer Astra. She had told him that she would marry him even if he were a beggar, and he understood now what she had meant. The love they felt for each other was wealth enough to last a lifetime.

He glanced backwards to see his squire bouncing on the broad back of the black warhorse. He smiled. He had not told Nicholas yet, but he had made up his mind. He was going home, home to Astra. He meant to offer her the only thing she had ever asked of him—his undying love.

The boredom and gloom of winter had hung heavy on everyone's spirits at Riversmere. As the weather suddenly turned sunny and mild, the manor residents grew almost giddy with the reprieve. One morning two horses were spotted in the distance, riding slowly toward Riversmere, and the excitement built even more. Astra tried not to let herself hope. Travelers arriving from the direction of London meant nothing, she told herself sternly. Even if Richard had come home, he likely would have sent a message to her so she could expect him. The nearing riders could be anyone.

Still, the disappointment struck her like a blow to her chest when she stood at the wooden palisade and saw that they were about to welcome only a traveling peddler. She glanced behind him and saw that the second "rider" was no more than a stack of merchandise piled high on the back of a mule.

The peddler was covered from head to foot with a long cloak, and he seemed to have some sort of deformity that made him hunch over awkwardly. Astra sighed and went to greet him. For all that she was disappointed by the peddler, the rest of the manor was elated. A traveling vendor brought a wealth of much needed goods to the manor, as well as something even more precious—news. They crowded around the man, asking a dozen questions at once. "Do you have salt, man? What of needles? Knives? Any spices?"

The peddler started to answer them in a strange muffled voice. Astra stepped forward and interrupted.

"For shame, Lettia, Croth, Ian. It's not fitting that we make the poor man stand in the courtyard and do his business when he is certain to be tired and hungry. Bring him in."

The peddler turned to her as she spoke. Astra could not see his face clearly beneath the cloak, but a strange chill ran through her. There was something odd about him. He was surprisingly tall, and despite his ungainly posture, he seemed to be a very substantial man. She could not recall any of the peddlers who had come to Stafford being anywhere near so big.

No matter, she told herself as she turned to go into the hall. If he had good merchandise and fair prices, she would be content. She must remember to ask him about candles. The tallow ones they made at Riversmere reeked terribly as they burned. She would so like to have a few beeswax ones to burn in her bedchamber at night.

There were a dozen things to think of in the next few minutes. They could serve the man some of the leftover pottage, but he must also have fresh bread and some of the good ale. She also needed to find her list of supplies and see Hereward about money. Before winter had set in for good, the steward had traveled to Oxford and sold some of Richard's loot for silver. A cache of pennies was hidden away in one of the storerooms, and she would need Hereward's help to dig it up.

"All this fuss for a peddler," Hereward grumbled as they pulled the wooden box from the dirt.

"It's good fortune to show a traveler hospitality," Astra pointed out. "Besides, there are many things we need, and it would be nice not to have to wait until I can travel to Wallingford and get them myself."

"What of your husband, Lady Astra? Will he not be coming soon with supplies?"

Astra blushed and ducked her head, avoiding the look in Hereward's eyes. She feared the steward had begun to doubt that "Lord Reivers" even existed. How much longer could she put him off with stories of her husband's business in France?

By the time they reached the hall, the peddler was seated at the trestle table surrounded by food. He still wore the hood of his cloak around his face, and Astra could see little more of him than she had before. She watched his brown scarred fingers as they reached again and again for the bread and ale. God in heaven!—he certainly was eating enough.

Astra waited impatiently with the rest of the manor inhabitants, wondering if she could bargain for better prices since the man had already consumed half her larder. At last, he pushed the food away and rose. He went to his bundles—which had been unloaded off the mule and nag and piled on the manor floor—and grabbed the top one. He opened it, and spread the contents out on the table. There was a gasp of excitement from the waiting customers.

The people of the manor crowded around the table, talking eagerly. They had little coin, but they bargained fiercely for the few trifles they could afford. Astra stood back, waiting for the others to finish their business. In her mind she went over the things they needed, things she'd rather not do without another month. She hardly heard the man when he called to her.

"The lady—what does the lady of the manor wish to buy?"

Astra straightened. The servants and villeins of Riversmere stepped away from the table and watched her expectantly.

The peddler spoke again. His voice was clear and even this time.

"Alas, I have nothing fine enough for the Lady Astra. I have no jewels to rival the blue of her eyes. No ribbons as bright and fair as her hair. No cloth excellent enough to array such a beauteous form."

Astra blinked. The peddler's twisted shoulder seemed to have straightened. He was even taller than she had imagined. His voice sounded odd to her, and even more so his words. She wondered if he were mocking her.

His hands sifted casually through the pile of goods laying on the table, spilling them to the floor.

"Alas, I can see I have nothing here for her. Nothing at all."

He stepped around the table and walked toward her.

Astra did not breathe. She could not think, and her vision seemed to waver and fade.

"What could tempt the Lady Astra, I wonder. She cares not for fancy gowns and jewels. What think you that she wishes for?"

The people in the hall watched, transfixed. Before their eyes the hunch-backed peddler changed. Now he stood straight and tall, a powerful man, a warrior. They watched as the hood of his cloak fell away, revealing long dark hair and a face both elegant and dangerous.

They gasped as the man's arms encircled their lady's waist, and he pulled her tightly against the dark bulk of his body.

"You might have warned me," Astra murmured. "You did not have to appear out of nowhere and nearly give me the vapors." She was lying naked on Richard's chest, nestling against the smooth, silky heat of him. It was the only way the narrow bed could accommodate both of them, not that either of them minded.

"I wanted to see for myself how you had fared. I was not sure you would still want me. I was afraid you might have changed."

"It has only been a few months, Richard," she teased. "Surely you did not think I would forget you quite so soon."

His eyes met hers, hot blackness against soft blue. "You *have* changed, Astra."

Her eyes widened in doubt, and she lifted her head from his chest.

"You are no longer the sweet little convent girl I fell in love with." His hand moved to cup her chin, his thumb softly caressing her cheek. "You are a woman now, Astra. I look around Riversmere, and everywhere I see the comforts and small pleasures only a woman knows how to provide. You have made Riversmere into something more than a clean, prosperous manor, Astra. You have made it into a home."

"Oh, Richard," she whispered. "That is all I ever wanted. A home, a peaceful haven for the man I love."

He shook his head. "I'm afraid it is not what I have always wanted. It took me so long, so very long to discover how much it means to me."

"I only wish you did not nearly have to die to learn what you need."

Richard stiffened. "You know?"

"Sweet Mary! Surely you do not think I would welcome my husband back without inspecting every inch of him. It is appallingly hard to miss the freshly-healed wound on your back, and from the size and position of it, I can easily guess that it near killed you."

Richard nodded. "I believe I was as close to death as a man can be and still return to walk among the living." He shook off the morbid mood and grinned. "When I awoke and knew my surroundings, my first thought was for you. That was when I knew I would live—when all I could think about was bedding you."

"For shame," Astra scolded, looking anything but displeased. "You spare no thought for the future of your immortal soul, and instead dwell upon the beastly urges of your wicked flesh."

Richard regarded her for a moment with eyes as lazy and heavy-lidded as a cat's, then he adjusted her body over his, sinking his shaft within her until she gasped with the size and heat of it.

"Tell me now, Astra, tell me what you think of my beastly urges."

"Oh, Richard," she groaned, nearly insensible with pleasure. "How I have missed you!"

Forty-one

"Isn't it marvelous?" Marguerite murmured as she leaned her squirming, red-faced son, Fulke, against her chest and patted his back. "Even Will was astounded when he heard the King had given Richard Castle Falaise along the Marches. It's a very wealthy *demesne.* You need never again worry about affording comforts or servants."

Astra smiled tranquilly. "Living on a large estate means little to me. In fact, Richard and I have decided to spend summers at Riversmere. It's more of a home than any dark, drafty castle could ever be. I wish the babe could be born there, but the midwife says it won't come until well after the Yule season, and we are to keep Christmas with the King and Queen at Canterbury."

Marguerite handed Fulke to a nurse and smoothed her gown. "Speaking of the King, you'll never guess the delicious gossip I heard not a fortnight ago."

"What?"

Marguerite leaned forward, her eyes bright with conspiratorial glee. "Guy Faucomberg has fallen out of favor with Henry. Apparently they had an awful row, and Rathstowe accused the King of being henpecked."

"He didn't!"

Marguerite grinned. "Aye, apparently he did, or at least that's the explanation given for the King banishing Faucomberg from court. Witnesses said that it was one of the worst rages Henry's ever had; his face turned bright red and his eyes practically bulged out of his head. There were those who feared for his health."

"And Faucomberg?"

"Apparently he left London calmly enough, but you know the man, he won't forgive Henry. He'll be plotting every minute to revenge the insult."

"At least things didn't come to such a pass between Richard and the King." Astra gave a little shiver. "I would hate to have Henry bear a lasting grudge against my husband. As my father found, crossing kings can be a dangerous thing."

Marguerite shrugged. "Henry isn't made of the same stuff John was. There are those who say that if all the barons with grievances joined forces against him, Henry would be compelled to meet their demands."

Astra's eyes widened in alarm. "You speak as if the barons mean to go to war against the King!"

Marguerite nodded. "Will says armed confrontation is very possible if Henry does not curb his greedy relatives and his own bad temper and extravagance."

"War! How awful. If it comes to that it won't be only men like Rathstowe who suffer, but the common people as well."

"Don't fret, Astra. Will says that the reckoning between Henry and his barons may be a long time coming. The barons lack a leader, and they would never unite behind a man like Rathstowe." She paused and flipped her dark curls carelessly. "God's blood, why are we conversing on such a dreary topic? I haven't seen you in months—you must tell me everything that's happened since Richard returned to England."

"There's little to tell, Marguerite. Richard and I live very quietly. We haven't even been to court. Richard meant to return to London a few weeks ago, but I was so sick with the babe, he wouldn't leave me."

"You were sick?" Marguerite grasped her arm in alarm.

" 'Twas nothing," Astra protested. "Merely the normal queasiness of the early weeks. The midwife even said it was a good sign; she believes it means the babe is taking well."

"Dear Astra, how awful. Myself, I felt wonderful up until the last few months. Then I swelled up like a bloated pig's bladder." She made a face. "I was grateful Will has no interest in me that way, or I would have been too embarrassed to share a bedchamber with him. I have never felt so repulsive."

"I don't feel repulsive at all. Richard says I have never looked more alluring, and I believe that, in his eyes at least, it's true."

"Richard would say that. He fair dotes on you. I can't believe the change in him. The arrogant, ferocious knight is no more; these days the Leopard is as mellow and sweet-tempered as a pet kitten."

"Except in bed," Astra said shyly. "There he is the same as ever."

"Really, Astra, you needn't brag. Will is a very indulgent husband, but I've yet to find the lover that satisfies me."

"How are things with you and Will?" Astra asked cautiously.

Marguerite smiled. "I said he was indulgent. Truly he outdoes my father the way he cares for my happiness. You were right, sweeting. I can have no regrets about marrying Will; he likely suits me as well as any man."

"You are satisfied then, Marguerite?" Astra asked. "It has been a year since we left Stafford. Are you happy with the way things have turned out?"

"Well, I have not found a great love as you have, but then perhaps I am not destined for it. I'm too selfish, I suppose. But otherwise, it has been an adventure, Astra. What else can one hope for?"

What else indeed?—Astra wondered, splaying her fingers across her slightly swelling belly. She had a handsome, loving husband and a babe on the way. What more could one wish for?

She looked up as Richard entered Thornbury Hall. He had been out hunting with Will, and his face was flushed with ruddy color, his hair charmingly wind-blown. He leaned over her, his dark eyes making a lazy perusal of her blossoming form. Then his gaze met hers invitingly.

"You ladies are missing a fine, fair day. Come outside with me, Astra. Enjoy the sunshine and sweet breezes."

She basked in the warmth of his eyes for a moment, then looked at Marguerite. Her friend gave a delighted laugh. "Go then, Astra. I'd not keep two such shameless lovebirds apart."

Astra stood to put her work away. Richard took her arm and led her toward the door.

"Do you wish to go riding, madame?" he asked as they went out into the castle courtyard.

"I think not," she answered with a regretful smile. "For all the practice I've had in the last year, I fear I am not much of a horsewoman. I can't quite get over the fear I will fall off."

"We could ride pillion. Kismet would not mind."

Astra turned to glance at her husband's face. "What are

you planning, Richard? Are you trying to get me off alone?"

"Alone?" he asked innocently. "Why would I do that?"

"You know very well why! You are forever enticing me to hidden corners to have your way with me."

Richard grinned. "What will it be then? It seems a shame to spend such a beautiful day inside."

"Very well, you lecherous wretch. We'll go to the garden."

Thornbury was a very old estate, and its garden seemed as ancient as the one at Riversmere—and almost as neglected. Astra followed Richard through tangled rose bushes and overhanging oak branches until they reached the orchard. The apple trees were in bloom; and the fragrant white blossoms drifted down on them with dreamlike slowness. Richard led her beneath the resplendent canopy of a large, gnarled tree and drew her to him. He pressed his face against her neck.

"I have found heaven with you, Astra," he said softly.

"You scarce deserve heaven," she teased as she reached her fingers into his thick, silky hair. "A miscreant like you ought to burn in hell for certes."

"Ah, but I have been redeemed. Some fair angel took my soul away many months ago, and she still holds it in safekeeping."

"An angel was it? Are you sure?"

He leaned back to look at her face, smiling. "Well, it could have been a wood sprite. They look much the same, don't they?"

Astra glanced down at her midsection. "I fear I shall not resemble a sprite much longer. In a few months, I shall be quite plump and ungainly." She looked up and met his eyes intently. "Are you pleased we shall have a babe, Richard?"

"Of course, I am pleased. Why would I not be?"

"I thought perhaps that it might distress you, that it might somehow remind you of your own unhappy childhood."

"That was different. This babe shall have a father who acknowledges him and protects him and a mother who loves him. He shall never have to endure what I did."

"Your mother loved you," Astra said softly. "If she had not, she would never have done what she did. She could have given you up and entered a nunnery. Instead, she sold herself so she could buy you a place in the world."

Richard nodded. "Perhaps I see that now. I have thought recently that my anger at her was nothing more than a child's anguish that he could not save someone he loved from pain."

Astra leaned close to stroke his face. "You speak of our babe as if it is for certain a boy. What if it is a girl?"

He smiled. "A girl would be delightful. I could pet her and spoil her and tease her." His expression grew rueful. "Of course, when she grew into a woman, I would have to lock her away. It would be my duty as a father to protect her from all the hot-blooded, young knaves who would try to steal her heart."

"As you have stolen mine, Richard?"

He smiled devilishly, and before Astra knew what was happening, he slid a long, lean leg between hers, disrupting her balance. He caught her in his arms, and they glided to the ground as gently as an apple blossom floating down from the tree. Richard eased himself next to her. Astra expected him to reach for the laces on her gown, but instead, he rested his face on her breast, nestling with a sigh against the place where her heart beat.

She looked up at the dazzling white boughs above them and twined her fingers in his hair. The sense of peace that filled her was as sublime and timeless as the earth they rested upon. "I love you, Richard," she murmured.

"As I love you, sweet Astra," he whispered back. "The Leopard has found his mate. He is content at last."

Dear Readers,

Leopard's Lady is my "rock and roll romance"—live hard and fast, 'cause you'll probably die young. The medieval age was a brutal one. Women died in childbirth or from disease so often that most men had several wives, and men faced the gruesome hazards of war on an ongoing basis. Children and young adults perished easily, and it was not unknown for whole families (even among the nobility) to die out completely.

With the specter of early death haunting them from cradle to adulthood, I believe the people of medieval times were both much more pious and much more reckless than we are. This gives a vibrancy and a passion to their time period that I find very compelling. In *Leopard's Lady* I sought to capture that mood of immediacy and *joie de vivre.* For all the seriousness of some of my themes, it is meant to be a fun book, a playful one.

In the midst of severe religious repression, horrible health conditions, and terrifying political upheaval (Simon de Monfort led an uprising of the English barons against Henry III a few years after *Leopard's Lady* takes place, and the revolt was eventually suppressed by Henry's son, Edward I, in very vicious fashion.) the people of medieval times never lost their sense of humor nor their passion for life. Perhaps that is why their time period appeals to me so much. They seem so *human,* so *real.* To do my research for the tavern scenes in *Lady,* I had only to go down to the local bar. It is all with us still—the humor and pathos, the sex and passion and danger. The story of life is played out before our eyes.

My interest in fiction arises from a competing desire to portray this drama realistically and yet contrive to create the happy ending that often eludes us in real life. I want to believe that good conquers evil, that generosity and kindness is stronger than greed and avarice, that sweetness and love can heal pain and anger and make us whole.

A fantasy, you say? Perhaps, but I'm a writer, and we're crazy enough to believe that fantasies really *can* make a difference in people's lives!

Happy reading,

Mary Gillgannon

P.S. I love to hear from readers. Please write to me at P.O. Box 2052, Cheyenne, WY 82003.

If you liked this book, be sure to look for the August releases in the **Denise Little Presents** line:

***Just a Kiss Away* by Jacqueline Marten** (0166–6, $4.99)
"Jacqueline Marten is one of my favorite writers!"
—Jude Deveraux

"Nothing short of brilliant" —LaVyrle Spencer

Just a Kiss Away is the story of orphaned Katie Coffee. At the age of twelve, she leaves Florida and the world she knows for a completely different life in Pennsylvania Amish country. As Katie grows older, she yearns for something beyond the boundaries of her simple existence. But finding a new life in a larger world could mean losing the man she loves more than life itself.

Just a Kiss Away is a stirring story of what happens when two cultures touch and two hearts unite. It's like nothing you've ever read before!

***Fearless* by Alexandra Thorne** (0165–8, $4.99)

Raina DeVargas is the kind of woman it took to tame the wilds of Texas. She was the daughter of a *vaquero* and a reformed whore, and there wasn't a soul in Texas in 1885 who'd let her forget it. Ulysses Pride was a man with power, money and a past. He was the scion of a Texas dynasty, seemingly secure on the path to the governor's mansion. The last thing he needed was a woman with a shady background to derail his plans. But Raina and Ulysses have more in common than a childhood spent on the same ranch. They are fated to share a love as big as the state that spawned them, to defy convention in the search for a truth that only they share—and in the end, to be fearless enough to commit to each other in a world that would keep them apart.

AVAILABLE IN AUGUST